D1579036

0 0 0 0 0 4 1 3 7 8 2

Stained Glass

GEORGE MARZOCCHI

RED
PENGUIN
Books

A big, love-filled thank you to my wife and muse, Terry, who was the wind at my back in finishing this book that I started in 2008. Her faith and encouragement made me get in front of the laptop and write, write, write.

To our sons, Damien and Julian, who have always been my inspiration and have never disappointed.

To our dear friend Loria Parker, who introduced us to Stephanie Larkin at Red Penguin Publishing, who brought this project to life.

CONTENTS

PROLOGUE

Hi. My name is Maxie and I'm a numbers guy. I could've worked on Wall Street with Goldman Sachs, Morgan Stanley, and J.P. Morgan, but they didn't pay enough for me. I was a math genius at twelve and went to prison at nineteen for check fraud and credit card scams. I guess I wasn't as smart as I thought. I got 8 years in the slammer and it wasn't white-collar prison like most guys. They made an example out of me.

Now, you're probably asking yourself, 8 years seems like a long time. Well, honestly, it would have been less than five if I didn't slug the arresting officer. I was a lot stronger back then. When I got out, I couldn't work in the finance racket. So I got mixed up with a guy named Dom, who introduced me to Richie DiNapoli, who introduced me to the wonderful world of organized crime. DiNapoli gave me a job managing his money and, oy vey, was he a tough boss!

I knew it was dirty money, but I needed a job and it paid better than Wall Street. I was skimming off the top and it helped pay the bills. At the age of thirty-two, I had a five-bedroom house on Long Island with a private dock, a couple of nice cars, and a small boat, if you call twenty-five feet small. But sometimes the best-laid plans, as they say, get messed up and that kinda happened to me.

CHAPTER 1
MEET THE FELLAS

Four men are sitting at a table in an old-fashioned espresso cafe—Little Italy style. They call it the "Social Club." The man at the head of the table is the boss. Coffee cups and Italian pastry are on the table, and on the wall is an old-school payphone—the kind you would see on every street corner in the city back in the day. The boss thinks calls made from this phone can't be traced. The phone rings and the boss says, "Hey Dom, get the phone."

Dom gets up and goes to the phone, "Yeah." The voice on the phone says, "Gimme Richie."

Dom covers the mouthpiece, looks over to the table and speaks to the boss. "It's that guy."

The boss says, "What guy, Dom?"

"You know, that spic."

The boss gets up and takes the phone from Dom. The boss speaks.

"Go ahead."

"I'm ready, are you?"

"Yeah, Tomorrow night at eight o'clock at that dump you hang out in. Be there."

"I'll be there. Make sure . . . "

The boss hangs up in the middle of the voice's sentence.

The boss is Richie DiNapoli. Richie is a real gangster, not a Hollywood stereotype wannabe. Made his bones during the cocaine wars in the 80s and 90s. He came up through the ranks with Dom partnering with cocaine dealers in Colombia. They sold to upscale clients, stockbrokers, celebrities, and millionaires in the Hamptons and Montauk. They amassed a fortune, all of it in offshore accounts. Richie has movie-star looks—black hair slicked back with dark eyes. He has a great fashion sense, and is very dangerous.

Dom is Richie's capo—stocky, looks like he lifted weights a long time ago. Not as well dressed as Richie, but he's trying. Dom makes sure Richie gets what he wants.

Maxie is Richie's consiglieri and accountant, and he looks the part. Meek and humble, he handles the family's finances. He's under a lot of pressure to make sure the numbers add up. When it comes to the family money, Richie is unforgiving.

The man at the end of the table is Primo. Primo cleans up after Richie - witnesses, informants, whatever. He wears black a lot. He has big hands that he uses as weapons when it comes time to do Richie's bidding.

The boss returns to the table and says to the men seated there, "Tomorrow night at 8. Maxie, I'll need 50 grand."

CHAPTER 2
A BIRTHDAY FLIGHT

A 1959 Cessna 170 is flying over Long Island. The plane is red and white and it contrasts sharply against the blue sky. The plane is being flown by a skilled pilot as it banks, climbs and dives. The pilot is looking left and right as he handles the controls. He's flying over the ocean and waves break on the shoreline. The plane banks and is now over land.

The radio in the plane comes alive. "Charlie Delta 472, this is Baltimore ATC. You're clear to land on runway 9 at Suffolk Airport. Do you read?"

"Confirm Baltimore ATC. I read you."

"Approach from Northwest #9, over."

The plane lands and taxis down the runway. At the end of the runway, it turns right and rolls toward a hangar. The engines sputter and go quiet with the propellers coming to a full stop. The pilot's door opens and Tom Hartford steps out. Tom was a sergeant with the Suffolk County PD, now retired. He flew medivac assist choppers called Pale Hawk helicopters in the Gulf War. They provided air cover for evacuations on the battlefield. He was awarded medals for bravery, including the Purple Heart. He always keeps himself in good shape. Blue eyes with graying hair, about 6'2." Flying was his passion ever since he can remember he's wanted to be a pilot.

A short black man with greasy coveralls and a Red Sox cap walks toward Tom. The man is Scott (Scottie) Harris. He owns the hangar. Wealthy people store their planes there and Scottie maintains them. As he gets closer to the plane, he stops and looks underneath. As he's looking, he says, "I don't think she's leaking anymore. How'd she feel?"

Tom answers, "No problem, she's handling well."

"That's good."

As Scottie and Tom are talking, mechanics are working on other planes. Scottie is distracted by the activity around him and he barks orders to his mechanics. "Billie, make sure you tighten up that manifold."

Billie shouts back, "You got it."

Tom walks around the plane making sure everything is okay. He returns to Scottie. "Scottie, I gotta go. I'm running late."

"What's the hurry? Hang out a while."

"I can't. I'm meeting some of the guys for drinks."

"Oh yeah, what's the occasion?"

"It's my birthday."

"Oh, shit. Happy Birthday."

"Hey, Scottie, why don't you come with me?"

"No, I can't. I gotta stay. I'm behind on repairs but go ahead. We'll grab a drink next time you come by." Scottie extends his hand and gives Tom a hearty handshake.

"Thanks, Scottie. I gotta go."

"Go ahead, I'll take care of the plane."

"I'll see you, Scottie. We'll get that drink soon." Tom leaves and walks to his car. In the background, Scottie is still barking orders to his mechanics.

Tom walks into O'Hanlon's Bar and Grill in Oceanview, Long Island. Once inside, he's greeted by cheers from the five men seated at the table. The men are all policemen and friends of Tom. One of the men is Bob Fuller. Bob is a close friend of Tom, even though they never worked together. The men have their bottles raised in a toast to Tom. Bob is giving the toast.

"Alright, guys. Let's toast to Tommy. One of the finest men I know. Happy Birthday, you old bastard." Laughter and then an off-key, alcohol-soaked version of Happy Birthday. Bob takes a sip from his bottle and talks to Tom. Bob is a big man, 6"3", 220 pounds, dark brown hair, and brown eyes. He's been a sergeant for many years. He and Tom have partnered on cases before. Bob liked to drink, sometimes too much. Bob asks, "How's the plane? Did you go flying today?"

"Yeah, it was beautiful."

"Shit, why didn't you tell me.

"I was, but I wasn't sure.'

"Wasn't sure about what."

"Wasn't sure your heart can take it, you old bastard."

"Hey, Tommy, go fuck yourself." The two men share a laugh and drink from their bottles. Bob asks Tom, "Did you decide about the house?"

"No, not yet."

"What are you waiting for, Tommy? It's been over two years."

"You're right."

"What about Eric? What'd he say?"

"We don't talk about it."

"Hey, Tommy, do something for me."

"What."

"Give Eric a call and talk to him about it. See how he feels."

"Yeah, good idea. I'll call him."

"You hungry?"

"Starving."

"Good, cause we're going to Gallagher's on me, alright?"

"Holy shit, Bob. Did you hit the lottery or something?"

"Come here." Bob throws his arm around Tom's neck and kisses him on top of the head. The other men at the table clap and catcall. Bob is looking around the table and laughing. "Hey, fellas, one day I'm gonna marry this prick.

CHAPTER 3
WHAT HAPPENS IN VEGAS

The sun is setting in Las Vegas. A car is parked in a facility adjoining a 4-star hotel. A man sits inside waiting. He's Hispanic in his 30s, a manila envelope by his side. He's impatient and looks at his watch. He scans the facility to make sure he's alone. From the other side of the garage, a car with four men inside drives in and parks.

Two men exit the vehicle and walk towards the Hispanic man's car. With the envelope in hand, he also exits and approaches the men walking towards the middle of the garage. He pretends to adjust his jacket, but he's really feeling for the 9mm gun in the waistband of his pants. The men get closer and they're both Middle Eastern. One of the men is carrying a briefcase. He's large and muscular.

The men meet in the middle and there are no pleasantries exchanged. The man with the briefcase addresses the Hispanic man as "officer." The officer is Special Agent Rodriguez with the Las Vegas DEA. The large man asks, "Is everything in the envelope?"

The officer nods yes and he asks if the money in the briefcase. The large man nods yes, and they exchange the envelope for the brief-case. The large man asks, "Are these the only copies?"

The officer answers sarcastically, "Maybe." The large man is staring at the officer and he says, "the Ambassador bodes you no harm and wishes you a long and prosperous life." With that, the other men exit the car as the large man reaches for his gun. The officer gets off the first two shots and hits the man twice. He falls mortally wounded.

At that moment a car drives into the parking facility, the headlights distracting the men. The officer uses the opportunity to run to the elevator directly behind him. One of the men makes it to the elevator with him as the doors close behind them. Both men are in the elevator as it goes to the penthouse, fighting for their lives. The officer smashes the man in the face with the briefcase and blood comes from the man's mouth. The man is disoriented and he's flailing punches as the officer hits him again with the briefcase to the side of his head. The man recovers and takes a knife from his sleeve. He attacks the officer and the first thrust misses. The second is thwarted by the briefcase the officer uses as a shield. He's not so lucky as the third thrust penetrates his jacket and slices his upper arm. The next attempt to stab the officer fails as the briefcase smashes on the man's head and he loses consciousness. In the scuffle Rodriguez loses his gun.

The doors to the elevator open and the officer is on the penthouse floor. The wound is bleeding steadily and blood is running down his arm. He makes his way down the hall towards the exit door and he hears the ping of the elevator in front of him. He picks up the pace but the elevator opens and the other two Middle Eastern men step out and he's spotted. He finds an open door behind him that says Sky Jump, and he climbs the two floors to the top with the men in pursuit. He encounters a security guard who shouts, "Hey, you're not supposed to be up here."

The officer shows his badge and he tells the security guard, "I'm a cop. Give me your gun." The security guard reaches for his gun when the Middle Eastern man fires and hits the security guard in the shoulder. The guard returns fire and hits the Middle Eastern man, and he falls wounded. The other man comes out of the shadows and attacks the officer. The officer is slammed against a concrete wall, knocking the wind out of him. The man is punching the officer in his wound, and the officer fights back and digs his fingers into the man's eyes. The man screams as the officer head-butts him. He opens a gash on the man's nose that gushes blood.

The officer has his arm around the man's neck and he tightens his grip. The man punches the officer's wound several times causing the officer to loosen his choke hold. The men are rolling around on the floor. The officer is now on top and pounding the man's face. The man again punches the wound causing the officer to scream in pain and this allows the man to get on his feet. The men are now fighting close to the edge of Sky Jump, 800 feet in the air. The guard is able to fire a shot in the air, distracting the men.

The officer seizes the opportunity and he kicks the man in the chest and he goes over the edge. The officer tries to help the man back onto the platform, but the man slips out of his grasp and he falls to his death. In the background, sirens are getting closer. The officer goes to the security guard to check his wounds. "How are you doing, pal?"

"Who are you?" The officer doesn't answer and continues checking the guard's wound.

"You'll be okay. Help is on the way." The officer gestures to the Sky Jump control. "Do you know how this works?"

"Yeah, that's my day job."

"Lucky me."

The guard adds, "Hope you're not afraid of heights. You see that red lever? Push it up." The officer does it.

"Now push the two green buttons and get into the harness."

"I don't have time."

"Help me up and grab the harness." The officer helps the guard as the sounds of sirens get closer. "Get over there and grab the harness. Don't look down."

The officer grabs the harness and says, "Do it." The guard triggers the descent of the officer at 40 mph to the street. The officer walks away from the crowds and the lights of the emergency vehicles. A taxicab turns the corner and the officer flags it down. Once inside, he leans back in the seat and closes his eyes.

Tom calls his son, Eric. "Hello, dad."

"Hi, Eric. How's Atlanta treating you?"

"Great, I'm on my way home. How was your birthday?"

"Good. I had drinks with some of the guys. Bob Fuller was there. He took us to Gallagher's for dinner."

"Gallager's is nice. I'm thinking about coming up to see you. I'll let you know when. I owe you a birthday dinner."

"Eric, I want to ask you something."

"Go ahead, dad."

"How would you feel if I sold the house?"

There's a pause, then Eric says: "I think you should. We had some good times there. But you're alone now in a big house. Maybe you can find an apartment in the area."

"You're right, Eric. It's something I've been thinking about for a while. On the way back from the airport, I drove past this good-looking house on Meadow Lane. The house is on a dead-end and kind of secluded. It was beautifully landscaped. From the outside it looks like a pretty big house. There was an apartment that had a for rent sign in the window. I'm gonna stop in tomorrow."

"Great. Go see it. You got nothing to lose."

Tom laughs, "With my luck, the Addams Family lives there."

"Hell, if that's the case, I'll take it."

"I'll let you know how it goes with the apartment. Once I get settled in, take some time off and come up. We got some catching up to do."

"Okay, dad. Sounds like a plan. We'll talk soon. Bye."

CHAPTER 4
ANNA SANCHEZ

Tom arrives at the house the next morning. It's a beautiful restored Victorian on one acre of land. It's isolated from the heart of town. Tom rings the bell.

The apartment for rent sign is in the window. No one answers the bell. He waits a bit then rings again. The door opens just enough for the woman inside to look out. Tom introduces himself. "Hi, I'm Tom Hartford about the apartment."

The woman says, "Hi, can you wait a minute?" The door closes and Tom hears the chain being removed. The door opens and standing there is a beautiful Latin woman with long black hair, brown eyes, about 35 years old. She gives a first impression of being a classy lady. She's dressed casually in jeans and a white shirt. She extends her hand to greet Tom. "Sorry about that. I'm Anna Sanchez."

Tom takes her hand, being careful not to squeeze too hard. "I'm Tom Hartford. Nice to meet you."

"Come in, please." Tom walks into a large, beautifully decorated house with early Spanish-style furniture. Rugs and tapestries decorate the interior. Artwork and antiques are everywhere. Daylight filters in and beautiful plants are placed around the room. Tom exclaims, "This place is gorgeous."

"Thank you."

"Did you decorate it yourself?"

"Yes, well, not exactly. My husband did the construction and I did the decorating."

"It looks professional."

"Thanks, I studied interior design in Madrid, that's where I'm from. So, do you want to see the apartment?"

"Yeah, I'd love to."

"Wait here, I'll get the keys." Tom waits in the living room, admiring the antiques and the artwork. Anna returns with the keys. "Come with me." They go out the front door and up a set of stairs on the side of the house. Anna describes the apartment to Tom. "This is your private entrance. Everything inside is brand new. We painted it a light color, but you can change it if you like." Anna opens the door and they walk in. The interior is illuminated with daylight. Tom is impressed. "It's nice, lots of light."

"It's bright, it's a great place for plants. The kitchen and bathroom are brand new. There's an extra bedroom that we added. Would you like to see it?"

"No."

Anna is surprised and she asks, "No?"

"No, I mean I'll take it."

"Just like that, Mr. Hartford? Don't you want to talk about the rent and…" Tom interrupts, "How much could it be?"

"It's fifteen hundred dollars a month."

"That's fine. I guess you'll want one month's rent and a month's security."

"Yes, if that's not a problem."

"When can I move in?"

"It's ready now, so any time, I guess. Let's go downstairs. I'll make some coffee and we can discuss it."

"I don't know. I should—"

Anna interrupts, "I insist. Let's go downstairs." Tom and Anna are sitting in the dining room. Anna asks, "Are you married, will you be moving in with your wife?"

"No, my wife died a few years ago."

"I'm sorry to bring it up."

"It's okay, I've been living in the house alone and it can get a little overwhelming at times."

"I understand, where is the house?"

"Oak Street."

"Oak Street. It's a very nice area."

"Yeah, we loved it."

"Do you have children, Mr. Hartford?"

"Yeah, I have a son, Eric. He teaches in Atlanta."

"A teacher. I have lots of respect for teachers. What does he teach?"

"He teaches history, 6th-grade history." Tom asks, "What about you? Any kids?"

"No, no kids."

Tom is looking around. "Is that what you do for a living?"

"What?"

"Decorate houses."

Anna replies, "No, two nights a week I teach interior design at Long Island College."

"So, you're also a teacher."

"In a way, but not like your son. I teach people who have nothing else to do. Some take it seriously, but most don't."

Tom is looking at his watch, "Well, I better get going."

"I'll walk you out." Tom gets up and begins to talk to the door and Anna walks with him. "By the way, forget the security deposit. Just one month's rent will be fine."

"Are you sure? I thought we agreed."

"It's okay. Just give me a call when you're ready to move your stuff."

"I was thinking of bringing some stuff over this week."

"Okay, let me know which day. May I call you Tom?"

"Sure."

"Call me Anna." They reach the front door. Anna unlocks and opens it and extends her hand. "It was nice meeting you." Tom takes her hand and gives her a firm handshake. She responds by tightening her hand, also.

"I'll talk to you. Bye."

"Bye, Tom."

Tom turns to leave and Anna watches as he goes down the stairs and closes the door.

CHAPTER 5
ANTONIO SANCHEZ

A nna and her husband, Antonio Sanchez, are having dinner. Antonio is a large man, athletically built with black hair, dark eyes. He is quiet but tense and menacing. They eat together in silence. Anna seems to be looking for the courage to speak. She puts her fork down and drinks from her glass. Anna reluctantly speaks to Antonio. "The man I told you about came to look at the apartment this morning."

"Oh, yeah, what happened?"

"He's gonna take it."

Antonio is still eating and he says, "Did he give you any money?"

"No, not today. He said he's coming back . . ." Antonio interrupts her, "That's bullshit, Anna. He ain't coming back. They all say that."

"No, Antonio. He said he wants to start moving in this week. He was serious."

"So what did you tell him?"

"I told him it would be okay to . . . " Antonio interrupts again, "That's not what I'm talking about, Anna. What did you tell him?"

"About what? What do you want to know?"

Antonio is growing impatient. "I want to know about money, Anna. That's what I'm talking about."

"I told him the rent was fifteen hundred dollars." Antonio is agitated and says, "That's good. One month's rent and one month's security in advance. Right."

Anna says nervously, "No, I told him one month's rent." Antonio is angry and he asks, "What about the security?"

"I told him just the first month's rent, Antonio."

"What? Why would you do that? What the fuck, Anna? What's wrong with you? You pissed away fifteen hundred bucks just like that."

Anna is intimidated and she says, "Please calm down and listen to me. I felt bad for him. His wife died and he's alone . . ."

Antonio interrupts, "His wife died. So what, this is business. I want the money. When he calls, tell him you want it. You hear me?"

"I can't do that. I already told him . . ."

"I want that money, Anna, and you better get it. Fuck this, I'm out. I gotta meet some fucking wops." Antonio grabs his coat and heads out the door. The door slams loudly behind him.

CHAPTER 6
OCEANVIEW—A QUIET LITTLE HAMLET

Officer Rodriguez is reporting for work a few days after the incident on Sky Jump. He fast walks past his boss's office, hoping she doesn't notice. His boss is Sergeant Elizabeth McMahon. She's African American and has been with the Las Vegas DEA for 15 years. In those 15 years, she's been awarded numerous medals and citations. She's cracked major drug trafficking cases and has helped take thousands of pounds of drugs off the streets. She's known for her "take no prisoners" approach to police work. This morning she's in an especially bad mood.

She sees him walk past and shouts, "Rodriguez, can you come in here?"

He enters and says, "Morning, Sarge." McMahon doesn't answer the greeting. On the desk are several folders. She insists, "Sit down, Rodriguez."

"You took a few days off, you feel better now?

"Sure thanks, what do you want to talk about?

"Have you been watching the news the last couple of days?"

"You mean that Sky Jump thing at the Stratosphere Hotel?"

"Yeah, that Stratosphere thing."

Rodriguez says, "What a shit show that was." McMahon sits back in her chair and stares at Rodriguez. She says, "I got a hit on my confidential phone this morning straight from the Nevada head-quarters of the DEA." Rodriguez says, "Damn, Sarge, you got a secret phone? I'm impressed."

"Cut the crap and pay attention, Detective." It seems the head of our division was impressed with the work you did earlier this year when you and your team broke that Reno meth distribution case. You took a lot of meth off the streets and locked up some big play-ers. Well, it seems he's sending up the Bat Signal again. I'm sending you to New York, Rodriguez. Well, not the Big Apple exactly but a town in Long Island called Oceanview." Rodriguez is surprised by this news and he says, "Oceanview sounds like a fucking nursing home."

"Maybe so, but this town with a population of 10,000 people could become a major player in a drug trafficking case involving the Delacruz cartel.

"Delacruz? Shit, that's big. What does Delacruz want with a small town like Oceanwaves?"

"It's Oceanview, Rodriguez. Our agents south of the border are picking up some increased activity with Delacruz's cartel. Some of this activity involves the DiNapoli family in Brooklyn."

"Damn, two of the biggest crime families north or south of the border. What's going on, Sarge?"

"We suspect Delacruz wants to use DiNapoli's distribution network to sell a dangerously potent form of cocaine in this area." That's why you're going to Oceanview to look around and report back to me."

"But Sarge, I don't want to go to Oceanview."

"What I'm about to tell you may change your mind. Consider this transfer a favor."

"What are you talking about Sergeant?"

"I got an update yesterday from Captain Steiner." He's with Vegas P.D. and he said the guard that was shot can ID the guy who took Sky Jump to the ground. He said the guy flashed a badge and said he was a cop."

"Did the security guard get the guy's name?"

"No."

"So how did he know he was a cop? Anybody can say that."

McMahon sits quietly, letting Rodriguez speak, then she says, " I'll tell you why—because the man went back to make sure the guard's wounds weren't life-threatening. Only a cop would do that. He also said the man's left hand was covered in blood. Vegas PD found a gun that can't be traced and a briefcase stuffed with stacks of paper and on top of each stack was a hundred dollar bill. According to Captain Steiner it was about eighteen hundred bucks. It was made to look as if the case was loaded with money." " Those fuckers," Rodriguez says, surprised.

McMahon looks at Rodriguez and says, "Expecting more? Let me see your left arm."

Rodriguez sighs and looks up at the ceiling. "There's something else. Two of the guys were carrying State Department IDs from Kuwait. I think we're gonna be in the middle of an international incident soon."

"I don't know what the fuck you're involved in with these mooks, but for you, you're going to Oceanview. You'll be in Sergeant Bob Fuller's precinct. As far as anybody is concerned you're Detective Rodriguez with the Las Vegas P.D. Captain Steiner was your C.O. You were transferred because you're a disciplinary problem."

"Sarge, you hurt my feelings."

"Focus, Rodriguez, this is important. This is a joint effort with the Brooklyn organized crime unit. The guy in charge is Captain Danny Ebersole."

"When do I meet him?"

"Not yet. I'll let you know. As of right now, keep your eyes and ears open."

"Anybody, in particular, I should pay attention to?"

"Yeah, Antonio Sanchez. Introduce yourself, but don't make a mess."

"What's the story with Sanchez? You got any history on him?"

"Yeah, plenty. He started with the Delacruz family in its early days. He lived in California for a while doing odd jobs—you know, construction type of work. He went off the grid for a while and he showed up in Oceanview. He married a local woman and settled in. He was arrested a few times—mostly for fighting, the most serious arrest was for a serious beating he gave some guy once but the guy didn't press charges. He's had some drug arrests in Oceanview but he always manages to squirm out of it. Take a few days, Rodriguez, and read the file. Sergeant Fuller has your papers. All you need to do is show up."

Rodriguez says, "I'll be out by the end of the week."

"One more thing. I don't have to tell you these men are dangerous. We had an agent in Columbia who was able to smuggle a sample of this new cocaine to one of our chemists. It's true, Rodriguez. It's the strongest shit we've ever seen. We haven't heard from him since. Unfortunately, the agents we can trust are being frozen out by the corruption. We don't know who's on our side. Listen to me carefully. Don't trust anybody, including Fuller."

"Thanks, Sarge. I'll take your advice."

McMahon slides an envelope across her desk and she says, "Everything you need is in there, including your plane ticket. It's an open ticket. You can fly when you're ready. Sign the transfer papers and give them to Fuller when you get there."

"Thanks, Sarge." He gets up and heads for the door but he stops, turns back, and speaks to McMahon. "By the way, I almost forgot. These are for you," and he puts a set of keys in front of her.

"What's this?" She notices the name stamped into the keys: Las Vegas National Bank Number 37 "What's this about?"

"It's about a few nights ago. "Those keys are for a safe deposit box and the contents will explain everything."

McMahon picks up the keys and says, "When this Delacruz thing is done, we're gonna talk about that night, Rodriguez. Remember, don't trust anybody."

Rodriguez says, "I'll be in touch," and closes the door behind him.

CHAPTER 7
THE TEST

It's 8:00 PM in Oceanview, Long Island. A black town car drives down a dark, isolated street and parks in front of a rundown building. A large sign outside the building says, "Ball Breakers." It's a combination pool room and low-rent strip club. This is Antonio Sanchez's hangout. This is where he conducts his drug deals. He has a private room in the back where he has sex with strippers. He's the only one with a key. He's meeting DiNapoli here tonight in what could be the beginning of the biggest drug deal of his life.

Right now Antonio is doing coke with a stripper. The stripper is leaning on Antonio with her hand on his crotch. She's wearing a robe and stripping music plays in the background. She kisses and plays with his ear. Antonio says, "Not now, baby. I got some business to do."

"What kinda business?"

"Don't get fuckin' nosey. You get it—nosey? Here, take another hit." Antonio hands the stripper a straw. She takes a hit and laughs, rubbing her nose.

Richie, Dom and Primo walk into Ball Breakers. Dom is carrying a briefcase. Primo stands by the door looking over the room. The people in the room pause and look at them. They know it's Richie DiNapoli from the newspapers and television and they quickly return to what they were doing. Richie and Dom walk to the bar as they scan the room. Primo's eyes are moving between the door and the room. The bartender walks over. He pauses and looks at the men and asks, "What can I get you, gentlemen?"

Richie says, "Bourbon, no rocks and no watered-down shit, either." The bartender looks at Dom. "What about you?"

"Same. Gotta be top-shelf. What'ya got?" The bartender goes to the top shelf behind the bottles and comes out with a bottle of Knob Creek unopened. He holds the bottle up for the men to see. He says, "Is this good—brand new bottle."

Dom says, "Yeah, that's good." The bartender brings two glasses and he pours. As he's pouring, he looks at Richie and he asks, "Ain't you Richie DiNapoli?" Richie picks up the glass and without looking at the bartender, he takes a sip. He turns to the bartender with a cold stare. "No."

The bartender is no longer smiling; he knows it's Richie and he stands there not knowing what to do. Dom is looking at the bartender and he says, "You waitin' for a tip. Get the fuck out of here." The bartender scrambles to the other side of the bar. Richie looks at his watch, then looks at the dancer on the stage above him. He smiles and says to Dom, "I hope you wake up next to that tomorrow."

Dom looks at the dancer, tilts his head, and says, "I wouldn't mind."

"Come on, Dom. She's a crackhead, probably doing tricks in this joint ."

"In that case, the wedding's off." They both laugh and Richie says, "You're a class act, Dom."

Richie looks at his watch again and takes another sip. He's growing impatient. "He's late." He turns to Dom. "If this guy doesn't show, we're leaving. Fuck him. I'll let Primo talk to him." The back door opens and the stripper comes out and goes to the ladies' room. Antonio pokes his head out and motions to the men to come in. Richie looks at Primo and nods, and Primo nods back. As they walk to the back, Richie whispers to Dom, "Be ready. I don't trust this guy." Dom pulls a gun from under his coat and holds it to his side. The men enter the room and Antonio locks the door. Richie looks around the room and he sees cocaine residue and empty beer bottles on the table. He says sarcastically, "Is this a bad time, Sanchez?"

Antonio sees the gun at Dom's side and he gets nervous. He points to the gun. "What're you gonna do with that?"

Dom is glaring at Antonio. "I don't know. I was thinking maybe I'll shoot somebody." Antonio stands with his hands in front of him.

Richie looks at Dom. "Put it away."

"He kept me waiting."

"Put the fucking thing away."

Dom puts the gun in his coat pocket, still staring at Antonio. Richie adds, "Put the case on the table."

Dom does what Richie says. Richie turns the briefcase around so the lock is facing Antonio. Richie says, "Open it." Antonio opens the case and looks inside. The case contains rolls of bills bound together in stacks. Antonio says, "Fifty grand, right?" Richie nods and gestures towards the case. He says, "That's for you. Now gimme mine and hurry up. This place is making me itchy."

Antonio gets the message and clears the table. He goes to the back of the room to a row of lockers. He grabs a locker and pulls it to the side revealing a wall safe. He moves to shield the combination and opens the safe. He reaches in and pulls out two clear baggies filled with white powder. Dom has his testing kit out, ready to test the product. Antonio puts the bags on the table. Dom takes out a vial with clear liquid. Richie takes a small amount of coke and puts it into the vial. Slowly, the liquid turns purple. Dom holds it to the light and looks at Richie smiling and he says, "This shit is no joke."

Antonio smiles, "See, Richie, I told you it's good shit."

"The other bag—is it the same?"

"Yeah, Richie, it's the same stuff." Dom looks at Richie waiting for the word. Richie says, "Test it."

"Come on, Richie, don't you trust me?"

"No, I don't." While Dom does the next test, Richie looks around the room and notices roaches crawling on the walls and he checks his clothes. Dom tests the second bag with the same result.

"It's the same."

"Good. Take the money out of the briefcase, put the coke in the case, and let's get out of here before we catch a fucking disease." Dom does as he's told. Antonio extends his hand to Richie and he's ignored. The men turn to leave.

Antonio says, "Why don't you come by one night? We'll have a drink and I'll get you laid." Richie stops and says "Get this straight. We're not friends. This is business. Tell Delacruz I like his product. Let me know when he's ready." Dom and Richie turn to leave.

Antonio says, "Richie, can you close the door?"

"No problem." The men walk out, leaving the door open. Antonio stands there with the money still on the table. He mumbles, "Fucking grease balls."

Richie and Dom are heading for the door when Richie stops at the bar. He looks up at the dancers and one of them stands out. The dancer is the girl-next-door type, stunningly beautiful with auburn hair with long, flowing curls. She catches Richie's eye and returns his gaze. He yells for Dom, "Dom, come here and call Primo over." "Let's have a drink." The bartender walks over. "What can I get you, same as before?"

"Yeah, let's do it again."

"What are we drinking, Richie?"

"It's bourbon. Try it, Primo. You'll like it." Richie leans closer to Dom and asks, "What do you think about that shit? How many times can we cut it?"

"Two or three times and it's still better than most of the shit out there."

"Hey, Primo, what do you think of the bourbon? Pretty good, right?"

"Not bad, boss, but I prefer red wine."

"Hey, Primo, sometimes you gotta try something new."

Richie looks up at the girl-next-door type dancing above him and he says to Dom, "Check out that dancer."

"Nice piece of ass."

Richie calls over the bartender and he asks "What's her name?"

"Cinnamon."

"My favorite spice." Richie makes eye contact with her and she leans over and gets closer to him. He puts a fifty dollar bill in her G-string and whispers "What are you doing in a dump like this? You're too good for this place."

She replies, "Yeah, you too," and moves to the middle of the stage.

Primo says, "Hey, boss, I think she likes you." The men laugh and Richie motions to the bartender to come over. Richie gives the bartender a one hundred dollar bill wrapped around his business card and tells the bartender, "Do me a favor. Give her my card and keep the hundred, that's for you. If she tells me to go fuck myself, it is what it is."

"I don't think too many people tell you shit like that."

"You'd be surprised what people tell me. Don't worry, I'm not an asshole. I don't abuse women. No matter what happens, you keep the hundred bucks."

"Okay, I'll give her the card." Richie and the others leave the club.

Primo is driving Richie and Dom to Brooklyn. Richie asks, "Hey, Dom, who did she remind you of?" Dom thinks for a minute. "You know that movie with the masks where everybody's chanting some weird shit? She looks like the babe in that movie."

"You mean 'Eyes Wide Shut?'"

"Yeah. That's it, Primo. That was some kinky shit in that movie. Hey Richie, what's her name, you know the star?"

"Beats me. Ask Primo."

Primo answers, "Nicole Kidman."

Richie says, "Very good, Primo. Nice job. Must be the bourbon."

"Nah, I just like going to the movies. I watch a lot of them on TV and I like going to the aquarium, too". "That's where I go when you guys have meetings at the Social Club. My favorite is the Brooklyn Aquarium."

"Holy Shit, Primo lets his hair down. Surprise, surprise, the Brooklyn Aquarium. I would've never guessed."

CHAPTER 8
MOVING DAY

Sunlight is streaming into Anna's living room. Anna is relaxing on the couch reading a book. The phone rings. Anna puts the book down and picks it up. "Hello."

"Hi Anna, it's Tom. How are you?"

"Okay, Tom. It's a lovely day."

"Yes, it is. I'd like to bring some things over tomorrow."

"It's okay, Tom. What time?"

"Can I come over about ten?"

"It's fine. Ring my bell. I'll give you the keys."

"Okay, Anna. Thanks, I'll see you then. Bye."

The following morning, a moving truck stops in front of her house followed by Tom's car. Tom gets out and greets Anna. "Good morning."

"Hi, Tom, I see you're all set. Right on time."

"Yeah, these guys are gonna start bringing some stuff upstairs."

"Would you like some juice or coffee, Tom?"

"No, thanks. I'm good."

"Okay, let me get the keys. I'll change and give you a hand."

"No, it's okay. We can handle it. These guys are pros."

"Okay, then I'll make you lunch. How long will you be?"

"It's okay. You don't have to."

"It's my pleasure. You won't let me help, so I'll make lunch."

"Okay, if it's no bother. They told me about three hours."

"Okay, about one o'clock. Sandwiches ok?"

"Sure."

CHAPTER 9
DISPLAY OF BRAVADO

Antonio is in Ball Breakers playing pool. A waitress brings beers to the players. She's wearing a short skirt and tight top with black hair, and looks Italian in her late 20's. The waitress walks past Antonio and makes eye contact. Antonio nods and motions to the back. The waitress walks into the back room and closes the door. Antonio hands his pool cue to a guy sitting on the side waiting to play, saying, "Here, finish this for me."

The player circles the table, sizing up his shot. The player is Felix Reyes. He's twenty-six years old and a crack addict. Felix is 5' 4" tall with black hair and a thin goatee. Due to his lifestyle and drug addiction he's skinny with rotten teeth. He has no friends and he idolizes Antonio. Antonio has used Felix's addiction and his admiration for him to his advantage.

The waitress is sitting on the table with her legs crossed. She looks at Antonio as he enters. Antonio reaches into his pocket and pulls out a vial of white powder. He waves it in front of her face. He opens the vial and looks her up and down. "Stand up." She stands. "Take off your top." She takes off her top and she's not wearing a bra. Her breasts are firm and perfect. Antonio shows her the coke again. "You want some of this?"

"You know I do."

"You want some of this and I want some of you. Come over here and get up against the door." The waitress walks to the door and puts her back against it. He gets close and puts a small amount of coke on one of her breasts and snorts it off as she smiles. He puts some on a spoon and puts it under her nose while his hand slides up her thigh. She takes a hit of the coke and begins to writhe. He kisses her and she pulls away teasingly. He attempts to kiss her again and this time she returns the kiss. "You like that, baby?"

She takes more coke. "Yeah, I do."

"What do you want?"

"You, baby."

"Say it again, baby. I want to hear it again."

"Give it to me, Antonio."

"You want it now?"

"Yeah, do it now."

Antonio picks up her leg to make it easier to penetrate her. She moans as he enters her. She grabs him around the shoulders and holds onto his shirt. They begin a rhythm and with every stroke, her back hits the door with a steady boom-boom-boom.

Felix is still playing pool and he begins to hear the boom-boom on the door. He realizes it's the sound of Antonio and the waitress. He waves his arms to everyone. Felix shouts, "Yo, listen to this shit." Some players haven't stopped playing. Felix shouts again, pointing to the door. "Yo, bitches, stop playing and listen." The small crowd quiets down. All we hear is the music and the boom-boom and the waitress begins to moan loudly. The stripper on the stage continues to dance, oblivious to what's going on. Felix shouts again, "Yo, turn the music down." Antonio and the waitress are both into it and they're reaching the peak. The thrusts are stronger now. Felix says, "He's doing her real good." One of the players says, "No shit." Another says, "What the fuck is going on in there?" "What the fuck do you think? Keep playing, stupid, so I can beat your ass."

The noise coming from the back room stops and the men go back to playing. The music goes back up as Antonio exits the room. He walks out prancing like a rooster, smug and sure of himself. He knows they heard it and that was his plan. This guy can't get enough of himself. He walks past the pool table and looks at Felix. Felix looks at Antonio with a big grin. "Yo, you the man! You want your stick back?"

"No, I'm out of here." Antonio struts out of the bar and doesn't look back. The waitress comes out of the room wiping white residue from her nose. Everybody stops and stares. The waitress goes behind the bar, pours a double shot of vodka and drinks it down, slams the glass on the bar and looks at the men playing pool. Some of the men are gawking at her. She says angrily, "What the fuck are you looking at? Go back to your game, assholes." She goes to the ladies' room and slams the door.

CHAPTER 10
FINALLY WE MEET

T he movers are finished and are gone for the day. Tom and Anna are sitting in Anna's dining room having lunch. Anna is talking about her family. "My father was a carpenter and eventually he started his own company and did very well. He died when I was young. Thanks to him, I was able to attend good schools in Spain."

"Your husband is also a carpenter, isn't he?"

"Well, he does a little bit of everything. He's very talented and he renovated your apartment."

"He is talented. The place looks great."

"So, you really like it?"

"I love it. I'm gonna move in next week."

"Do you have more stuff?"

"Yeah, the guys who were here today are gonna be back."

"Would you like another sandwich?"

"No, I'm okay. Thanks, Anna."

"You should get some plants for the apartment."

"I don't know. I'm not a plant kind of guy."

"Come on, they'll do well up there."

The door opens and in walks Antonio. Anna sees him and tenses in her chair. Antonio takes off his jacket, throws it on the sofa, and walks over to Anna. As he approaches, she sits upright in her chair, obviously tense, and Tom notices. Antonio leans over and kisses Anna on the lips and Anna does not react. He looks at Tom and says, "I'm Antonio, Anna's husband."

Tom stands and extends his hand. "Tom Hartford. I'm your new tenant."

Antonio sits down. "So, how was the move?"

"Okay, but I have more stuff to bring over."

Anna interrupts, "Antonio, do you want a sandwich?"

"Sure, baby."

"What do you want?"

"Whatever, it don't matter. You know what I like." He looks at Tom with a smug look on his face. "So, Tom, what do you do?"

"Nothing these days. I'm retired."

"From what?"

"I was a sergeant with Suffolk County P.D. I flew choppers for them."

"Oh, shit, a cop. How come you never arrested me?"

"There's still time, Antonio."

"You gotta catch me first." Both men laugh as Anna returns to the table with Antonio's sandwich and places it in front of him. The laughter stops and the two men are looking at each other suspiciously. Anna breaks the tension. "When did you retire, Tom?" she asks. "About four years ago." Antonio looks at Anna seemingly upset that she asked the question first. Tom says, "Anna tells me you do construction." "Yeah, when there's work. Right now, there ain't shit out there. Maybe I'll start selling drugs." Antonio pauses for effect, then he says, "Just kidding, Tom. Don't get excited."

Anna changes the subject. "Tom's son teaches sixth grade history in Atlanta." Antonio interrupts, "You think they care about what happened a hundred years ago? Nobody cares. All they want to do is play fucking video games and talk shit about the other kids in class." "Antonio, please." Antonio asks Tom sarcastically, "Hey, Tom, what do you think?"

"I think it's important. It affects how we live today."

"Trust me, Tom. They don't give a shit."

Tom looks at his watch, gets up, and says, "I gotta go." He looks at Antonio and says sarcastically, "Take care of yourself." He responds, "Yeah, see ya around." Anna comes around the table and walks Tom to the door. Antonio brings his sandwich to the couch. He throws himself down on the sofa and grabs the remote.

Anna and Tom reach the door, and she says, "I'm sorry for Antonio's behavior. Sometimes he can be rude."

Tom replies, "It's okay. Thanks for lunch. Bye." Anna closes the door and tries to walk past Antonio on her way upstairs. Anna says, "I'm going to take a bath." Antonio grabs Anna's hand and asks her, "What's going on?" Why're you upset?" Anna says, ``I don't want to talk about it." And she pulls away.

"So what's up? Why're you upset? You on the rag?"

"You wanna know why I'm upset? You could've been nicer to him."

"Why, he said something?"

"No, but you made him uncomfortable."

"Me? What did I say?"

"It's not what you say. It's your actions. I can't explain it."

"Well, Anna, if you can't explain it, I don't know what the fucking problem is."

"You don't understand. You were rude to him."

"I wasn't rude, I was honest. And don't forget he owes me money. I want the fucking money, Anna. Get it from your rich uncle if you have to. Just get me the fucking cash."

Anna is angry and she storms up the stairs. From downstairs, Antonio yells, "Did you ask him for the money?" Anna slams the bathroom door.

CHAPTER 11
INTERNATIONAL INCIDENT
OR NOT

Sergeant McMahon is sitting at her desk reading the contents of the envelope that was in the safe deposit box at the Las Vegas National Bank. The documents reveal that the Kuwaiti Ambassador is selling weapons to terrorists. The documents also show that officials with the Turkish government are fellow conspirators.

McMahon puts the papers down on the desk. She walks to the door and motions to two men in suits sitting outside her office. The men enter and one of them closes the door. McMahon says, "Have a seat, gentlemen. Before we get involved in these papers, I just wanna say I'm not gonna tell you how I got the documents. I spoke to your boss at the State Department and she told me you were the best techs she had to authenticate these papers. If you don't think you can do it, let me know and I'll call her and tell her how disappointed I am. Take a look."

McMahon slides the envelope across the desk. The men open the envelope and thumb through the papers and glance at each other. "One of the men looks at McMahon and says, "these documents name names and places." Shit, if these are genuine there's going to be a lot of people going to prison including some of our guys."

They exchange the documents amongst themselves and one of the men says." It's going to take us some time to determine if these are real, is there some place we can study these in private?" "Is there an empty office we can use."

"Sure, there's one next door. But don't leave the building with 'em.

"So if these are authentic and the weapons were going to terrorists what happens then?"

"If it's for real, then we report back and the big boys get involved. You know - FBI, NSA and probably Homeland Security. When they get involved you're going to have to tell them where they came from. Do you want to tell us about it and save yourself a lot of bureaucratic bullshit?"

"No, I don't but I'm curious. Now that you've got 'em, what the fuck are you gonna do with 'em? Thank you gentlemen. I will leave you alone," and she closes the door.

CHAPTER 12
WHO IS THIS GUY?

Tom calls Bob Fuller and the Sergeant picks up. "Hi, Bob," Tom says.

"Hey, Tom, How's it going?"

"Good, can I come buy or are you busy?"

"Sure, come on. Grab a couple of coffees on your way."

"Tom walks into the precinct and is greeted by the officers on duty."

"Can we talk privately?"

"Sure, my office. Come on." The men enter the office and Bob gestures to Tom to sit down as he closes the door. "So, Tom, what's going on?"

"Antonio Sanchez. Do you know him?"

"Yeah, I know him. Did you have a run-in with him?"

"Kind of. I'm renting the upstairs apartment in his house."

"No shit. You finally made the move. Good for you, Tom. So I guess you met his wife, Anna."

"Sure, I met her."

"She's stunning, isn't she, Tom?"

"Certainly is."

"Antonio is a really jealous husband. He's obsessed with Anna. So, you wanna know about Sanchez? Let's see what we got. Hang on, let me get Detective Rodriguez in here. He's the new guy, transferred from Vegas. I think they wanted to move him out, discipline issues, at least that's what it said in his file. He hasn't been here that long, but so far he hasn't been a problem." Fuller gets up from his desk and opens the door. He pokes his head out and calls for Detective Rodriguez.

"On the way, Sarge." Rodriguez shows up at the door and enters the room. "What's up, Sergeant?" Fuller makes the introductions. "Detective Rodriquez, meet Tom Hartford. Tom's an old friend of mine. We go back at least 10 years."

"Did you work with Sergeant Fuller in this precinct?"

"No, I was with the eighteenth over on the north shore, but we worked cases together. Tom is a war hero from Desert Storm. Has the medals to prove it. Shit, he even flies his own plane. Yep, he's my hero."

Tom laughs. "Bob's my biggest fan."

"Hang out, Detective. We're looking at Antonio Sanchez's file. It seems Tom is living in his house—the lucky bastard." Fuller is punching information into a keyboard and he asks Tom, "How far back do you wanna go?"

"Whatever you got, Bob."

"Let's see. He lived in California about ten years ago. It seems he was involved with the Delacruz cartel in the early days. He was arrested in California three times for drug possession. Well, well—this is interesting..."

"What's that?"

"One of the arrests was for cocaine possession with intent to sell. Lots of cocaine. He was convicted and sentenced to eight years, but, get this, he only did ten months."

"Ten months—are you shitting me?"

"I kid you not."

"Sounds like friends in high places."

"No doubt, Tom. Maybe a politician or the prosecutor."

Rodriguez listens intently even though he's heard some of this from Sergeant McMahon.

"About five years ago, Sanchez showed up here. He's doing odd jobs, finally settles into construction, carpentry, and general contracting work. He's pretty talented from what I hear. He met Anna when she asked him to do some work in her house. They got married and he moved in."

"I saw the work he did in the house and he's good at what he does, real good."

"Anna owned the house for about three years, she lived with her mother until she died a few months after she bought the house. Supposedly she came from a wealthy family from Spain, I think. She studied interior decorating and was quite successful at it. She worked a lot in Manhattan redecorating lofts, brownstones—that sort of thing."

"That would explain the house."

"Yeah, I heard it's gorgeous inside."

Rodriguez questioned, "Was he ever in trouble here?"

"Oh yeah, he certainly was. I had a few, shall we say, differences of opinion with him. He's been arrested here mostly for drug offenses. There was one major arrest two years ago for assault, he beat somebody pretty bad, which could have turned into an attempted murder rap but the victim didn't press charges. We think he was intimidated by Sanchez and some of his asshole friends."

"What was that about, Bob?"

"Antonio and Anna were out one night at a dance club. A man asked Anna to dance. She accepted, which was ok, until Antonio felt that the man had his hands all over her. I would guess his jealous imagination got the best of him. It was probably innocent, but we're talking about a very jealous asshole. Well, that's about it, gentlemen."

Rodriguez asks, "Was Sanchez in California around 2009-2010?"

"Yeah, he was there at that time and he had some issues with the law."

"Wasn't that the time when he got busted and got out early?"

"It was about that time, wasn't it, Sergeant?"

"Yep, he was there."

"Do you remember the cocaine wars around that time?

"It was pretty bad, dealers were killing each other and users were OD-ing all over the place."

Tom asks Rodriguez, "Do you think Sanchez was involved?"

Fuller answers, "He was there, but there was no connection to him."

"He has to be involved. He was in California at the time, then he came here.

"I'm with you, Tom, but there was never any evidence."

Rodriguez asks, "Does he have a favorite hangout?"

"Yeah it's a place called Ball Breakers. It's a dive, a combination pool room and strip joint down by the ocean."

Fuller says to Rodriguez, "Can you excuse us for a minute, Detective?"

"Nice meeting you, Tom." Rodriguez leaves the room.

Bob warns Tom. "Be careful around Sanchez. You just heard how jealous he is. He's fucking nuts."

It's a cloudy night in Oceanview, a mist covers the ground. Sanchez is driving home after a night at Ball Breakers. The drive is lonely along a strip of road bordered by the ocean on the right and the sand dunes on the left. The road is dark with no lights and no other cars in sight. As he drives, he struggles to stay awake. He has enough drugs and alcohol in his system to get him locked up. He notices a black sedan following close. Eventually, he hears the chirp and sees the unmistakable lights of a police car.

A tall figure exits the police car carrying a flashlight. His hand is on his gun. When he gets close enough, he shines the light into the car. He moves the light around the inside of the car checking the interior. He does this to deliberately aggravate the driver. He shines the light into the driver's face and motions for him to roll down the driver's side window. The driver complies and the officer says "License and registration." The officer continues to shine the light into the front seat.

The driver barks back, "Get that light out of my face."

"License and registration."

"Why'd you stop me?"

"I've been following you for about a quarter mile and I noticed you were swerving and driving erratically. One more time, give me your license and registration."

"Alright. Can you kill that light?"

"Not yet."

The driver lets out a groan and says "My license is in my pocket. I'm gonna reach for it. Don't get trigger happy."

"I won't as long as the only things in your hand are your license and registration.

He hands the papers to the officer. The officer takes them from him and reads the name 'Antonio Sanchez.' "Mr. Sanchez, where were you tonight?"

"I was at Ball Breakers. You heard of it?"

"Yeah, I heard of it—strippers and pool."

"You got that right."

The officer adds "and drugs."

"Don't know about that, Officer," answers Sanchez.

"Come on, Mr. Sanchez, we know what goes on in places like that."

Sanchez asks, "What's your name? Are you in Fuller's command?"

"My name is Rodriguez. How do you know Fuller?"

"Don't worry about it. You gonna give me a ticket or can I go?"

"Have you ever been arrested, Mr. Sanchez?"

Sanchez is surprised and he says "You can't ask me that."

Rodriguez hands the license and registration back to Sanchez.

"So that's it, I can go?"

Rodriguez replies "Not yet. I need you to do something for me."

"What do you want?"

"I wanna know what goes on in that shithole you hang out in. You know, drugs, hookers and underage girls stripping and don't tell me it doesn't happen."

"Fuck that! I don't have to tell you shit."

"You're right, you don't, but you stink of booze and weed and I get the feeling if we search the car, we'll find all kinds of illegal shit inside. Consider it a public service and a way to save your ass. I'll give you a pass this time. Think about what I said, next time I won't be so nice. I'll be in touch. Drive carefully."

Rodriguez turns and walks back to his car. The lights on his car continue to flash blue and white.

Rodriguez is driving back to town and his phone rings. The number is not familiar, but it's from Vegas so he answers it.

"Yeah" the voice on the other end says. "After one week, that's the best you can do?"

Rodriguez recognizes the voice and he asks "Hi Sarge, how're you doin'?"

McMahon responds "I'm here in the middle of a shitstorm. Those papers are real, and now I'm front page fucking news. Thanks, Rodriguez."

He asks "Who's phone is this? This ain't your number."

"I figured with all that's happening, I better use a different phone. So I went to evidence and got a phone that belonged to some mook doing time for murder in Nevada State Prison."

"I'm learning a lot of shit from you, Sarge."

"Save it, Rodriguez. You've got a lot of explaining to do when you get back to Vegas. I got people following me. Today it's this young agent, probably FBI, so right now I'm shopping."

"You're shopping?"

"Yep, I'm in my favorite mall. I know this place like the back of my hand. I lost the kid about half an hour ago. I'll catch up with him later. I think he's in Victoria's Secret."

McMahon says laughing, "So did you meet Sanchez yet?"

Rodriguez says "Yeah, about ten minutes ago."

"Oh shit, Rodriguez, tell me about it."

"I pulled him over for a DUI stop. I followed him from that dive Ball Breakers."

McMahon interrupts "What the fuck is Ball Breakers?"

Rodriguez responds "It's a combination strip club and pool room and who knows what else. I pulled him over and I told him that he was all over the road, which he wasn't. I shined the light at him and I knew he was stoned."

McMahon asks "You didn't arrest him, did you?"

"No, I let him go, but I told him to let me know when things go down at Ball Breakers."

"What did he say?"

"He was polite and basically told me to go fuck myself."

McMahon laughs, "Yeah, sounds about right. Listen, Rodriguez, you're not working this alone. I got an agent in Oceanview. For right now, I want you in the shadows. When, and if, the time is right, you'll meet. You're playing Sanchez just right. Keep at it, but don't scare him off. Be careful, Rodriguez. I'll take care of things here. Now, let me see if I can find that guy. Maybe I'll buy him a drink. He's kind of cute."

Laughing, McMahon disconnects.

CHAPTER 13
WAR HERO

Anna is setting the table for dinner.

Antonio is standing behind her and takes her wrist. Anna reacts and pulls away slightly but catches herself and looks at Antonio. He says "You know I love you, right?"

Anna pauses and says, "I know."

He asks "Are you thinking about leaving me?

"No, why are you asking me?"

"Cause I need you to be with me. Nobody's good enough for you. You know what I'm saying."

"Yes, Antonio."

Antonio has a menacing look on his face and it scares her. Antonio releases Anna's wrist and picks up his beer. Just then the phone rings.

"I got it. Fucking telemarketers." Antonio picks up the phone on the third ring.

"Yeah." The voice on the other end is Tom. "Hi Antonio. How's it going?"

"Oh Tom. Sorry, man. I thought it was somebody trying to sell me some shit."

Tom says, "It's ok. Actually I should be apologizing to you."

"Why?"

"The last time I was there, I forgot to bring the check for the rent."

Antonio speaks softly so Anna can't hear. "Oh yeah, the three thousand. Right."

Tom is confused. "I thought it was fifteen hundred. One month's rent.

"No, Anna made a mistake. It's rent + security. Three grand."

"Ok. I'll bring the check in the morning. It is what it is. I'm moving in tomorrow."

Antonio says, "That's cool, but can I get the security in cash?"

"Cash is ok, so you want fifteen hundred in cash and a check for the other fifteen hundred, right?"

"Yeah, that's right. Can you give it to me early cause I gotta go to work."

"What time?"

Antonio says "At seven, and do me a favor, don't tell Anna about the cash."

"Yeah, I got it. Seven's ok." Tom hangs up the phone angrily and says to himself, "What an asshole."

The next morning, Antonio is standing next to a pickup truck talking to the driver. Tom drives up and stops behind the pickup. He steps out of the car and Antonio walks toward him.

Antonio greets Tom, "What's up, Tom?"

"Not much. Here's the money." Tom reaches into the side pocket of his jacket and hands him the cash and the check. "I'll take the cash. Give the check to Anna if you see her today."

"There's a lot of twenties in there. I didn't have large bills."

Antonio takes the envelope and makes believe he's weighing it in his hand. He says, "That's cool. Money is money. Remember Tom, keep this cash thing between us, okay? You know, man to man."

"Yeah, no problem."

Antonio pats him on the shoulder and hops into the pickup. The truck leaves with the tires screeching. Tom watches it leave and heads towards the stairs leading to his apartment.

Anna is stepping out of the shower. We see her silhouette against the light coming through the bathroom window. She puts on a robe and walks to her bedroom and opens the blinds to let in the sunlight. A figure in the backyard catches her eye. She opens the blinds a little more, carefully so he doesn't see her. It's Tom dressed in sweatpants and an Army T-shirt. He's practicing TaiChi. Anna is impressed by his ability and concentration. Tom continues as Anna closes the blinds.

Anna and Antonio are sitting on the couch. Antonio is watching TV and Anna is reading a book.

Antonio asks, "Was Tom upstairs today?"

"I don't know."

"You didn't see him?"

"No Antonio, I didn't."

"He told me he was moving in today."

"When did he tell you?"

"Last night when he called."

"He called when?"

"You remember. Dinnertime."

"You didn't tell me."

"I guess I forgot."

"I guess. Why don't you call him and see if he's there?"

"Why Anna?"

"I don't know. I thought we'd invite him down. After all, we're neighbors."

Antonio is raising his voice and he tells Anna, "Oh, so now we gotta invite him every night cause we're neighbors? "

"I didn't say that."

"Anna, he's the tenant and I'm the landlord. That's the relationship."

"Ok Antonio. Let's leave it alone."

Antonio is getting angry. "You know what, Anna? I'm gonna invite him down cause you have been ignoring me. So, what the fuck, I'll talk to him. Where's his number—I'll call him now."

Anna is frustrated. "Do what you want. His number is on the fridge."

Antonio adds, "The Yankees are playing. Maybe he likes baseball."

Antonio goes to the phone and punches in the numbers as he reads them aloud. The phone rings and Tom answers.

"Hello."

Antonio returns the greeting. "Hey Tom. How's it going?"

"Ok. I have your check. I didn't see Anna today."

"Did you move in today?"

"Yeah, all the big furniture is in."

"Hey, Tom, you like baseball? "Yeah." "The Yankees are playing. Why don't you come down?"

"I'm a little busy right now…."

"Come down, we'll have a few beers."

"Ok. I'll be down in a minute. I'll bring your check."

Antonio hangs up the phone and returns to the couch. Anna says "Is he coming?"

"Yeah. We got beer?"

"Yeah, there's plenty, and there's snacks in the cabinet."

"Snacks, not for me. All I need is beer."

The doorbell rings and Anna goes to the door. "Hi, Tom. Come in."

"Thanks. Before I forget, here's the check."

Anna says, "Thanks" and walks to the dining room and puts the check on the table. She picks up some books and papers and says, "Excuse me. I have work to do for class." Anna goes upstairs, carrying her papers.

Antonio says to Tom, "Sit down. The game is on TV."

"Who's pitching?"

"I don't know. Some new guy. Are you getting used to living upstairs? Feeling good about it?"

"Yeah, I'm getting used to it."

"You can use the yard if you want."

"I know. Anna told me."

Antonio gets up and goes to the fridge and gets two beers. He returns to the sofa and hands a beer to Tom.

Tom says, "I was out there today."

The crowd roars as the Yankees score two runs.

"Antonio claps his hands and makes a big deal out of it. "Fucking Yankees! Yeah, go baby." He calms down and turns his attention to what Tom was saying.

"You said you were out in the backyard today."

"Yeah, I was. I was doing Tai-Chi."

"Isn't that some kind of martial art or something?"

"Kind of."

The door upstairs opens and Anna comes down the stairs. She enters the living room and sits on the sofa next to Antonio. He gets up and goes to the kitchen. Anna asks "What's the score?"

Antonio responds from the kitchen, "Two nothing. Where's those snacks, baby?"

Anna looks over to Antonio, "In front of you to the left."

Antonio returns to the couch next to Anna with the bag of snacks. "Tom told me he was in the yard today doin' What did you call it - Tai key?"

Tom says, "Tai Chi."

Antonio says, "Yeah, it's like a martial art."

Anna says, "I heard of it. Where'd you learn it?"

"In the Army."

Antonio asks, "Were you in Iraq?"

"Yeah, two years."

"Did you kill any of those assholes?"

"I did my duty."

Anna says, "Tom's got three medals."

Antonio looks at Anna, "Oh yeah? How do you know?"

Tom says, "I told her."

Antonio says, "No shit. You got 'em upstairs?"

"No. They're at my house. I'll bring them over this week."

Antonio asks, "How'd you get 'em?"

"It's not that important. I'd rather not talk about it."

"Come on, Tom. I don't know any war heroes. Anna wants to hear it, too. Right, Anna?"

Anna says, "It's up to Tom. I don't want to push it."

"Well, I want to hear it, Anna. Come on Tom. What'd you say?"

Tom leans forward in his chair. He puts the bottle down on the table. Anna turns off the TV.

"In the Iraq war, I was a pilot on a medivac helicopter escort called the Pave Hawk. Our job was to provide cover while the Black Hawk hospital choppers picked up the wounded and the dying."

Antonio interrupts, "Those are the big ones, like in that movie, Apocalypse Now."

"Our gunner was a guy from Brooklyn named Rocco. In the chopper, we had a gunner, two pilots and one flight engineer. We had two fifty-caliber machine guns."

Antonio says, "Damn! Those'll cut a guy in half."

"That day, we were going to pick up four wounded. We were told the pickup zone was cool and there was no enemy in the area. We flew in with two Pave Hawks escorting the extraction ship. As we got closer, we spotted the smoke and the wounded."

Antonio asks, "What's smoke?"

"It's a smoke grenade that's used to pinpoint the landing zone."

We could see Rangers waving us in. I saw the stretchers and body bags."

Antonio says, "So you were cool. Nobody was shooting at you?"

Tom says, "That's what we thought. As we got closer, we took on heavy fire."

Tom pauses and takes a sip of beer. He looks at Anna, and she's sitting cross-legged on the sofa, her eyes focused on him.

Tom continues. "Our sister ship gets hit, but is still airborne. We're firing into the desert and the sand is being kicked up by chopper blades. My co-pilot is yelling for an air strike. We needed it to give us a chance to get into position to evacuate our men. In the first ten minutes, we lost three men on the ground. The remaining men on the ground start bringing the wounded closer to the Medivac chopper. I hear a thud and I see blood splatter the inside of the chopper. Billie Rudowski, one of my gunners, was dead. I knew there was no way those three men were gonna get those stretchers out of there without help. My corpsman in the Medivac chopper is taking fire from a sniper in a mound of sand. He radios his location and Rocco pounds the area with gunfire and takes him out.

Tom pauses and takes a sip of beer. Antonio is leaning forward on the sofa.

"Two men on the ground grab one of the stretchers and they get hit. That left only one man on the ground, Corporal Hernandez. I didn't think about it too long. I took off my harness and yelled to my co-pilot to get me closer to the ground. I hit the ground and ran to Hernandez. We grabbed the stretchers one by one and began loading the choppers. Rocco was laying down ground fire to cover us. Rocco contacts HQ to let them know we're coming in. We're still taking fire as we're loading the stretchers on to the Black Hawk." "A Ranger from the Black Hawk is giving us cover as we load up."

I turned to Rocco and I saw part of his head was shot away. The round came through the windscreen. He was twenty-six years old. I feel a sharp pain and my left arm goes numb. We get into the chopper after loading the last stretcher. "We get the chopper in the air and it's climbing slowly." "At this point we're an easy target, apparently the chopper suffered some damage affecting the rotors." "The next shot hits me in the leg.". "It came through the left side of the chopper." "I remember landing at base, then everything went black."

The room is silent. Antonio is staring at the floor. Anna says, "Excuse me" and goes into the bathroom.

Antonio asks, "Did those guys make it?"

Tom answers, "We lost seven men that day."

"You saved four of them!"

Tom says, "Like I said, I did my duty."

Antonio says, "That's what I'm talking about. Those fools I hang out with at the pool hall are suckers. They just talk a lot of shit. Blah, blah, blah. Not you, man. You walk the walk."

Anna returns to the living room.

Tom says, "I should go, it's late."

"When you bring the medals, can I see 'em?"

"Yeah, sure."

Tom rises and starts for the door. Antonio gets up and extends his hand. Tom looks at Antonio and shakes his hand. Anna asks, "Tom, can I walk you to the door?"

Antonio goes to the fridge and gets another beer. He sits on the couch and puts on the TV. Anna and Tom are standing by the door. Anna unlocks the door. She looks at Tom and says, "Thank you!"

"For what?"

"For allowing me to know a little more about you. Good night."

"Good night, Anna."

She closes the door and locks it. Anna walks to the couch and sits next to Antonio. Antonio says, "Wow, that was some crazy shit."

Anna doesn't hear Antonio. Her mind is on Tom. She's falling in love with him.

CHAPTER 14
THE NIGHTMARE

Tom is lying in bed, he's having difficulty sleeping. He hears the sounds of Antonio and Anna making love. He tries to sleep but can't, the sounds of passion playing in his head. The steady beat of the headboard hitting the wall and the sounds of Anna reaching climax and her cries of ecstasy are keeping him awake. The beat begins again and Tom sits up listening but the sounds have changed. They were no longer the sounds of love making, it was more aggressive and violent. He hears slapping sounds as if someone is being hit over and over. He gets off the bed and goes to the window to hear better. He hears breaking glass and Anna screaming. He lunges for the door bare-foot and runs downstairs. He breaks through the front door and runs up to their bedroom. The slaps now sound like punches and the screams are low and muted. The bedroom door is open and Anna is lying on the bed. Antonio is beating her; her face is bloody. Tom lunges and grabs Antonio around the neck to pull him off Anna. Antonio fights him off and punches Tom in the face sending him against the wall. Tom retaliates and kicks Antonia in the chest that sends Antonio into the night stand. Anna is lying on the bed not moving. Tom lunges at Antonio again but this time he's grabbed from behind. Tom feels… strong arms around him pinning his arms at his side. The arms were not warm like human's but cold and icy. They were clad in a flight suit just like the one they wore in Iraq. Over his shoulder Tom could feel a cold chill. He struggles to turn to see who's behind him. He manages to break free and turns to face his attacker. It's Rocco, his gunner, half his head is missing and blood stains the right side of his flight suit. Tom wants to scream but he can't. Antonio and Rocco now come at Tom together. Antonio is laughing maniacally. Tom is backed into the wall. Rocco gets closer and reaches for Tom. Tom wakes up his heart pounding. His breathing is heavy and he feels as if he may hyperventilate. He puts on the light and looks around the room to make sure he's alone. He breathes more normally and sits on the edge of the bed for a while.

The next morning Tom awakens and opens the blinds to let in the sunlight.

The nightmare is now just a bad memory. He decides to take the plane for a flight and he calls Scottie. Scottie is sitting behind a desk in his office. The office is spacious but not organized. Airplane parts are stacked along one wall. Scottie's doing paperwork. A single window, large and gated, is behind him. His cell phone is on the desk and it rings "Scottie's." Tom says, "Good Morning, Scottie." Tom hears mechanics working on planes and it's noisy. Scottie is having a hard time hearing Tom. He walks to the door and closes it.

"Hey, Tom. How're you doing?"

"I'm alright. You want me to fuel her up?"

"I was thinking about Friday morning."

"Ok, Tom. I'll have her ready around ten."

"You got it. See you then."

CHAPTER 15
PAY DAY

I t's a misty night in Oceanview; a black car is parked with the engine running. A street light bathes the scene with a soft glow. Another car comes alongside and stops. The driver's side window lowers and it's Dom. Primo is in the passenger seat and on the dashboard is a plastic bag. On the seat next to Dom is a gun. The man in the other car lowers the window. Dom says sarcastically, "Well if it ain't Sergeant Fuller. Lovely night, ain't it, Fuller?"

"Throw it in, Dom."

"What's up Fuller—no small talk this evening."

Fuller responds angrily, "Put it in the fucking car."

Dom takes the bag full of money and throws it into the open window of the car. Sergeant Fuller is staring straight ahead.

Dom says, "Good night, Fuller." Fuller's car window goes up and his car drives off and disappears around the corner. Dom and Primo are still in the same place as a soft rain continues to fall.

Dom says "I'd like to shoot that fuck right in the face."

"You can't. Richie said it's bad to kill a cop."

"I know what Richie said, Primo. I didn't say I was gonna do it."

"But Richie don't want the guy dead. He says never kill a cop."

"Primo, listen carefully. I'm not going to kill Fuller."

"Ok, Dom. I get it."

"Jesus Christ, Primo, do me a favor on the way back to Brooklyn. Don't say a fucking word."

"Hey, Dom. Why're you getting upset?" The window of the car goes up and it drives off. At the corner it makes a right.

CHAPTER 16
TOM'S HOUSE

Tom hears stirring on his porch. He opens the door and is startled, what he thought was a person standing there was actually a plant.

He brings the plant inside, smiling. He goes to his car and he sees Anna on her porch. Anna calls, "Hi, Tom. How are you?"

"I'm good, Anna."

"How's the apartment? Is everything ok?" Tom wasn't going to mention the plant yet. He was going to toy with her.

"Yep."

"So are you done with the boxes?"

"Not yet. There's a lot of years in those boxes."

"Are you bringing more today?"

"Yeah I'm going back for more now." As if on cue Anna opens the passenger door and jumps in. Tom pokes his head into the window and looks at Anna. "And where are you going?"

"With you, in case you need help."

"I'm ok."

"I insist. Besides if I don't help you, you'll be bringing boxes for the rest of the year. So come on. Let's go."

"Fine, but just one trip, ok."

"Ok Tom. Besides, I got some shopping to do."

Tom gets into the car, buckles up and starts the engine. He looks at Anna and she returns his gaze and smiles. Tom smiles back.

Anna is looking out the window and she asks "So, everything was ok upstairs?"

"What do you mean?"

Anna turns to Tom. "Nothing unusual with the apartment."

Tom says "Let me see. Well something did happen when I got upstairs. There was this big green thing in front of the door. Thanks for the plant."

Anna says with a confused look "What plant?"

They both laugh. Anna shifts her position and moves closer to Tom. Tom welcomes it and he can smell her perfume. The car drives and stops in front of Tom's house. Anna leans out of the window and looks at the house. Tom exits and comes around to open Anna's door. She steps out and continues to look at the house.

Anna says "I can see why you liked it. It's beautiful."

"Thanks, let go in." They go up the stairs. Tom unlocks the door and ushers Anna inside.

The interior looks like a house in the middle of a move. Furniture is in one corner, rugs are rolled up, and boxes are piled up in another corner. Anna looks around. "Looks like you're serious about this move."

"Yeah. You want something to drink?"

"No, not now, thanks."

"Come on, I'll show you around." Tom takes Anna to the living room. There's boxes piled up against the walls. Paintings are neatly placed in one area of the room. Anna admires the fireplace, then her attention shifts to the stained glass windows on one side of the house.

"I love the stained glass windows."

"Thanks, Rebecca did them. My wife."

"Wow, she did those?"

"Yeah she took some courses and practiced a lot. About six months and some broken glass later, that's the result. She got good at it eventually."

"They're fabulous and she learned quickly."

"Yeah, she was something else."

"I'm going to bring them to the apartment today and hang them in front of the living room windows."

"I love the fireplace."

On the fireplace are several pictures. They're pictures of Tom and his family. In the middle is a glass covered mahogany box standing upright. Inside the box on black velvet are 3 military medals. In the center of the three is the Purple Heart. Anna asks, "Are these the medals you told us about."

"Yes, they are." Also on the mantel are pictures of Tom's family. She picks up a framed picture with three people in it. It's a formal portrait with Tom in his police dress uniform. Anna asks, "Is this Rebecca and your son?"

"Yes it is."

"She's beautiful. Your whole family is."

"Thanks. Come on, I'll show you the kitchen. I think you'll like it." Tom and Anna walk to the kitchen. Anna is walking closer to Tom, her body language becoming more seductive. They reach the kitchen and her eyes light up.

"A country kitchen. I love it!"

"It was Rebecca's idea."

"It's wonderful, the whole house is. It feels like a real home with lots of love."

"Thanks. There was." Anna is sensing a change in Tom's mood.

"Maybe we should get back," Tom says. "Do you still wanna take a few boxes."

"Of course, that's why I came."

"They're over here, let's take six or seven."

"I don't think we can fit more than that in the car." Tom and Anna walk over to where the boxes are. They're piled up in a small room to the left of the empty dining room. Tom says "I'll take the heavy ones and you take the light ones."

"Why, don't you think I'm strong enough?"

Tom looks at Anna and smiles. He turns to pick up the top box on the pile. He grabs the box and turns to Anna, she is now standing directly in front of him. Again he gets a whiff of her sweet scent. Anna extends her arms as if to take the box. Anna asks, "Is it a light one or a heavy one?"

"Light one, it's yours."

She takes the box and her hand brushes against his. Tom asks "Think you can handle it?"

"Yeah I got it." Anna takes the box and walks toward the door. She turns to Tom and asks, "Are you coming?" Tom bends to pick up a box. He lets out a groan as he lifts it. Anna says, "Not too heavy, is it?" Tom says, "Shut up."

After the last box is loaded Anna sits in the passenger seat. Tom locks the door and comes down the stairs carrying two books. He hands them to Anna, she looks at the books, they're both about stained glass. Tom says "I thought you might find 'em interesting. Give 'em back when you're done."

"Thank you Tom, I'm gonna try it." They drive away.

Tom is hanging the stained glass frames in front of the living room windows.The light coming through them bathes the room in muted colors." The furniture is in place and Anna's plant is in the corner by the window. the doorbell rings and Tom opens the door. Anna is standing there holding a large plate covered in aluminum foil.

Tom is surprised to see Anna and he invites her in. "Hi Anna. Was I making too much noise?"

"No, not at all, I bought you some food. Chicken and rice, black beans and some salad." Tom takes the plate from Anna. "That's nice, Anna. I'll have it for dinner. Thank you." Tom walks into the kitchen and says, "Have a seat in the living room." Anna looks around at the artwork on the walls.

"I love your paintings. Are they from local artists?"

"Yeah, Rebecca insisted we support local artists. I have more at the house. I gotta bring them over." "The stained glass panels look beautiful."

"I see you hung up your medals. Good for you. You should be proud. The place looks nice. I see the plant is still alive."

Tom says laughing "I'm trying to, so far so good. Don't you have a class tonight."

"I do, but it's later on."

"How is it? Do you enjoy it?"

Anna responds, "It's alright, but the people are coming from work. They're tired, hungry and not very focused. I try to make it interesting."

"I'm sure you do."

"Tom, I didn't come up just to bring you food. I wanted to apologize for Antonio the other day. I know he makes you uncomfortable."

"It's ok. Already forgotten."

"I don't want you to avoid us because of Antonio. We're neighbors, we may need each other one day. The other night when you left all he talked about was you."

"Me?"

Anna says, "Yes, you. Antonio considers himself a very Macho guy. He thinks he's better than any man but you really impressed him."

"Because of the war?"

"Yes, and your medals. You're a tough man, Tom, but you have inner strength and confidence. You have nothing to prove to anybody. From the little time I've known you I see that you're a kind man. You don't need to be alone." Tom is feeling uncomfortable and he says "I have to get back to work."

Anna replies "It seems I've made you uncomfortable. I have to get ready for class." Anna stands and Tom walks her to the door. Anna looks at Tom and says "I'm sorry if I made you uneasy."

Tom says, "It's fine. I appreciate what you said. Bye Anna." Anna says, "Bye, Tom." She turns and goes down the stairs. Tom closes the door behind her.

CHAPTER 17
FELIX AND THE STRIPPER

Later that day Anna is cooking. As she cooks, she's reading one of the stained glass books. The door opens and it's Antonio. Antonio walks in, throws his coat on the couch and takes off his work boots. He walks to the kitchen and says, "Hi, baby. Shit, I'm tired." Antonio puts his arms around Anna's waist. He sniffs her hair and kisses her on the neck. Anna turns and acknowledges the kiss. Anna says "That was nice."

Antonio asks "You got class tonight."

"Yeah."

"What time are you coming back, baby?"

"I'm usually home by ten. Why're you asking, Antonio?"

"How about I stay home tonight and wait for you?"

What'd you got in mind?"

"You'll see when you get back, baby."

"Promise me you won't drink too much." You scare me when you drink. I don't enjoy being with you when you're drinking.

Antonio says, "But babe, I gotta have a couple."

"Please, Antonio." Antonio gives in. "Ok, I promise."

They're still hugging when Antonio notices the stained glass book. He lets go of Anna and walks over to where the book is. He asks, "What're you reading."

Anna says "It's a book about stained glass."

"Stained glass, like church windows."

"It's a book about how to put stained glass together. I was thinking of trying it."

"Oh yeah? Where did you get it?"

The question took Anna by surprise and put her off guard. She didn't think Antonio would care about the book. He never asked about her other books. She didn't want to tell him the truth, she knows how jealous he is. She hesitated, making believe she didn't hear the question. Antonio asks again "Where'd you get the book, Anna?"

"At the library, I picked it up today."

" So you're really going to try it."

"Yeah I think so. Sit down, dinner is ready."

Felix is playing pool in Ball Breakers. He's hustling somebody, stoned as usual. He's in the middle of the game when he's approached by Antonios's stripper girlfriend. She's in need of a hit and she's frantically searching for Antonio. She's wearing a red robe with just a G string underneath. She's scheduled to dance next. She stands next to Felix and says, "Felix, can I talk to you?"

"Yeah what's up? I'm in the middle of a game."

"Can you give me something?"

Felix says quietly, "Where's Antonio?"

"How the fuck do I know."

"What do you want?" Felix is paying attention to the game as he talks to her.

"Anything, it don't matter."

"Meet me in the ladies room. Give me 5 minutes to beat this chump." The stripper walks to the ladies room. Felix continues to play and runs the next 5 balls. If he sinks the next 3 balls he wins the game and takes 50 dollars from his opponent.

Felix states, "If I get these three in, you're done. I hope you got the money fifty bucks, right?" His opponent says, "I got it. Go ahead."

Felix makes the three shots and wins the game. Angrily the player reaches into his pocket and gives Felix fifty dollars. Felix peels the bills one at a time and counts out loud smugly. "Want a rematch?"

"No, that's ok." Felix hands the stick to the next player and walks to the bathroom. He opens the door and the stripper is leaning against the sink. The bathroom is small, and a single bulb hangs in the middle. A steam pipe with rust stains is in one corner. The sink has a leak and the toilet has no cover. The walls are painted a loud red and the room smells of urine and bleach. Felix reaches into his pocket and takes out a baggie with rocks of crack in it. He asks the stripper "You got a pipe?" She answers, "Yeah."

The stripper reaches into the pocket of her robe and takes out a pipe. She takes out a lighter and hands it to Felix. She puts the pipe to her lips. Felix gets the lighter ready. "You ready?" The stripper nods yes. Felix lights up the rock and she takes a slow deep drag and holds it. Her head goes back, her eyes half closed as she exhales. "Nice hit. Is it good?" She doesn't answer, she just looks at him with half closed eyes. She says "Hit me again."

"Sure, baby." The ritual is repeated. The stripper getting deeper into the high."

Felix asks "How do you feel?"

"Nice, aren't you gonna take a hit?"

"Not yet, you got some money for me?"

The stripper is a little surprised by the question and she looks at Felix.

"You know I got no money."

"Well, this shit ain't free."

"You didn't say shit about money, Felix."

"It don't have to be money." She says, "Sex. You want sex. Is that it?"

"You know I was always hot for that ass."

She says sleepily, "Can I have the other rock?"

"You gonna fuck me for it?" Felix asks.

"Yeah, but give me the rock first."

"No, after."

"Later. I'll fuck you later. Let's do the other rock."

Felix takes the pipe out of her hand and takes a hit himself. He takes a deep drag and lets out the smoke. He puts his hand around her neck, not squeezing just holding her in place. He gets in her face. She could smell his rotten teeth breath. Felix says, "We're gonna do it now." The stripper tries to pull away from his grip. "Come on, Felix. I said later. You're scaring me." He tightens it as she struggles. It's gonna get scarier if you don't give me what I want." Felix tightens his grip. "Get your fucking hands off me." Felix tries to rip off her robe and she fights him off. He holds her by the neck and pushes her into the corner. "Let me go, Felix. I told you after, you fucking asshole. Now you ain't getting shit." Felix pins her to the wall and tries to kiss her. She pushes him off and takes a swing at him but misses.

"You tried to hit me, you bitch." Felix punches her in the face and her head hits the steam pipe. She tries to scream but Felix covers her mouth. Her eyes are wide open and she's terrified. She pushes him off her again. She says "I'm telling Antonio."

Felix lunges at her and grabs her neck with both hands. Her eyes bulge as his grip tightens. She slowly sinks to the floor. Felix says "You ain't telling Antonio shit." Felix continues to hold her by the throat and she goes limp. Felix catches himself and realizes she may be dead. He panics and calls her name "Evelyn! Evelyn, wake up! Come on, wake up. Don't fuck around." Felix shakes her and slaps her face trying to wake her but she's not moving. He begins to talk to himself: "Felix, what the fuck did you do? You killed her, you stupid fuck! Antonio's gonna kill me. Shit! what the fuck do I do?" And he begins to sob." He pulls himself together and calls Antonio.

Anna has already left for her class. Antonio sits on the couch, watching the ballgame. He promised Anna he wouldn't drink but he's drinking anyway.

He's out of his element. Being home at night is something he's not used to. He's bored and he's looking for something to do. He promised Anna he would be home and he's trying his best to keep it. He notices the book about Stained Glass and he picks it up and leafs through the pages. Toward the end of the book he sees a picture. It's a photo of Tom's family, the same portrait hanging in Tom's house. Antonio is getting angry and begins to connect imaginary dots. They're both home all day, she lied about the book, the medals, the whispering all feed his jealousy. He shoves the picture into his pocket and puts the book back where he found it. He paces, thinking what to do. His cell phone rings but he's not in the mood to talk to anyone. Caller ID tells him it's Felix.

He picks up and he's angry. "What Felix?"

Felix says "Antonio, Antonio I fucked up, man. You gotta come."

"What happened Felix, you get busted again?"

"No Antonio. This is bad. Real bad."

"Where are you?"

"I'm at the club. You gotta come."

"I got my own shit I'm dealing with. This better not be some dumb shit."

"No, man. Antonio, you gotta come."

"Wait there, don't you go nowhere." Antonio grabs his coat and heads for the front door and it slams behind him.

Antonio walks in to Ball Breakers and he's greeted by the regulars. He looks around for Felix but doesn't see him. He walks over to his crew playing pool and he asks, "Yo, anybody see Felix." Some of the players say they haven't seen him. One player says "He's in the back." Antonio walks to the back room, and it's empty. He turns to the pool players and yells angrily "Which fucking room is he in?" One of the players says, "The ladies room—must be having his period." There's laughter as Antonio goes to the ladies room and knocks. No answer. He pounds the door with his fist. He yells, "Felix, open up." From inside Felix says, questioning, "Antonio, is that you?"

"Open the door." Felix has to move the stripper's body to open the door. Even then the door doesn't open all the way. The door opens wide enough for Antonio to squeeze through. He sees Felix against the sink, looking down.

"Felix, what the fuck did you do? Did you drop acid or . . . " Antonio stops in mid-sentence when he sees the stripper's legs. He slams the door and locks it. He stares at the stripper and looks at Felix. Antonio asks, "Is she dead?" Felix nods, still whimpering. "What the fuck did you do?"

"I don't know - we did a few rocks and she went nuts. Look, she scratched me on my face and my arms. I was trying to get her off me."

"So you're telling me she got high and tried to kill you. Was it my shit, Felix - and don't bullshit me."

"Yeah, the shit you gave me."

"No way, man. My stuff is clean. She never did that with me."

"I swear."

"No Felix, let me tell you what happened. You got high together and you decided you wanted some pussy. She told you no so you figured you'll just take it. She wasn't giving it up to a piece of shit like you."

Felix is crying now. "I swear she came after me. I didn't . . . "

Antonio doesn't give Felix a chance to finish the sentence. He grabs Felix around the neck with his right hand. Felix is shocked with how fast Antonio moved and grabbed his neck. He stares at Antonio with his eyes wide. He can't speak.

Antonio says, "It happened like I said, right? Tell me the truth or there's gonna be two dead people in this room." Felix nods in the affirmative. Antonio doesn't let go right away. He stares at Felix, holding onto his neck. Felix's eyes are bulging and his head is going from side to side. Antonio finally lets go. Felix wheezes and coughs, trying to catch his breath. Antonio paces in the tight space.

"What the fuck are we gonna do?"

Antonio is tapping his forehead with the heel of his hand.

Felix says, "Antonio."

"Felix, shut up."

"I'm sorry, Antonio."

"I'm gonna kill you, Felix, if you don't shut up." He says to himself, "Come on, Antonio. Think." He paces, looking at the stripper and Felix. He takes out his car keys and hands them to Felix. He says "Go get my car and back it up to the back room and open the trunk. Come back here and don't talk to anybody. You hear me?"

"Ok, you got a plan."

"Do what the fuck I say. Felix. Do it now." Felix leaves the room and Antonio is now alone in the bathroom. He looks down at the stripper's body. He's disgusted by the sight of her swollen face and bruises. He takes some paper towels and covers her face. Just then there's a knock on the door. Antonio listens and says, "Yeah." It was one of the strippers; her set just finished.

She says "Hey, pal. That's the ladies room and I gotta pee."

Antonio says, "It's out of order."

"Bullshit. Open up."

Antonio shouts back, "Get the fuck out of here." The stripper goes to the men's room as she mumbles to herself "fucking drug addicts."

Antonio listens by the door for Felix. The knock comes, startling Antonio. Antonio says, "Yeah."

"It's me, Antonio." Antonio opens the door and Felix comes in.

"The cars in the back by the door."

"Listen to me. Here's what we're gonna do. We're gonna stand her up, you on one side and me on the other. We take her to the back room. It'll look like she's drunk or stoned or something. When we get to the back, we put her on the table. I got garbage bags back there. Wait here. I'm gonna go unlock the door."

Antonio comes back to the bathroom. He says, "The door's unlocked." He takes the paper towels off her face, wets them and wipes off the dried blood.

Antonio says "Come on, grab one side. Let's get her on her feet." The men struggle with the dead weight. Antonio thought her body would be colder. Felix, the weaker of the two, is having a hard time. Her head is resting on Felix's shoulder and he begins to sob. "Man up, motherfucker Were you crying when you killed her? You can't go out there crying."

"I'm ok, I'm ok. Let's go."

The two men have control of the body. It looks like she's passed out as the men carry her to the back. Nobody pays any attention as the music keeps playing and the dancers keep dancing. This is a common occurrence in a place like this. The men open the door to the back room and go in. Antonio locks the door. They put the body on the table. Antonio says "Get the bags." Felix gets the garbage bags and hands the box to Antonio.

They begin wrapping the body in the bags.

Outside in the club, the bartender is looking for her since she's next on stage. He goes to the ladies room and knocks on the door. He shouts "Evelyn, you're on. Let's go." No answer from inside. He pounds on the door with his fist. "Evelyn! Open up. You're on." He opens the door and sees the bloody paper towels on the floor. He leaves the bathroom and knocks on the back room door.

"He shouts, "Evelyn, Evelyn!"

The body is partially wrapped on the table. The men stop and don't make a sound. Antonio whispers to Felix, "You got my keys?" Felix says, "Yeah."

The bartender says, "Come on, Evelyn. Are you getting high in there? Open up."

Antonio asks Felix, "Is the trunk open?" Felix says, "Yeah." Antonio says "We're gonna pick her up and put her in the trunk. "Go ahead, Felix. Take her legs." Antonio asks, "You ready?" The men lift the body and half carry and half drag her to the car.

They unceremoniously throw her into the trunk. The body lands with a thud. Antonio closes the trunk and gives Felix the keys.

He says, "Here, go park the car on the corner and wait for me. Don't come back into the club."

Felix drives away and Antonio closes the back door. He looks around the room to make sure it looks normal. He unlocks the front door and sits at the table drinking a beer. The bartender knocks again, calling Evelyn's name.

Antonio yells, "It's open."

The bartender walks in, sees Antonio and asks, "Why didn't you answer the door?"

Antonio says "I just got back."

The bartender says "Got back? I didn't see you leave."

Antonio says, "Yeah, Evelyn was fucked up. We put her in a cab. Me and Felix took her out the back."

The bartender, now agitated, says, "How come nobody told me she was leaving?"

Antonio replies angrily, "She was fucked up. We put her in a cab. What's the big deal?

"The big deal is she works for me. I gotta know this shit."

"Like I said, she was fucked up and we sent her home. Besides who are you to question what the fuck I do?"

"I'm her boss, that's who the fuck I am," the bartender says.

Antonio says, "You're the boss, so call up another bitch or get your fat ass up there and dance."

The bartender says, "What did you say to me?"

Antonio stands up with the bottle in his hand. He goes face to face with the bartender. He says "Fuck you, why don't you dance maricon?"

The bartender takes a swing at Antonio and connects. Antonio drops the bottle and stumbles into the main pool room. The bottle shatters on the floor getting everyone's attention. Antonio gets to his feet and grabs a pool cue. The pool players scatter and give the men room.

The bartender lunges at Antonio. Antonio swings the pool cue hitting the bartender on the side of the head. The bartender collapses and grabs the edge of the pool table to keep from falling to the floor. Antonio hits him again on the back of the head. The bartender tries to get up and Antonio hits him again snapping the cue in half. This time the bartender falls to the floor. One of the players says, "Stop, man. You're going to kill the dude," and he grabs the pool cue from his hand.

Antonio looks down at the bartender and comes to his senses. He remembers there's more important business at hand. Antonio runs from the club and to the car waiting on the corner. Felix is sitting in the passenger seat. Antonio jumps in and drives off.

Felix says, "Where were you, man?"

"We're fucked. I think I killed the bartender."

"What happened?"

"He was fucking with me, so I hit him with one of the pool sticks."

"Antonio, what if the cops stop us? We gotta…"

Antonio cuts him off, "Ain't nobody gonna rat me out. Don't worry."

Antonio drives to the waterfront area past junkyards and scrap metal salvage businesses. He stops in front of a gated auto junkyard. He jumps out of the car with a set of keys in his hand. He unlocks the gate and motions to Felix.

"Come on, help me with the gate. Help me get it open."

"Yo, where'd you get the keys?"

"I got 'em from some people I know," Antonio answers.

"Who? Those Mafia chumps that came to the club?"

"None of your business."

The men return to the car and drive into the yard. There are cars piled up in rows. Some are fairly new, some are rusted out hulks. Car parts are strewn everywhere. Antonio drives to the back of the junkyard and stops next to a big machine, a car crusher. Antonio gets out and opens the trunk.

Antonio turns to Felix and says, "Let's go, Felix."

FELIX AND THE STRIPPER 95

Felix gets out of the car. Antonio is looking on the ground for something.

Felix asks, "What're you looking for?"

"See if you can find a pipe or something."

Felix comes up with a long piece of metal. He says, "Is this good?"

Antonio says "Yeah, help me pry open the trunk on that car." Antonio points to a car on the bottom of the pile next to the car crusher. The men struggle with the lock and, eventually, it pops open.

Antonio says, "Let's get her."

The men return to the car and lift the body out of the trunk. They carry the body to the rusted out hulk and put it in the trunk.

Antonio says, "I got some rope in the trunk. Go get it."

Antonio lowers the trunk lid on the junked car. Felix returns with the rope. The two men tie the trunk shut, "that's it Felix." Antonio looks around to make sure nothing was left behind.

Antonio says, "Let's get the fuck out of here."

The men get into Antonio's car and Felix has tears in his eyes. He's coming down from his high and the reality is hitting him. Antonio starts the car and drives to the front gate.

He tells Felix, "Go close the gates and don't forget to lock 'em. Here's the lock." Antonio hands the lock to Felix and rolls up the window. Antonio stares straight ahead. Felix closes the gates and gets back in the car.

As the men leave the waterfront, Antonio breaks the silence. They're gonna crush these cars. Then they melt 'em down. It takes seven thousand degrees to turn the metal to liquid. There'll be nothing left."

Felix is crying now and Antonio hears him and he says, "Cry all the fuck you want, but you owe me."

"I killed her. I ain't never killed nobody."

"Too late. She's dead."

"I'm sorry. I didn't mean it. I just wanted some pussy."

Antonio pulls the car over and stops. He sits quietly listening to Felix cry. Felix picks up his head and looks at Antonio, his eyes red. Felix says, "Why did you stop the car?"

Antonio is staring ahead and he says, "I helped you. Now you gotta help me."

Felix is whimpering and he says, "I'm sorry. I'm sorry. What do you want me to do?"

"You still driving that piece of shit car?"

"Yeah, why Antonio?"

"Cause I want you at my house tomorrow morning early."

"Your house. Why?"

"I want you to follow my wife."

"Your wife. Why?"

"Keep an eye on her. I wanna know everything she does."

There's silence in the car and Felix pulls himself together.

"I think she's fucking the guy upstairs."

"No way. You mean the old guy you told me about?"

"Let me tell you something about this guy, Felix. He's the real deal. He's a war hero and an ex-cop. He even does some martial arts shit. This guy's not soft."

"So what? Do I watch her?"

"That's what I said. Follow her."

"How long, Antonio? All day?

"Until I get home, Felix. You better be there at sunrise and make sure she doesn't see you."

"I'll be there. I won't fuck it up."

"There's the bus stop. Don't forget, Felix. Early. Now get out."

Felix gets out and Antonio drives off.

CHAPTER 18
ANNA'S FLIGHT (THE TRUTH HURTS)

Tom exits his apartment and walks to his car. It's a beautiful day with unlimited visibility so he decides to go flying. He's carrying a briefcase with his flight plans and charts. As he opens his car door, he notices Anna standing on her steps. He says, "Good morning Anna."

She walks toward his car and says, "Where are you off to so early?" - her hair wet from her shower.

Tom says, "I got a few things I need to take care of." Tom is standing by the open door, looking at Anna.

She's wondering what he's staring at and she says "What?"

Against his better judgment, he asks Anna to go with him. "Do you have plans for today?"

"No, not really."

"Would you like to come with me?"

"Where?"

"It's a surprise."

Anna hesitates, "I don't think it's a good idea. Antonio's working and I usually have his dinner ready when he gets home."

"What time do you have to be back?"

"By 2, I guess."

"Done. We'll be back before then."

"Why can't you tell me?"

"It won't be a surprise if I do."

"No, you go. I'm not dressed."

"Are you sure? I'll wait."

"You don't mind?"

"No, go ahead. I'll be here."

"What do I wear?"

"Something comfortable."

"I don't know, Tom. Can I trust you?"

"Of course you can trust me."

Anna asks, "Back by 2?"

"I promise. Back by 2."

"Ok, I'll go, but I have to change."

Tom is reading the flight plans when he looks up and sees Anna locking her front door. Anna is wearing a white flowing dress, her hair, still damp, is curly and thick. She opens the door and gets in.

"Did I take too long?"

"Nope."

Tom starts the car and they drive towards the airport. The car drives past Felix who's parked on the corner. He starts the car and follows.

Tom asks Anna, "You don't get air sick, do you?"

"No, are we going to Paris for dinner?"

"Can't. Gotta be back by two, remember?"

"Are you kidnapping me, Tom?"

"Yep, you guessed it."

"And the plane is your hideout."

Tom laughs and he makes a left turn onto the highway. Tom says, "We're almost there."

Anna is looking out the window and notices they're on the airport access road.

"Are you serious? We're going to the airport."

"You'll see." He follows the signs to Hangar G, which is Scottie's shop. Tom reaches the hangar and is pleased to see his plane is at the front of the runway.

Felix stops across the road and watches from inside his car. Tom exits the car and opens the passenger side door and helps Anna out. The mechanics stop to look at Anna as they walk into the hangar. Tom says to Scottie, "Hey, Scottie. How's it going?"

"Great, Tom. And who's this lovely lady?"

"This is Anna. Anna meet Scottie."

Scottie takes Anna's hand and kisses it. Tom says, "Watch out for Scottie. He's a ladies' man."

"Used to be." "These days my love is these babies you see in her," and he gestures to the planes in the hangar. So are you all set?"

Tom says, "Yeah, we're good."

Tom hands Scottie his flight plan. Scottie quickly looks at it. He says, "I'll get your paperwork. Be right back."

He leaves and goes to his office. Anna asks, "Tom, are we flying somewhere? Like a tour or something?"

Anna looks at the planes and says, "These planes are beautiful." She points to Tom's plane and says, "I love the red and white one."

"Well, this is your lucky day."

"Are we going in that one?"

"Yeah, that's the one."

Ann walks around the plane admiring it. Scottie returns and hands Tom some papers. He folds them and puts them in his jacket pocket.

"Thanks, Scottie."

"Happy flying. See ya when you get back."

Tom turns to Anna, "Are you ready?"

"I think so," Anna answers.

Tom takes Anna by the arm and walks her to the plane.

"Wait, isn't Scottie coming?"

"Nah, three's a crowd."

"But who's gonna fly the plane?"

"You're looking at him."

Anna says, surprised, "You?"

"Are you surprised?"

"How come you never told me?"

"Are you nervous?"

"A little. I've never been in a plane that small before."

Tom helps Anna into the plane and climbs in himself. They buckle their safety harnesses. Anna has a little trouble and Tom helps her buckle up.

Felix drives his car to the side of the hangar so he can see Tom's car. He settles in to wait until they get back.

The plane starts up and purrs as it taxies to the head of the runway. Tom is checking the gauges on the control panel and running a pre-flight check. Tom speaks into his mic on the headset. "Suffolk Airport Tower, this is Delta Charlie 4732. I'm ready for take off."

The voice on the other end says, "Good morning, Tom. Good flying day, ain't it? Proceed to #3 and climb to 8,000 feet. Baltimore ATC will pick you up. Over."

Tom says, "Copy. Going to 8,000. DC4732 Out." He pulls back on the throttle and the plane rolls down the runway picking up speed as it goes. The plane gets airborne and Anna holds her stomach as the plane climbs.

Tom says, "That was the toughest part."

Anna looks at Tom nervously and holds onto the arms of her seat.

"When we level off, it'll be a lot smoother. You sure you're ok?

Anna is still holding onto her seat. "I'm a little scared, but it's fun."

Anna is looking out the side window and she asks, "How high are we now?"

Tom says, "3,000 feet on the way to 8,000. That's the Long Island Sound down there."

Anna says, "It's beautiful."

The radio squawks, "Good morning DC4732. This is Baltimore ATC. We got you. Climb to 8,000 feet and hold. Do you copy?"

Tom says, "Good morning. This is DC4732. I copy. Over."

Anna is more relaxed and she asks, "How long have you been flying?"

Tom answers, "Since I left the military - about fifteen years. Do you like my plane?

"I love it. How old is it?"

"She was built in 1959. It's a Cessna 170. I found her in a boneyard."

"A boneyard?"

"It's a scrapyard. The owner was selling her. She belonged to his father."

"Was it in bad shape?"

"No, not that bad. I made him an offer and he was happy to get rid of her. You should have seen Scottie's face when I got it back to his hangar. He and I restored it. He's quite a mechanic."

"Is Scottie a pilot too?"

"Yeah, he's a great pilot. He helped me when I was learning how to fly.

"Wow, how long did it take you guys to fix it up?

"Two years and a little more than $27,000."

"She's beautiful. What's her name?"

Tom is confused and asks, "Her name?"

"Tom, she's gotta have a name."

"She does. Delta Charlie 4732." Tom says.

"No, a regular name. People name their boats, why not your plane?"

Tom smiles and shakes his head.

"Why are you smiling; you think I'm crazy."

Tom gestures out the window, "No, you're not crazy. Look out the window. Paris is 3,000 miles away.

Anna is looking out the window and she says, "The ocean is so vast, so scary."

"I was thinking about having lunch in Mystic, Connecticut."

"How far is that?"

"We could be there in an hour."

"If we go, we'll never get back by two, will we?"

"Is it really that important?"

"It is to Antonio."

"What about you?"

"Me? Antonio is my husband and there's things he expects from me."

"Like?"

"Like dinner, Tom. It's the least I can do. He works all day." Anna says. "Can we talk about something else?"

"We can, but I think he expects more than dinner from you."

"Tom, drop it, please."

"I just want you to be honest with yourself Anna."

"About what?"

"About your feelings for Antonio."

"My feelings for Antonio are none of your business."

Tom looks out the side window.

Anna says, "Why did you ask me to come today?"

Tom looks at Anna and says, "I thought you might need a change."

"From what? My boring life?"

"I didn't say that. You're right. It's none of my business."

The radio squawks, "This is Baltimore ATC, come in DC4732."

Tom responds, "Baltimore ATC, this is DC 4732. I'm at 8,000 feet."

"Hold at 8,000 DC 4732. Do you copy?"

"Copy Baltimore ATC, will hold at 8,000."

"Happy flying DC4732."

Anna is looking out the window.

Tom says, "We're gonna see Montauk pretty soon."

Anna is still looking out the window. She says, "Tom, you're a policeman. What do you know about my husband?"

"Nothing Anna. I retired before he got here."

"Did you ever ask your friends about him?"

"I don't have to. I already know."

"Know what, Tom?"

"I know you're in an abusive relationship."

"Don't talk to me that way, Tom."

"I know the signs, Anna. Like you said, I'm a policeman."

"You don't know anything about me and Antonio."

"I know you're afraid of him. When he's near you, you're tense and scared."

Anna turns away and looks out the window again. She is tearing up, but she doesn't want Tom to know. The cabin is silent for a while.

Anna asked, "When you were a policeman, did you ever kill anybody?"

Tom doesn't answer.

"I'm sorry Tom. You don't have to answer."

Tom finally says, "Yes."

Anna turns and looks at Tom, looks back outside the front window. She says, "I feel like I can stay up here forever. It's beautiful, quiet and peaceful, but at the same time, it's dangerous, just like you Tom. Please take me back."

"If that's what you want."

"Sorry if I ruined your day, Tom."

Scottie and a mechanic are in the hangar and Scottie hears Tom's plane coming in. He looks at his watch and says, "That ain't right. He's back too soon."

Scottie walks fast to the front of the hangar as Tom's plan taxies in. Scottie says, "You're back early. Is everything ok?"

Tom says, "Yeah, with the plane."

"Do me a favor, would you help Anna down?"

Scottie walks around to the passenger side as Anna struggles with her seat belt.

"Scottie, could you please help me with this?"

Scottie points to the red button in the middle of the belt and tells Anna "Just give it some slack and push the red button."

"Thank you, Scottie." Anna says.

"You're welcome Anna. Tom went to get the car."

"I'm afraid he's not very happy with me right now. I kinda messed up his plans."

Scottie says, "He'll be ok in a little while. He won't be upset for long."

Tom's car drives up and stops by Scottie and Anna. Scottie opens the door and Anna gets in the car. Tom's window goes down and he says, "Scottie, take care. Thanks."

Scottie says to Anna, "Don't forget what I told you."

She extends her hand and Scottie kisses it. "It was nice to meet you."

Scottie says, "See ya."

Tom and Anna are sitting silently. Anna is looking out the side window.

Tom says, "I need to go to the house. I have more stuff to bring to the apartment."

Anna says, "Can you drop me off at the market? I'll walk from there."

Tom's car drives into the parking lot of the market. Anna reaches into the back for her bag. She retrieves it, looks at Tom and says, "Tom, it's my fault the day turned out this way."

"I never should've brought it up."

Anna pauses and says, "You were right about Antonio."

"What?"

"You were right about him."

Tom is looking at Anna and he says, "A couple of days ago, you told me I don't have to be alone. Do you remember?"

Anna nods and says, "Yes. We were in your apartment."

"Well, you don't have to accept the abuse."

Anna looks at Tom. She opens the door and exits the car. She walks towards the market, turns and waves goodbye to Tom. Tom turns out of the parking lot. Felix is tailing him as he drives towards his house on Oak Street.

Tom arrives at his house and goes up the stairs and enters, the door closing behind him." Felix parks across the street and watches. Tom grabs a beer from the fridge and sits on the couch. He looks around the room and admires the remaining stained glass panels still hanging in the windows and thinks about Rebecca. He wonders if taking the apartment in Anna's house was a bad idea.

CHAPTER 19
FELIX BEARS WITNESS

A cab stops in front of Tom's house and Anna gets out. Felix is half asleep having smoked half a joint, which is typical for Felix. Seeing Anna going up the steps snaps him out of his stupor. He says to himself, "What the fuck?"

Anna gets to the door and rings the bell. Tom opens it and is surprised to see Anna standing there. She walks in and says, "Tom, I need to talk to you."

"Come in, Anna. Are you ok?"

"No, Tom." Anna stands in front of Tom and Tom tries to go around her to the living room. She blocks his path and she says, "Tom, look at me and tell me what you're feeling right now."

"Anna, this is no good. You're married."

Anna says, "Please tell me."

Tom tries to go around her again, but she follows him, takes his arm and turns him so they're face to face. Tom looks into Anna's eyes for a few seconds, then takes her into his arms and kisses her passionately.

Felix watches from his car as Anna returns his kiss and puts her arms around his shoulders, their silhouettes visible through the stained glass in the window. He thinks to himself, "Antonio's gonna kill that dude."

Tom picks her up and carries her to the couch. They fall to the couch and continue kissing as they begin to undress each other. The sunlight coming through the stained glass casts colors on their semi-naked bodies.

Felix has his head back. He's still stoned and he looks at his watch. It's 1:15

Tom and Anna are lying in bed. Anna says, "Be careful Tom. Antonio carries a gun."

"I figured as much. I can take care of myself. Do you know if he ever used it?"

"We don't talk about it. I never wanted to ask how your wife died. I felt I didn't have the right."

"Do you want to know?"

"Not now, Tom. Not if it upsets you."

"She died in surgery—a routine operation."

"My God, Tom. I'm so sorry."

Tom continues, "I was at work when Rebecca called me. She told me she was having bad stomach pain. I drove to the house and my neighbor told me she was taken by ambulance to Hampton General. When I got there, a nurse told me that she was in surgery. Her appendix almost burst, but they caught it in time and she would be out of surgery in a few hours. I felt relieved, but two hours became three and then four. I was trying to find someone who could explain why it was taking so long. When a nurse came out, I feared the worst. The look on her face said it all. She told me that Rebecca didn't survive the surgery. A lot of emotion went through me, shock, anger, and sorrow.

"I asked her why didn't the doctor come out to speak to me. I demanded to see him. She told me he was unavailable. My darling Rebecca was dead and he couldn't come out to tell me how or why. In a fit of anger, I went to the operating room with the nurse attempting to calm me down. When I burst into the room, I saw Rebecca's body under a blood-soaked sheet. Again, I demanded to see the doctor. I picked up a tray of instruments and threw them across the room.

I pulled back the sheet and lying there was Rebecca, her eyes closed. The color had left her face. I fell to my knees. I felt hands grab me by the arms and shoulders and drag me out of the room. I was taken to a small chapel. A deep voice told me if I didn't calm down, they would have to call the police. As a cop, I understood they were just doing their job. Damn rent-a-cops stayed with me until a doctor came in. He told me he was the chief of staff. I asked him what happened to Rebecca. He told me while they were getting a team together, her appendix burst and caused severe bleeding. They couldn't get it under control. He said they tried everything but the infection and bleeding was too much. He told me he was sorry. About a month later, I got a call from a nurse who was in the operating room. That night, the resident on duty was not experienced to handle a complicated surgery. Dr. Weeks, chief of surgery, was called to come in. When he arrived, he was obviously intoxicated, and in our opinion, should not have been in the O.R. Dr. Ramos, the resident, said he would do the surgery if Dr. Weeks would talk him through it. We felt this was the best way to proceed. At least the instruments would be in steady hands. Dr. Weeks refused and he told Dr. Ramos that he was only a resident and he should watch and learn. We objected and Dr. Weeks silenced us. With time running out, we had to give in. You see, Dr. Weeks threatened us with disciplinary action if we protested. Dr. Ramos tried his best to assist, but from the moment the surgery began, we realized hope for Rebecca was fading. She was bleeding and we couldn't stop it. As her vital signs were fading, Dr. Weeks stormed out of the O.R. Rebecca died a short time later. Drunk and unsteady, Dr. Weeks cut into the appendix and caused bacteria to spread. He didn't clamp the veins properly and the bleeding was uncontrollable. I haven't had a good night's sleep since it happened. I had to tell you."

I asked her if she would testify against Dr Weeks. She told me if she did she would never work in nursing again. There's a code of silence that runs through the medical profession. She told me she wanted to be a nurse since she was a little girl. She loved being a nurse. I didn't want to do anything to destroy her future. I felt bad for her. She was innocent in this."

"What did you do?"

"It took me a few months of searching for him. I called hospitals but nobody knew him. He had a pile of malpractice suits and a drug rap. I tracked him down and finally I found him in Costa Rica."

"What happened when you found him?"

Tom is staring at the ceiling and he says "I killed him."

Felix has his seat back, his eyes half closed and he looks at his watch. Anna has been in Tom's house for three hours. He's looking forward to telling Antonio what he saw. Felix is a crack addicted loser who lives vicariously through Antonio. It gives him pleasure to see turmoil in other people's lives.

A taxi stops in front of Tom's house. Anna exits the house in a hurry, goes down the steps and into the taxi. The taxi leaves and drives past Felix. Felix starts the car and follows the taxi. It stops in front of Anna's house and she goes in. Felix drives off excited about telling Antonio what he saw. Antonio is playing pool with the regulars. His cell phone rings and he answers "Yeah, Felix. What's up."

"Yo, it's like you said, man. Your wife is playing you."

"Don't fuck with me Felix. You better be sure."

Felix can hardly contain himself "Yeah, I'm sure. They went into a house on Oak Street. I could see them through the window."

Antonio's anger is now at its peak "That motherfucker! Where are you now?"

"I'm outside your house. Your wife is home. I'll meet you at the dude's house. We'll fuck him up."

"You're a stupid man, Felix. I got something else planned for the war hero. Meet me at the junkyard. Remember - the one where we dumped that girl you killed?"

"Come on, man. Don't say it like that. It was an accident."

"Be there in an hour."

Tom leaves his house on Oak Street and drives to his apartment. He goes into the bedroom, reaches under the bed and pulls out a metal box. He opens the box and inside are three guns and two boxes of Ammo. Tom picks up a small gun in a holster with velcro fasteners. He takes the gun out of the holster to see if it's loaded and attaches the holster to his ankle. He takes a bottle of beer out of the fridge, goes outside and sits on the steps to his apartment.

Felix is sitting in Antonio's car, telling Antonio what happened that day. Antonio is angry. "So how long were they in the house?"

"Three hours."

"Just what I thought - the war hero is messing with my wife."

"I know what his plane looks like. Let's go burn that shit."

"Nah, Felix I don't give a shit about his plane. It's him."

"So whatcha gonna do, Antonio?"

Antonio stares straight ahead as he speaks. "We're gonna kill the war hero."

"We, Antonio? I can't kill nobody."

"Oh no, you already did, remember."

Antonio turns to Felix with a cold stare and he points to the junkyard "She's over there in one of the cars."

"I ain't gonna do it, Antonio."

"Yes, you are. We're gonna do him together. You're gonna help me."

"I ain't killing nobody. I'll tell the cops you wanna kill the guy." Antonio looks straight ahead. A sick smile on his face. He reaches into the side pocket of his jacket. Felix jumps not sure what to expect from him. Antonio takes out a video cassette from a camcorder and shows it to Felix. Antonio says, "Relax, you little pussy. Do you know what this is?"

"Yeah, some kind of film."

"You wanna guess what's in this film?"

"What?"

"You and the stripper, Felix. I put a camera in the ceiling so I could watch those bitches. You'd be surprised what they do in there."

"Yeah but you're in there, too."

"It's funny, but that part of the tape got erased. You still wanna go to the cops?"

Felix's voice is cracking and he says, "Why are you doing this to me, man? I don't want to kill anybody."

"You're gonna help me, Felix, and that's it. I gotta big score coming soon. You and me are gonna kill the war hero. I get paid and then I'm out."

"What about me, man?"

"What about you? You keep playing pool and hanging out with those pendejos. Now get out. I'll let you know when."

Felix exits the car and walks to the bus stop on the corner. The driver's side window goes down, and Antonio looks at the film cassette in his hand with a smile on his face. "What a stupid fuck! Who uses camcorders anymore?" He throws the cassette out the window and drives off.

CHAPTER 20
CINNAMON CALLING

DiNapoli is in the social club playing cards. He's sitting at a table with his crew, Dom, Primo, and two local button men. The old school phone on the wall rings. Richie says "Hey, Dom. Get the phone."

"Hey Richie, why is it always me who gets the phone?"

"Come on. Get the fucking phone. Don't be a dick." Dom slams his cards down on the table and walks to pick up the phone. Richie picks up Dom's cards and shows them to the other players.

"Don't worry, Dom. I won't let them see your cards." The men snicker as Dom picks up the phone and answers, "Yeah?"

A female voice asks, "Is this DiNapoli Carting."

"Ahh yeah, DiNapoli Carting. That's right."

"Is Mr. DiNapoli there?"

Dom covers the phone and shouts to Richie, "Hey, Richie. You here?"

Richie responds, "Depends on who it is."

"Some broad."

"Don't say broad! Do you live in a fucking cave? I'll be right there."
Richie walks to the phone, "This is Richie, who's this?"

"Mr. DiNapoli, was that your secretary? Does she have a cold?"

Richie laughs. "That's not my secretary, that's a friend of mine. He
works for me, who are you?"

"I'm someone who's holding your card."

"A lot of people hold my card. Let me guess, auburn hair, body to
die for, too good for that place you dance in."

"You're getting warm."

"You remind me of a spice."

"Very good, Mr. DiNapoli."

"You working tonight, Cinnamon?"

"Yeah, till midnight."

"You like champagne?"

"Champagne? Who doesn't?"

"I know a place that's got fountains of it. See you at midnight."

"Sure of ourselves, aren't we?"

"Just say no and I'll go away."

"See you at midnight."

It's a little after midnight and Cinnamon is leaving the club. She
sees a black limousine and walks toward it. The back window goes
down as Primo goes around the back of the car to open the door for

her. From inside the car Richie says, "Come in, Cinnamon. I don't bite. Don't be afraid."

Cinnamon responds, "Maybe you should be afraid of me," as she steps in and sits next to DiNapoli.

DiNapoli looks at Cinnamon and asks, "Were you dancing all night?"

"Yeah, about six hours."

"Well, if you look this good after work, I'd like to see you after a good night's sleep."

"That's original. I never heard that before."

"It's not a line—you're gorgeous!"

"So, Mr. DiNapoli, where's this place with fountains of champagne?"

"Please, call me Richie. Primo, to The Empire Club."

"The Empire Club, that's posh."

"You've been there?"

"No, over my budget I'm afraid."

"That's 'cause you're dancing in a dump out on the island. What're you making now, two-fifty a night? A dancer with your looks and that killer body should be pulling down five, six hundred a night. I got some people in Manhattan who run some high-end clubs I can . . ."

Cinnamon cuts him off. "Thanks, Richie, we can talk about it some other time."

Richie asks, "What's your name."

"Cinnamon."

"No, I mean your real name. Isn't Cinnamon your stripper, I'm sorry, dancing name?"

"No, it's my name and don't apologize. I know what I do to pay the bills."

"So how did you get into it?"

"It's a long story. I needed money for rent, food, credit cards. You know. Things didn't go according to plan. I thought I'd be making some big money."

"You can, but not there."

She glances out the window and sees the New York Skyline from the Queensboro Bridge and says, "Beautiful, isn't it?"

"Yeah, but it hides a lot of shit."

"What do you really know about me - who I am, what I do? You gave me your card. It says you're in the carting business." "Come on. You know what I'm asking."

"Just what I read and hear."

"Does it bother you what you hear about me."

"We're in a limo together and we seem to be getting along. I don't have a problem with it." They both chuckle.

Cinnamon asks, "How'd you get into it?"

"I'm taking the fifth. It's too complicated. Primo, didn't I tell you to take the tunnel, it's faster."

"Yeah boss, but I just saved you about twenty bucks."

"But it's costing 25 bucks in gas."

Cinnamon asks, "Does he work for you?"

"Yeah, I got a big payroll to look after." Richie lowers his voice.

"He's not the brightest bulb, but he's so loyal, it's scary. To me, loyalty is very important.

Cinnamon asks, "What does he do, is he like a bodyguard or something?"

"You don't want to know what he does, let's leave it at that. Besides, we're almost there."

"Ok, Richie."

"You hungry?"

"Yeah, starved."

"This place has the best fillet mignon in the city. You're in for a treat. The owner is a friend of mine. Here we are."

They leave the car and enter the restaurant. Hours later they arrive at Richie's house on Long Island by the shore. It's four a.m. Primo opens the door and helps Richie out of the car. Richie has had a lot to drink and is feeling the effects. Primo extends his hand to Cinnamon and she exits the car much soberer than Richie.

Richie asks, "Hey Primo, how many times have you been to the Brooklyn Aquarium?"

"What, boss?"

"How many times have you been there, you know, the Aquarium?"

"I don't know, boss. Maybe ten or twelve times, I guess."

"Do you like fish that much, Primo?"

Cinnamon is a little embarrassed for Primo and she tries to inter-cede. "I like the Aquarium, too, Richie."

"That's nice, but I'm talking to Primo."

"Tell you what Primo. Take tomorrow off. Go see some whales or sharks or whatever the fuck. It's Wednesday and I got a meeting at the club."

"You sure, boss?"

"Yeah, I'm sure. Take the day off. Why do you go there anyway, Primo?"

"Cause it relaxes me from all this bullshit."

"So Primo, you're saying what we do is bullshit—is that what you think?"

"I'm not talking about that. I mean the world, you know, war and all that shit."

Richie asks Cinnamon, "You like fish, too. Do they relax you, babe, or is it bullshit?"

Cinnamon says, "They're fun to watch, and yeah, they relax me. Now can we go inside, please? I'm fucking exhausted." Richie says, "I decide when we go inside."

He turns to Primo and says, "What the fuck are you doing here?"

"We were talking about fish. Remember, boss?"

Richie says "We're done talking. So go, get the fuck out of here and be careful driving. You're drunk."

Primo walks to the limo driver's side and turns to Richie and says, "I'm not drunk, boss. Am I off tomorrow?"

"Sure Primo, take off, do whatever the fuck you want."

"Thanks, boss."

"Hey, Primo, say hello to Flipper."

Richie turns to Cinnamon and says, "We love Flipper. Don't we, babe?"

Cinnamon replies, "Richie, can we go inside now? I'm freezing out here."

"Ok, babe, let's go. Primo's gonna go visit Orca tomorrow. I hope a shark bites him on the ass." Richie laughs as he staggers into the house, being helped by Cinnamon.

CHAPTER 21
PRIMO DELICATO

Primo is enjoying his day off. He made a fine marinara sauce with meatballs and sliced the garlic hair thin so it would dissolve in the sauce. He sautéed some fresh broccoli rabe and got a loaf of just-baked Italian bread. He pours himself a glass of MontePulciano 2012 and sets the table for one, with cloth napkins and silverware. His apartment is neat but hasn't been updated since his mother died ten years ago. He's dressed for dinner with a black suit, white shirt, and black tie, and his gun is always with him in a shoulder holster. Family pictures and pictures of patron saints are hung around the living room. In a display case is his mother's collection of thimbles from all over the world, a collection she was very proud of and she would show them to everyone who came to the house. Opera music plays in the background while Primo mimics the conductor with a wooden spoon, waving the spoon all around like a conductor's baton. He even sings along with the music, entirely off-key.

The pasta is ready, al dente of course, and he drains it and lets it drip. He puts the right amount of sauce on top and sprinkles freshly grated cheese on the sauce. He sits at the table, tucks a napkin into his collar and turns on the television. He surfs the channels looking for a movie but he stops at the six 'o'clock news. They're breaking a story about an organized crime murder from two years ago. They're reporting the authorities have new evidence regarding the murder of an organized crime associate, and the associate's name was Salvator 'Sallie Boy' Nardo. He was a member of the Scarpello crime family. Authorities believe the DiNapoli crime family ordered the hit on 'Sallie Boy' through their many associates. As of now, investigators are tight-lipped about the identity of the killer or killers. Nardo was found face down in an alleyway, with his neck broken and shot twice in the head. Investigators see a connection between this murder and two others with the same MO.

"We'll have more information …" Primo changes the channel, and he is staring at the TV as if in a trance. He shakes his head from side to side hoping to wake himself from a nightmare, breathing heavily, he takes a sip of wine to calm himself. He begins to sweat and he takes a fork full of pasta and shoves it into his mouth. His anxiety is growing and he pushes the plate of pasta away, while on the stove his broccoli rabe is beginning to burn. He gets up and turns off the burner and sits back down. He takes another sip of wine and begins to mumble to himself. "It can't be. I was careful. There's no way they know. It's bullshit." "Yeah it's just bullshit." He has more wine and he's beginning to calm down.

He's channel surfing one reality show after another, and finally, he finds something that interests him. It's a documentary about sharks. Primo stops and is fixated on the image of sharks killing and devouring a small whale. Blood and flesh litter the water as the sharks tear apart the whale. The whale thrashes in the water as the sharks continue to prey on the whale, as the blood in the water increases the frenzy. Primo is aroused by the power of the sharks and the blood as they rip flesh from the whale, and he takes another sip of wine. His right-hand goes to his zipper, he opens his pants and masturbates. Watching the feeding frenzy brings him to the point of no return and he climaxes. The table shakes and the plates rattle as he holds on the table in ecstasy. It's over, his head goes back, his eyes close and he begins to snore.

CHAPTER 22
MOMMY ISSUES

Cinnamon calls Sergeant McMahon. "Hello, Cinnamon. How's it going? Talk to me."

Cinnamon responds. "Our boy Sanchez had some visitors a few nights ago."

"Who?"

"Richie DiNapoli and a few of his paesans. They went into that back room that Sanchez hangs out in. The Bartender told me Sanchez is the only one with a key. He uses it as some bullshit office. One of the guys was carrying a briefcase and a big dude was watching the door."

"Let me see. The guy with the briefcase was . . . "

Cinnamon cuts her off. "Dom, and the other guy was Primo. From my vantage point, I saw the whole thing."

"Vantage point, what do you mean?"

"I'm on stage, Sarge. Remember, I'm a stripper."

"What about Sanchez, anything else on him?"

"No, except he's a real piece of work. He tried to talk me into that back room of his."

"No shit! What did he say?"

"He promised me drugs and all the shit he can do with his tongue......"

McMahon cuts her off—"That's enough of that."

"I told him if he didn't leave me alone my boyfriend was gonna break his legs."

"Shit, Cinnamon. Who's your boyfriend?"

"Richie DiNapoli."

There was silence on the other end of the phone. "Are you serious? How the fuck did that happen?"

"It's called irony, Sarge. I was dancing the night DiNapoli and Sanchez had their meeting. Richie came out and watched me dance. He gave me his card and here we are."

McMahon is angry and it shows in her voice. "Here we are, that's it? I'm hearing about this now. Are you sleeping with him, agent?"

"Did you just call me 'agent'? Goddamn, you must really be pissed off! Look Sarge, I'm sleeping with him, but it's not what you think."

"Then what is it? Why're you sleeping with him? Do you want me to pull you from this case?"

"No, I don't. Please hear me out. Richie's got issues, Sarge."

"Issues, what do you mean?"

"I think it's mommy issues. He doesn't touch me—he just wants to cuddle, and he calls for his mommy in his sleep."

"Are you kidding? Shit, how weird! We got a tough guy with mommy issues. You can't make this shit up."

"There's more. He talks in his sleep and keeps me awake."

"What does he say?"

"He babbles most of the time. But there's something he does every night in his sleep. He repeats the number 82 over and over."

"82? What do you think it means?"

"I don't know Sarge, but I'll try to find out."

"Be careful Cinnamon. Mommy issues or not, DiNapoli is a dangerous man."

CHAPTER 23
THE SHEFFIELD DINER

ntonio is in the club shooting pool with Felix when his phone rings.

"Who's this."

The voice on the other end says "You forgot me already—my feelings are hurt. I think we should continue our talk from the other night."

"No way, Rodriguez. We're done. Stay the fuck away from me."

Rodriguez ignores him and asks, "You know the Sheffield Diner? Be there tonight at ten."

"For what?"

"See you there," Rodriguez replies forcefully. The diner is about 12 miles out of town on Rt. 25. It's a hole in the wall that always seems to survive the health inspector. Rodriguez gets there early and takes a seat overlooking the parking lot. A little after ten Sanchez arrives and sits across from Rodriguez.

"So I'm here. Now what?"

Rodriguez asks, "How are things at Ball Breakers?"

"You dragged me out here for that shit?"

"You banging strippers, Antonio?"

"You know I'm married, Rodriguez. So don't try that shit on me."

The waitress shows up and asks, "You boys want anything?" Rodriguez says, "Sure. A cup of coffee and a toasted bagel - well done."

Rodriguez asks Sanchez, "You want anything?"

"You crazy—look at this place—it's filthy!"

The waitress glares at Sanchez, as Rodriguez says, "Don't worry, darling. He's in a bad mood, and you're a great waitress."

"Fuck you. Rodriguez! Eat your bagel by yourself. I'm out!" He reaches into the pocket of his jacket and takes out a baggie full of white powder and puts it on the table and asks, "What does that look like to you?"

Sanchez says, "Come on, man. Put that away."

The couple at the table next to them look over at the men. Rodriguez again asks "What is this stuff?" Just then the waitress brings the bagel and coffee for Rodriguez. She places the food on the table, notices the baggie with the powder, shakes her head and walks away.

Rodriguez nonchalantly takes a teaspoon of white powder, waves it around and asks, "You want some?"

Sanchez looks around and says, "You crazy, man."

Rodriguez puts the white powder in his coffee. He stirs the coffee looking at Rodriguez. "This time it's sugar. Next time, who knows?

Ten or fifteen of these baggies filled with something other than sugar found in the trunk of your car would cause a lot of trouble for you."

"You gonna plant shit on me? That's illegal, and you gotta prove it's mine. This ain't nothing but a shakedown! You can't keep me here, I'm out."

Rodriguez sits sipping his coffee unfazed by what Sanchez said. He looks up at Sanchez and leans back in the booth. "I heard you got a private room in the back. What goes on there, Sanchez?"

"How the fuck should I know. Maybe lap dances?"

"You should know Sanchez, you're the only one with a key."

"I'm out." Sanchez storms out of the coffee shop. The waitress brings Rodriguez the check and he says, "Told you he was in a bad mood."

CHAPTER 24
JORGE DELACRUZ

Jorge Delacruz is sitting at a long table with his associates. Delacruz is the head of the most powerful drug cartel in Colombia. He's short in stature, pudgy with pox marks on his face. He's in his mid-50s and has gray hair that he dyes an awful shade of brown. People who know him say he's a humble, sophisticated and educated man, but people who have crossed him are dead. He's on Interpol's 'most wanted' list, but massive payoffs to police and politicians insulate him.

The men are gathered at a beautiful hacienda in Medellin, Colombia. Tapestries, priceless artwork and expensive rugs from around the world adorn the walls and marble floors. Ornate fountains and pools are located throughout the hacienda, and frolicking in these pools are beautiful women. Delacruz and his associates are having lunch. There are plates of caviar, lobsters, fine wines and champagne.

A manservant comes to clear the table while Delacruz sits back and speaks.

"Gentlemen, did you enjoy your lunch?" The men at the table nod in agreement. "Yes, gentlemen, I know—lobster, caviar, the finest wines—who can deny it? Look at me, do I look like a movie star?"

The men look at each other, not understanding the question.

"Come on, don't be afraid. Be honest."

One of the men at the table named Miguel says, "No, Padrone, but…."

Delacruz cuts him off. "An honest man, but allow me to answer. I'm a rather unattractive man but look at how I live, the Palacio, the art, the food, but best of all the women. Look at them laughing and enjoying themselves. Anytime I want I could select one or all if I choose, go to my bedroom and we'd make love until the sun comes up. On the other hand, if I choose to kill one and bury her in the jungle I could do that too."

The men are uneasy, and they shift in their seats and glance at each other. Delacruz says "I see I made you uneasy, tranquillo gentlemen. Why would I hurt such beautiful creatures?"

At that point, the manservant brings cigars to Delacruz. He places the cigars on the right side of the table, and Delacruz says to his manservant, "Thank you. Gentlemen, cigars! They're not from Cuba—fuck Cuba. These are specially made for me. Let's enjoy them." Delacruz passes around the cigars. The manservant lights Delacruz's cigar first then proceeds around the table, and Delacruz says to his manservant, "Thank you. You can go home to your family now, I won't need you the rest of the day."

"Are you sure, Padrone? It's still early."

"Yes, you may go." The manservant thanks him and leaves. Delacruz speaks to the others. "My manservant is the wealthiest servant in Colombia. He has a beautiful hacienda not far from here, a beautiful wife, drives a nice car, anything he wants. Do you know why, gentlemen?" The men at the table glance at each other. "Loyalty. I buy it with money. Some of you at this table may be wondering why Tomas is not here. It'll tell you why. He betrayed me and he stole some of my merchandise. It seems he was offered a better deal across the river with that pendejo, El Moreno." He looks around the table at the men seated there. He takes a drag from his cigar and points to the men. "Gentlemen, if any of you are looking for advancement, a raise, so to speak, go ahead - work for whomever you wish. However, if you steal what's mine, I'll bury you in the jungle next to Tomas. Now, down to business. It's my understanding that Mr. DiNapoli is an honorable man. I have no reason to doubt it. However, for the first transaction, I insist on having the 20 million dollars before the Italians get the merchandise. Money upfront, as the saying goes. If this arrangement is acceptable to Mr. DiNapoli, then I'll proceed. We'll have the money deposited in several of our accounts. When the deposits are confirmed the merchandise will be stored in the usual manner. Diego, Miguel, and Carlos will go to New York to handle the transaction. Diego, you will stay with the Italians until the merchandise is tested and DiNapoli is satisfied. Make it clear to DiNapoli that the first shipment is merely the beginning and larger shipments are available if he chooses. Your contact is Sanchez. He is making the arrangements with the Italians. You've met, of course."

Diego responds "Sanchez is a puto. I hate that pendejo."

"That's good, because before you come home I want you to kill him."

"My pleasure, Padrone."

"Our warehouse #10 in the Brooklyn Navy Yard will be at the disposal of the Italians for as long as they need. So, gentlemen, if there's nothing else, it's time for relaxation. I have friends for you to meet." He motions to the women, and they stop what they're doing and gather around the men. "Enjoy yourselves and have anything you want, but remember to treat these women tenderly or answer to me."

CHAPTER 25
DINAPOLI CALLS FULLER

Fuller is reporting for work, and as he walks to his office his phone rings. Caller ID says DN, DiNapoli is on the other end. Fuller hesitates and then answers. "What can I do for you, Richie?"

"How's it going, Fuller?"

"I guess it depends on what you want."

Richie laughs. "Alright, I'll get to the point. You gotta detective working for you named Rodriguez, is that right?"

"Yeah, transferred from Vegas. All the way from Vegas to Oceanview."

"Doesn't that seem strange from Vegas to a small town in Long Island?"

"Not to me, Richie. I was short-handed and they sent me this guy. I didn't have a choice. He was a disciplinary problem according to Vegas PD., so now I'm stuck with him. Why all the questions, Richie."

"Why, cause something ain't right with this guy. He's harassing Sanchez, and this deal better not get fucked up. Rodriguez is sniffing around, asking questions and I want him to back off. That's where you come in, Fuller."

"Careful with the names, Richie."

"Don't worry, Fuller. I'm on the café phone. Stupid ass feds been trying to bug this phone forever. We're ok."

Fuller offers, "I got a missing person case I can put him on, that should keep him busy."

"I don't give a shit how you do it. Just keep him away from Sanchez."

"Sanchez is a piece of shit."

"Yeah, he is a piece of shit, but Delacruz won't do business with anybody else but him, at least on this deal. Stay focused, Fuller. After this deal is done we'll all be walking around with fuck you money. You can retire to a nice island somewhere and drink pina coladas all day and bang broads half your age all night."

"Ok, Richie. I'll take care of it."

"Yeah, I know you will. It's time to earn your money. Keep your cops, especially this fucking Rodriguez, away from Sanchez."

CHAPTER 26
GETTING TO KNOW YOU

Fuller calls Rodriguez into his office. Rodriguez enters and sits down. Fuller says, "We never had a real face-to-face talk since you got here, Detective. So how do you like Oceanview so far?"

"I like it. It's quiet."

"Don't let the quiet fool you. We get a lot of cases out here. Assholes commit crimes in the boroughs then come out here to hide out." Fuller does air quotes with his fingers for effect. "Coming from Vegas, this must bore you to tears. What made you choose Long Island?"

"I didn't, someone else picked it for me."

"That's right detective, your captain called me. Captain. . . I forgot his name."

"Steiner," Rodriguez fills in the blank.

"That's right, Steiner. He told me you were a disciplinary problem. You wanna explain?"

"Sure. You see Sergeant, I'm not subtle when it comes to police work, and I guess that pissed off my superiors."

"What do you mean subtle?"

"Well Sergeant, if I need to bury a foot in some body's ass to get what I need, I bury the foot. It's that simple."

"Well, before you start that shit in Oceanview, make sure you check with me first. I'll decide who's ass you put your foot in. The folks in Oceanview don't appreciate aggressive policing. As long as they feel safe, we try not to expose them to the underbelly of law enforcement. Have you toured the town yet? People pay millions for their homes; let's not give them cause for concern. So how long have you been a cop?"

"About fourteen years, the last nine in Vegas."

"Where were you before Vegas?"

"I was in Florida and Arizona."

"Did you work big cases in those states, Detective?"

"Sure, we had some good cases. A lot of 'em were drug cases. The biggest case was a meth distribution case in Arizona."

"I'm sure you worked with the DEA in those drug cases."

"Yeah, sure. We collaborated. You know how it works."

Fuller leans back in his chair and asks, "So, you know people in the DEA?"

"Some. It's been awhile since I spoke to them."

Fuller is eying Rodriguez suspiciously, and after a while, he asks, "What made you become a cop?"

"It was either law enforcement or football, I think I made the right choice."

There is silence in the room, then Fuller says, "Alright detective, I'm gonna give you a case. It's a missing person case—her grandmother reported her missing. Here's the file, look it over." "Her name is Evelyn Lynch."

Fuller slides the file across the desk, and Rodriguez picks it up and flips through the pages.

"This girl has been missing for one week and I'm just getting the file now?

"What do you want me to do, Rodriguez? I'm short detectives. Do you want the case or not?"

"Yeah, I'll take the case."

Rodriguez gets up and opens the door. He turns back and says to Fuller, "One week and we're here jerking off."

"Easy, Rodriguez. Don't forget who your boss is."

"Yeah, sure," Rodriguez replies and closes the door.

CHAPTER 27
EVELYN'S GRANDMOTHER

The next morning Rodriguez drives to the grandmother's house. The house is on a tree-lined street in a middle-class neighborhood. It's a midcentury brownstone with a brick exterior and nicely maintained landscaping. The grandmother's name is Janet Cooper. Rodriguez rings the bell; the voice on the intercom is loud and strong.

"Who is it?"

"I'm Detective Rodriguez. I'm here about your granddaughter."

"Ok, just a minute." Rodriguez looks around the neighborhood. It's a blue-collar area, well kept but by no means affluent. The door opens slightly and a tall grey-haired woman in her late sixties asks, "Do you have an ID, Officer?" "Of course," Rodriguez responds and he shows her his badge and ID. The woman motions him inside to one of the rear two apartments. As they walk to the apartment she says, "I had to move down here some years ago, the steps were too much for me. Besides, when my husband George died, our granddaughter moved in with me 'cause the apartments are bigger down here." They both sit down and the woman asks if he would like a cup of coffee. Rodriguez declines and takes a pad and pencil from his inside jacket pocket. He says "Mrs. Cooper I just want to let you know we'll do everything we can to find Evelyn. Can you give me her full name?"

"Evelyn Lynch."

"No middle name or aliases."

"No, just Evelyn.

"When did you see her last?

"Monday night, as she was leaving for work around six p.m."

"Where does she work?"

"Not sure. She never mentioned the name. The only thing she told me is that it's an upscale, very expensive Italian restaurant."

"Do you know the address, Mrs. Cooper? Anything you can tell me to help me find the place."

"Only that it's on Main Street by the library."

Rodriguez asks how far is that from here, and Mrs. Cooper replies "About 3 miles."

"You said it's an upscale place?"

"Yes. Evelyn told me that dinner for two could cost 100 to 150 dollars. I can't afford that. I think that's pretty upscale, don't you, Detective?"

Rodriguez nods and asks, "Is Evelyn in a relationship with anybody?"

"She never mentioned anybody, but kids have a lot of secrets these days. I pray nothing happened to her."

Rodriguez puts his hand on hers and says, "We'll do our best to find her. Do you know if Evelyn did any type of drugs or if she drank alcohol to excess?"

"No detective, not that I saw. She always came home after her shift. I'm so worried about her."

"Did she mention names of friends or wanting to take a trip somewhere out of town?"

"No, Detective." She said she had friends at work and sometimes they would go out but, like I said, she always came home."

"Do you mind if I take a look in her bedroom? I may find something with the restaurant's name on it."

"Sure, that's a good idea. It's back here."

They walk to a well-kept, neat room in the back of the apartment. Rodriguez looks around the room and sees a photograph that appears to be a college graduation picture. He asks if he can have the photo, and she replies "Yes." Rodriguez removes it from its frame and puts the 4x6 photo in his pocket. He searches the drawers of the night stand and bureau and finds a pipe and some drug paraphernalia and quickly removes it and puts it in his pocket.

He turns to Mrs. Cooper and says, "I'm done. I'll have to canvas the restaurants on Main Street till I find out where she works. It should be easier now that I have her picture."

"Thank you, Detective. Let me walk you out. Please find her. I'm alone and I miss her so much."

"Mrs. Cooper, I have one more question if you don't mind. Evelyn's parents, where are they?"

"My daughter died years ago, and her father is an abusive drunk."

"We'll find her. I'll be in touch. Bye, Mrs. Cooper."

"Thank you, Detective. Goodbye."

He turns and walks down the steps as Mrs. Cooper closes the door. Rodriguez drives along Main Street and finds the library. He stops into two nearby restaurants and no one recognizes the woman in the picture. The third restaurant named "Loria's" is an upscale white table cloth establishment with a young good-looking wait staff, an amazing bar, murals of Italian landscapes and designer lighting. Rodriguez enters and is approached by a maître d' who says, "Sorry, sir. We open at 5 pm."

Rodriguez shows his badge and the maître d' asks, "How can I help you, officer?"

Rodriguez shows the maître d' her picture.

"This girl is missing and I'm looking for her. Her grandmother is worried sick. May I show her picture to some of the wait staff, maybe they know her? I was told she works at an upscale restaurant on Main Street."

"Yes, but please hurry. We're setting up for dinner."

"I get it. I'll keep it brief." The maître d' steps to the side and Rodriguez asks if he would have the wait staff gather in the middle of the room.

"It would be easier if I showed everyone the picture at one time, and then I'll be out of your hair."

The maître d' shouts, "Will the wait staff come to the middle of the room? The detective has a photo he would like you to look at."

The wait staff forms a line by the bar. "Is that everybody?" The maître d' says, "Yes, unless you want the kitchen staff out here also." "Yes, please. If you don't mind." The maitre'd sighs and hurries into the kitchen. The full staff is now assembled in front of the bar. The maître d', stressed, now walks away and checks on the table settings.

Rodriguez takes out the photo and walks up and down the line. "This girl is missing. Does anybody know her? She works at a restaurant. Does anybody know where?" One by one they say no. One girl makes eye contact with Rodriguez and discreetly tilts her head towards the back door once, twice, till Rodriguez understands the gesture. He puts the picture in his pocket and thanks everybody, including the maître d' who groans in response. Rodriguez leaves the restaurant and walks around to the back. The girl is there waiting for him. She says to him, "Can I see the picture again?" Rodriguez shows her the photo. "That's Evelyn, Evelyn is her real name."

"What do you mean real name?"

"Detective, she doesn't work in a restaurant. She's a stripper. We work together at Ball Breakers. Her stripper name is Candy Willow. That's all I know. Please keep me out of it. If this place finds out I'm a stripper, they'll can me, and the money's better here."

"Was she doing drugs at the club?"

"Once in a while when she could get 'em. She hangs out with a bunch of assholes and really messed up people. I gotta get back, I'm gone too long."

"If anything else comes to mind you have my number," and he hands her his card. He asks, "What is your name?"

"Susan. I gotta get back." She begins to walk to the restaurant when Rodriguez asks, "About those messed up people—can you give me a name?" Susan walks back to him, gets closer and says—"Antonio Sanchez."

CHAPTER 28
THE CONFRONTATION

S anchez is at home drinking and watching a ballgame when his phone rings. He recognizes the number as Rodriguez's. and he ignores the call. The phone continues to ring, then he picks up the phone and shouts "What?!"

Rodriguez asks "Where are you?"

"I'm in my house, why?"

"Stay there."

"Why should I? You can't tell me what to do."

"Cause I'm taking a field trip out to your hangout tonight and I don't want you there or I'll embarrass you in front of your crew."

Sanchez asks "Why are you going there anyway?"

Rodriguez replies, "I'm curious."

"Stay home, Sanchez."

Sanchez slams the phone down.

Antonio is angry and he calls Felix who answers, "Where are you, man? We're waiting for you."

Sanchez responds, "I ain't coming tonight, but I need you to do something for me."

"What is it, Antonio?"

"I want you to get some of the players together, three or four. I want you to fuck somebody up for me."

"What, who?"

"His name is Rodriquez. He's a big dude, black hair, dark eyes, ain't never been there before, you'll know when you see him. Be careful, he carries a gun so make sure he doesn't see it coming. Get some of your junkie friends together, you know that crack head Angel, Freddie and that crazy Irish guy Tommy—he's a fucking psycho—tell 'em there's a grand each in it. Just hurt him, and one more thing—tell him to stay away from Antonio Sanchez. There's a grand in it for you. You gonna do it?"

"Sure, Antonio, sure."

The black Lincoln drives to Ball Breakers and parks on the side of the club. Rodriguez walks into Ball Breakers and all eyes are on him. He looks like he doesn't belong, and nobody knows him. He walks to the bar, orders a beer and puts ten bucks down. As he's drinking his beer he looks around the room and notices the men playing pool. Felix catches his eye and Rodriguez turns back to the bar. Felix whispers to his friends. "Yo, I think that's the dude. We'll get him outside and bring the sticks. Hurt him real bad."

Rodriguez motions to the bartender and he walks over. Rodriguez shows the bartender the picture and asks, "You know her?"

"Yeah, that's Evelyn, but she hasn't been here and I can't reach her, so I stopped trying. You look like a cop?"

"Yeah, I'm a cop, and I'd rather not flash a badge in this joint if you know what I mean. Her grandmother reported her missing. When did you see her last?"

"I think it was Monday night. She went home in a cab. I think she was sick or stoned or something. A couple of the regular assholes told me they put her in a cab."

"Assholes. Who are these assholes?"

"A guy named Sanchez and this guy Felix. A couple of douchebags."

"Let me ask you something—how long have you been working here?"

"About seven years."

"In all those seven years, how many cabs have you seen in this neighborhood?"

The bartender thinks for a minute and says, "Now that you said it, I ain't never seen one. They don't come down this way." Rodriguez nods and asks, "You got cameras in this place?"

The bartender laughs. "If we put cameras in this place we wouldn't have any customers."

Rodriguez points to the locked door in the back by the men's room and asks, "What's in there?"

"I don't know. I don't have a key."

"Who does?"

"Sanchez, but you didn't hear it from me."

Rodriguez finishes his beer and slides 10 dollars to the bartender and says, "Keep the change."

"There is no change, the beer is 15 bucks."

"Fifteen, wonderful." He places another 10 on the bar.

"You want change?"

"Nah, keep it. Oh, one more thing. The guys you mentioned—Sanchez and Felix. I know what Sanchez looks like. Is Felix in here now? Just a yes or no."

"Yeah, he's the skinny ugly one with the shitty goatee."

"Thanks. Men's room back there?"

"Yeah. just before the exit."

Rodriguez walks to the back and out the unlocked exit door. He looks around and sees what looks like a warehouse building with two men standing outside. He looks up and notices two cameras, one facing Ball Breakers. Rodriguez approaches the men.

"You guys work here?"

"Yeah."

"Is this place 24/7?"

"Yep, unfortunately. Are you a cop or something?"

"Yeah, looking for a missing person." He gestures to the cameras. "Do they work?"

One of the men says, "I don't know. Ask the boss. He's inside, but I gotta tell you he's in a shitty mood."

"So am I."

One of the men uses a key card to let Rodriguez in. "Go straight back, his office is right there," he says, pointing to the back. Rodriguez walks to the back of the warehouse and, as he walks, forklifts and people are working and moving around him. A worker approaches him and asks, "Can I help you?" Rodriguez shows his badge and says, "I'm looking for the boss." "Keep walking straight back. You can't miss him."

Rodriguez finds the 'Boss' in a dingy office with stained walls, a wall calendar that's two months behind and a dirty and dusty Mr. Coffee machine. Not looking up from his computer, the boss says, "What can I do for you?"

Rodriguez shows his badge and says, "I'm Detective Rodriguez. I'm searching for a missing girl. Do those cameras outside work?"

The boss is a short pale and pudgy man with thick glasses, thin hair and a lazy eye. He replies, "Yeah, they work, otherwise they'd be no damn good. Ain't that right, Detective?"

"Do they record to tape or live stream?"

"I don't know. They're right there all nice and neat. My security guy is anal about shit like that."

"Can I see last Monday night?"

"Not now, I'm busy, up to my ass in work."

"I see. If I called OSHA, Immigration and got a warrant, would that make you less busy?"

"Look, detective, I got 30 guys out there just on this shift. Half of 'em are ex-cons, some are doing drugs and the rest are probably sleeping somewhere in this building. I can't watch everybody, and you're just adding to my shit to-do list—you get it?"

"Yeah, I get it, but it's important to her grandmother." Rodriguez sees a picture on the desk of a family. "Nice picture. Is that your family?"

The boss says, "Thank you, Detective. My wife Jennie passed a few years back—cancer took her, but she fought. Boy did she fight; beat the odds. The genius doctors gave her 6 to 8 months—she hung around for two years. That handsome guy is me and my daughters, Allison and Sara. They're all I got and I love 'em to death. In medical school, both of 'em."

"You must be proud. I sure am. They're in medical school because they're smart."

"Look around you, Detective, what do you think they pay me here? They got scholarships—both of 'em—damn right I'm proud."

"I'm sorry about your wife. The girl I'm looking for is about the same age as your daughters. I promised her grandmother I'd find her. That tape would be a great help."

The boss says, "Same age as my daughters, you said?"

"Yeah, she's about 25-26." The boss shakes his head and points to two cassettes and says, "Monday during the day and Monday night."

"Thanks. Is there any way I can watch in private?"

"Sure, I gotta make rounds, anyway." The boss points to the VCR on the desk and asks, "You know how to use it?"

"I think I can figure it out. If I see some evidence on the tape, can I take it?"

"Sure, don't worry about it."

"Thanks." The boss grabs a clip board and leaves the office. Rodriguez hears him shout, "Everybody line up for attendance check. If anybody out there is smoking, put 'em out and get in here."

Rodriguez loads the tape and begins to watch, the back exit of Ball Breakers is grainy but visible on the screen. He goes through the tape. At 9:10 pm a man staggers out and pees against the wall of the club, obviously drunk. Rodriguez mutters to himself, "Nice move. There's a bathroom inside, asshole." At 10:10 a stripper who's half-naked and a male patron are taking a marijuana break. As he takes a drag on the joint she leans against him and rubs his crotch. They finish the joint and go back inside. At 10:20 a man leaves the club and he goes off camera range. A few minutes later a car comes into range and backs up to the rear door. The same man exits the car, opens the trunk and goes back inside. Rodriguez notices the man is using the private office that is used by Sanchez. Rodriguez continues to forward the tape. At 10:40, two men exit the club carrying what appears to be a heavy object wrapped in black garbage bags and taped all around. The men struggle with the bag and finally maneuver it into the trunk. The shorter man gets into the driver's seat and drives away. Approximately five minutes later, the taller man bolts from the office locks the door and runs out of camera range. Rodriguez is convinced that the taller man is Sanchez. He grabs both tapes and is leaving the warehouse when the boss intercepts him at the door.

"Find what you were looking for, Detective?"

"Yeah, thanks for helping out."

"Hope you find her."

Rodriguez goes back to Ball Breakers and tries the rear door to the mysterious office but it's locked. He uses a knife to jimmy the lock and the door opens.

The room smells of cheap perfume and stale beer. He looks around and notices white powder residue and empty beer bottles on the table. In the background, he hears music as the dancers perform on stage. He sees a row of lockers and attempts to open them, but he finds that some are locked and others are empty. One locker has been moved and is out of line with the others. Behind it is a wall safe. He photographs the room and the wall safe with his phone. He leaves the room the same way he came in and closes the door behind him. He walks back into the club and sits at the bar. The bartender comes over and says, "I thought you left. Do you want another beer?"

"Not at fifteen dollars a pop I don't."

"The boss doesn't like when we buy back but this one on me."

"Thanks." He looks up at the dancers behind the bar and notices the differences between the two girls. He calls the bartender over and asks him, "The girl on this side of the stage, you know the girl next door type, what's her name?"

"Around here we call her Cinnamon."

"Cinnamon," Rodriguez says. He finishes his beer straight from the bottle, gets up, puts 10 dollars on the bar and walks to the door. He looks at Felix on the way out and it dawns on him that Felix is the other man on the tape. Felix and three of his crew stop playing pool and follow Rodriguez out.

Rodriguez has his back to the club as he makes it to his car. The element of surprise was on the side of the thugs as the first blow strikes Rodriguez in the lower back. Stunned Rodriguez turns to see another pool cue coming for his head. He dodges and grabs the pool stick and smashes the base of it into the thug's nose which immediately gushes blood. Crazy Tommy who's been in and out of prison most of his life hits Rodriguez in his midsection with the end of the cue. Rodriguez hardly feels this due to his many hours in the gym. Tommy is surprised by this and it gives Rodriguez an opening to leverage the cue to flip Tommy to the concrete. Tommy's head hits the floor with a thud. Rodriguez turns his attention to the two remaining men and one pulls a knife on Rodriguez. He lunges at him and Rodriguez uses the pool cue as a club and disarms the thug. At that moment the other thug strikes Rodriguez to the back of the head. The blow stuns Rodriguez and he is struck again as he slides to the floor against his car. At that point the parking lot is spinning and the men begin to kick him. Rodriguez is still conscious as Felix sticks his face two inches from his and says, "Stay the fuck away from Sanchez." The combination of Felix's intensely bad breath and adrenaline in Rodriguez causes him to grab Felix by the neck and squeeze. Felix is surprised by how much strength he has left and he tries to get Rodriguez's hands from his throat. The next blow to his head causes him to let go of Felix and go into a state of semi-consciousness. He lies in the deserted parking lot for half an hour. A voice begins to wake him and he pulls himself up. He feels warm blood on the back of his head. His ribs are aching and he's almost on his feet. He feels two arms around him trying to help him up. The same voice comes into focus, "I'm gonna call an ambulance." Through the fog he sees the outline of a woman. It's the dancer Cinnamon.

He says, "No ambulance."

Cinnamon replies, "You may have a concussion. You should get to the hospital." Rodriguez ignores her and turns and opens the car door. He says, "Thanks for the help, Cinnamon."

She closes the door to his car and asks, "You sure you can drive?"

"Yeah, I'll be alright. Thanks again." He drives off.

CHAPTER 29
THE REAL FULLER

F uller is shaving, the mirror is steamed up. A young girl comes from behind him wraps her arms around him and whispers "When you're done I'll be waiting in bed."

"No, you won't. Get dressed and take your money, it's on the bed."

"Just one more time, daddy, then I'll go."

"Get lost! I spent enough money for one day. Now take the cash and get the fuck out."

"I've been a bad girl, don't you want to discipline me?" Fuller stops shaving and throws the blade into the sink. He grabs the girl's clothes and money and throws them into the hall. He grabs the girl by the hair and says, "I told you to get the fuck out." He drags her into the hall and slams the door. The girl is shouting and banging on the door.

"I'm telling everybody what kind of a prick you are and how you like to play with underage girls, you motherfucker! That's right, Fuller, I know you're a cop."

The door opens and Fuller pulls her back in. "Listen to me, you little junkie bitch. If you ever tell anybody about me or mention my name again I'll kill you real bad. You'll wind up just another dead hooker. Now get your shit and leave. Don't force me to hurt you. You understand me?" The girl doesn't respond, so Fuller grabs her by the neck and says, "You got it?"

The girl nods furiously. He opens the door and pushes her into the hall. She picks up her clothes, sobbing loudly. A door opens and an old woman peeks through the opening and sees the young girl. She asks "Are you hurt, child?" The girl says "No, go back inside." The door closes.

CHAPTER 30
THE SCORE IS EVEN

Sanchez hasn't heard from Rodriguez since the beating and figures Rodriguez got the message. On the third day, his phone rings and it's Rodriguez. He ignores it. On the third try he picks up. Rodriguez says, "We need to talk."

"About what?"

"About money. You want me to back off, it's gonna cost you."

"How much?"

"Fifty grand, and you won't hear from me again."

"Fifty thousand's a lot of money."

"Yeah, and I know you got it—you're dealing drugs out of that club you hang out in. So fifty grand—and I want it tonight. Ten 'o' clock at the spot."

Sanchez arrives at the diner late as usual. Rodriguez is sitting at the usual table. Sanchez slides into the booth and looks at Rodriguez and says, "I guess you met my crew" with a smirk on his face.

Rodriguez responds, "Yeah I was pissing blood for a few days."

"Wow, they really fucked you up. I heard you put up a fight. You think you're a real tough guy, don't you, puto?"

"You got my money?"

At that point the waitress comes to the table and says, "Good evening, gentlemen. Would you like the usual bagel and coffee for the nice man, and nothing for Mr. Personality?"

Sanchez barks at her, "Get lost, bitch!"

Rodriguez asks the waitress to give them a minute, and then asks again, "Where's the money?"

"Give me a few days I'll get it. So I give you the cash and then what happens?"

Rodriguez is staring at Sanchez and says, "What happens? This happens." The speed at which Rodriguez grabs Sanchez by the collar of his jacket, dragging him across the table, totally catches Sanchez off guard. He's pinned to the floor with Rodriguez's fist in his throat. Rodriguez tells him, "If you ever get your junkie friends on me again I'll kill the whole bunch of you." Sanchez is gasping for air and he punches at Rodriguez but his hand is swatted away. Sanchez's eyes are bulging as Rodriguez continues, "You just made this personal, maricon. I'll be in touch." Before he loosens his grip he pats him down and finds a gun and states, "I'll keep this," as he gets on his feet. He hands the waitress a twenty dollar bill and leaves the diner. Sanchez is on the floor trying to catch his breath, coughing and cursing Rodriguez, his eyes tearing and bloodshot. The waitress approaches Sanchez and asks, "You sure I can't get you anything?" to which Sanchez responds, "Fuck you!"

Later that week, Rodriguez is on his way to the precinct when his phone rings and he answers. "Good morning, Sarge." McMahon sounds annoyed. "Good morning, my ass. I got a call a few minutes ago from Captain Steiner. Do you know who that is?"

"Sure, he signed my transfer papers."

"Well, Rodriguez, it seems Fuller called him. He's claiming you threw Sanchez a beating at some coffee shop in front of about ten witnesses."

"Ten? It was about three. The place is a dive - nobody goes there."

"Don't crack wise, Rodriguez. I'm in no fucking mood. The bottom line is you gotta back off Sanchez."

"But Sarge, didn't you tell me to introduce myself?"

"I said to introduce yourself, not choke the guy out."

"So maybe I did get a little carried away, but that was a revenge beating. He sicced some of his playmates on me outside that strip club he hangs out in."

"Why am I finding out about this now? Assaulting an officer is serious shit."

"What about murder, Sarge, how serious is that?"

"Murder? What are you talking about?"

"About a week ago Fuller gave me a missing persons case. A young girl by the name of Evelyn Lynch. Her grandmother reported her missing. What her grandmother didn't know was that she was working as a stripper where Sanchez hangs out. I went out there to interview the people that work there. I spoke to the bartender, and he told me that Sanchez and a guy named Felix were the last people to see her alive. Sanchez told him she was drunk and they put her in a cab."

"So what do you think happened, Rodriguez?"

"I think the cab story is bullshit, Sarge. I looked around outside the place and I saw a building across the street with cameras. One of the cameras caught a piece of the strip club exit. There's a room in the back of the club by the exit and only Sanchez has the key. On the tape there's two people carrying a black garbage bag out of that room. The bag looks heavy, they're struggling with it and finally they get the bag into the trunk of a car."

"And Rodriguez, you think there was a body in that bag?"

"I think it's the missing girl, Evelyn Lynch."

"Shit, Rodriguez. You think Sanchez killed her?"

"I don't know who killed her, but one of the people is his size and body type and I'll bet the other guy is Sanchez's pet chihuahua, Felix."

"Can you see any faces on this tape?"

"No. Sarge. It's dark and the film is grainy."

"How did you get this tape? I hope you didn't take it without permission."

"No, the manager of the warehouse gave it to me."

"Did he give it up voluntarily?"

"Yeah, he did, Sarge. I noticed some family pictures on his desk. It was his wife and two daughters. I told him his daughters are about the same age as the missing girl. I guess he felt he had to help under those circumstances."

"Whatever works. I guess for right now keep the tape in a safe place. We can't make a move on Sanchez yet."

"But Sarge, it's a murder rap. We could use it for information on DiNapoli."

"I appreciate your enthusiasm, Detective, but based on what you just told me, there is no murder rap. "If we pick him up now and he's involved with DiNapoli, we'll have nothing. You can't see anybody's face on the tape, it's the bartender's word, no witnesses and nobody saw them leave together. Leave Sanchez alone for now. Let him think he won. When we get him on the drug rap we'll push for a murder conviction on top of it."

CHAPTER 31
READY TO MOVE

Richie and his crew are at the social club playing cards. The phone rings and Dom picks it up. "It's Antonio, give me Richie."

Dom yells over to Richie, "Hey Richie. It's Sanchez."

Richie throws his cards down and says "Now what?" He goes to the phone. "Yeah, what's up Antonio?"

"We're ready to move."

"Come to Brooklyn tomorrow at two. I'll buy you a coffee." Richie hangs up and returns to the table and says, "We're on, gentlemen."

It's 2:20 the following day. Richie and his crew are seated at a table in a corner of the social club. Antonio Sanchez is twenty minutes late, and Dom looks at his watch and is growing inpatient. At 2:30, Sanchez walks in and heads toward the table. Richie puts up his hand and says, "Hold it Antonio. Primo, check him. Sorry Antonio, house rules."

Primo frisks Antonio and finds a 9mm gun and a straight edge razor and says, "That's it, boss. He's clean."

Dom sees the razor and says "Hey Primo, let's see that." Primo hands the razor to Dom.

Dom opens the Razor and tests the blade on the back of his hand. Without looking up he says "You kept me waiting again. Are you ever on time for anything?"

Sanchez replies, "Traffic, couldn't help it."

"I like this blade. I see you keep it sharp."

"Yeah, otherwise it's just a toy."

Dom says,"Back in the day when I was coming up, it was my weapon of choice when I needed to be quiet. Know what I mean? I like it. It's old school, black handle diamond in the middle. Real nice." Dom turns to Primo and adds, "You could learn something about tradition; it's what's missing today—finess. You like it, Primo?"

Primo replies, "It's ok, but I prefer these," and he shows Dom his large hands and a 45-caliber Glock from a shoulder holster. Dom is still admiring the razor, and he asks Antonio, "Did you ever use it?"

"Yeah when I was in Colombia, working for Delacruz."

"You mean Colombian neckties and all that shit?"

"Yeah, that's what snitches get in Colombia."

Dom says "Badass Sanchez, you wanna give me a Colombian necktie?"

Sanchez stares at Dom and says, "No, but keep fuckin' with me and …"

Richie steps in mid-conversation and says, "Enough of this shit, we got business."

Richie turns to Primo and says, "Thanks, Primo. Now we got business to discuss." Primo gets up and walks to a different table. Richie asks Sanchez, "So what's the word from Delacruz?

"The first shipment is 1500 pounds of merchandise, the cost to you is 20 million. After that you decide when and how much. Mr. Delacruz only asks that your next purchase happens within ninety days of the first fifteen hundred pounds. Delacruz is willing to give you an exclusive to sell you his product, but you gotta buy more before ninety days is up or he goes to the competition."

"How do I know he won't sell to the competition, anyway?"

"You don't, Richie, but if you don't buy more, it's guaranteed he's going somewhere else, and you'll be out. There's a warehouse at the Brooklyn Navy Yard. It's number 10. It's at your disposal - compliments of Delacruz. Use it to test the product or store it for a few days. Delacruz wants you to be happy. Your contact will be Diego Vargas—treat him with respect. He used to be Delacruz's enforcer but now he's his business manager. He enjoys killing—you hear me Dom—so be careful."

"See how scared I am, asshole."

"Knock it off, Dom. Go ahead, Sanchez."

"Five crates each containing three hundred pounds of merchandise will be waiting for you. How will you transport it?"

"In the back of a garbage truck, how else?"

"That's original. Richie says we'll keep the truck in the warehouse for a few days. When the time is right we'll drive it to Long Island City."

Sanchez reaches into his pocket and takes out his cell phone. He shows the screen to Richie. On it are 10 account numbers. "Mr. Delacruz requests that you place two million dollars in each of ten banks. Don't worry. These deposits can't be traced. Your money and where it came from is protected. Mr. Delacruz doesn't take chances when it comes to his money."

"So let me get this straight—it's money before product?

"That's the only way he'll do business. It's your decision. You can walk away if you don't like it."

"So Richie, when do I get paid?"

"It depends."

"Depends on what, Richie?"

"What's Delacruz paying you?"

"No offense, but that's between Delacruz and me."

Richie thinks for a minute and says, "Ok, Antonio. That's fair enough. Now answer me this—who was in that garbage bag you and one of your fucking friends threw in the back of your car?"

"How the fuck do you know about that, Richie? "Were you following me? Dom says,"I was. Richie don't do that no more."

"The question hasn't been answered—who was in that bag?"

Antonio nervously answers, "A stripper. She won't be missed."

Richie looks around the table at the men gathered there and asks, "Did you kill her?"

"No, it wasn't me. It was one of the guys I hang out with."

"Does this guy, this fucking hero, have a name?"

"His name is Felix. They were doing drugs together and he wanted some pussy—you know—for the drugs, and she wouldn't give it up."

Richie is leaning forward in his chair staring at Antonio with his hand up to his chin. He opens his other hand in front of Dom and says, "Give me your razor."

"What're you gonna do?" Antonio is visibly scared.

Richie takes the blade and opens it. He holds the razor close to Antonio's face.

"Back in the day, I did my share. I did what I had to do, but killing a woman—that's a line I wouldn't cross." Richie moves the razor closer to Antonio's face. "If I took this razor right now and cut your fucking throat it would be a soul for a soul." Antonio is staring at the blade as Richie moves it back and forth in front of his face. He asks Dom, "Hey Dom, would this be the first time I killed somebody in this place?"

"No, Richie it wouldn't."

Antonio shudders. "But Richie, I didn't kill her, it was Felix."

"It doesn't matter. God wants a soul, a soul for a soul." Richie is still holding the blade and is staring at Antonio. He finally folds the blade and gives it back to Dom. "Tell Delacruz he's got a deal, we'll wire the money soon. Maxie, take care of it. Antonio, get with Maxie and give him the numbers." Sanchez lets out a sigh of relief. Richie adds, "If the merchandise is like the stuff we sampled, we're gonna do a lot of business. As for you getting paid, when the deal is done I'll pay you two million dollars, like we agreed." One more thing before you go, Sanchez. I was told you and that hero friend of yours dumped that girl's body in one of my scrap yards without my permission. I need you for this deal, otherwise you and that piece of shit friend of yours would be in the back of one of my trucks." Richie motions to Primo. "Empty his gun and give it back to him. Get your shit from Primo and get the fuck out of here."

Sanchez opens the door to leave and, as he does, the church bells from across the street begin to ring.

A member of Richie's crew approaches the table. Richie waves him over and the man whispers in Richie's ear and motions towards the storeroom in the back. Richie nods and says to Dom, "Let's go." Both men walk to a store room in back of the social club. Primo leaves his table and joins them. In the room are two refrigerators that fill the room with a low pitched hum. Bright fluorescent lights cast an annoying blue cast throughout the room. Tied to a chair beneath one of these lights is Joey Palumbo. He's in and out of reality, having taken a more than usual dose of heroin. Joey is one of Richie's dealers who broke the golden rule of drug dealing—do not use what you sell. The men enter the room and close the door behind them. Richie pulls up a chair and sits directly in front of Joey. He calls out, "Joey, Joey wake up." He slaps Joey's face and continues to call, "Joey, it's Richie, wake the fuck up. Let's go, Joey." Joey comes to his senses and sees it's Richie. He's sleepy and trying to focus. He realizes it's Richie and he panics. "Richie, I'm sorry I'm back on the shit. I'll get straight Richie—give me a chance."

"I'm tired of giving you chances, you fucking mook—this one's number three. You know me and your old man go back 20 years at least. When he went to prison, he begged me to bring you into my crew. He knew you were a fuck up, Joey. He knew you couldn't make it on your own. He begged me, Joey, and I gave in 'cause your old man was like a brother to me."

"Richie, I'm a good earner. I always was."

"You were, Joey, and then you started using my shit. What did I tell you when I took you in? I told you 'don't use what you sell.' Ain't that right, Joey?"

Joey begins to nod out again, and Richie calls him but there's no answer from Joey. Richie gives him the back of his hand across his face. "Wake the fuck up, Joey. I'm talking to you." Dom and Primo who are standing behind Joey glance at each other. They're witnessing Richie at his worst. "When you use what you sell, it costs me 'cause it's my drugs, Joey. You're stealing from me. Do you know that?"

"Please Richie, give me just one more chance."

Richie looks at Dom and nods, "So you want one more chance, Joey? Hey, Dom, should we give him one more chance?" Joey begins sobbing and begging Richie, but it falls on deaf ears. Dom has a syringe filled with a lethal dose of heroin. Joey sees it and begins to scream. Primo covers Joey's mouth with his big hand as Dom stabs Joey in the neck with the syringe. Joey is kicking at Richie as Richie moves his chair back and watches Joey as he convulses and goes limp in the chair. Primo says, "I think he's dead, boss." Richie takes a handkerchief, wipes his hands and says, "Say hello to your old man. Hey, Dom, get a few of the boys and dump this piece of shit."

CHAPTER 32
MCMAHON MEETS EBERSOLE

McMahon is in her office when her phone rings. It's Captain Ebersole from Brooklyn organized crime. "How are you, Sergeant McMahon? I've got some news that'll make your day. We have new evidence linking Primo to the murder of Sallie Boy several months back. I'm giving you a call cause I know you DEA guys are working on a trafficking case involving the DiNapoli family. We have a tape that puts Primo at the scene. His face is clear—there's no doubt it's him. We made some prints from the tape, and we're thinking we can use the evidence to turn him against DiNapoli. There's a phone in the Social Club, an old school payphone that we can't seem to tap remotely. Maybe we can get Primo to bug the phone and different areas of the club. The only problem we're having is getting Primo alone long enough. Do you want in?"

Sergeant McMahon responds. "Sure I want in, and I can help you with getting Primo alone. Every Wednesday DiNapoli has a family meeting at his Social Club. He doesn't let Primo in on the meeting, and as it turns out Primo goes to the aquarium—we can grab him there."

"How do you know that, Sergeant?"

"Let's just say it comes from a reliable source and leave it at that."

"Ok, Sergeant, I get it. Today's Monday. Can you get here tomorrow?"

"I'll get on a flight tonight."

"Ok, great. We're at 17 Water Street in downtown Manhattan. When you get here I'll introduce you to the team and I'll go over the evidence with you." "That's good, Captain. See you tomorrow."

McMahon arrives at the organized crime headquarters. The entrance to the building is a plain stone facade with two glass doors. Written on one of the doors is "NYPD Organized Crime Unit —Brooklyn Division." McMahon wonders to herself why they would advertise. She goes in and notices the lack of security. Sitting at a desk is a man in uniform reading a newspaper. He looks up, hands McMahon a clipboard and says, "Sign in and go through the metal detector. That guy on the end will tell you what to do."

McMahon shows her badge and says, "I'm a Sergeant with the Las Vegas DEA and I'm armed."

The man answers, "You gotta check the gun, cuffs or whatever is on this list," and he shows McMahon a list of prohibited items.

You're telling me nobody in this building carries a weapon?"

"They do, but they work here. You don't." He grabs a plastic tub from the floor and puts it on the desk "Put your stuff in here." The man gives her a visitor pass and says, "You need to wear this while you're in the building. Take your stuff to that guy and go through the metal detector."

The other man takes the tub and puts it on the other side of the metal detector as she goes through. He asks, "Who are you here to see?"

"Capt. Danny Ebersole."

"I couldn't help overhearing you're from Vegas."

"Yes I am."

"I go there a lot. Last time I was there, I beat the crap out of those slots and took 'em for eighteen hundred."

"A whole eighteen hundred—let me know the next time you go. I'll let the casinos know there's a high roller in town, just as a heads up."

The man just looks at McMahon, not knowing how to respond. McMahon adds, "Listen, I wanna keep my gun. Who makes that call?"

"Ebersole. He's in charge of the building. I gotta ask him."

"Would you, please? I'm already late."

The man slowly and purposely picks up the phone and dials, and after a while says, "Hi, Captain. I got a woman down here who says her name is McMahon, and she wants to keep her gun." There's a pause. "Ok, Captain, I'll give it to her. Thanks."

The man hands her the gun and says, "Go to the 9th floor. He's in room 9F." McMahon says thanks and walks past the man to the elevators.

McMahon walks into room 9F. The room is busy with agents, people at computers and uniformed NYPD officers. Captain Ebersole is a 30 year veteran of the NYPD. He worked homicide, vice, and finally ended up in the organized crime unit. In his 30 years of service he's been shot, stabbed and beaten up, he's due to retire but his love of the job keeps him going. He's gathered around a table with a few agents. They're gesturing and talking loudly, and the conversation is dominated by Ebersole. He looks past the agents and sees McMahon, excuses himself, and comes to greet her. "Hi Sergeant, I'm Danny Ebersole," he says, extending his hand.

McMahon replies, "Did you hire those guys downstairs?"

"Well, good morning to you, too."

"I'm sorry, Captain. I'm a little short on patience this morning. I'm Elizabeth McMahon."

"Nice to meet you," he says, and they shake hands. "Come over. I'll introduce you to the team." They walk over to the table where there's agents waiting for Ebersole and he makes the introductions. "This is the team you'll be working with tomorrow. This is agent Alex Ruiz—he'll be driving the car. This handsome gentleman is agent Johnny Powell—he'll cover Primo to make sure he doesn't get out of line. In the backup car we got agent Anna Flores and John Harris—you'll meet them later. Sergeant, come into my office. I wanna show you the pictures we got." Ebersole takes a manila envelope from the top drawer of his desk; he turns it over and six pictures land on this desk. "Look we got six shots off that tape. Primo's face is clear in four out of the six."

McMahon asks, "Where did you get these?"

"There's one building at the end of the street among the abandoned buildings in that alley. The only occupied floor of that building was used to shoot pornography. The cameraman heard the commotion in the alley, turned his camera out the window, and got the murder on tape. Turns out a few of the people in these films were under-age." "Kiddie porn? "No, but borderline. His lawyer traded the pictures for less jail time. We don't know who ordered the hit. There's no doubt it's Primo."

"Let me see those pictures." McMahon looks at the pictures and says, "There's no question that's Primo. These are pretty brutal."

"Yeah, they sure are. Primo breaks his neck then shoots him in the head twice."

McMahon asks, "What was Sallie Boy doing there in the first place?"

"Don't know. Maybe Primo can tell us. Let's go outside and talk about the details with the rest of the team."

They approach the rest of the team and Ebersole gives them their instructions. "Tomorrow morning we'll be at the Social Club at 10 a.m. Primo normally gets there between 10:30 and 11. We'll follow Primo to the aquarium or wherever he goes. The cars will leapfrog to avoid being spotted. When he gets to where he's going, Agent Flores and Harris in the backup car will bring him to you, McMahon. Remember, if he goes to the aquarium there may be families with children there so be careful. Catch him off guard, and bring him to McMahon. If he agrees to turn on DiNapoli, we'll drive him to the safehouse and brief him. If not you've got to take him into custody. Be careful. He's a killer."

McMahon says, "I wanna be the one that talks to him."

Ebersole asks,"Any objections?" It's quiet, and nobody speaks up. "Ok then. McMahon will do the talking. But remember, Agent Ruiz is in charge. Ok, people, let's break and meet up here tomorrow morning at 8 a.m."

Ebersole turns to McMahon and asks,"Do you have plans for dinner? Would you like to join me? I know a great Italian place nearby."

"Thanks, Captain, but I'm exhausted. I just wanna get back to my hotel and sleep. Any other time I would take you up on it."

"I understand, Sergeant. Get some rest. Tomorrow we'll do this thing."

"Good night, Captain."

CHAPTER 33
PRIMO'S DAY OF RECKONING

Primo is driving Richie and Dom to the Social Club in Brooklyn. He doesn't notice the two cars parked near the Club as he drops off his passengers. Richie says, "Primo, take the day off. We got a late meeting tonight, so take the day off and go say hello to Orca. Enjoy yourself." Richie and Dom chuckle as they enter the Social Club. "Thanks, boss," Primo shouts.

Primo is happy because he gets to spend time at his favorite place, the Brooklyn Aquarium.

Primo arrives at the Aquarium, exits his car and fast walks to the ticket booth excitedly with money in hand. A car parks next to his, and a man and a woman in suits exit. The other car with McMahon and the two other agents goes around to the back of the parking lot. The two agents approach Primo from either side. Agent Flores shows her badge and says, "Come with us, keep your hands at your side. There's kids here, let's not have a bad scene." Agent Harris puts his gun against Primo's back and says, "Make a fuss, and I'll put a hole in your kidney. Move to the back—somebody wants to talk to you." They reach the car, and McMahon opens the door. Harris pats Primo down and removes Primo's weapon. Harris looks at the size of the gun and says, "What do you do with this fucking cannon?"

Primo responds, "Give it back and I'll show you."

Agent Harris says, "Get in the car, asshole." A female voice adds, "Get in, Primo."

Primo gets in beside McMahon and asks "Who are you?"

"I'm Sargent McMahon with the DEA. This is Agent Ruiz and Agent Powell; they're with the organized crime unit. They're here to make sure you're polite."

"So, Mr. Delicato. Delicato, isn't that 'delicate' in Italian?"

"Yeah, so what?"

"So how's Sallie Boy doing? It wasn't too delicate the way you killed him."

Primo says "Sallie who?"

"Sallie Boy. Somebody broke his neck."

"Too bad for Sallie Boy, but I don't know shit about that. Can I go now, is that it?"

"No Primo, that's not it. Here, open it," and she hands Primo the manila envelope.

Primo asks, "What's this?"

"Open it, Primo."

"Why, what 's inside?"

"Open it and find out." He opens the envelope, and the pictures fall out of the envelope and onto his lap.

Primo picks up the pictures, goes through them and hands them back to McMahon.

McMahon says, "You were thorough that day, Primo. You didn't leave any clues."

Primo stares straight ahead with no emotion, and asks "Where did you get these?"

"There were cameras in the alleyway, but none of them were working. At the end of the alley there's an abandoned building, abandoned except for one floor. You wanna know what they did on that floor, Primo?"

"What?"

"Porn."

"So what? It ain't against the law."

"Depends on what state you're in. But you know what's against the law everywhere? "Using minors for porn."

Primo hangs his head and says "Fuck."

"Yeah, fuck, you piece of shit. You knew there were minors in there and you didn't say shit."

"No, I thought it was the regular stuff."

"It seems the scumbag that was operating the camera heard a commotion in the alleyway, turned his camera out the window, and guess what—his lawyer just traded these pictures for less jail time for the scumbag. That's good for the guy with the camera, but too bad for you, Primo. I read Sallie Boy's record and, to be honest, you did us all a favor. But murder is murder, and you gotta answer for it, Primo. How did you do it?" McMahon asks.

Agent Powell turns and looks at McMahon.

Primo answers, "You know."

"Yeah I know, but we wanna hear it from you. How did you know Sallie Boy was gonna be there? Did you follow him?"

"No, I waited for him."

McMahon asks, "Was DiNapoli behind the hit?"

"No, it was an open contract and I took it. I would have done it for free. I hated that prick. Everybody knew he liked to watch."

"Watch what?

"You know, porn. One of my associates told me he was gonna be there. I hid out in one of the doorways. When he got close I stepped out. I wanted him to see me face to face when I killed him. I wanted my face to be the last thing he saw before I snapped his neck."

Agent Powell again turns and looks at McMahon. McMahon looks back at Primo who's still staring straight ahead. Primo continues "When he saw me, he was fucking with me, and he said something that really pissed me off."

"What was that, Primo?"

"He said, 'What're you doing here, Primo? Looking for something to eat?'"

Powell turns to McMahon with a half smile on his face. McMahon says, "Go ahead, Primo."

Primo continues, "The dumb prick didn't realize he was about to die. I put my hands around his skinny neck and I broke his neck in less than five seconds. He didn't have time to reach for his gun. Fuck him."

"What happened next, Primo?"

"I held him there for a while to make sure he was dead. He pissed himself and I let him drop to the floor. I took out my gun and put two in his fucking head." Agent Powell turns to McMahon and shakes his head from side to side.

McMahon asks Primo, "You broke his neck and you knew he was dead, so why did you shoot him?"

"It's my signature, that's how I sign my work." There's silence in the car. After a while McMahon speaks. "Primo, do you know what *modus operandi* means?"

"No."

"It means you're in deep shit cause your signature can tie you to two other murders."

Primo is still staring ahead, and he says "What do you want me to do?"

"You know the phone, the old school payphone on the wall at DiNapoli's Social Club?"

"Yeah, I know it."

"Well, we want you to put a bug in it, and put a few more around the club so we can listen in."

"I can't do that. If Richie finds out I'm a dead man."

"If you don't, you'll have to answer for one—possibly three murders. Take a minute, Primo. Think about it."

"Why are you guys always after Richie?"

"Why?" McMahon responds "Cause he's a killer and a drug dealer. He extorts people, and has people killed if they cross him. You ever kill for him, Primo?"

"I ain't saying nothing about that. But I did overhear something Richie said once at that strip club, Ball Breakers. Something about cutting some drugs, and Dom said it'll still be stronger than most shit on the street."

Agent Powell asks, "Did you overhear where it's coming from or when?"

"No, Richie never tells me anything about his business."

McMahon says, "I'm afraid that's not good enough, Primo. So did you decide?"

Primo looks at McMahon and pauses. Finally he says, "Can I tell you a story?"

"Sure, Primo. Go ahead."

"My mother died a couple of years ago. She made a great sauce, and she always told me to learn how to cook. She used to say 'your mother won't be here forever.' She had a thimble collection from all over the world, and she was very proud of it. She showed her collection to everybody who visited the apartment. I was at her bedside the day she died, and I promised her that I would take care of her collection."

McMahon and the agents look at each other with puzzled expressions. Primo continues, "Once a week I take them out and I clean them. It takes a long time cause there's at least 100 of 'em. If I go to prison there'll be nobody left to do that." The words are not fully out of Primo's mouth when he grabs the seatbelt of Agent Powell, wraps it around his neck and yanks it back, pinning him against the seat. His left hand is wrapped around McMahon's throat. Agent Powell is struggling to get the belt from around his neck. The strength of Primo is overwhelming, and McMahon struggles to reach her gun. Agent Ruiz pulls his gun and aims it at Primo but before he has a chance to shoot, Primo lets go of the seat belt and slams the agent's head against the driver side window, temporarily stunning him. Agent Powell is gasping and coughing, still trying to free himself, as Primo grabs the belt again. McMahon is on the verge of blacking out. She pulls her gun and fires point blank into Primo's gut. The bullet passes through Primo's massive body and shatters the car window behind him. Primo is still holding McMahon by the throat but now his body weight is on top of her. His face is beet red and he's wheezing from his wound. His mouth is filling with blood. He and McMahon lock eyes and McMahon puts the barrel of her gun against Primo's forehead. He mouths the words "Kill me."

Agent Ruiz yells, "No!" He knows what a 9mm bullet will do to a skull at that range. For McMahon, it's now life and death and she fires. Bits of skull, brain and blood splatter the inside of the car and its occupants. Agent Powell shouts "Drive, fucking drive!" The car peels out from the parking lot with tires screeching, followed by the other car. With sirens and lights flashing they reach speeds of 100 miles an hour. Agent Powell shouts, "Get to the safe house!" His voice is dry and raspy. McMahon is leaning against the corner of the back seat, shaking and unable to compose herself. Primo's body is at her feet, and it twitches its last second of life like the whale being torn apart by the sharks. She stares out the window to avoid looking at the bloody mess at her feet. She begins to compose herself and feels pity for Primo and anger at herself for not having more control over the situation. Agent Powell turns and asks McMahon,"Are you alright?" She looks at him and says, "What the fuck do you think?"

A few blocks from the safe house the cars run silent so as not to draw attention. The warehouse gate goes up and the cars drive in. The safe house is an old warehouse garage. It's large, cold and most of it is dirty. There are several desks with computers and large monitors on the wall. The monitors keep vigil on the street around the building. Ebersole comes from behind his desk and walks to the cars. As he gets closer he notices the smashed window and the blood splatters. He walks quickly to the car as McMahon jumps out, covered with gore. The other men exit the car in the same condition. Ebersole looks inside and sees what's left of Primo. He screams, "What the fuck happened?"

Agent Powell says, "Ask Miss Las Vegas here—she fucked it up."

McMahon responds, "You had your back turned—you were supposed to cover him, asshole. Where were you?"

Agent Powell says, "I was getting choked, bitch."

Captain Ebersole shouts, "Everybody shut up, shut the fuck up!" He asks Agent Powell to tell him what happened. Agent Powell replies "We put him in the back seat with McMahon. She told him about the evidence we had. He copped to the murder of Sallie Boy. Told us how he did it in detail—even that Sallie Boy pissed himself before he died."

"Was he gonna cooperate?" Ebersole asks.

McMahon answers, "No."

Ebersole turns to the driver, "And then?"

The driver continues, "He started talking about his mother and her collection."

"Collection, collection of what?"

"Thimbles, Captain."

"Thimbles, a collection of thimbles, who the fuck collects thimbles? Then what happened."

"He went crazy and wrapped the seatbelt around Powell's neck and then he grabbed McMahon by the throat and he was choking her."

Ebersole turns to McMahon. "Is that the way it happened."

"Yeah, he was trying to kill me, so I blew his fucking brains out."

Ebersole asks, "How'd he get his cuffs off?" There's silence. Again he asks, "How'd his cuffs come off? Did you cuff him?" Ebersole gets in Agent Ruiz's face. "Was he cuffed?" Agent Powell responds, "No, he wasn't." Ebersole says it louder. "Was he cuffed?" "No, Captain. He wasn't," answers Agent Ruiz. Ebersole turns to McMahon and asks, "Why wasn't he cuffed, McMahon?"

"Don't know, it wasn't my call."

Ebersole screams angrily, "You're fucking cops—that's the first thing you do, especially with a guy like this. He's a suspect in 3 - count 'em, 3 - murders. You acted like a bunch of rookies. What made you think he wouldn't kill you, assholes? Didn't I tell you to be careful? What the fuck were you thinking?"

The other people in the room are silent. McMahon asks "Where can I get cleaned up." A woman at a keyboard answers, "there's bathrooms upstairs." McMahon says thanks and walks to the stairway. Ebersole turns to the two men and says "Take the car and that fucking mess in the back seat and get rid of it. All of you get the fuck out of here."

Ebersole is sitting at his desk staring into space. McMahon comes down the stairs and sits down at Ebersole's desk. There's silence and the people in the room continue to work.

Ebersole looks at McMahon and says, "This turned to shit quick. Now what, McMahon? He was gonna be the guy to help us put the puzzle together."

"Now we go back to square one. I gotta go." She gets up to leave. Ebersole says, "Primo was gonna die one way or another—it just happened to be you. You're a mess, you can't go outside like that. I'll have one of my agents drive you to your hotel."

"Thanks, Captain."

CHAPTER 34
PRIMO'S BODY FOUND

DiNapoli is waiting at his home in Oceanview, Long Island. It's not like Primo to be late. You could usually set your watch to him, but today he's over an hour late. Richie's phone rings. "Yeah, Dom, I know you're waiting. He ain't here yet."

"Did he call you?"

"No, and this ain't like him. Hope he's ok. Is Maxie with you?"

"Yeah we're both waiting." "Hey, Dom. Do me a favor. Go over to Primo's place and see if you can find out what's going on. Maybe he's sick or something. He ain't picking up his phone. Something's up."

"Maybe he did a Mama Cass and choked on a ham sandwich."

"Don't be an asshole, Dom. Go ahead over there, I'll pick up Maxie. We'll meet at the club."

Dom arrives at the Social Club and tells Richie he had no luck at Primo's house. "I looked through the windows, rang the bell, all that shit. Even his car is still there. You don't think the feds grabbed him, do you, Richie?"

"Don't know. But even if they did, he doesn't know shit, and what he knows will implicate him, too."

Dom gets up to leave and Richie asks, "Where the fuck you going? It's early."

"Home. It's my wife's birthday. I told her I would take her to a nice restaurant."

"Hey, Dom. Why don't you take her to Bella's across the street? Tell her to meet you there."

"Sure Richie, that's real classy. See you tomorrow."

Dom is driving the seven miles to his house. He hears breaking news on the Radio. "Primo Delicato, an alleged member of the DiNapoli crime family, was found dead this morning behind an abandoned factory in the Bayshore section of Brooklyn. The victim was shot twice at close range. We'll have more news stories on our 11 pm report."

Dom pulls over and turns off the engine. "Motherfucker," he says to nobody in particular. He calls Richie. Richie answers, "Yeah, Dom, ain't you home yet?"

"Get ready, Richie. I just heard Primo's dead, he was shot twice." There's silence on the other end of the phone. Dom continues, "They found him in Brooklyn behind some old factory."

"Shit, Dom. Sounds like a hit." Richie says to Maxie, "Primo's dead —they found his body in Brooklyn. What the fuck! I can't believe it! We would have heard if he overstepped his bounds and pissed somebody off. If this was sanctioned I wanna know who ordered it."

Maxie says, "Primo was made—if somebody took a contract, it had to be sanctioned."

Richie pauses. "I can't believe Primo's dead. Find out what you can, Maxie."

"I'll call Fuller to see if he knows anything."

"If this wasn't sanctioned, I wanna know so I can return the favor."

"I'll ask around, Richie."

"Thanks, Maxie. I can't believe he's dead."

McMahon is at the airport waiting for her flight back to Las Vegas. She decides to call Rodriguez to let him know about Primo.

Rodriguez answers "Hey, Sarge. How's it going?"

"I'm at JFK."

"No shit! You're in New Yoek? That's great!"

"Yeah, I was, but I'm going back to Vegas."

"Back to Vegas—what do you mean?"

"I got a call a few days ago from Brooklyn organized crime. Remember Captain Ebersole? He's working the case with us. They had new evidence linking Primo to one - possibly three - murders. Ebersole had a plan to pick up Primo and use the evidence to flip. They wanted to bug the phone in the Social Club. They've been trying to bug it for a long time. This was their chance."

"Sounds like a good plan, but I'm getting the feeling something went wrong."

"It's worse than that, Rodriguez. We had Primo in the car and we were talking, just talking when suddenly he went crazy and things went into the shitter real fast. He started choking me, everything was spinning, I couldn't breathe and I was about to pass out, so I put my gun against his forehead and blew his brains out."

There's silence on the other end of the line. After a while McMahon says, "I gotta go—they're calling my flight."

CHAPTER 35

SANCHEZ AND DINAPOLI—THE DINNER

F our men are seated at a table in an Italian restaurant owned by a friend of Richie's. Richie is becoming paranoid, especially after Primo's death. He doesn't know who to trust. The people at the table are Richie, Maxie, Dom and Sanchez. Sanchez says, "Mr. Delacruz will have the merchandise available for pickup on Sunday at 11pm. Warehouse number 10 at the Brooklyn Navy Yard. Diego Vargas will be there to handle the transaction. The security guards all have the night off except for the front gate. He'll let you in." Richie looks around the table at the men seated there and he says, "The four of us at this table are the only ones who know about our arrangement with Delacruz."

Dom asks, "What about Fuller?"

"Yeah, about Fuller, my trust for him ran out a long time ago."

"I'll take care of Fuller, I'll figure something out."

"Like I said, nobody knows, only us and Delacruz. Got it, Antonio?"

Richie is staring at Antonio. "Why are you looking at me?"

Richie replies, "'Cause you're a loose cannon with a big mouth. Can I trust you to keep this quiet? Can I, Antonio?"

"Don't worry about me, Richie. When this deal is done I'm gettin' outta Dodge. Pay me and I'm gone, Richie."

Richie is still staring at Antonio and he takes a sip of his wine. "Ok, Antonio. After we get the product, you get paid. Don't fuck with me and things will go smoothly."

Richie picks up the menu and asks who's hungry. Dom says, "I could eat."

After dinner, Richie goes across the street to the Social Club and calls Fuller. Fuller picks up the phone though he's half asleep. "Yeah," he answers.

"Did I wake you, Fuller? Sorry for the late hour. I got some news that's gonna put a smile on your face."

"What's that Richie?"

"What are you doing Sunday night at 11:30?"

"You tell me."

"We're having a party on Pier 86 at my warehouse and you're invited. Make sure to wear something festive."

"Got it, Richie. I'd be happy to attend."

"Good night, Fuller.

CHAPTER 36
FULLER, RAT OR NOT

The next morning, Richie and his crew are in the Social Club. Dom and Maxie are talking and laughing loudly— probably on espresso overload. Richie leans over to Dom. "Dom!" Richie calls. Dom keeps talking and laughing loudly. Again Richie calls Dom, but he still doesn't respond. Richie says a little louder, "I got rid of Fuller last night." All of a sudden there's silence. Dom says, "You didn't …" and he makes a pistol gesture with his hands.

Richie says, "I see I finally got your fucking attention. No, he's still alive. What did you hear about Primo? Did you find anything out?"

"No Richie, my contacts don't know shit. If it was sanctioned, nobody's talking. Fuller doesn't know shit, either."

"Speaking of Fuller, how long has he been on our payroll?"

"About five years."

"He's about to be tested. I called him last night and I told him the drop was 11:30 at our pier. Pier 86, where we keep our trucks. Half hour later and 10 miles from the actual drop. Next to our warehouse there's a storage facility—put one of our guys in there. If he sees police activity, we'll know he's a rat. If Fuller is standing there by himself with his dick in his hand, maybe I was wrong about him."

"What if he did turn on us, Richie? He knows our business."

"What does he know? He knows nothing. Let me tell you something about Fuller—he's a pedophile fucking freak—he's got a thing for underage girls. He goes to this joint in Flushing owned by some Asian scumbags."

"How do you know?"

"I did some business with these gook pricks and they owed me a favor. They told me Fuller's a regular there. It was either pay him off or shoot him in the face, and killing a cop is not a good idea."

Dom says. " So Fuller's a pedophile. What do you know? The sick fuck."

"Why don't we just blackmail him, boss?"

"Not a good idea, because when the shit hits the fan, who are they gonna believe? Don't worry about Fuller. Sunday we'll know where he stands."

CHAPTER 37
FULLER REVEALED BY MRS. SADIE KLEIN

Rodriguez is at the precinct talking with the other officers. From across the room an officer shouts, "Rodriguez! You might want to take this on line 2. It's a woman calling about a young girl, could have something to do with your missing person case."

"Hello, Mrs. Cooper."

"Hello, I'm not Mrs. Cooper. My name is Sadie Klein, Mrs. Sadie Klein."

Rodriguez says, "I'm sorry, Mrs. Klein. I thought you were someone else. I'm Detective Rodriguez. What can I do for you?"

"Well, detective, there was quite a ruckus outside my door a few nights ago."

"Ruckus? What kind of ruckus, Mrs. Klein?"

"You see, Detective, I'm a virtual shut-in, and since my Maxwell died—he was my husband—my health is getting worse. I can hardly walk around my apartment."

"I understand, Mrs. Klein. Tell me about the ruckus."

"Well, a few nights ago I was watching my favorite television show. At around 10:30 I hear loud noises from the apartment next door. There was a man talking loudly as if he was angry. Then I heard the door slamming a few times."

"Go ahead, Mrs. Klein."

"I heard sobbing in the hallway and I opened the door just a little, and I was mortified by what I saw, Detective. Standing in the hall was a girl of no more than 17 or 18 years old. All she was wearing were her tops and bottoms."

"What do you mean, Mrs. Klein?"

"Just her underwear, Detective."

"I get it, go ahead."

"Her clothes and some money were strewn all over the floor."

"Are you sure she was in the apartment next door?"

"Oh yes, Detective. You see, there's only four apartments on this floor. She was definitely next door."

"Do you know the person who lives next door?"

"No, I only hear him leave, and sometimes when he comes home. Since I don't get out much, I hardly see anybody."

"May I have your address, Mrs. Klein?"

"Of course, Detective, but I don't need to get involved, do I? You see, I'm 77 years old, and I'd prefer not to be a witness or anything like that."

"I'll make sure of it. Tell me your address, please."

"It's the condominiums on the water. 724 Oakwood Drive. in Oceanview."

"I know the building well, Mrs. Klein. And what is your apartment number?"

"I'm in apartment 3B."

"Ok, Mrs. Klein, apartment 3B. I have your phone number. I'll keep you informed. Is there anything else?"

"Yes, there is. It's a name that she said, but my memory is failing me lately."

"Take your time."

"The girl said the man's name and it started with an F… it's coming to me, I'm playing it over in my head … yes, Detective. She said Fuller."

"Fuller. Are you absolutely sure, Mrs. Klein?"

"Yes, and it's all coming back to me. She said he was a cop and she knew it. But I don't think that's true. A policeman would never treat a young girl like that."

Rodriguez is silent.

"Detective? Are you there, Detective?"

The voice snaps him back. "Thank you, Mrs. Klein. You've been very helpful. I'll be in touch. Good bye, Mrs. Klein."

"Good night, Detective."

CHAPTER 38
THE DISCUSSION ABOUT FULLER

M cMahon is at home a few days after Primo's death. Rodriguez calls her.

"Hi Sarge, how're you doing?"

"I'm ok."

"Listen, Sarge, about the Primo thing - I'm here if you wanna talk."

"Thanks. I appreciate that, Detective, but that's not the reason you called, is it?"

"No, not entirely. I got a call today from a woman who lives next door to Sergeant Fuller. She told me that a few nights ago she heard noises from the apartment. It sounded like people arguing, then she heard the door slamming a few times. She peeked into the hallway, and saw a girl about 17 years old. She was crying and picking up her clothes, and there was money all over the floor."

"And you think it's Fuller's apartment?"

"Yeah, I do. I checked the address and the apartment number, and

Fuller lives next door. Right after the door slammed, the woman, her name is Sadie Klein, heard the girl say 'I know you're a cop.' She also said his name was Fuller."

"Shit, Rodriguez, this is nuts. Can Mrs. Klein ID the girl if we found her?"

"I suppose, but she asked me to keep her out of it."

"So what do you want to do, Sarge?"

"There's not much we can do. Our chances of finding the girl are practically zero."

"May I make a suggestion, Sarge? I want to follow him. I think there's more to Fuller than meets the eye."

McMahon answers, "I'm not comfortable with this—after all, he's your boss."

"He's not my boss, Sarge. You are."

"So, Detective, I assume you want my seal of approval to follow him."

Rodriguez answers, "It would be nice, but I'm gonna do it anyway."

There's a pause. "Ok, Rodriguez. Go ahead." McMahon disconnects.

CHAPTER 39
FULLER (SHORT EYES)

Fuller leaves the precinct a few hours before his shift ends. He drives west on the Long Island Expressway towards Flushing. He's unaware that he's being followed by a black sedan. He exits at the Main Street exit, and proceeds down dark streets past old buildings and boarded up Asian restaurants, 'for sale' signs are everywhere.

He stops in the middle of a row of apartment buildings that are not as run down as the others in the area. The address is 47-18 Murray Street. The building is one block from Flushing Bay. Rodriguez stops on the corner of the block behind Fuller's car. He watches as Fuller exits his car and walks towards the building.

Rodriguez is following Fuller undetected.

Fuller walks up the front steps to the outside doors. He rings the top bell and he gets buzzed in. Rodriguez watches as Fuller goes in and walks up the steps to the left. He sees the camera over the bell and stays out of its range. He's able to catch the door just before it closes. He goes to the bottom of the stairs and listens for Fuller's footsteps. He ascends the marble steps one floor below Fuller as Fuller reaches the third floor. Rodriguez is just below that floor and slowly moves into position that enables him to see which apartment fuller goes to. He knocks on the door of apartment #2. The knocks are more like a code—there's three knocks with a long pause, then two knocks. The door opens and Fuller enters. He's greeted by name when he enters. It's a woman's voice. Rodriguez waits on the landing above. About one hour later Fuller opens the door to leave and a woman says goodbye to Fuller. She speaks with an Asian accent. Fuller goes downstairs, and the outside door closes behind him. Rodriguez goes down one staircase and approaches apartment #2.

He doesn't have a plan of action. He suspects it's human trafficking, but what he finds inside will shock him. He uses the same code Fuller used and knocks on the door. A voice from inside says, "You forget something?"

"Yeah," Rodriguez answers.

The door opens and a small Asian woman stands in front of him. She's blocking his path, but that doesn't stop him and he pushes past her. He makes believe he's drunk. The Asian woman says, "Get out. I don't know you." He scans the room and sees girls as young as 14, some with bruises on their bodies. He continues his drunk act.

"You don't know me, I don't know you, we don't know anybody—where's Harry? I'm looking for Harry."

The Asian woman tries to push him out, saying, "You go—no Harry here."

Rodriguez replies, "Yeah, he told me to meet him here."

He looks to the back of the apartment and sees a long corridor with 5 rooms on each side. He hears sobbing coming from the back. He begins to walk towards the back when the Asian woman shouts something in a language Rodriguez doesn't understand. From the back of the room two men approach and block his path. "Get out," one of the men says. Rodriguez says, "You're not Harry."

The other man says, "Go, or we throw you down the stairs."

"Ok, Ok. I'm leaving. I don't like Chinese food anyway, it gives me gas."

The Asian woman yells at Rodriguez and the two men make sure he goes down the stairs. Rodriguez turns and says, "If you see Harry tell him I was looking for him. Thanks and good night." He goes down the stairs singing as loud as he could—"Everybody was Kung Fu fighting"—while still acting drunk."

CHAPTER 40
MCMAHON LEARNS ABOUT THE PEDOPHILE

Rodriguez calls McMahon. "Two calls in a row, Detective. I'm honored."

"I've got some news about Fuller and it's not good. A few nights ago I followed him to an area of Queens known for teenage prostitutes and runaways. He cruised the area for a while and left."

"Maybe he didn't like the merchandise."

"But tonight I saw Fuller's dark side. He drove to a location in Flushing. There's a building right off Flushing Bay on Murray Street. He entered and went to apartment #2. He was in there for about an hour. When he left I was able to get inside and I saw underage girls, very young girls."

"How did you get inside?"

"It's a long story, Sarge. Let's just say I was not welcome and I was shown the door. I noticed that some of the girls had bruises on their bodies. In the back of the apartment there was a long corridor with private rooms, about 5 or 6 on each side. The witch at the front apparently knew Fuller. She called him by name."

"The witch at the front? What do you mean?"

"There's a camera downstairs before you get inside right above the door bell. The woman at the front desk monitors who rings the bell, and she can see who's coming in. If you stay close to the wall she won't see you."

"What time did Fuller get there?"

"Seven 'o' clock on the dot. He leaves at six 'o' clock a few nights a week."

"Let's suppose Fuller has an appointment with a particular girl at seven 'o' clock once or twice a week—would that make sense?"

"It makes a lot of sense—if it's by appointment, the witch can control who comes and goes."

"When you were inside, you said you were shown the door. By whom?"

"Two big guys threatened to show me out and throw me down the stairs if I didn't leave."

"Is there a back way out, Detective?'

"Yes, there's a fire escape in the back, Sarge."

"Did you see anybody else inside?"

"No, just the two assholes and the woman in the front."

"Are you thinking what I'm thinking, Sarge?"

"Yeah, I am. With Primo gone, Fuller is our only hope of getting DiNapoli."

"But what if he's not on DiNapoli's payroll? This whole thing could blow up in our face."

"I got a feeling about Fuller when I first met him. If we hit the place with him inside we can squeeze him and he'll make a deal. Next time he leaves early—follow him. If he heads to Flushing, we'll be there."

"I'll notify Ebersole and let him know we need his help. I'll catch the next flight out."

.

CHAPTER 41
THE PINCH

Rodriguez is at his desk in the precinct. Fuller pokes his head through the door and says, "I'm out—dentist appointment. See you tomorrow."

"Ok, Sarge. See ya." The clock on his desk says 6 o'clock. He goes down the back stairs to his car parked around the rear of the precinct, and waits in his car until Fuller drives by. He follows him at a safe distance and calls McMahon. "Fullers heading towards Flushing. I'll let you know when he's close."

"He's going to 47-18 Murray St. Approach from 18th Avenue—you can't see it from the apartment. I'll meet you there."

McMahon calls Ebersole. "He's on the move heading towards Flushing. It's 47-18 Murray Street—we'll meet on 18th Avenue."

"I got 6 men leaving now, and we got 4 uniforms on loan from NYPD."

"I'm almost there, see you on 18th Avenue."

Rodriguez calls McMahon: "Fuller is about ten minutes away—what about Ebersole?"

"He's en route," McMahon says.

Rodriguez is the first to arrive; he turns the corner and parks on 18th Avenue. Fuller is inside the apartment. McMahon arrives and walks to Rodriguez's car. "When Ebersole gets here we'll figure out how to get inside."

"Don't worry, Sarge. I'll get us inside."

Ebersole arrives on the scene. McMahon walks over and says, "Thanks, Captain. We appreciate your help on this one. Is he in the apartment, Sergeant?" "Yeah, he's in there." "Detective Rodriguez says he can get us inside." "At that moment Rodriguez walks over and addresses Ebersole. "You must be Captain Ebersole. I'm Detective Rodriguez," and he extends his hand. They shake hands, and Rodriguez says, "He's up there, got here about ten minutes ago."

Ebersole asks "Any ideas on how to get in there?"

"Yeah, leave it to me—we're old friends. Where is he?" Ebersole asks.

"He's on the third floor—Apartment #2."

In the background, Ebersole's officers are donning bullet proof vests and checking weapons. Ebersole says, "I understand you've been inside, Detective—what are we up against?"

"Two, probably more, armed and with a bad attitude. There's a woman at the front of the apartment who controls who comes in and out. I like to call her the witch. When you meet her, you'll know why. There's a bell on the outside doors and a camera. Stay close to the wall and the camera won't see you. I'll get us inside."

Ebersole addresses his officers. "There are civilians up there so be surgical, let's not go up there with guns blazing." He turns to McMahon and asks, "What about the girls?"

"Child Protective Services is waiting to take the minors. As for the adults, your guess is as good as mine."

Ebersole addresses his men again: "I want you uniforms to cover the back—there's a fire escape back there if anybody comes down grab 'em. Two of my agents will cover the front, nobody in or out. The rest of you with me. Once inside, McMahon will take over. You good with that, McMahon?"

"Sure. I got it, Captain."

"Ok, Rodriguez. Lead the way."

Rodriguez says, "Stay close to the wall—when they open the door, we move."

Rodriguez has his gun in hand and he climbs the front stairs of the building. McMahon and Ebersole's officers are on either side of Rodriguez. He rings the bell and a voice answers: "What do you want—go away." Rodriguez acts drunk again. "Is Harry there?" There's no reply from the intercom. He rings again and the ring is answered again.

"Go away!"

"Tell Harry I'm here." McMahon and Ebersole look at each other and they're not sure about what's going on.

The woman tells two of her enforcers to "go downstairs and fix it, teach him a lesson." Rodriguez rings the bell again, and the two men open the door. One of the men says, "You asked for it, asshole." Rodriguez lifts his gun and points it in the man's face as Ebersole's officers run inside. Rodriguez tells the men to drop their weapons, and they are cuffed by Ebersole's officers and taken away.

McMahon and Rodriguez run upstairs to where Ebersole and his officers are waiting. They hear a woman yelling in a language nobody understands. Ebersole signals one of his men to break down the door. McMahon says, "I got the witch." The officers rush in, and the witch is reaching for something under the desk. McMahon points her gun at her.

"Keep your hands where I can see them." The woman keeps speaking in the same language. McMahon says, "I think we need a translator."

Rodriguez replies, "Don't let her bullshit you. She speaks English."

He goes to the back and empties the rooms. The girls and johns are led to the middle of the apartment. In room number 8 he finds Fuller, and with him is a young girl of no more than 15. Rodriguez takes her robe, hands it to her and motions to her to go outside. He tells Fuller to get dressed and stay in the room. One of Ebersole's agents stays with him." Rodriguez returns to the middle of the apartment. Ebersole's men are in control of the situation, questioning the johns and processing the underage girls. The four NYPD officers come back in with three suspects in handcuffs. One of the officers says, "We found these guys going down the fire escape; they had some serious firepower on them." The officers walk past Rodriguez. One of the suspects glares at Rodriguez, and he's recognized. Rodriguez tells the officer: "Wait a minute, hold up," and he walks over to the suspect, gets in his face and says, "Hey, tough guy, you still wanna throw me down the stairs?"

The suspect says, "Take the cuffs off, cop."

Rodriguez looks at the officer and says, "You got the keys." The officer glances nervously at McMahon and Ebersole.

McMahon says, "Knock it off, Rodriguez. Have your pissing contest some other time."

The suspect says, "Yeah, cop, some other time."

Rodriguez leans in and sings in a low voice: "Everybody was Kung Fu fighting."

McMahon says "Enough, Rodriguez. Get 'em out of here, officers."

CHAPTER 42
FULLER FLIPS

Rodriguez and McMahon go into room number eight; the room is barely big enough for a twin bed. A red bulb hanging from the ceiling is the only illumination. By the bed is a nightstand, and on it is a glass bowl full of wrapped condoms. Fuller is staring at the floor while seated on the bed.

McMahon says, "You're under arrest. I'll take your gun and badge."

Fuller says to Rodriguez, "You can't do this to me. I'm your boss..."

Rodriguez replies, "No, you're not. She is."

"I'm Sergeant Elizabeth McMahon with the Las Vegas DEA. I'm gonna skip past the bullshit, Fuller. How old is that girl?"

Fuller responds, "I don't know."

Rodriguez looks at McMahon and says to Fuller: "Just being in the same room with a girl her age can get you five years. Plus all the other shit we're gonna pile on top."

"What's the DEA doing in Flushing, raiding this joint?" Fuller asks.

McMahon says, "We're investigating a shipment of cocaine that's coming from Colombia. An alliance between Delacruz and DiNapoli, and we think you have information that could be helpful to us."

"Me, no way. I don't know anything about it."

Rodriguez says, "We know you're on DiNapoli's payroll."

McMahon looks at Rodriguez with a puzzled expression on her face. Rodriguez continues, "You heard about Primo?"

"Yeah, somebody whacked him."

Rodriguez says, "Yeah, he got whacked, but before that he told us about a deal between DiNapoli and Delacruz, and how you were involved."

"Bullshit! DiNapoli never discussed business with Primo around."

"How would you know that, Fuller?" McMahon asks.

Fuller realizes he said too much. He doesn't say another word and continues to stare at the floor.

Rodriguez asks, "Is Sanchez involved?"

Fuller asks, "You gonna read me my rights?"

Just then there's a knock on the door. It's Ebersole. "We're wrapping it up out here, just letting you know we're out." The door opens and Ebersole goes inside. "Shit, this is a tiny room."

Rodriguez says to Ebersole, "This is Sergeant Bob Fuller from the 18th."

At that point McMahon asks Ebersole, "Can we speak privately, Captain?" They leave the room and go to the outer foyer. "We're gonna need your safe house for a while."

"For what?"

"Fuller's not part of this operation. He's a suspect."

"Continue."

"It seems Sergeant Fuller has short eyes. We also think he's on DiNapoli's payroll. With Primo gone, he's our last chance. We wanna take him to the safe house so we can interview him further."

"What do you expect to get out of him?"

"We wanna find out about this shipment from the Delacruz cartel. We wanna know where and when."

"Did he ask for a lawyer yet? If he does, this whole thing falls apart."

"Then we gotta make sure he doesn't."

Rodriguez comes out of the room with Fuller, who says, "I'm not saying another word without a lawyer."

McMahon asks, "Do you really want a lawyer involved? If you lawyer up, it all comes out—the underage girls, cruising for hookers, that girl you assaulted and threw out of your apartment. How old was she, Fuller? Your involvement with DiNapoli, it's going to be out there for all to see. It's your choice. Help us out and we'll see about returning the favor. Lawyer up, and there's no deal."

Fuller thinks for a minute and says, "Ok, I wanna deal. Now what?"

"Now we go with Captain Ebersole to a house in Brooklyn where you'll be under, shall we say, house arrest. If any information you give us is good, we'll talk about a deal."

Captain Ebersole adds, "We're ready to roll."

McMahon says, "Cuff him."

"You think that's necessary, Sarge? He's unarmed and he ain't going anywhere."

"I said put the cuffs on him."

"Ok. Sorry, Fuller, but you heard the lady."

Rodriguez cuffs Fuller and asks McMahon, "Can we at least go down the backstairs?"

"Sure, as long as he's cuffed." They go downstairs and climb into three cars. Ebersole says to McMahon, "Fuller is gonna ride with me." McMahon and Rodriguez are riding together and there's silence in the car. Finally Rodriguez asks McMahon, "Why did you insist I cuff him? He didn't have any weapons, and after all, he's a cop. I didn't want to humiliate him in front of the other officers."

"When we picked up Primo we didn't cuff him, and we were talking to him in the car. He was calm, he didn't say much. We confronted him with the evidence against him, and he admitted he killed Sallie Boy. We told him we wanted information on DiNapoli. He refused to help us and then he started talking about his mother. He went crazy and wrapped that big fucking hand of his around my neck like he did Sallie Boy. I pulled my weapon and fired one round into his gut—nothing, no reaction. I put the next round between his eyes. It was murder by cop. And that's how Primo died. Now you know why I wanted him cuffed."

"And what was that shit about Primo telling us that Fuller was involved with DiNapoli and Delacruz?"

"It worked, didn't it, Sarge?"

"Yeah, I guess whatever works."

CHAPTER 43
PLANNING TOM'S DEMISE

Sanchez and Felix are playing pool at Ball Breakers. Sanchez finishes his game and tells Felix, "Let's go to the room. I gotta talk to you. It's time to pay your debt to me."

"What are you talking about, Antonio?"

"Not here. Let's go to the office."

The men enter the backroom and close the door behind them. Antonio opens the fridge and offers Felix a beer. Felix declines, but Antonio opens one and takes a big swallow. He says, "Sunday night we're gonna do the war hero."

Felix asks, "Why Sunday?"

"Cause Sunday I get paid after I do this deal."

"This guy didn't do nothing to me. I don't want to kill him."

"Listen Felix, you owe me. I helped you get rid of the body, and you didn't get caught. Without me you'd be in jail right now—just another sad sack inmate looking at serous time."

"I can't do this, man."

"Yes, you can and will. I'm gonna give you a gun and you're gonna shoot the war hero." Antonio's plan is to have Felix shoot Tom. When Tom is dead, Antonio kills Felix. No witnesses, no evidence —Antonio gets his money and leaves the country.

"Here's the plan, Felix. Sunday night we drive to the house and park a block away. I'll go upstairs and get him to open the door. When he does, you shoot him."

"What if he ain't home?"

"Don't matter to me—if he's home, he dies. If he ain't, I got the keys. We go in and we wait. Live or die don't mean a fucking thing to me 'cause either way I'm leaving town. We wait. If he don't show, I'll go take care of my business."

"What about Anna?"

"I'm done with Anna—the bitch played me. Killing the war hero will be punishment enough, knowing she caused this shit."

"What if she's home?"

"She won't be home. She has a class that she never misses. After class they all go out for tea or whatever the fuck. Sunday night I'll pick you up at eight—that's when I'll give you the gun. We drive to the house, we do him, and I'll drive you back to the club—that's your alibi. They'll think you were there all night."

"What about you, Antonio?"

"I got business to take care of."

"What about me, Antonio? We've been friends a long time."

"All good things must end, Felix," Antonio says sarcastically. "I'm gone after Sunday."

CHAPTER 44
AT THE SAFE HOUSE

The car arrives at the safe house. In the lead car is Ebersole, Fuller and two of Ebersole's men. Ebersole steps out of the car and tells McMahon, "Let's go upstairs. We can talk to him there." They all go upstairs into a room with a desk and four chairs. In front of the desk is a camera on a tripod. Fuller is still handcuffed, and he sees the camera. He says, "I'm not saying a word till you turn the camera off and take off these fucking cuffs."

McMahon says the camera and the cuffs stay put." "You gotta buy those privileges, Fuller. Give us information and you get something back."

Rodriguez whispers to McMahon, "I wanna take his cuffs off."

McMahon says "No, not yet."

"Trust me—take his cuffs off. I'll have him eating out of my hand."

"No Rodriguez, not yet."

"Can I at least talk to him?

"Sure. Go ahead and talk." Rodriguez walks over to Fuller and whispers, " Listen to me, Fuller I wanna take your cuffs off but my boss won't let me. If I take them off, will you do anything stupid?"

"No, I won't fuck around. Take 'em off."

Rodriguez looks back at McMahon, and she shakes her head no. McMahon tells Ebersole, "Captain, would you ask your agents to excuse us, please?"

Rodriguez says, "It seems I might be the only friend you've got in this building. Sergeant McMahon says they stay on. Sorry, Fuller, I tried."

Fuller says, "I get it, a bad cop, good cop routine, is that what this is? Ain't gonna work with me, I've been a cop too long."

"Let me tell you what this is, Fuller. If I get the feeling that you're not being honest with us or you're fucking with me, I'll throw you around this room, cuffs or no cuffs."

McMahon says, "Easy, Rodriguez. Rodriguez continues, "I don't care what you did for DiNapoli in the past, Fuller, but we're trying to stop a shipment of cocaine, actually cocaine on steroids, from hitting the streets. People who use this shit could die. Tell us when and where, Fuller."

Fuller says, "If I tell you and they find out it was me, I'm a dead man, just like Primo." McMahon and Rodriguez glance at each other. Ebersole says, "Let me tell you something—when you get to prison, you're gonna be a dead man, anyway. You got short eyes and you're a cop. So the way I see it, you've got a better shot with us. Tell us what you know and we'll protect you."

Fuller hesitates for a moment and then he asks, "Is that camera on? If it is, I want it shut off and moved away from me or I'm not saying shit."

Ebersole shuts it off and turns it to the wall. "You happy now, Fuller."

Rodriguez says, "Now tell us about the shipment."

Fuller says, "This Sunday, Pier 86 at 11:30 pm. That's where DiNapoli keeps his trucks. It's at his warehouse."

McMahon asks, "Who else is involved?" Fuller is silent.

Rodriguez says, "Antonio Sanchez. Ain't that right, Fuller?" Fuller nods yes. "How is the merchandise being transported?"

Fuller responds, "I don't know—all I know is the drop is at Pier 86."

McMahon asks, "Who told you?"

"The man himself."

Rodriguez says, "Shit, that only gives us a day and a half."

Ebersole says, "Let me know how I can help. This is your parade, Sergeant."

"Thanks, Captain."

Fuller asks, "What happens now?"

Ebersole answers, "Now you're gonna be our guest for a while."

McMahon and Rodriguez leave the room. McMahon asks, "Do you think the information is good?"

"If it's not, he's fucked. Good night," and he walks down the hall.

McMahon yells, "Where the hell are you going?"

"I'm tired, and I don't feel like driving back to Long Island. I'm looking for a place to sleep in this dump."

CHAPTER 45
SADDLE UP

DiNapoli and his men are preparing for the exchange at the Brooklyn Navy Yard. They're in an empty warehouse in Long Island City. The warehouse is owned by RDN Importing, one of DiNapoli's many shell companies. The cocaine will be tested, cut to the desired potency, and distributed from this warehouse.

The men prepare their weapons and DiNapoli tells them, "When we get to the Navy Yard, fan out. Keep your eyes open. Don't be too anxious. The last thing we need is a fucking war."

Dom says to DiNapoli, "What about Sanchez? Richie, what do you want me to do?"

"Leave him alone, Dom. If Delacruz wants him dead, let his guys do it."

"I don't want to get on Delacruz's bad side in case Sanchez is his golden boy."

"When we have the product, I'll keep my word and pay him. But if he fucks us, he's yours, Dom. Maxie, let's roll."

Maxie yells, "Saddle up, fellas. Let's go."

CHAPTER 46
SUNDAY NIGHT MASSACRE—TOM IS THE TARGET

Sanchez is on his way to pick up Felix when he arrives at Felix's building. Felix is waiting downstairs, and he enters the car.

"Here, Felix." Antonio hands Felix the gun. "It's loaded. Safety's off —just aim and pull the trigger. Wait till he's close—you can't miss."

"I can't kill nobody. The stripper was an accident—we were both fucked up."

"Yeah, you were both fucked up, but she's dead and you're alive. Now man up, you pussy. You're gonna kill the war hero."

Felix is quiet the rest of the way. They arrive at Tom's house and the lights are out. Sanchez says, "Wait here I'll get the keys." Antonio goes into his house and comes out with the keys to Tom's apartment upstairs. "Come on, Felix, let's go up."

"He ain't home, let's go."

"No, we're gonna wait awhile. If he don't show, he gets to live. It's his lucky night."

The men climb the stairs and Antonio says, "We're gonna wait a while, but not too long, there's some place I gotta be. When he comes in, start shooting and keep shooting till he's dead."

"Antonio I'm shaking. I ain't never shot nobody. I hope he don't come home."

"Hide behind the couch. I'll be in the kitchen." A few minutes later headlights skim the inside of the house. "You better shoot him, Felix, or I'm gonna shoot you."

Tom climbs the stairs and is about to enter the apartment. Felix panics and fires a shot through the door. The bullet strikes Tom in the shoulder. Tom fights through the pain and pushes the door in. Felix continues to shoot wildly as Tom moves about in the dark apartment, deliberately drawing fire. Felix runs out of bullets and screams for Antonio. Felix attacks Tom, trying to pistol whip him. Felix is no match for Tom's 6'3" 200 pound frame. Tom is strong from his days in the military and workouts in the police gym, but Tom is taken by surprise by the strength of Felix, probably drug fueled, who is determined to kill him. The gun comes down on Tom's head and stuns him. Tom's right side is blood soaked from the bullet wound in his shoulder. Tom regains focus, and the two men wrestle for the gun in Felix's hand. Tom wins the battle, and takes the gun from Felix. The gun crashes down on Felix's nose, opening up a deep gash that immediately gushes blood. This shocks Felix, and he again yells for Antonio. He feels the impact of the second blow to the side of the head. Felix punches at Tom's wound, causing pain, but this seems to energize Tom. The gun in Tom's hand comes crashing down on Felix's head again. The feeling of being airborne overtakes Felix, and he wonders if it's because he's going into shock or because of the blows to the head. Felix is lapsing into semi-consciousness as he is thrown through the front window. The last thing he sees is the jagged piece of stained glass protruding from his chest. Felix dies on the porch below. Tom hears

Antonio moving around the kitchen and takes cover behind the couch. "You're a dead man, war hero. I know about you and my wife, and now you're gonna die." Tom moves about to draw fire in the dark. Antonio fires and misses. Tom pulls the gun from his ankle holster. Again he makes noise to draw fire and again Antonio misses. Tom aims at the muzzle flash and fires. Antonio is hit by the bullet grazing him just above his hip. "Motherfucker, you got me! I'm gonna kill you slow, war hero." Antonio fires again and again till he's out of bullets. Tom fires and misses. "You missed, war hero I'm gonna cut you into little pieces, you fucking cabron." Tom moves toward the kitchen, and as he turns he sees Antonio lunging at him with a knife. Tom deflects the attack and punches Antonio in the face. Antonio swings the knife and again it's deflected. Antonio tries to punch Tom in his wound but Tom blocks the punch again and backs up to avoid another lunge of the knife.

Tom reverts to his martial arts background and kicks Antonio in the chest. The speed and the power behind the kick stuns Antonio. Antonio charges Tom with the knife over his head. The knife misses as Tom sidesteps the attack. Antonio punches Tom directly on his wound and Tom reels from the pain. Antonio lunges again and Tom is able to disarm Antonio with a kick to Antonio's wrist. The knife slides across the floor. Antonio feels vulnerable, and he throws his full body weight at Tom. They both fall to the floor with Tom on the bottom. Antonio is flailing punches which Tom is able to deflect. Tom delivers a punch to Antonio's throat causing Antonio to gasp for air and lose focus, which allows Tom to get to his feet. Antonio is attempting to stand, but Tom kicks him in the face. In desperation, Antonio grabs a lamp with a marble base and hits Tom in the knee. Tom falls to the ground and reaches for the knife. Both men struggle for the knife but neither one is successful. Antonio grabs the lamp and swings it towards Tom's head. He strikes a glancing blow and Tom is stunned, but attacks as the lamp crashes against the wall. Blood covers the men and the furniture.

Tom hits Antonio with the lamp and he falls to his knees. Tom wraps the wire around his neck and as Antonio struggles Tom tightens the wire. Antonio's arms are flailing trying to punch Tom from an impossible position. Tom puts his knee in Antonio's back for leverage. Blood and saliva pour out of his mouth. Antonio continues to struggle, but Tom is determined to end it here. Antonio's face is a grotesque death mask with bulging eyes and lips slightly blue.

Tom continues to keep pressure on the wire. He knows Antonio's dead but hatred and adrenaline fuel his strength. Finally, he relinquishes his grip and falls to his side. The room goes dark and unconsciousness overtakes him.

CHAPTER 47
INTRODUCING DIEGO

Three large black cars drive through Brooklyn. They're on their way to the Brooklyn Navy Yard to meet the shipment and close the deal. Not far behind is a carting truck belonging to the DiNapoli carting company. They drive through the main gate, and the guard gives them a knowing nod. The group arrives at warehouse #10. The trucks stop in front of the warehouse, and the cars form a semicircle. In the lead car is Richie, Dom and Maxie. They wait till the men in the other two cars exit, carrying semi-automatic weapons. The men fan out, covering the area near the warehouse. When the men are in position, Richie, Dom and Maxie exit the car. From the other end of the pier two cars approach, their headlights lighting up the warehouse and the men waiting there. In the headlights there is a silhouette of three figures, and they approach DiNapoli and his men. When they get close, the man in the middle waves his hand and the night is dark again as the headlights go out. The men are now face to face. The man in charge is Diego; he looks more like a Hugo boss model than a Cartel business manager. With him is Miguel, Delacruz's enforcer and the third man who is very large. Dom leans over to Richie and says, "Don't that guy remind you of somebody?"

Richie replies, "Yeah, Primo must be his twin."

Diego is the first to speak. "Gentlemen, I'm Diego Vargas." He extends his hand to the man in the center, assuming he's the man in charge.

Richie takes his hand and says, "I'm Richie DiNapoli. This is my Lieutenant, Dom, and Maxie, my Counsellor."

Diego now makes his introductions. "This is Miguel. He is, as you would say, Mr. Delacruz's Lieutenant, and this large gentleman is Carlos, but we call him Gordo Carajo."

Richie asks, "what does that mean, what you just said?"

"Fat fuck."

"Don't that bother him, that you call him that?"

"No, you see he's a little slow." He points to his head and lets out a laugh. "Because of it his adversaries underestimate him. But he can snap your neck just like that," and he snaps his fingers in the air for effect.

Maxie says to Richie, "Yeah, just like Primo."

"As for me, my job is simple. I'm Mr. Delacruz's business manager. I put together deals just like this one, and I am paid quite handsomely. So now down to business. Mr. Delacruz wants you to know he thanks you for your trust in him and looks forward to working together."

"Yeah, sure. Me, too."

Richie looks up and down the dock, and all he sees is a crane at the end of the dock. He looks at Diego and asks, "Where's the boat."

Diego looks at Richie as if he doesn't understand. Richie asks again: "The boat with the merchandise—where is it?"

Diego says, "The boat" as he laughs, and his men laugh with him.

DiNapoli's men lift their weapons as do Delacruz's men, anticipating trouble.

Diego says, "There is no boat."

Richie replies, "What the fuck is going on?"

Diego says, "Relax gentlemen. Please, no weapons," and he gestures to his men to lower theirs. "Tranquilo, muchachos. Your merchandise has been here for several days, safe as a baby in its mothers arms. Gentlemen, please observe the crane at the end of the dock." He gestures to the crane's operator and shouts, "Bring it up!" The crane is old and worn, with faded yellow paint and rusted metal. All eyes are on it as it starts up. It makes a roaring sound and black smoke billows from its stack. Richie looks around nervously. Out of a container in the floor of the dock comes a pallet with five crates on it. Maxie says, "Holy shit, look at that."

Diego hears him and explains: "A few years ago Mr. Delacruz purchased some warehouses along these docks. Some were foreclosed, and others were put up for sale by their owners. Those in ground storage units were used to store grain, a long time ago, of course. When shipping moved to containers, that form of storage became obsolete. We converted them to humidity and temperature controlled rooms. That 'free sample' Sanchez gave you to test came from there." He points to the palette. "The Merchandise is the same throughout."

Richie says, "Did you say that was a free sample?"

"Yes, an investment towards future business."

"That fucking Sanchez charged me for that sample."

"He made you pay? How much?"

"Fifty grand, that motherfucker."

"That's typical of that puto. Speaking of Sanchez, where is he?"

"I don't know, he was supposed to be here. All the more reason to get the fuck out of here."

"Too bad Sanchez isn't here. Mr. Delacruz wanted me to give him a present," Dom says, "Colombian necktie."

Diego smiles. "Yes, something like that. Richie says, "Let's load up and move out."

Richie gives the signal, and the back of the truck opens up and the men move the crates into the back of the truck. The truck closes again like the mouth of a giant creature. Diego motions and the warehouse gates go up.

"Mr. Delacruz gives you the use of his warehouse; it has all the comforts of home. I'll be in New York until you test the product and are assured it's as advertised. In the future we'll do business with tons—not kilos—of product."

Diego hands Richie a card and says, "I can be reached at that number."

Richie reads the card—it says "Vargas International Shipping, Diego Vargas, President."

Diego says, "It's bullshit. Call me when you're ready to move the merchandise." He turns and begins walking to a waiting limousine. He turns to Richie and says, "I'll let you buy me dinner at the best restaurant in New York. Italian, of course. Good night, gentlemen."

Richie shouts, "Hey Diego, how did you get the merchandise to New York?"

Diego turns and responds, "By boat, of course." He laughs as he gets into a limousine and it drives away followed by his men.

Richie says to Dom, "Bring the truck inside and stay with the merchandise tonight. Take a few men with you. We'll move it in a few days to Long Island City."

"Why me, Richie? I don't wanna spend the night in some shitty warehouse."

"Dom, who else can I trust? There could be one hundred million bucks of street value in that truck."

"Ok, Richie, I get it. I'll stay tonight."

"Thanks, Dom. I'll get Maxie to stay tomorrow. Tell the men to stay alert, we can't trust anybody. I appreciate it, Dom."

Richie and the remaining men leave the Navy Yard. Minutes later Richie's phone rings. It's Dom.

"Yeah, Dom?"

"Holy shit, Richie, you gotta see this place. It's hooked up like a Park Avenue pad. It's got a full kitchen, champagne in the fridge, cable tv, designer bathrooms, unfuckingbelievable."

Richie laughs and tells Dom, "See Dom, like Diego said—all the comforts of home. I'll ask Maxie about tomorrow night. Ok, Dom?"`

"No, that's ok ,Richie. I'll do it tomorrow night, too."

"That's what I thought. Good night, Dom."

Ebersole and McMahon are looking at a map of Pier 86, planning the raid on DiNapoli's warehouse. Ebersole speaks to his people. "Gather round, we're almost ready to go. To my right is Sergeant McMahon, she's on loan from the Las Vegas DEA, with Special Agent Rodriguez. The Sergeant will be second in command on this operation. She knows the drill. She's done this more than once. On the table is a map of Pier 86. Agent Ruiz, take 3 agents and cover the rear of the building here and here. Agent Harris, you take 6 and cover the front. Nobody gets in, nobody gets out. We're gonna run silent and put our cars up here on the street. If you see any security on the pier, flash your badge and bring them up to the cars or tell them to duck and cover. Last thing we want is a bunch of civilians getting hurt. Remember to meet force with force. There's a swat team standing by if we need 'em. Get your vests on and check your weapons."

Ebersole walks over to Sergeant Fuller and says, "You can get comfortable in my office, Sergeant. A couple of my men are gonna stay with you. I'll tell 'em to keep the cuffs off. I'm trusting you to do as they say and don't do anything stupid, otherwise they're gonna cuff you to a chair. This is a courtesy, Fuller. Don't fuck it up."

Fuller says, "if DiNapoli doesn't see me there, he's not making the deal."

"Bullshit, Fuller! It's too late for DiNapoli to turn back now—this ain't a social call. When we hit the pier, the last thing on DiNapoli's mind is gonna be you."

Ebersole motions to his men and they walk over. Ebersole says "I told Fuller as long as he behaves you'll keep the cuffs off, but if he fucks around, handcuff, him to the chair in my office. Don't let him out of your sight."

Ebersole yells to his men, "Let's go, it's an hour to Pier 86."

Two cars and a van leave the safe house, leaving Fuller and three agents behind.

CHAPTER 49
THE ESCAPE

Fuller is sitting at one of the desks in the safe house, and one of the agents assigned to watch him says, "Let's go to Ebersole's office. There's a cot in there you may want to grab some sleep."

"Nah, I don't want to sleep. You think there's a gun in one of those drawers?"

"Ebersole says I should cuff you to the chair if you get stupid, so watch your mouth."

"Sure, no problem." Fuller sits behind Ebersole's desk and the agent sits across from him.

"So Fuller, how long have you been a cop?"

"About 30 years."

"And now you fucked it all up."

"I'll be alright. What about you? What's your story, Agent?"

"I've been with Ebersole 8 years, been a cop for 21."

"You wanna play cards? You got cards around here?"

"Nah, I don't play cards with pedophiles."

"Too bad, I'm fucking bored to tears."

"Matter of fact, I'm gonna leave and send someone else in to watch you. I don't like the air in here." The agent leaves. While he's gone, Fuller tries opening the drawers in Ebersole's desk but they're all locked. A young agent comes into Ebersole's office and sits across from Fuller.

Fuller says, "Hi, Rookie. You must be the A-Team. How long have you been with Ebersole?"

The young agent answers, "18 months."

"Shit, 18 months—I got condoms older than you. You are a fucking Rookie. You got a deck of cards, Rookie?"

"No I don't, and don't call me Rookie any more."

An agent from the other side of the room yells, "Hey, Fuller, leave the kid alone or I'll cuff you to the fucking chair."

"Yeah, sure. You got a girlfriend, Rookie?"

"Stop calling me rookie."

"Sorry, so you got a girl?"

"Yeah, I do."

"Is she young?"

"She's my age."

Fuller says "I like 'em young, too. Real young." The other agent yells, "Last warning—one more and you get cuffed to the chair, you fucking freak."

Fuller gets closer to the young agent and says, "Your girlfriend got a younger sister?"

The young agent says, "Fuck you!"

The other agent says, "I'm cuffing you to the chair and if you don't shut up I'm gonna shove a gag in your mouth."

Fuller yells, "I gotta pee!"

The other agent walks over and tells the young agent, "I'll take him upstairs. Come on, Fuller. Let's go. You got five minutes." They go upstairs and the agent waits outside the bathroom door.

Fuller is in the bathroom looking for a weapon. He reaches under the sink and unscrews a pipe about 18 inches long, puts it behind his back and into his waistband. He flushes the toilet, grabs some paper towels and makes believe he's drying his hands. He steps out of the bathroom, puts his hands in the air and tells the agent, "You wanna search me?"

"Put your hands down, let's go back downstairs."

The agent turns his back to go downstairs. Fuller takes the pipe from his waistband and hits the agent. The agent tries to yell for help, Fuller covers his mouth and hits him two more times. The agent is unconscious, and Fuller takes his gun. He drags him into the bathroom and closes the door. Fuller goes out the back and down the stairs. He goes to the garage and is approached by an officer. "Can I help you?"

Fuller says, "Yeah, I'm Sergeant Fuller. I need a car. I'm meeting up with Ebersole—he's on assignment."

"Ok, let me check the list." The officer checks the clipboard for Fuller's name." Sorry, Sergeant. I don't see your name. Ebersole has to approve the cars going out. Do you have an ID?" Fuller reaches into the inside pocket of his jacket and produces the gun. He pistol whips the officer until he's unconscious, grabs a set of keys from a locker and drives away.

CHAPTER 50
BAD INFORMATION

Ebersole and the team arrive at pier 86. They park the cars on the street overlooking the pier. From inside the cars they look for activity but it's quiet. McMahon radios to Ebersole. "We need to get a look inside the warehouse."

"You trust Fuller's information, Captain?"

"His ass is on the line—I think he knows better than to fuck with us."

"I hope you're right, Captain. I see an open window—I'll see if I can get inside."

"Careful, Rodriguez." McMahon radios Ebersole. "Rodriguez is gonna try to get inside." Ebersole radios the swat team and his men. "Stand down—one of ours is gonna try and get inside. We move on my signal. Just wait for instructions." Rodriguez crawls through the open window and the back room stinks of garbage. He sees men milling about and trucks with their engines on. The gate to the warehouse goes up and several trucks are lined up to leave.

Rodriguez shouts into his radio "Move in" lights and sirens pierce the quiet on Pier 86. The team moves in and shouts of "Don't move" and "Let me see your hands" echo through the warehouse.

Ebersole walks into the warehouse with gun drawn. The men who were milling about are now lined up with their hands behind their heads. They're not sure what's going on and glance nervously at each other. Ebersole barks: "Who the fuck is in charge here?"

A voice in the line replies, "I am, sir."

Ebersole barks again: "Get over here and keep your hands where they are. What's your name?"

"My name is Joe Delgado and I'm the night manager."

"What's going on, Mr. Manager? And don't bullshit me."

"I don't understand."

"Where's DiNapoli? Is he here?"

"No sir. He never comes here.

Ebersole turns to his men. "Don't stand around—search this fucking place." He asks, " Are these trucks coming or going?"

The manager answers "They're empty. They're going to the city to pick up garbage. They were leaving when you guys got here."

Ebersole pauses and walks up and down. He puts his gun down to his side and turns to McMahon. "Any ideas, Sergeant?"

McMahon replies, "Search the trucks."

Ebersole tells the manager to open a particular truck. The manager steps to the front of the truck and signals the driver to open the back. Even though the truck is empty, the smell is overpowering as the back opens. Ebersole tells two of his men to check it. "But Captain, it stinks!"

Ebersole shouts: "Check the fucking trucks."

The men search the truck and yell back that it's empty.

"Search 'em all, I don't give a fuck if it takes all night."

Captain Ebersole calls over an NYPD officer. "Check these guys for priors. If they got open warrants, hold 'em. The rest can get the fuck out of here. I'm gonna have a look around."

Ebersole's radio squeaks: "Fuller's gone and two of your agents are in bad shape."

Rodriguez says, "I got this. I know where he's going. He's gonna fly his way out of here. He's got a friend—Tom Hartford—who's a pilot. I'll contact you when I find him." Rodriguez takes one of the cars and speeds away.

Ebersole says to McMahon: "Well this was a fucking disaster, McMahon. That's two for two—what's next?"

McMahon responds, "You were there when we questioned him, and your men let him get away. I'm out of here. His information was bullshit; there's nothing here." McMahon contacts Rodriguez and asks, "Detective, where are you?"

"I'm on my way to Sanchez's place. I can't explain now, but it's a house on Meadow Lane that belongs to Sanchez's wife. Give me a head start, then call for backup.

Fuller arrives at Tom's house and runs from his car. He stops when he sees Felix on the porch. He draws his gun and goes upstairs. He looks through the window and sees silhouettes of the men on the floor. Cautiously he enters the apartment and turns on the light. He's shocked by what he sees, blood is splattered everywhere. Sanchez is lying on his side, his face blue and distorted. Tom is unconscious and Bob feels for a pulse. Tom is alive and Fuller calls his name. "Tom, Tom can you hear me? It's Bob." He shakes him a few times, still calling his name. Bob goes to the kitchen and grabs a towel and places it on Tom's wound. He applies pressure and Tom winces. Tom begins to regain consciousness and the room slowly comes into focus. He looks at Fuller and says, "Bob, Sanchez tried to kill me."

"Looks like you got him first. Who's that asshole on the porch?"

"I don't know, he was with Sanchez. He's the one that shot me."

"I think that's Felix; he's one of Sanchez's lackies. Tom, I need your help—you've got to get me out of the country. If you don't, one way or another, I'm a dead man."

"What're you talking about?"

"I'm a dirty cop, Tom. I got involved with DiNapoli years ago and I'm on his payroll. I need you to fly me out of here."

"I can't fly Bob, look at me! I couldn't fly even if I wanted to."

"I got a lot of money stashed away, Tom, there's enough for both of us. We can live like kings, just help me get out. I can fly the plane— just talk me through it."

"I can't Bob, I'll be breaking the law."

Bob aims his gun at Tom and says, "Don't make me shoot you, Tom. I don't want to hurt you."

Just then, head lights light up the windows and Fuller goes to see who it is. He sees Rodriguez coming out of the car with his gun drawn. "It's fucking Rodriguez—how did he know I'd come here."

"You told him I flew a plane, remember."

"Shit, don't make a sound or I'll kill you both." Fuller turns off the light. Rodriguez is walking up the first set of stairs. He sees Felix's body on the porch, he wonders to himself what the fuck is he doing here. If Felix is here, Sanchez is also lurking close by. He rethinks going up the front steps and instead goes to the back of the house. Fuller is tired of waiting and he slowly peeks out the front window looking for Rodriguez. Tom tries to reach for the knife dropped by Sanchez but his attempt is thwarted by Fuller who hits him with the gun on the side of the head. "Try it again and I'll kill you. Now shut the fuck up and I won't hurt you again." Rodriguez is making his way up the back stairs and Fuller turns to face the back door. Rodriguez shouts "Come out, Fuller. Give it up."

Fuller responds, "Come get me, motherfucker."

Rodriguez sees the outline of Fuller and he moves across the door to draw his fire. Fuller fires two rounds and misses. Rodriguez returns fire and also misses the bullet crashing through the window. Fuller fires again and misses, the bullet whizzes past Rodriguez. Tom is regaining his senses and he is able to reach the knife dropped by Sanchez. He stabs Fuller in the leg causing him to fall to one knee. Fuller screams in pain and he turns his gun towards Tom. Rodriguez takes advantage of the distraction and aims towards the noise. As Fuller turns his gun Rodriguez fires twice, hitting Fuller and he falls to the floor mortally wounded. Rodriguez runs over to Tom to see if he could treat his wounds till the ambulance arrives. He stops at Fuller and feels for a pulse. He says to Tom, "Hang in there—help is on the way."

"What about Bob? Is he …"

Rodriguez interrupts. "Yeah Tom, he's dead. He left me no choice." In the background the sound of sirens and lights penetrate the sky.

———

Richie and Maxie are at the social club the morning after the delivery at the Brooklyn Navy Yard. The pay phone on the wall rings and it's Dom. Maxie picks it up. "Hey Maxie, put on Channel 4 news. Hurry up." Maxie yells across to the waiter, "Put on Channel 4 - quick." On the news there's a special bulletin about the shooting and the three deaths at Tom's house. Richie and Maxie just stare at the TV, not believing what they're hearing. After the bulletin, Richie is still staring at the screen; after a while he goes to the phone. He says to Dom, "See, Dom, like I always told you, there is a God. They're all dead, and last night died with them. Wednesday morning we move the truck to Long Island City. Let Diego know."

"Do you want Maxie to relieve you tonight, Dom?"

"No, Richie. You kidding? I like it here."

'Yeah, that's what I thought."

CHAPTER 51

82

Rodriguez is sitting in his office at the precinct. He's typing reports about the events of Sunday night. The phones at the precinct are ringing off the hook with reporters, and photographers and television stations are outside the precinct hoping for an interview with Rodriguez. McMahon walks into the office, carrying her luggage for the trip back to Las Vegas. "Damn, Rodriguez, you're a popular guy!"

"I could live without it. Are you off to Vegas, Sarge?"

"Yeah, I've got a flight out of JFK. I've had enough of the Big Apple."

"I wanna thank you for your efforts on this one. I know leaving Vegas wasn't easy for you."

"Oceanview wasn't so bad. I got used to it. The peace and quiet, you know what I mean."

"Peace and quiet, my ass—six dead plus a girl you think was killed by Sanchez, a pedophile police sergeant, and a missing drug shipment. Some peace and quiet."

How're you going to the airport, Sarge?"

"I don't know. I guess I'll take a cab."

"I'll give you a ride. I gotta get out of here for awhile."

"That's okay, Detective, I see you're busy."

"I insist, Sarge. We can chat, give us a chance to bond."

"Cut the crap and give me the keys."

"Why?"

"Cause I've seen you drive, Rodriguez, and the idea is to get to the airport before the plane leaves the ground."

"Very funny, Sarge. Okay, let's go." Rodriguez yells to his officers, "I'm heading to the airport. Come on, Sarge, let's go down the back."

Half an hour later they're stuck in traffic. "Well, Sarge, here we are. Any suggestions?"

"Don't worry. I have a lot of time left, I'll make it. So tell me, Detective, what are your plans? Are you thinking about staying in Oceanview? Think when the dust settles you'll get Fuller's spot?"

"I'm not sure. I think I'd miss Vegas. So tell me, Sarge, who else did you have on this?"

"I guess I can tell you now. I had an agent in Ball Breakers posing as a stripper."

"No shit, Sarge!"

"Yeah, I brought her up from Virginia. She went by the name of Cinnamon."

"We've met, Sarge. She helped me the night I got beat up outside the joint."

"Well, well, it's a small world. Take a few weeks, detective, and make your decision. There's a place for you in my Command."

"Thanks, Sarge. So tell me about Cinnamon. How did that work out?"

"It worked out too well, Detective. She and DiNapoli got close, too close for her own safety. I pulled her out on Saturday before the raid at the pier. This traffic is nuts. I'm gonna get out and go through local streets—this traffic sucks."

"Yeah. Good idea, Sarge. We should be at the airport soon. So, this turned out to be a shit storm, didn't it, Sarge?"

"Yeah, Rodriguez, and anybody who knows anything is dead."

"So Sarge, now what, do we just suck it up?"

"What about this guy, Tom? What do we know about him?"

"Tom is above all this, he's a retired officer, served his country and was defending himself against Sanchez and Felix. He fell in love with Anna and he was completely focused on her. Tom was the victim here. Antonio's jealousy almost killed him."

"I get it, Detective."

The car winds though city traffic, making better time than the highway. Rodriguez says, "Looks like we're moving now." The car stops at a light and a truck pulls up to the right side and it catches Rodriguez's eye. It's a carting truck, and the name on the side is DiNapoli Carting. "Look at this, Sarge. Ain't this some shit. Look who's on the right."

McMahon looks out the passenger side window. "Yeah, ain't that some shit. The motherfucker."

The light changes and both vehicles jockey to get ahead of each other. "Let' em go, Sarge. They're bigger than we are. Besides, it would be a shame to bang up a nice new truck." The truck pulls out ahead of their car.

McMahon sees the back of the truck and there it is right above the compactor—the number 82. "Holy shit, Rodriguez! There it is—82 —it's the number of the fucking truck! Son of a bitch! I'm gonna follow it."

"What're you talking about, Sarge?"

"I'll explain later." McMahon follows the truck at a safe distance. "I'd love to see who's driving that truck." They both stop at the next light and the truck is on the right side of the car again. The light changes and the truck moves. Rodriguez grabs the wheel and jerks it to the right hitting the rear of the truck.

McMahon is startled and shouts, "What the hell are you doing?!"

"Stop the car, Sarge! Stop the car—just sit and don't react. Let's see if anybody comes out of the truck."

The truck goes through the intersection and stops. The driver's side door opens and the driver steps out, dressed in a sport jacket and white shirt.

"Does that guy look like he's picking up garbage?"

"Not dressed like that. Let's not spook him. The last thing we need is a 20-ton garbage truck rolling through the streets of Queens at 60 mph."

The man from the truck walks to the back to see what caused the noise. He looks around but doesn't see any damage. He drives on, followed by the car.

"What's with the number 82, Sarge?"

"Ok, Detective, let me give you a quick summary. Cinnamon was supposed to get information on Sanchez. Instead she wound up with DiNapoli."

"What do you mean 'wound up with,' Sarge?"

"DiNapoli saw her dance, gave her his card, and one thing led to another. They wound up sleeping together."

"Shit, talk about taking one for the team."

"It's not what you think, Rodriguez. He never touched her."

"That's hard to believe, Sarge. She's gorgeous."

"Yeah she is, but DiNapoli has issues, Mommy issues—he likes to cuddle. He never touched her, they just cuddled. He talks in his sleep, and he keeps repeating 82 over and over. We couldn't figure it out till now—it's the truck."

"If this is the real deal we should radio for help."

"Yeah, I'll call Ebersole." McMahon calls Ebersole and he picks up. "Hello, McMahon. Are you at the airport?"

"No Captain. Looks like I'm gonna miss my flight. I'm calling for backup."

"That's not funny," Ebersole says.

"I'm serious, Captain, we're following one of DiNapoli's trucks—truck number 82. Don't ask me to explain now, but I think this is what we missed Sunday night." "A carting truck filled with drugs."

"Well, too bad, Sergeant. My men are in the field."

"Not good enough, Captain, we're on Astoria Boulevard Near 101st Street."

"I got nobody. I'm afraid you're on your own."

Rodriguez says, "Put out an 'Officer Needs Assistance' call—he has to respond."

"This is an 'officer needs assistance' call, Captain, you HAVE to help. I'll let you know when we stop moving and I'll give you a location. Get NYPD involved."

Ebersole says, "Dammit, McMahon. Why are you dragging me into this?"

"Cause I wanna make you a hero, Ebersole."

They follow the truck through Queens and they arrive at a desolate section of Long Island City. The area is known for abandoned buildings and old factories. It borders the East River and Brooklyn. The truck turns the corner and stops in front of a large brick building with a sign that reads RDN Importing.

Rodriguez says, "Stop here." The truck's doors open and the men step out and look around.

McMahon says, "I wish I had binoculars. I swear the passenger looks like Dom, DiNapoli's right hand man."

Rodriguez opens the glove compartment and takes out a pair of opera glasses and hands them to McMahon. "Will these do?"

"Opera glasses? What are you doing with opera glasses?"

"I love the opera! 'Carmen' is my favorite ...and he sings, 'Toreador, Toreador.'"

McMahon laughs. "Shut up, Rodriguez, you can't sing for shit. But I'm glad you like opera. It shows you have some culture. I love it, too, but I'm a 'La Boheme girl.'"

McMahon looks through the glasses. "I think we found our shipment. That's definitely Dom." Seconds later the warehouse doors open and a different driver takes the truck inside.

"I gotta get in there—call Ebersole." Rodriguez leaves the car and runs across the street and behind the truck. As the truck enters the warehouse he darts to the right side and hides behind some boxes. McMahon is on the radio with Ebersole. "I need backup now! I'm at 14th Avenue and River Street in Long Island City. The truck is in a warehouse owned by RDN Importing. Rodriguez is inside. Get here quick." Ebersole says, "On the way."

Rodriguez texts McMahon. "The back of the truck just opened. I see crates in the back. I count about 8-10 men, heavily armed. I hope the cavalry is on the way. There's a guy looking at monitors, and there's cameras around the building. I'm gonna get closer to see if I can pull the plug."

McMahon texts back, "Rodriguez—stay put. Ebersole is on the way."

"I can't, Sarge. It's no good if they're spotted. I'm gonna take him out."

Rodriguez slowly comes alongside the man at the console. The fork lift begins unloading the drugs. Rodriguez moves into position using the noise of the machinery to cover his movements. When the opportunity presents itself, he lunges. He grabs the man around the neck and pulls him to the floor. He continues to squeeze cutting off the man's oxygen temporarily rendering him unconscious. He sits at the console and texts McMahon. "All clear."

"Got it!" McMahon answers.

"Where's Ebersole, Sarge? They're unloading now."

"He's on the way. Stay away from the front gates—SWAT's gonna bust through."

Rodriguez moves around the room to get a better position for the element of surprise. Dom is overseeing the unloading with Diego when he spots Rodriguez. Rodriguez doesn't know he was spotted as Dom tells Diego, "I'll get this guy." Dom opens his straight edge Razor and tries to catch Rodriguez off guard. Rodriguez sees him and runs for the stairs to the roof. Dom is in pursuit, razor in hand. Rodriguez gets to the roof and kicks the door open as Dom gets closer. Rodriguez uses the door as a weapon and slams it into Dom as he reaches the roof. Dom pushes it open and the men confront each other. Rodriguez pulls his weapon and tells Dom to drop the razor. "You must be Rodriguez. I heard you're a real hard ass. You think you can take this blade away from me."

"Give it up asshole—troops are on the way. You're done."

"Come on, put your gun down. Let's go one on one. Take my blade, tough guy."

"I'll take it and shove it up your ass. You wanna do this, let's do it." He removes the clip from his weapon and puts his gun on the ground. Dom doesn't hesitate to attack swinging the blade at Rodriguez. He's able to fend off the attack, his jacket protecting his arm. Dom swings at Rodriguez's neck and misses. As he misses, Rodriguez punches him in the face. This stuns Dom and he's getting frustrated, swinging more widely. Dom swings again and catches Rodriguez off guard slashing his right arm. Dom says, "How's that, tough guy?" Dom takes another swing at Rodriguez's stomach and misses, which allows Rodriguez to punch Dom in the face with a series of lefts and right. Dom is reeling and his legs go rubbery. Rodriguez kicks the razor out of Dom's hand. They're now fighting with no weapons mano a mano, and Dom is no match for Rodriguez's strength and youth. Dom realizes he's in trouble and he reaches for his gun thinking Rodriguez is unarmed. Rodriguez falls back and removes his weapon from his ankle holster. He fires two rounds hitting Dom in the chest; he falls back-ward through the skylight to his death three floors below. The NYPD crashes through the front gates and gunfire breaks out, and there's yelling and screaming from below. Rodriguez finds his gun and reloads. His arm is bleeding and he makes a tourniquet to stem the flow.

He slowly makes his way down the stairs. He sees McMahon taking cover behind some boxes and he makes his way over to her. Ebersole and his men are engaged in a fire fight with DiNapoli's men. Rodriguez reaches McMahon and she sees his wound.

"Is that Dom lying there?"

"Yeah, but he got me with his blade."

"Get out of here, Rodriguez. There's some medics outside. They'll treat that wound."

"No, I'm gonna hang with you, Sarge. Somebody's gotta watch your back. Some of DiNapoli's men are beginning to surrender. This is over."

On the balcony above them Diego is taking aim. He fires at Rodriguez and the bullet goes past them and hits the wall behind them. McMahon and Rodriguez look up to the balcony. McMahon recognizes the man.

"Shit, Rodriguez. That's Diego Vargas."

"Who is he?"

"Somebody we need to catch alive. He knows all about Delacruz's operation."

Diego fires again, the bullet ricocheting off the floor near Rodriguez.

"Shit! That was close, Sarge."

"He's Delacruz's business manager. He used to be his enforcer, but he got educated."

"Drug dealers need business managers—who knew?"

McMahon looks at Rodriguez and shakes her head. She gets on the radio to Ebersole. "Captain, that guy on the balcony is Diego Vargas. We need him alive."

Rodriguez says, ``I'm gonna try and get up there. Cover me."

McMahon tells Ebersole, "Rodriguez is going up there. Hold your fire."

Ebersole replies, "I ain't making any promises. He wounded one of my guys, and he's got us pinned down."

"He's Delacruz's money man. We want him alive."

"Like I said McMahon—no promises."

Diego reloads and fires again and yells, "Fuck you, cop."

Rodriguez is on the balcony and getting closer to Diego and he signals to McMahon not to shoot.

He fires again at Ebersole's men. Some of DiNapoli's men have escaped, but those that couldn't have surrendered. McMahon shouts again, "Come on, Diego. You're alone. Drop it and come down."

Diego begins to run across the balcony, firing at both McMahon and Ebersole's men. Agent Harris fires and hits Diego, and he falls—his wound is fatal. McMahon yells "Fuck, I wanted him alive." They run up the stairs to check on his condition.

Agent Harris asks, "Who's this guy?"

"This guy is Delacruz's business manager. We should have taken him alive."

"Business manager—drug dealers need business managers?"

"In 2020 they do. We should have taken him alive."

"Well, McMahon, if somebody's trying to kill me, I kill 'em back. Does Primo ring a bell?"

"Fuck you, Harris."

"Go back to Vegas, McMahon. You're over your head."

Rodriguez runs over and shouts, "Didn't you see me up there, asshole? You could have shot me. I should throw your ass off the balcony."

Harris says, "Anytime, Detective."

Ebersole says, "Walk the fuck away, Harris. Sorry, Sergeant, he was firing at us. He already wounded one of my agents."

The NYPD and Ebersole's men are making arrests and sealing the warehouse.

"Any sign of DiNapoli?" McMahon asks.

"No," replies Ebersole. Rodriguez and McMahon are leaving the warehouse when Ebersole shouts from the warehouse. "Hey, McMahon! My agents just picked up Maxie at the airport."

Rodriguez yells back, "Was he alone?"

"Yeah, Detective. He was alone. No DiNapoli."

CHAPTER 52
MAXIE BEHIND BARS

It's been a month since the Sunday night massacre. Rodriguez calls Ebersole to ask if Maxie has cooperated and given any information. Maxie is not cooperating, and Ebersole is no closer to finding DiNapoli, and Delacruz is even further out of reach. Ebersole figures that perhaps Rodriguez may have better luck. Rodriguez arrives at the Suffolk County detention facility. He checks in at the security desk. Ebersole made sure he would be brought in to see Maxie immediately. He's led to a corridor painted institutional green and down the fluorescent lit walkway to a door. He enters. In the room are ten chairs on one side, separated by a plexiglass partition and ten chairs on the other. He sees Maxie waiting for him. He sits down and he notices Maxie is looking tired and drawn. The two men don't talk for a while. Finally Rodriguez breaks the ice. "So, Maxie. How're you feeling?"

"How am I feeling? Are you fucking with me, Sergeant? I'm feeling like I want a bowl of pasta with sauce that doesn't taste like ketchup, a nice plate of broccoli rabe sautéed with garlic, and olive oil washed down with a glass of Chianti and a nice blowjob for dessert. So I guess you're a hero now. I heard you got Fuller's spot. Fucking Fuller. I'm glad he's dead, the pedophile prick. So what brings you to see me, Sergeant? Are you here to make a deal? Ebersole tried and I told him to go fuck himself. Unless your deal cuts me loose and all is forgiven you can fuck off, too."

Rodriguez let Maxie talk—now he asks: "Are you ok in here? Is anybody fucking with you, Maxie?"

"Thanks for asking, but I got two things working for me here. Nobody wants to fuck an old nerd like me, and the jerkoffs in this place know I'm with Richie DiNapoli's crew. No, Sergeant. I don't need shit from you."

"Hey, DiNapoli's crew left town. You're alone pal, the old gang is dead."

"It's a temporary thing, Rodriguez. Don't sell Richie short—he'll be back. In the meantime his money is safe cause I'm the only one who knows where it is."

"So Maxie, where do you think Richie is right now? Costa Rica? Somewhere in South America? Maybe he's with Delacruz, eating lobster and banging Colombian chicks. Columbian women are beautiful, aren't they, Maxie? What do you think?"

"I think you're trying to fuck with my head, Sergeant. You know, turn me against Richie. Let me tell you something you cops don't understand. It's called loyalty. Richie's been more than a boss to the family—he's been a dear friend for many years."

"So what do you expect him to do, Rodriguez? Walk in here with his hands in the air and say 'I'm here. Lock me up?'"

"If the situation were reversed, I'd do the same thing—bide my time and when the time was right start up again somewhere else. Yeah, Richie will be back, Sergeant. Now let me ask you something. Do you think this case is solved and closed? Most of DiNapoli's crew are either hiding or in jail. You can't touch them. Delacruz, he's protected by crooked cops and politicians south of the border. Now be honest with yourself—do you really think the mastermind behind this was Antonio Sanchez?"

"No, it was Diego Vargas."

"Well, you're right about one thing—Sanchez was a loose cannon dumb spic who couldn't mastermind a circle jerk. That leads us to Diego Vargas. Now I agree that he's got ten times more smarts than Sanchez - you know, cool, collected, rational - but he was in Colombia setting this up down there. No, Sergeant, I'm talking about here in New York and Long Island. Come to think of it, you stumbled your way through this case."

"What're you talking about, Maxie?"

"Well Rodriguez, for starters you didn't get DiNapoli, Delacruz is untouchable unless the CIA sends in a hit squad, which ain't gonna happen, and you took a detour on your way to the airport and found the drugs. I read all about it in the papers. I think you need to resume your search for the person pulling the strings, catch that person and you'll redeem yourself as a detective—just saying. Come back and let me know how you make out."

"Why are you so interested in this mastermind, Maxie? Is there something you wanna tell me."

"No Sergeant. What I know I'll take to the grave. It's dinner time. I gotta go and eat some slop."

───────

Rodriguez is driving back to Oceanview with Maxie's words playing over and over in his head. He calls McMahon and she answers. "Hello, Sergeant Rodriguez. I believe congratulations are in order. We're peers now. How's it feel, Sergeant?"

"It feels great, but you know you'll always be my boss. So guess who I saw today."

"Who?"

"Maxie. He and I had a long talk."

"Did he give anything up?"

"No, he said he's never gonna give Richie up. He also said something that got me thinking. He said we never found out who the mastermind was behind this deal. He told me this person is still out there."

"Did it occur to you that he was messing with your head?"

"Yeah, it did, but he made his point, and now I'm thinking about what he said."

"Listen, Rodriguez. The opinion of everybody involved was that the brain behind this was Diego Vargas. But I get the feeling that's not good enough for you, is it? So what do you want to do about it, Rodriguez?"

"I want to keep digging. This thing is beginning to eat at me. I may need your help."

"You've always had good instincts, Rodriguez. How can I help?"

"Thanks, McMahon. Can you send me all you got on Delacruz?"

"That's a lot of material. How far back do you want to go?"

"I'll take whatever you got."

"Ok, Rodriguez, but it's gonna take awhile."

"It's ok. I'm gonna stop by and see how Tom's doing, so I'll be away from the precinct for a few hours. Thanks, Sarge. We'll talk later."

CHAPTER 53
WHY OCEANVIEW?

Rodriguez arrives at Tom's house and is welcomed by Anna, and she invites him in. Tom is sitting on the couch reading a book. He greets Rodriguez. "Congratulations, Sergeant! Nice of you to stop by. I'd like you to meet Anna."

Anna extends her hands and says, "Nice to finally meet you, Sergeant. Thank you for everything you've done for us."

"You're welcome, Anna. I was just doing my job. So Tom, how are you feeling?"

"Today is not so bad, but it can change when the headaches get bad. I get vertigo, my vision blurs, and what's worse is, it can happen anytime. What bothers me the most is I'm still not cleared to fly."

"That's too bad, Tom. I know how much you love it."

Anna asks, "Are you going to stay a while, Sergeant? Have a seat and I'll make some coffee."

Rodriguez says, "Is it ok if I ask you a few questions about that night, Tom? Is it ok, Anna? I know Antonio was your husband."

Anna replies, "Do you need me for this? I was about to run some errands."

"No, it's ok Anna. Go ahead. I just have a few loose ends to straighten out."

Rodriguez helps Anna with her coat. He extends his hands and says, "Very nice to meet you, Anna. I hope to see you again."

"Nice meeting you also, Sergeant. Goodbye."

Anna says to Tom, "I'll be in town. If you need me, just call. Ok, Baby?" She kisses Tom and leaves.

Rodriguez says, "So Tom, now that Anna's not here, why do you think Sanchez wanted you dead?"

"I think you know the answer, Sergeant. We were having an affair."

"Yeah, I heard about Antonio's insane jealousy. How much do you know about what happened that night?"

"Just what I read in the papers, Sergeant."

"Did you ever suspect Sanchez was involved in something this big, from a cop's perspective?"

"No, I knew he was a scumbag, but I thought he was a nickel and dime scumbag. But from what I read it was quite a score."

"Cut the right way, the street value could be fifty million to seventy million. That's a conservative estimate. In the right hands it could go for ten to twenty million more."

"I know DiNapoli got away. Any idea where he is, Sergeant?"

"No, we got people working on it. It seems like he fell off the face of the earth."

"And the cartel in Colombia—any word on Delacruz?"

"I'm afraid he's gonna be a lot tougher to find. You know, Tom, everybody's getting paid, crooked cops, politicians—they keep him insulated. Let me be honest with you, Tom. I'm not convinced that it's over. I think there's still a part of this that's not finished. Do you think Sanchez was smart enough to put something this big together?"

Tom laughs, and Rodríguez laughs along with him. "You wanna know what I think, Sergeant? I think Colombia was pulling the strings." "Yeah, Tom, I agree. I think Sanchez was taking orders from Medellin."

"So Sergeant, what brought you to Oceanview? What's the real story?"

Rodriguez thinks about the question for a while and he answers: "I was with the Las Vegas DEA for about eight years. My commanding officer was Sergeant Elizabeth McMahon, and being in law enforcement, Tom, I'm sure you've had some tough commanders. Well, McMahon is someone you don't want to get into a pissing contest with. She'll slap your dumb ass around real quick. She and I worked many cases together, including this one. So back to your original question. About six months ago a journalist friend of mine called me and told me he had documents that showed a certain middle eastern royal family was supplying weapons to terrorists. He gave me the documents and I contacted the consulate. I told them I had this evidence, and I wanted two hundred thousand dollars for it.

"Shit, Sergeant—you were blackmailing them?"

"Yeah, in the technical sense, but I wasn't gonna keep the money— it was going to a good cause."

"Good cause? What good cause?"

"I'm gonna tell you something, Tom, that nobody knows. Not even McMahon, who I'm very close to. I'm a twin. My sister was born with a rare childhood disease that affects the nervous system. There's no cure, but it's being worked on. The only thing missing is money. That was the plan—the two hundred grand was going to the scientists trying to find a cure. We were making the exchange at a hotel parking lot in Vegas when things went south. We were changing the money for the documents when one of the assholes asked me if those were the only copies, so of course, being a smartass I said maybe."

"Shit Rodriguez—what happened when you said that?"

"Well, these guys obviously had no sense of humor and they tried to kill me."

Both men laugh, then Rodriguez added, "I regret that I had to go outside the line that I drew for myself, but I'm desperate to help my sister. She's incapable of doing anything for herself because of this disease. Two people died that night and two were wounded. I knew going in that no matter what I did these guys were gonna kill me. A few days later McMahon sent me to Oceanview to keep an eye on Sanchez. A couple of these guys had State Department ID's so it became an international incident. I know McMahon was protecting me by sending me here to work on this case. She's still dealing with the fallout, and you'll never see this on the news because it's being covered up. I know there's things going on behind the scenes—you know, investigations and all that shit, but the public will never know about it. I'm not proud of what happened that night, somebody died, but I would do it again. There was no money, the whole thing was a set up. They were going to get the documents and kill me. So that's my story." Rodriguez looks at his watch and adds, "Damn, time flies. I gotta take off, Tom. My crew will be wondering where I am."

"Ok, Rodriguez, come back soon. Next time we'll have something stronger than coffee."

"Sounds good. Give my regards to Anna. You're a lucky man to have her by your side."

"I know, thanks. Bye, Sergeant." Tom closes the door and sits on the couch. He puts his head back and closes his eyes.

CHAPTER 54
THE MASTERMIND

Anna is walking on Gold Street in the city of Oceanview. Gold Street is the Rodeo Drive of Oceanview with high end boutiques lining both sides of the street. She's been shopping most of the afternoon at some of these boutiques - boutiques like Gucci, Versace, and Ferragamo. Get the picture? Her phone rings and it's a number she doesn't recognize, but it has an international area code and she answers "Hola!"

The voice on the other end says, "Hola, mi corazon."

"Tio, how are you? I've been worried about you."

"Don't worry about me, my darling. Can you talk?"

"Yes, I'm out shopping. Tom is home. I feel so bad for him. He's still getting those headaches."

"That's too bad. How is he treating you, my dear?"

"Tom is wonderful, Tio. He's a good man."

"I wish I could've gotten my hands on that pendejo Sanchez. I would have fed him to my dogs. Every day I would think about the way he was treating you—that piece of shit."

"Tio, be careful. You always tell me someone might be listening."

"Perhaps, but not on this phone. You see, I have a friend in the C.I.A.—his daughter needs braces to straighten her crooked gringo teeth so when she grows up she won't be so ugly. So I traded him his daughter's perfect smile for a phone that can't be traced. I paid for her braces, that's how things are done down here, clean and simple."

"You make me laugh, Tio."

"Well it's true, cara mia, he had something that I needed, and I had something he needed. See, simple - like I said."

"Now tell me about Tom. Do you love him."

"Yes I do, Tio. I've never felt this way about any man before."

"Tell me about him."

"Well, he's a war hero from the Gulf War, and he's got medals for saving his men under fire. He's a retired policeman."

"A policeman, how ironic. Go ahead. Continue."

"He has a plane and it's beautiful. It's red and white. I went flying with him. It was wonderful. I felt so free."

"What does he know about our business, about us?"

"Nothing Tio. I would never tell him. Do you think I would reveal what we do?"

"No, no, never. But let me ask you a question. Do you feel that he would ever want to join our family?"

"Family, you mean marriage?"

The voice laughs. "Marriage? You are in love! No, no. I'm speaking of the business."

"No Tio, not Tom. He's too honest. He would never break the law."

"I see—so we have a decorated war hero, a policeman who's honest and can't be persuaded to join our family. That's a dilemma, my darling."

"A dilemma? Why, Tio?"

"It's a dilemma because, for instance—and this is just a 'for instance'—if he were to find out about our business, what are you prepared to do?"

Anna stops in front of a Gucci store to admire a pair of shoes. The voice continues: "You haven't answered my question, my darling niece."

"Tio, you know family comes first, I'd have to kill him. I have to go. I just saw the most wonderful pair of shoes that I must have."

"Wait, before you go. I just want you to know that not a minute goes by when I'm not thinking of your brother Diego."

"I know, Tio, me too."

"One day we 'll have our revenge but I can't move freely now. The policia and their counterparts from America are watching. I'll be in touch, my dear. Adios."

CHAPTER 55
THE FACEOFF

Rodriguez is back at the precinct, and as he walks to his office, his men hand him phone messages. He quickly reads through the messages and he stops at a message from Mrs. Cooper. He goes into his office and throws the messages on his desk. He sits at his computer to see what McMahon sent him. The files paint a picture of Delacruz as a strong member of the community, whether it's receiving an Award for charity work, golfing with politicians and precinct captains or building a church. Rodriguez continues going through the file on Delacruz. He's convinced there's some things in the files he's missing.

Tom awakens from his nap and calls for Anna. He goes, to the kitchen looking for a snack. He says to himself that if she's not home in a half hour he'll call to make sure she's ok. He's getting bored and he begins to wander the house. He's always respected Anna's privacy, but now the detective in him is taking over. Next to the master bedroom in the rear of the house there's a room he's never seen. The door is always locked, and he felt it would be a betrayal of trust to even ask about it. He feels around the top of the door frame for a key. As he enters the room he notices that like the rest of the house it's beautifully decorated. It's very masculine—a cross between an office and a man-cave. On the wall is a wide screen TV opposite a queen size sofa. The walls are painted a forest green with baseball memorabilia on display. Some of the items could be worth thousands of dollars, not bad for someone who doesn't have a steady job. A beautiful antique bookcase occupies half a wall. It's filled with books, and as Tom gets closer, he notices that some of the books are collectables. He sees that Rebecca's books about stained glass are on the book shelf, and he wonders why Anna would lock them in a room. Tom sees a book that seems out of place—it's a copy of The Bible. He finds it strange that this book would be among the others since Anna never discussed religion or had never gone to a house of worship since they've been together. He notices a white piece of paper, perhaps a bookmark, protruding from the center of the book. He takes the book off the shelf and removes the folded piece of paper. He slowly unfolds the paper and is shocked to find a certificate of confirmation for a Mercedes Delacruz. His heart is racing as he continues to look through the book. Nestled between the pages toward the back of the book he finds a photograph of a young girl of about fourteen years old and a boy of about twelve. They are standing with an older man, a rather unattractive man. The young girl is wearing a white dress with a tiara. In her right hands is a book that looks a lot like the bible he's holding. Tom is thinking that there's a rational explanation for it. His love for Anna is clouding his logic. He plays various scenarios over in his head but a closer examination confirms that it's Anna. He puts the certificate and the photograph in his pocket. He places the book back on the shelf in the same position and leaves the room. He locks the door and puts the key back on the door frame.

Rodriguez is at his desk going through the files McMahon sent him. He glances at the message from Mrs. Cooper and dreads calling her. He's been occupied with the drug trafficking case and hasn't devoted the time to continue the investigation into the disappearance of Evelyn Lynch. He's positive she was murdered by Sanchez and Felix, but he needs to find the remains so her grandmother has closure. He plays over in his head what he's going to say to her.

Tom is pacing the living room. He's experiencing many different emotions. He wonders how she could have deceived him for a long time and how he was so in love not to see through the charade. He decides to end the masquerade and calls Rodriguez, knowing full well he'll never be with Anna.

Rodriguez is ready to call Mrs. Cooper; he realizes he has to walk a fine line and not reveal too much but, at the same time not to squash her hope. He knows the fragile state she's in, and besides, nobody wants to hear that their granddaughter is dead over the phone. He picks up his phone reluctantly to call Mrs. Cooper. As he's about to dial, a call comes through and it's Tom. Rodriguez feels a little relief and he answers. "Hi, Tom. Is everything ok?"

"No Sergeant, I don't think so. I may have found our mastermind. Does the name Mercedes Delacruz mean anything to you? I found a certificate of Confirmation with her name and a photograph of a man with two children. One of the children looks like Anna. She's dressed in a white dress. You know, a Confirmation dress.

Rodriguez says, "Damn, is Anna in the house?"

"No, she's out but she may be back soon."

"Tom, you have to be one hundred percent sure."

"I'm sure it's Anna, and the certificate is signed by Jorge Delacruz as her guardian." Tom still has his back to the door and didn't hear Anna come in. She's heard part of the conversation and she moves closer to Tom, who's still not aware that she's back. Tom says to Rodriguez, "There's a boy in the picture. Do you have any idea who that might be?"

"No I don't."

Anna has a gun at her side; she lifts it and puts it to the back of Tom's neck. Tom feels the cold metal and he slowly turns and sees Anna. She signals to him to end the call. Tom says to Rodriguez, "Ok, McMahon, I gotta go now. We'll talk later."

Anna asks Tom, "Who the fuck is McMahon?"

"It's Rodriguez's boss."

"How did you figure it out?"

Tom holds up the picture and the certificate. Anna looks at the picture and she points to it with the gun. "The boy, you wanna know who he is? It's my brother, Diego Delacruz. Of course, he changed his name to Diego Vargas so he wouldn't be hunted like a dog. Your pig friends killed him, Tom."

"I had nothing to do with that."

"You're a cop, you're all the same."

Rodriguez says to himself, "McMahon? What the fuck was he

talking about?" He keeps scrolling on the computer until he comes across the same picture that Tom found. This picture was in El Colombiano, a local newspaper in Medellin. The caption reads "Jorge Delacruz, a philanthropist and a resident of Medellin, at the Confirmation of his niece Mercedes Delacruz at the Church of Our Lady of Miracles, the church he had built through his generosity." Rodriguez stops reading, grabs his jacket and bolts out of his office. He shouts to Detective Spinelli, "Spinelli you're in charge till I get back." Rodriguez jumps into his car and turns on the lights and sirens.

Anna says to Tom, "Move. Let's go to the car."

"You gonna kill me, Anna? Go ahead. Do it here, or are you afraid to get blood all over your designer couch?"

"Move, Tom, I'm serious. Get in the car."

Tom knows he has to stall, the precinct is ten minutes away. He's hoping that Rodriguez realized that something is wrong. He says to Anna, "I guess all that talk about loving me was bullshit, wasn't it, Anna?"

"Family comes first, Tom. I was praying you wouldn't find out. But now you leave me no choice. Go to the car Tom. Now."

He begins to walk to the car when Anna asks, "Where's your gun?" He points to the table by the couch but he's wearing his ankle holster with a loaded gun. He puts his hands in the air and says, "Do you wanna search me?"

"Keep walking and go to the car."

Rodriguez is a few blocks away—he turns off his lights and siren and turns onto Tom and Anna's street. He sees Anna and Tom getting into the car. Anna still has the gun pointed at Tom's back. "So where do you plan on killing me, Anna?"

"Drive, Tom, and shut your fucking mouth."

Tom looks in his rear view mirror and sees a black sedan parked behind them.

"I need air, Anna. Can I roll down the window?"

"I don't give a fuck, Tom. Just drive or I'll kill you here in the car."

Tom rolls down the window and begins to drive. He looks in the rear view mirror and sees the black sedan driving behind them. He puts his hand outside the window and signals to Rodriguez. Tom is waiting for the opportunity to pull the gun in his ankle holster. The car is driving down an isolated dirt road near the Oceanview city dump. They drive a half mile and stop at a secluded area with tall grass and rusted hulks of cars that were dumped there years ago. Anna tells Tom, "Get out and start walking towards the water." Rodriguez stopped his car and he's using the tall grass as cover as he's heading towards them, gun in hand. They walk down a small pathway to the water. To the right there's an abandoned ranger station. Rodriguez is about fifty feet away, hiding in the reeds. He continues to move inch by inch closer to them. "Get into the house Tom. Move!"

"Was this planned all along, just in case I found out?"

"Move, Tom. Get inside and shut up. Don't make this tougher than it is."

Rodriguez realizes now is the time to make his move. He runs toward Anna and screams, "Drop your weapon and don't move!"

Anna turns and fires at Rodriguez. Her first shot grazes Rodriguez in the leg. He returns fire and hits Anna. The wound is not serious and Anna turns her gun on Tom. Tom used the distraction to pull the gun from his ankle holster. Tom is facing Anna and both have guns drawn. Tom says, "Drop it, Anna. Don't make me shoot you."

Anna is bleeding from her arm. "Look what this fucking pig did to me, Tom. Kill him."

Rodriguez comes out of the tall grass. He tells Anna, "You can only kill one of us, Anna."

Anna says to Tom, "Go ahead, Tom. Kill him. We can be together forever. There's money, Tom, more than you can imagine. We can live the life people dream of. We can go to Colombia. My uncle will protect us."

Tom turns his weapon on Rodriguez and he says, "Sorry pal. I love her."

Rodriguez says, "You're not going to kill me, Tom. She was behind this whole drug deal. Tom, do you think she gives a shit about you? It's family first, Tom. You know how it is."

Tom drops his weapon and says, "Go ahead, Anna. Kill me."

Anna says, "What the fuck are you doing, Tom?"

"I knew you couldn't shoot me, it's between you and Rodriguez now."

Rodriguez still has his gun trained on Anna. He says, "Come on, Mercedes. It's over. Drop it. No me hagas Matarte."

"Don't speak Spanish to me! You're not one of us. You're a fucking gringo cop."

"What's it gonna be, Mercedes?"

Tom says, "Drop it Anna. You know he'll kill you if you don't."

Anna looks at Tom and back at Rodriguez and drops her weapon. Rodriguez moves in and cuffs Anna. He calls for backup and an ambulance for him and Anna; they're taken away to the hospital for medical attention. Tom is taken back to the house he shared with Rebecca.

CHAPTER 56
DELACRUZ'S DRONES

J orge Delacruz is seated at a table with seven of his closest associates. He's anxiously smoking a cigar and mumbling to himself. He suspiciously looks around the table at the men gathered there. The associates sense this and nervously glance at each other. His manservant brings newspapers and a beautifully carved ornate box. Delacruz tells his manservant to "put the box here." And he points to the table directly in front of him. He looks around the table and he speaks to his manservant. "Give them the newspaper—one for each." The manservant distributes the papers, the men glancing at each other. Delacruz takes a long drag on his cigar and throws it on the ground. He opens the box and takes out a silver-plated 357 magnum. He places it on the table in front of him. In one motion he sweeps the box off the table and it crashes to the floor with a thud, and the men jump in their seats at the sound.

"This gun was given to me by the Medellin Chief of Police. See? Here on the handle, it's engraved. Ironic, isn't it?"

'I keep it loaded, but I've never used it."

Delacruz speaks to the man on his right. "Read the headline out loud so we all can hear."

The man begins to read slowly his voice unsteady: "Mercedes Delacruz, the niece of Jorge Delacruz, was arrested in New York on drug trafficking charges and attempted murder."

Delacruz says, "Enough." He points to the next man and says, "You read it."

This continues around the table until Delacruz asks, "Was I betrayed by one or all of you? I don't sleep at night. I think of my nephew Diego, who was more man than all of you. My niece, my dear niece, in some fucking gringo prison. I'm being watched. Sometimes I hear the drones, I hear the helicopters. Why do I pay you fucking people? Isn't it your job to protect me and my family from these fucking gringos?" They look nervously around the table. Delacruz looks up at the sky and adds: "Look at them—flying around like little fucking mosquitos." He smacks his arm for effect. "See, I just killed one." He continues to look at the sky. "I have merchandise I can't move because I'm being watched. I can't touch my money. I'm being isolated from the rest of the world. Listen, listen to the drones buzzing around above us." The men look up at the sky and at each other.

The man to his left says, "Padrone, there's no drones above us." Delacruz looks at the man for a while and he says, "You don't see the drones?" He picks up the magnum and shoots the man in the chest. The man is wide-eyed and shocked and he sputters, "Padrone, you shot me!"

"Yes I know. Do you see the drones now, pendejo?" He fires again and again and throws the weapon down on the table. "The rest of you—bury him in the jungle and get the fuck off my land."

CHAPTER 57
EVELYN LYNCH FOUND

For the next two weeks the media is abuzz with the story. Rodriguez is in his office filling out reports and closing the file on the case. He's almost completely recovered from his gunshot wound. He's ready to leave for the day when his phone rings and he answers, "This is Sergeant Rodriguez."

The voice asks, "How's the leg?"

He sits back down at his desk and says, "Who's this?"

"It's Maxie. Why don't you take a ride and come see me tomorrow? We'll chat."

"About what? I thought we already had our chat. Listen, Maxie, the next time I talk to you is when you start giving me information, and how the fuck did you get my number?"

"I told you Richie still has pull in this joint. "Don't worry about where I got it, come see me tomorrow in the afternoon around three —I got something for you."

Maxie disconnects the call. Rodriguez gets to the prison at 2:45; the guards at the processing desk usher him in and take him straight to Maxie.

"Hi Rodriguez, how's tricks? I see you still got a little limp."

"Yeah, but it's getting better. What do you want?"

Maxie leans back in his chair and lets out a sigh. He leans forward again so no one else can hear. "Remember the last time you were here, I told you I would never give Richie up. Well, that hasn't changed, but what I will do is tell you how I used to skim Richie's money right off the top."

"You were stealing from Richie? Why are you telling me this?"

"Because I like you, Sergeant. You're trying to do the right thing. We don't have to hate each other. Do you wanna hear more?"

"Yeah. Go ahead, Maxie."

"Before I continue, you gotta promise me one thing—this doesn't go any further than right here."

"Go ahead, Maxie. It won't go anywhere."

"Like I told you before, I was always loyal to Richie, but I felt I wanted a little piece of the action. Now don't get me wrong, Sergeant. Richie took good care of his crew. I have been handling Richie's money for twenty years. You know, shell companies, offshore accounts, moving money around and making sure his money grows. Did you know some of these accounts pay interest on your money?"

"I know, some more than others."

"That's where I skimmed, on the interest. It worked like this—if the account paid 4% interest I'd have 2% sent to my account in the same bank under a shell company. Now, you're thinking to yourself, 'what's 2%,' right? Well, I'll tell you, after twenty years of two, three or more percent, I've accumulated millions."

"Shit, Maxie. Weren't you afraid Richie would find out."

"Nah. As long as his money was steady or growing, he was alright. In dealing with these banks I found out one thing, everybody has a price, even bank presidents. When Richie started this deal with Delacruz he deposited twenty million dollars in ten different accounts. In order to do that I had to have Delacruz's account numbers. I had to pay off a lot of bank presidents to get access to Delacruz's accounts."

"Goddamn, Maxie. You must have a death wish. Did you ever think what would happen if Delacruz found out?"

"Not really. You see, every time there was a movement on Delacruz's accounts, money out or money in, I would get a notification on my phone. All under the radar. I wasn't able to touch the money, but I got an activity report for every transaction. Once it was set up, it was on cruise control. If I told you how much that cocksucker Delacruz had in these accounts your head will explode." At that moment the bell rings, signaling the end of visiting hours. Maxie added, "What if I told you that I knew who the mastermind was months ago? I figured it out by following the money. Shit, I hate clichés, but it's true."

"How did you figure it out?"

"Next time you visit I'll tell you about it. Now I got something for you, Rodriguez. You got a pen and paper?" The guard walks over to remind the men it's time to go. Rodriguez flashes his badge and the guard says, "Ok, Sergeant. Five minutes." Rodriguez takes out a pen and paper and is ready to write.

Maxie says, "Santangelo Salvage on Dock Street in Oceanview, down by the water. Sanchez and some prick named Felix dumped a body there."

"How do you know that, Maxie?"

"While we were putting this deal together, Richie didn't trust Sanchez so he had him followed. We had a sit down at the social club in Brooklyn and Richie confronted that fucking Sanchez. He admitted to dumping the body in the salvage yard. The way Sanchez told it, Felix and the stripper…. "

Rodriguez cuts him off. "The stripper has a name, Maxie. It's Evelyn Lynch."

"Yeah, that's right. Sanchez said Evelyn was her name. How did you know, Sergeant?"

"I know because it was my case. I saw Sanchez and Felix dump the body in a car trunk on surveillance video. Thanks for helping me close the case, Maxie. I appreciate it. You didn't have to tell me shit."

"Like I said, Sergeant. You're doing the right thing. Come back soon. We'll chat some more."

———

Evelyn Lynch's body was found four days after the visit with Maxie. She was discarded like the rusted and dented skeletons of cars on death row, in line to be crushed and turned to liquid metal. Rodriguez was on the scene when her remains were found. One would never accuse Rodriguez of being sensitive, but the way life ended for Evelyn brought a tear to his eye. A girl who made bad life choices and wound up a victim to a lowlife drug addict. Rodriguez thinks to himself at least the grandmother will have closure now.

EPILOGUE

This was the first installment in the Rodriguez trilogy. In the second installment his courage and investigative instincts will be put to the test when he encounters the most diabolical and monstrous nemesis in The Cyclist Club.

Who or what will Sergeant Rodriguez confront in the third installment of the Rodriguez Trilogy? Coming soon…

Made in the USA
Middletown, DE
01 May 2022

Beyond
Words

In a broadcasting career spanning forty-five years JOHN HUMPHRYS has reported from all over the world for the BBC and presented its frontline news programmes on both radio and television. He has won a string of national awards and been described as a 'national treasure' – all of which he attributes to longevity and luck. He presents Radio 4's *Today* programme and BBC2's *Mastermind*. His previous bestseller *Lost For Words* was published in 2004.

Also by John Humphrys

Lost for Words

The Great Food Gamble

Devil's Advocate

Beyond
Words

JOHN
HUMPHRYS

How Language
Reveals the Way
We Live Now

HODDER

First published in Great Britain in 2006 by Hodder & Stoughton
A division of Hodder Headline

This paperback edition published in 2007

The right of John Humphrys to be identified as the Author
of the Work has been asserted by him in accordance with
the Copyright, Designs and Patents Act 1988.

A Hodder paperback

1

A CIP catalogue record for this title is available from the British Library

ISBN 978 0 340 92376 4

Cartoon on page ix © by John the Brush

Typeset in Sabon by Hewer Text UK Ltd, Edinburgh
Printed and bound by Clays Ltd, St Ives plc

Hodder Headline's policy is to use papers that are natural, renewable
and recyclable products and made from wood grown in sustainable
forests. The logging and manufacturing processes are expected to
conform to the environmental regulations of the country of origin.

Hodder & Stoughton Ltd
A division of Hodder Headline
338 Euston Road
London NW1 3BH

To my son Owen, who has learned to read since I began writing about English. So far . . . so good.

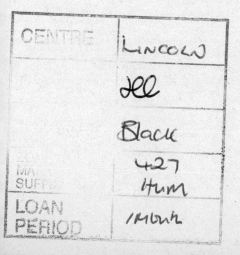

Acknowledgements

There would be no book without the help of many people. I am grateful to friends and colleagues who have shared their thoughts and frustrations. Among them are Philip Booth, Kevin Cecil, David Cox, John Dwyer, Charlotte Eilenberg, David Jordan, Dilip Lakhani, Theresa Marteau, Iain McGilchrist, Annie McManus, Helen Mountfield, John Smyth and Tony Travers.

Luigi Bonomi has done what all literary agents must do: offered praise even when it's not justified. Rowena Webb, my editor, can indicate disapproval with the merest pause or drawn-out 'yee . . . ss'. Also essential. And Hazel Orme has saved me from myself more often than I care to remember.

Above all, my thanks to the readers of *Lost for Words* who inspired me to write this book and who gave me so much wonderful material that I could write another dozen. But I promise I won't.

John Wakefield

John's name should have equal billing on the cover of this book. I could not – would not – have done it without him. What's truly re-markable is that this is the third book on which we have collaborated and we remain friends.

Contents

What Have I Started?

If I have learned anything in more than forty years of broadcasting it is that it's almost always a mistake to predict the way the audience will react. After a particularly lively interview on *Today* you might well walk out of the studio confidently expecting the plaudits of the nation for having exposed a politician's mendacity and single-handedly rescued the democratic process. Then you see the emails from those listeners who think you are an arrogant prat who could possibly have added a smidgeon to the sum of human knowledge if only you'd kept your trap shut for more than a few seconds during the interview. It is bad for the ego but probably good for the soul.

There are one or two certainties on *Today*. You know that a story about cruelty to animals will always get a bigger reaction than one about cruelty to children. You know certain subjects will stir great passion in the breasts of a certain section of Radio 4 listeners: 'elf 'n' safety rules; political correctness gone mad; anything about the Union Jack and, of course, anything about the English language.

Lost for Words was my first and, I thought, my last

book on English. I hoped it would stir things up a bit (though I was mildly surprised to be described on the Internet as a 'pendant') and indeed that was one of the reasons I wrote it. Don't believe journalists who tell you that they are interested only in informing the debate. They want to be talked about as well – or at least have their work talked about. What I was un-prepared for was how big a reaction there would be from readers and how it would be expressed.

The book was a cry from the heart of an ageing hack who has made his living using words. It was a protest against the cavalier approach we have taken to teaching children English over the past few decades and a lament at the way our language is mangled and manipulated by those who should know better. The response to it has been extraordinary and hugely encouraging – and that is partly what prompted this book and what the first couple of chapters are about.

But there was another motive. Language is more than a tool for expressing ourselves. It acts as a mirror to our world, reflecting back to us the way we live. Our choice of language and the new words we create reveal an enormous amount about how we lead our lives today and how society is changing. And that is what this book looks at.

In *Lost for Words* I was not saying that language should never change (because of course it always does) but that grammar matters. One of the daftest things we ever did in our schools was to stop teaching it to children. Academics who should have known better came up with the absurd notion that rules somehow confined children, restricted their imagination. I argued that the opposite is true. Understanding the basic workings of grammar – even if you don't observe all the rules to the letter – can liberate. If you don't know how to construct a sentence, how can you express yourself?

To judge by my readers' letters, I was pushing at an open door. Some of them came, as you would expect, from what is unkindly called the Green Ink Brigade (GIB). The GIB get a bad press mostly, I suppose, because of their predictability. Some really do use green ink and write in the margins of the letter when they have filled the page. Some even scribble a few lines on the back of the envelope after they've sealed it. Some clearly believe they are the only people on the planet capable of spotting a noun used as a verb or a dangling participle. Some are, quite frankly, a bit barmy.

Even so, I am a passionate defender of the GIB – just as I am a passionate defender of Brian Haw and people like him. Mr Haw is the man who made such a mess of Parliament Square by protesting about Iraq. He set up a ramshackle camp and managed to stay there for five years until the police came and evicted him. But it took a new Act of Parliament to do it. He, too, may be slightly bonkers. He may even be wrong. That's not the point. If someone believes in something it's good

3

that they say so – just so long as they don't hurt anyone else in the process.

The GIB hurt no one. Indeed, they boost the profits of the Royal Mail. They may exaggerate occasionally (I need a little more persuasion before I shall accept that ending a sentence with a preposition is the root cause of moral decay in this country) but their hearts and their heads are usually in the right place. So, let us salute the GIB for their eccentricity and their unflagging energy – though an author's life would be a little easier if they forsook their scratchy pens for a word-processor or even a typewriter.

Many people saw the book as an opportunity to share their 'pet hates'. The posher sent me their '*bêtes noires*'. The not-as-posh-as-they-think-they-are offered me '*bêtes noirs*', or maybe they thought such horrors could not possibly be feminine. My office became a menagerie of deformed and repellent creatures. We had become a nation of 'stores' not 'shops'. 'Drives' had become 'driveways'; 'windows' are now 'window areas'. There were no longer 'warehouses', just 'distribution centres'. You could no longer buy a blouse, only a 'top'. Small children routinely talk of their butts rather than their bottoms. Nothing was 'more than' something else, it was now 'in excess of'. Estate agents were blamed for that, as they are for so much else. And, to the horror of many, none of this was going to change 'any time soon'.

I began to feel I was at the centre of a web of

4

vigilantes who are forever on the look-out for some verbal-delinquency or other that has to be reported back to HQ. So I was the first to be informed when *The Times* printed a headline saying:

The Slowdown in the Housing Market is Gaining Speed

And when a farmer in the Lake District received a communication from the Department of the Environment talking about

the Sheep National Envelope

it was instantly put into a real one and sent to me. I was invited to squirm that a BBC newsreader had been heard to say:

Known offenders are being fed into a computer.

One long-suffering commuter shared my bafflement at trains being terminated and doors being alarmed. His own train was delayed, according to the announcer, because it hadn't yet 'platformed'. Someone else invited me to unmask the young MP Ed Balls, close buddy of Gordon Brown. How, the writer wondered, could he possibly be the rising hope of those stern and unbending Brownites if he could offer this comment on the notion of Britishness?

The danger with Remembrance Day is it becomes a purely backward-looking event.

5

Another wanted me to share his disdain for the Liberal Democrat leader, Sir Menzies Campbell, for having said in an interview during the leadership election campaign:

There is no silver bullet on carbon emissions.

'Is there a silver bullet to deal with *any* political problem?' my correspondent scoffed. 'They might as well say they "can't wave a magic wand" . . . which of course the idiots do say, all the time!'

The language of official bodies continues to get up the noses of lots of people, especially when it involves spending our money. One letter-writer was very upset that the Metropolitan Police had spent a small fortune changing its logo (think of all the stationery and signboards that would have to be redone) from 'Working for a Safer London' to 'Working Together for a Safer London'.

Another was exercised by the reported proposal (still 'out for consultation') that traffic wardens should be renamed 'civil enforcement officers'. Apparently these new beings would be given greater discretion, including imposing variable fines. Presumably this would mean you wouldn't have to remortgage the house for getting back to the meter five minutes too late although you would if you were a 'persistent offender'. But it was the change of name that really rankled:

Can you imagine ANYONE EVER storming into the living room, face purple with anger, and screaming: 'That f***ing civil enforcement officer has just given me a ticket!'

There's no getting round the fact that there is a whiff of sado-masochism among those of us offended by poor language. One woman wrote to me: 'I thought you would hate this so I had to send it to you!' What so upset her was a letter from a company that organises conferences:

We have the capacity next year to enable you, if you wish, the opportunity to meet with these delegates within your meeting schedule. Obviously if you didn't want to meet with them we will offer you the facility to negative preference them individually.

Technical jargon goes marching on, crushing all before it. In the IT business they use 'legacy' when they mean 'old' (probably best not to ask why) and this is how a company that sells barcode-readers described one of their *very* old systems:

A legacy narrowband wireless system that had served its purpose over 10 years but had gone end of life.

Isn't 'gone end of life' so much more evocative than 'obsolete'?

The Americanisation of English walks hand in hand with jargon:

> UK consumer goods manufacturers have gotten used to operating in this highly competitive market . . .

You might expect that in the *Wall Street Journal* or the *New York Times* but, no, it was the work of the Economist Intelligence Unit in a report sponsored by the German software firm SAP. Readers have noted the growing preference of European companies for so-called 'international English' over the real thing. Instead of discussions there are 'brain dumps' during which 'key learnings' may or may not be divulged. Recruits may be asked what they have in their 'skills basket', to which the response will probably be 'All righty!' A Swedish-owned company issued a press release from its London office about a collaboration with British Aerospace aimed entirely at the UK media but written in American English. They seemed surprised when this was pointed out to them.

And speaking of PR releases, a friend sent me this cheery greeting from a senior PR executive:

> Hope you are well and thank the lord for the rest-bite in the weather . . .

Businessmen have their own glorious way with words. Richard Lapthorne, chairman of Cable & Wireless, tried to defend a bonus package he wants to introduce for senior management. They'd get £220 million worth. He admitted the scheme was 'a bit idiosyncratic' but described it as a 'tool kit' [huh?] designed to introduce the sort of performance-related pay seen in the venture-capital industry. He said: 'It's not about instant returns. We don't get turned on *per se* by money.' Quite so. When last heard of, C&W was planning to cut three thousand jobs in the UK.

Even words and phrases that have long settled into our way of speaking still bring some people out in a rash of indignation. Sex, as ever, is a problem. Apparently it's quite absurd to say you want to 'sleep with' someone since the phrase refers only to the before and after and skirts the object of the exercise. And when it comes to the main event, my vigilantes are concerned with language again. Why do we talk of 'having' sex when it's the 'doing' that counts? And it's ridiculous to talk about 'going out' with someone when the whole point is to stay in – and not to fall asleep, either.

You begin to think you have found yourself in bed with lovers of lost causes. They never give up:

Billion. Yankspeak for 10^9 when it should be 10^{12}. The previous European term for *one-thousand-times-one-million* was 'milliard'; and I can't see why something with nine zeros has 'bi-' in its name.

Neither can I, but I don't know quite what I'm supposed to do about it. People are obviously looking for leaders:

Could you attempt to get the word 'fantastic' made illegal? One TV host uses it every other sentence and I'm sure gets paid enough to have a vocabulary.

Broadcasters are in the cross-hairs of many of my vigilantes – and quite right too. Weather forecasters probably get more flak than most, which is a shame because in my experience they tend to be very nice people. But there can be no pity in this business and a crime is a crime. Verbosity is regarded as an indictable offence:

They always say 'during the course of the morning' instead of simply 'during' and 'more in the way of sunshine/cloud' when they mean 'sunnier or 'cloudier'. 'More in the way of sunshine' must mean 'cloudier' to foreigners.

Nor does it help when they add that more in the way of sunshine will be 'on offer'. Has Tesco now cornered the market in fine weather too? The cartoonist John Smyth is baffled by 'sharp showers'. He says he asked what it meant but the man at the BBC didn't know. Since then, he says, the virus has spread and we now have:

The weather may become sharper.

He fears that sharp showers will come to haunt him like 'cold snap' does. But Mr Smyth – a self-confessed 'cheery soul' – is one of the many whose greatest loathing is for unnecessary words. When he went to buy a DVD the girl in the shop said she would 'pre-order' it for him. He told her he'd be perfectly happy for her simply to order it but she looked baffled. Nor does Mr Smyth approve of what he calls 'super-cool inversions'. Here's a flavour:

    Team Britain
    Travel Ireland
    Squash Welling [It used to be called Welling Squash
       Club]

There are many, many more and all equally baffling. And what about this word:

    worsenment

Someone told me he'd seen it in *The Guardian* – which turned out to be true. It was in the context of train delays: a 'worsenment' of services. *The Guardian* poked fun at it (quite right too) and claimed it didn't exist. But that was wrong. It does. Apparently it's the antonym of 'betterment'.

But let me not give the impression that all my correspondents were on my side. If only. I have been suffering a severe attack of the 'physician heal thyself' variety:

    On page 84 you have committed a monstrosity in
    writing 'marginally less ridiculous'. Permit me to

quote from Gowers . . . 'in recent years *marginal* has come to be increasingly used to mean no more than *small*. This misuse has now reached the status of an epidemic and every writer should make a habit of crossing out *marginal* as soon as he has written it . . .'

Quite so. I was a bit slapdash with some of my prepositions too. I'd written that my old friend, Rod Liddle, 'was fired from the BBC for writing rude things'.

The first reaction is, how did they do that? By cannon? Where did he land? Was he hurt? Surely it should be fired BY.

Mea culpa again. I'd also committed the solecism of writing about 'decent public schools' as though there could be such a thing as an indecent one. According to one reader I 'betrayed my provenance' by suggesting (slightly tongue in cheek) that 'cuppa' should be included in the *Oxford English Dictionary*. Another pointed out that it already is.

It's an intriguing thing, this business of what's right and what's wrong. I have always hated 'meet with' or, even worse, 'meet up with' and assumed it to be one of our less welcome American imports. More fool me for not reading my Kipling properly. After all, he tells us that when we 'meet with' triumph and disaster we should treat the two impostors just the same.

I was sniffy about 'outwith' but had to run up the

white flag after the umpteenth letter from angry Scots telling me it was not some modern version of guru-speak but a word used north of the border since long before I had uttered my first sentence.

'Test out' was another. I've always supposed the 'out' to be a redundant preposition. I reluctantly concede defeat to those who made clear that it is self-evidently a helpful adverb meaning 'thoroughly'.

I thought I was on safe ground when I scoffed at 'on a daily basis'. Surely 'daily' was more than adequate? Seemingly not. 'Day' is a noun and a noun may be turned only into an adjective and not into an adverb. So it turns out that it's wrong to say you swim daily and correct to say you do so on a daily basis. If we wanted a single word instead it would have to be 'dailyly'. But perhaps not.

Turning nouns into verbs is viewed as an even greater offence. You do not have to be a member of the GIB to wince at competitors in the Winter Olympics hoping they would 'medal'. By the time of the Commonwealth Games sports commentators were confident our national athletes would 'podium'.

In *Lost for Words* I'd confessed I was 'baffled' as to why the phrase 'wheelchair-bound' should be thought offensive while 'wheelchair-user' was fine. I wasn't alone. One helpful reader asked a disabled friend (not 'differently abled': one must hold on to something here) and here's what he said:

13

'I am wheelchair-bound only once or twice a year. I enjoy it very much but I'm a reasonable man and I do understand that my wife doesn't enjoy it as much as I do and it takes a great deal of setting up to get the knots just at the right tension. Now would you like to share with me one of your most intimate moments with your wife?'

Ambiguity, of course, is one of the sources of comedy as well as misunderstanding in language. I wasn't always sure whether I was being warned about genuine problems of usage or whether I was having my leg pulled. I was pretty sure that the person troubled by the phrase 'child psychiatrist' was not really worried about under-age practitioners. And even though the pendulum may be swinging back in favour of selecting children on ability, I was not persuaded that the sign 'Slow Children Crossing' was in itself discriminatory.

But you never can tell. Someone got very upset by my translating the ancient Greek advice about how to live life as 'nothing in excess'. How could I possibly believe there could be an excess of nothing? The only accurate way of using the word is King Lear's: nothing comes of nothing. I should have written 'Everything in moderation'.

I suppose that's right but where does it leave the advertising copywriter who came up with the catchy line 'Nothing acts faster than Anadin'? Perhaps he was actually trying to subvert the pharmaceutical company that made it. I once had a minor operation and the surgeon advised me not to take the painkillers offered to me afterwards. It was good advice. The pain was unpleasant for a day or two but then the endorphins took over. 'Nothing' really was more effective – and much cheaper.

One woman drew my attention to the ambiguity in the phrase 'family butcher'. She could see the funny side of it. Not so a friend of hers who had grown up in Germany in the thirties and much preferred the straightforward German word 'Fleischerei'. What intrigued me was why anyone should want to attach the word 'family' to 'butcher' in the first place. Was it simply to soften the impact of the uncompromising and graphic word 'butcher'? Is the phrase just a vestige of the era of warm beer and midwives cycling through villages on bicycles when the patrons of butchers' shops were, indeed, almost exclusively families?

If it is, maybe we should now have butchers labelled according to their more diverse contemporary clientele. Should their shopfronts read 'One-Person-Household Butchers', and 'Co-habiting Butchers'? Maybe gay butchers would become 'Pink Butchers', catering specifically to those who like their meat rare. Not that it matters. The way the supermarkets are taking over, there will be no butchers left soon anyway – except for the posh shops catering to only the most well-heeled customers and, of course, the Organic Butchers. Presumably the inorganic ones are made from plastic.

What unites the GIB, the vigilantes and the less militant readers is that we should give a hard time to all those (usually people trying to sell us things) who use language that is clearly intended to mislead.

I am partial to the occasional bag of crisps. The brand I buy claims to be 'handmade'. How? They sell tons of the things in shops across the land. Am I really supposed to believe that vast teams of workers spend their lives making crisps by hand? Don't they have *any* machines in their factories? And how do you 'hand make' a crisp anyway? A piece of pottery or a nice hand-knitted sweater maybe, but a crisp?

Like most people, I have failed to penetrate the mystery of hedge funds. The one thing I do know is that 'hedging' your bets is a way of reducing risk. Yet hedge funds are among the riskiest of investments on the market.

On one level it is reassuring to know that so many people share one's irritation and occasional amusement at this sort of thing. On another, it's slightly alarming. If my correspondence is a reliable guide, people out there are being driven to distraction by it. What can be said to the lady who complains that her life is made a misery by the contradiction in the phrase 'I don't know, I'm sure'? Or to the person who wrote:

I writhe in frustration at: 'What did you say your name was?'

Well, yes, I take the point about names not changing, but one shouldn't get too tense about tense. On the other hand, because of the sheer madness of the following, I warmed to the woman who wrote this:

Having called into Tesco's one evening on my way home from a girlie lunch, I arrived at the check-out where a young man in his mid-20s began to cash-up my purchases. I interrupted my packing to give him some money and as he handed me the change he said, 'There you go.' I looked him in the eye and the following conversation ensued.

'What does that mean?'

'I dunno.'

'Why do you say it, then?'

'I dunno.'

'Well, that's very interesting. Here we are with speech enabling us to communicate thoughts and ideas, yet you say something to me not knowing what it means or why you say it.'

The young man looked at me with his mouth open. (By this time the girl at the next check-out was on her feet, straining to hear what was going on and nudging the girl next to her to also pay attention!)

At this point my reader thought of quoting Henry Ford, the maker of the Model T. He not only said you could have it in any colour so long as it was black, he also said running a business would be a cinch if it weren't for the customers. But she decided against that. Instead she told the hapless young man:

> 'I think you say that because you think saying "thank you" is demeaning.' As no thoughts or ideas were forthcoming I resumed my packing, squashing into the bag the last item as I barked, 'And you haven't said it yet.'
>
> He managed a stuttered 'Thank you.'

The woman had the good grace to admit that in retrospect she felt a touch of sympathy for the target of her wrath:

> 'Poor young man! Whenever this episode surfaces I either scream with laughter or go hot and cold at my harshness.'

Quite so. But we shouldn't let embarrassment at our occasional excesses deter us from making a fuss about the mangling and manipulating of language. The campaign must go on. I take some comfort from the knowledge that I have more than the massed ranks of pedants on my side. I have the Goths too. Early in 2006 an article appeared in the *Sunday Times* head-lined:

Goth-rock Hero's Darkest Secret

It was by Robert Sandall and was about Ville Valo who (for those of you who may not know it) is 'the lead singer of the elegantly doom-laden Finnish band Him'. Mr Sandall wrote:

> An hour or so after Him finished their set at the Paradiso club in Amsterdam, Valo is back in the hotel bar studiously ignoring a gaggle of silently adoring female fans who have somehow managed to trace him here. This tiny fraction of the girl-led mob milling around the venue after the show ended are now disappointedly cradling drinks while their hero presides over an all-male coterie comprising his bandmates, manager and an English journalist (me).
>
> But the person who has helped him most recently in his battle with words and meanings is – no kidding – John Humphrys, the presenter of Radio 4's *Today* programme. 'I just finished his book *Lost for Words*,' says Valo. 'I love people who are passionate about their language and appreciate the history of it.'

I can't tell you how hurtful the 'no kidding' was.

CHAPTER ONE
Making Sense of Making Sense

There is one thing we have in common. All of us. You and I and the slightly menacing young hoodie hanging around on the street corner. We all care about language. Your concern may be different from the young hoodie's. You might contemplate climbing Everest naked before splitting an infinitive. He cares just as passionately about using language that proves his street cred. We each need to take care. His language is changing almost every day. A word that was a compliment yesterday may be an insult tomorrow. Ours is changing too – more slowly, but just as surely.

The point of this book is to look at what our changing use of language reveals about the way we live now. It is about our attitudes, about the way we see things and how we are seen by others: in public life; in politics and commerce; in advertising and marketing; in broadcasting and journalism. Language provides us with a revealing mirror on contemporary life. But we will be able to recognise what it shows us only if we know how words work and how they are abused. Yet the prevailing wisdom about language seems to be that 'anything goes'.

It's important to be clear about what should *not* worry us. I don't get at all agitated about the good-natured lad doing a dreary job on a supermarket check-out who tries to be amiable by passing meaningless remarks to a slightly batty customer. Nor does it worry me in the slightest that he may use an alien (to me) language when he's discussing the merits of one MP3 player against another. And he hardly needs to speak formally correct English when he's chatting up girls in a bar or talking about his football team with his friends.

He has his world and I have mine and we each speak our own kinds of English in them. But we also have a shared world where we need a dependable common language if we are all going to get by. And what matters is not so much how the lad on the check-out may use language in this shared world, but the attitude of so many academic experts to that common language.

As an interviewer, I spend my life asking experts questions for the very good reason that they know more than I do. The problem with a life spent in journalism is that you end up knowing a tiny bit about every subject under the sun but not a great deal about anything in particular. Like any halfway competent interviewer I can make a credible job of interviewing an expert for a few minutes on even the most arcane subject. Stretch that beyond five minutes and I start to flounder. But on this one issue – our common language

– I'm happy to mix it with the experts. That's because when they should be getting exercised and passionate they tend to relapse into a state of indifference. Their attitude to the condition of the very thing they have spent their lives studying amounts to little more than 'hey, whatever . . .'.

Professor David Crystal is the experts' expert, the *capo di tutti capi* of the linguistic Cosa Nostra. He has probably written more books on the English language than any other living soul: more than a hundred so far and he will almost certainly have written another in the time it takes me to finish this chapter. What Professor Crystal does not know about the structure and history of English is probably not worth knowing. He also writes brilliantly. Mere journalists like me are scarcely fit to hem the fabric of his academic robes. Yet he infuriates me.

Here's a small example. He does not think it much matters if we put apostrophes in the wrong place. So he would not, presumably, have given a fig if he'd read a press release entitled:

Lecturers Pay Dispute

that went on to talk about 'student's exam papers'.

I mention that one specifically because it happens to have been sent out by the office of Boris Johnson, the Shadow Minister for Higher Education. David Crystal selects the more common example of the greengrocer selling 'potato's'. He does not reach for his horsewhip;

23

he merely points out that in the eighteenth century it would have been perfectly acceptable. Indeed, he says, it is perfectly acceptable in the twenty-first century because there is no room for ambiguity. Everyone knows it must be a plural for the obvious reason that we know potatoes cannot possess things.

Well, that's true. But the great Keith Waterhouse, founder of the Association for the Abolition of the Aberrant Apostrophe, makes a different – and vitally important – point. Unless you get into the habit of being precise you'll be open to misunderstanding when something is capable of having two meanings. He once offered this example:

> Prudential – were here to help you.

Sometimes an apostrophe can be a copywriter's saviour. But experts as eminent as David Crystal have no truck with the likes of Waterhouse and Lynne Truss – or, indeed, with me – when we write about the use of English. He compares us to car mechanics who have had no training but 'write repair manuals about language and expect other people to live by their recommendations'. He goes further:

> In fact, the people who write manuals are more akin to doctors than mechanics, because they take the view that a great deal of language use is unhealthy, and that a large proportion of the population is linguistically sick without realising it. Having persuaded

others that they are unwell, they then offer remedies in the form of usage tablets of their own devising. Talk or write like me, they say, and you will be well again. The word *doctor* was wrong: these are the equivalent of the nineteenth-century quacks.

So that's us told, then. It's an interesting notion that the only people qualified to write about the use of English are those who have been trained to do so. For a hack (or 'quack') like me to square up to David Crystal may well be a bit like a go-kart challenging a Ferrari, but there's no reason not to try.

Professor Crystal seems to believe that so long as we are intelligible we can be as cavalier as we like with the rules and conventions of language. What's more, he thinks those rules and conventions can take quite a battering before we lose the sense of what someone means. In the most narrow sense that's true. One reader demonstrated it by sending me a letter that included this:

Aoccdrnig to rscheearch at Cmabrigde Uinervtisy, it deson't mttaer in waht oredr the ltteers in a wrod are, the olny iprmoatnt tihng is taht the frist and lsat ltteer be in the rghit pclae. The rset can be a taotl mses and you can siltl raed it wouthit a porbelm. Tihs is bcuseae the huamn mnid deos not raed ervey lteter by istlef, but the wrod as a wlohe.

Amzanig huh?

And, dammit, it's true. I did get the full meaning of what he had written in spite of the grotesque spelling. So does that prove we are making a fuss about nothing? No. Here's how the letter (which, by the way, came from a former head of English in a comprehensive school) continued:

> What is not made clear, of course, is that in order to decipher the jumble, your own mind has to have a semblance of order in the first place. This is exactly why we need rules and conventions. There has to be a common code of communication and this piece of research does in fact prove exactly the opposite of its hypothesis. Without a common code, it could not be understood.

In any case, the idea that intelligibility is all that matters is deeply suspect. Intelligibility itself is a slippery notion. When we hear something that's said in mangled language we may think we understand what's meant but we may be mistaken.

After Hurricane Katrina hit the Gulf coast of the United States an official from New Orleans said in a radio interview:

> The magnitude of this disaster is untenable.

People who heard it probably thought they knew what she meant. But what exactly did she mean?

The problem is that it doesn't make sense to say a magnitude is untenable. It could be that she meant the scale of the disaster was unbearable. She may have thought 'unbearable' was too personal and emotional a phrase for an official to use so resorted instead to 'untenable', which sounds more neutral, more 'official'. It is akin to the way many public figures avoid saying that something is 'wrong' (too loaded) and settle instead for saying that it's 'inappropriate'.

Or she may have been making the almost metaphysical point that the magnitude of the disaster was incomprehensible, impossible to get hold of.

Or perhaps this was just extreme shorthand. What she was saying was that the scale of the disaster was so great that Washington's slowness in getting to grips with it was becoming politically untenable.

Who knows? Probably most people would have thought she meant no more than 'Gee, it's awful!'

And that's the point. Mangled language may be intelligible but only when we settle for some lowest common denominator of meaning. If we're happy to let our common public language be used in this way, communication will be reduced to a narrow range of basic meanings. What we will understand (and all we will come to expect) from it is a rough, approximate meaning rather than anything precise or subtle.

That, of course, would be rather convenient for snake-oil salesmen, unscrupulous estate agents and (dare I say it?) even some politicians who might prefer not to be pinned down to anything too precise. But why should the rest of us settle for lowest-common-denominator communication when we have the great Voltaire on our side? He put it this way:

> Loss of your subjunctive is the loss of your civilisation!

A trifle over the top perhaps, but mere intelligibility is simply not good enough.

Bad language often buries meaning. A friend who does some work for a consortium of universities was presented with this proposition:

> The participants are increasingly identifying the need for radical change which weaves together renewed attention to a vision of citizenship for all, direct engagement with people using support and the major shift in culture required to ensure delivery prioritises person-centred support and connections to the wider community.

He had not the slightest idea what it meant – or, at least, he couldn't be bothered to work it out. If you make the effort you can just about discern a meaning, but why should we have to? Professor Crystal would say that if it's intelligible it's OK; I'd say that if it becomes so only through the sort of struggle that makes bashing your head against a wall seem pleasant, it isn't.

A vicar told me about his years as the chairman of his local residents' association. He was, as he put it, 'showered with bumph from the local council'. Most of it was written in extraordinary officialese. Not wishing to let them get away with it, he demanded simple translations even when he didn't really need them. For example, he had asked what was meant by 'low-profile landscape'. He was told it meant 'flat'. Well, of course it did, and of course he knew that, but he made a fuss about it for the best possible reason. If officials on your local council don't use the same language as you do, the impression comes across that they don't share your world and they don't want you to share theirs. Or, as the vicar put it:

> The danger is that bodies like governments and councils will get away with murder simply because they have wrapped up what they are doing in special language.

'Or careless language', he might have added. A woman whose father had recently died told me about the letter she received from a firm of solicitors:

> With regard to the estate of your diseased father . . .

It reminded me of the epitaph Spike Milligan said he wanted on his gravestone: 'I told you I was ill.' But it's funny only if it happens to someone else. You have to wonder what's going on when a firm of lawyers – the very profession whose use of language must be precise – can do something quite so idiotic and unthinking.

29

You wonder if they realise that a real, vulnerable human being is at the other end of their pathetic attempt at communication.

So, with great respect to Professor Crystal, intelligibility is not the only criterion by which our common language should be judged. It should also make us feel at home in a shared world and not alienated from those with whom we are supposed to be sharing it.

But there are good reasons to wonder whether, in the way we communicate with each other, we do still share a common world and, if so, how long we shall go on doing so. Some interesting new phrases are entering the language, which take us into a different world: 'digital native' and 'digital immigrant'. The immigrants are people like me, no longer in the first flush of youth, who have not so much embraced the digital age as accepted its inevitability and tried to learn as much as they need to cope. The natives probably learned to use a mouse before they could read a sentence and simply cannot imagine life without the ability to send text messages or join in conversations in cyberspace.

Some of them will speak a language that is incomprehensible to the other half of the population. Students and children at school will engage in 'wiki-thinking', which means exchanging ideas through digital networks. It derives from the Internet encyclopedia called Wikipedia, which has been built up not from the knowledge of individual academics and experts but the collective knowledge of thousands of contributors. Some of it is rubbish. Much of it will add to the sum of human knowledge.

Richard Woods wrote a thoughtful piece in the *Sunday Times* about the impact of this generational divide between the immigrants and the natives. I'm interested in its effect on language. Dr Anders Sandberg, who is researching cognitive enhancement at Oxford University, told Woods that anecdotal evidence suggests people are becoming more visual than verbal. He said some people are claiming that 'once computers gain good language understanding and we can speak to them, then reading and writing are going to seem cumbersome'.

That is an alarming prospect. Visual images are often more powerful than the same things described in words. I doubt that any of us will ever forget the pictures of the Twin Towers crashing to the ground. Photographs of a child starving to death or a mutilated body lying in the rubble arouse us to the heights of pity or anger.

But what the pictures cannot do is express the complexity that might help us understand why these terrible things are happening. Only words can do that. A world that depends more on images and dismisses reading and writing as 'cumbersome' will be a much cruder and probably an even more dangerous place. I hope I never see it.

Happily, it's not here yet. Until it is, language is what we'll continue to use to negotiate our way around our shared world – for better or worse. Let me give you an example of the worse. In the course of a year I get hundreds of requests for help from 'media study' students. I try to resist telling them that many (if not most) 'media' degrees are about as much practical use as a cat-flap on a submarine and I do what I can to help. But this particular email strained my courtesy to its limits. I reproduce it exactly as I received it:

Dear Mr Humpreys,

I am a 3rd year student of Politics and Communications at the University of Liverpool. I'm am currently writing my final year dissertation on the future of UK PSB. My specific research question is:

'Is the notion of universal public service broadcasting provision, institutionalized around traditional mainstream broadcasters, an obsolete one in the multi-channel media era?'

I was hoping you may be interested in offering a few comments for the 1st chapter which consider's whether UK broadcasting is seeing a return to 'the golden age' of television by way of programme variety and content. I am argueing that there is a return to that level of provision and that quality and range-while not perfect is getting better, particularly so across the BBC but is limited elsewhere, you may agree or disagree. As a senior broadcaster and vocal commentator on broadcasting issues, i feel you could offer some valuable general observations of the current broadcasting landscape on the topic of provision by PSB's – these would be of immense value to my dissertation if you could spare a couple of mins to share your thoughts. Of course i would happy to provide you with a couple of the final dissertation as a show of my appreciation.

Thankyou for your time,

I look forward to hearing from you,

Best wishes

I shall spare the young man's blushes by not printing his name but it raises a number of questions. The most obvious is how someone who is barely literate might seriously believe he has a career in a trade that requires him to write the odd sentence.

Another obvious one is how he has managed to get to the third year at university without being sent off on some sort of remedial course. It is a sad commentary on the state of English teaching in schools that most universities now offer such courses. The Oxford University Press has just published a new dictionary for students in response to lecturers' complaints that they're forced to waste time correcting basic errors of grammar. The dictionary's editor Catherine Soames says: 'Ideally it should have been learned at school but often it is not, so we are helping students redress the balance.'

The other question is how the young man made it to the third year without being advised to consider another course. I suppose the answer to that one is simple enough: universities need students to cover their costs and who cares if they waste three years of their young lives when they might be doing something to which they are better suited? Or maybe that's too cynical.

Or maybe it was *he* who didn't care. That may explain why he did not even bother to check how my name is spelled or pick up any of the howlers (I gave up counting when I got to twenty) in his email. Maybe he was listening to his iPod or chatting to his girlfriend as he typed it. Or maybe – and this is too depressing to contemplate – he simply didn't know. If that is the case, I suppose one must feel sorry for him.

Soon after I heard from the student, the Royal Literary Fund published a report about the state of literacy among British undergraduates. In 1999 the RLF had sent professional writers as RLF fellows into universities and colleges to help students with the basic skills of writing essays and the like. The report was a compilation of their accounts of what they had found. The biographer Hilary Spurling, the chairman of the scheme, wrote:

The individual accounts read like dispatches from a front line where students struggle to survive without basic training or equipment.

One of the recurrent themes of the report is the confusion, embarrassment and fear endured by students who find themselves confronted with written assignments they don't understand and can't begin to tackle. The inability to write, based on lack of preparation and practice, destroys young people's confidence.

'Anxiety is at the heart of many of the problems students experience with their writing,' reports one of our writers. 'Some of them have not been asked to write an essay or its equivalent for years, and few have ever been told how to do it in the first place.'

She concluded:

Learning to write is no longer a purely academic issue. It is a question of our social, economic and cultural future. What began as a private scheme devised primarily for the benefit of writers has exposed a public catastrophe.

I hope the RLF report was read very carefully indeed by all those academics and English 'experts' who say intelligibility is the only criterion and that grammar doesn't matter so long as we can understand what is being communicated. It's perfectly true that I understood (just about) what my emailing friend required of me, though it took a little more effort than it should have done. But that misses the point. All those people who have written to me about the value of what they regard as decent English cannot be dismissed as a bunch of cranks living in the past. They are not saying the language must never change, must always remain as they remember it in some mythical golden age. They know it must adapt to changing times as it always has. But they do not want to feel alienated in the public space that, at some time or another, we all occupy. They are entitled not to be offended by semi-literate rubbish.

And what of my student? I suppose he's well into his dissertation by now – but he's doing it without my help. Perhaps I should feel guilty. Maybe it's not his fault that he can't spell or use punctuation. Maybe his teachers let him down. Or maybe the teachers themselves were let down. I have had many letters over the years from teachers who say they themselves were never taught the basics. So why, to pursue this to the bitter end, were the failings of the teachers not spotted? We do, after all, have a system of inspection.

Ah, but that assumes the inspectors themselves were capable of spotting their failings. Allow me to introduce you to a little booklet produced by Ofsted, the body responsible for inspecting the nation's schools and trying to ensure that our children get a decent education. It is twenty-two pages long and entitled *Guide to Ofsted's House Style*. Among those who received it were the school inspectors. We all know about them. Most of us can recall at least one morning in school when the teacher was reduced to a nervous, stuttering wreck because a stranger had come into the classroom and had sat quietly at the back watching and listening. It was the dreaded inspector, the Grim Reaper himself, scourge of incompetent teachers throughout the land. These were the men (almost always men in those unenlightened times) who sat in judgement because they were the People Who Know Everything. Their word was law. Now even *they* are deemed to be in need of a little help when it comes to writing.

When I asked Ofsted about the guide, they told me it is to help people (including the school inspectors) write their reports 'in a clear and consistent style so that readers can readily understand their content'. Fair enough. Nobody's perfect. But let me give you a flavour of the content. Here's part of what it says about apostrophes. They are not to be used to indicate plurals but to . . .

> . . . indicate possession . . . Note the difference be-tween 'its' and 'it's'. The former is a possessive pronoun and does not take an apostrophe. The latter is the contraction of the words 'it is' or 'it has' and does take an apostrophe.

37

And here are some examples of apostrophe use that Professor Crystal presumably would think even Ofsted inspectors need not worry their little heads about:

'The children's books' (The children own the books.)

'The ladies' cloakroom' (The ladies use the cloakroom.)

'The women's singles tournament' (The tournament is played by the women.)

There is help, too, when it comes to confusion over when to use 'I' and when to use 'me' or 'myself'.

Use 'I' if you are doing the action of the verb (for example, the speaking in 'I spoke to him'). Confusion can arise when there is more than one person doing the action ('Claire and I spoke to him') or having the action done to them ('He spoke to Claire and me'). If you are unsure which is correct try removing the extra person from the sentence. 'He spoke to I' is obviously wrong.

Who can argue with any of that? The great Fowler himself could not have put it better. It's just the sort of stuff I hope my little boy will be taught over the next few years. But that's the point. He is barely six years old. Shouldn't we assume that the people who run our schools inspection system already know all this? Ofsted insisted this was not aimed at teaching basic grammar to inspectors, oh dear me no. It was aimed at all Ofsted people and is intended, as its title suggests, to 'provide guidance about stylistic conventions . . . to help ensure all Ofsted and other publications or reports adhere to a clear and consistent style'. I was told this was similar to a newspaper's style guide and that, it seems, makes all the difference.

Well, I'm afraid it doesn't. Grammar is not style and style is not grammar. Style is about whether you capitalise certain words or indent paragraphs or use single or double quotation marks and a thousand other stylistic things. It is NOT about the basic rules of grammar. Yet it is those very rules that Ofsted seems to be having to teach its own inspectors.

Of course, it is possible to make a case that in a changing language we shouldn't talk about anything as forbidding as 'rules'. A. A. Gill, the brilliant television critic of the *Sunday Times*, says there were never any rules, only conventions and habits. Fair enough: I don't need to go to the stake in defence of 'rules' rather than 'conventions'. But people who press this point then leap to the claim that anything goes. Here's how Gill put it in the course of writing a typically robust attack on a BBC programme *Never Mind the Full Stops* presented by the writer Julian Fellowes.

> Nobody speaks better English than you do, whatever they say or however they say it. The language doesn't belong to Lynne Truss, Julian Fellowes, Fowler, the BBC or the Queen. It belongs to everyone who has something interesting to say.

Notice something about that little extract? Yes, Gill has observed the rules (sorry, conventions). The punctuation is in the right place and the syntax would satisfy the most pedantic critic. It is one of the many reasons why his writing is so easy to read. Even if, as he says, it has nothing to do with rules, only convention and habit, an interesting question arises. Gill, like most good journalists, is an iconoclast, always challenging conventions and habits. So why does he not do so when he's writing? Because he knows language is at its best when there is no room for ambiguity and misunderstanding, when it is clear and simple and direct. Which is, of course, precisely why we have the rules, the conventions and the habits. And long may they be observed.

I am left with the impression that writers such as A. A. Gill and experts such as David Crystal are rather like people with a lot of money. They take it for granted, cannot imagine what it must be like not to have it so don't bother themselves with thinking about those who have none. For 'money' read 'knowledge of how to use language properly'. They have that knowledge and use it effortlessly, with style. But those who don't have it struggle. And our common, shared world is the poorer because they do.

So my conclusion? Bring back grammar! And then we can all understand what is going on in our world.

CHAPTER TWO

The Legion of Little Lies

One of the nice things about knowing someone who's famous is being able to compare the public perception with the private man. John Simpson has won every award worth winning and I've no doubt the public perception of him is that he's brave, authoritative, intelligent and everything else that's needed to become the finest foreign correspondent of his generation. And all of that is true. But I've known John for thirty years – he's one of my closest friends – and there's something about him that most people probably don't know. We worked together in South Africa during the ghastly apartheid era and in Rhodesia during the final years of the guerrilla war, and one of the things that helped keep me sane was his sense of humour. Unlikely as it might seem when you watch him analysing the latest foreign crisis on television, John would have made a good stand-up comedian. He'd be brilliant as one of those characters who assumes the guise of someone he despises and exaggerates it to the point of ridicule.

There are risks in this. We once had dinner in a Rhodesian restaurant with a reporter who'd come out from London a few days earlier. John began playing the part of a typical Rhodesian 'redneck' – one of those characters who had settled in the country because he rather liked the idea of having lots of black servants to boss around and expected the 'blicks' to treat him with respect for no better reason than the colour of his skin. It had become a form of escape mechanism for both of us. But the reporter didn't get the joke. Maybe we should have warned him. Anyway, after ten minutes or so he leaped to his feet and rushed out of the restaurant. When we got back to the hotel where we were all staying we found he'd checked out and was on his way to the airport, complaining bitterly to anyone who'd listen about how Simpson and Humphrys had 'gone native' and become more racist than the 'rednecks'. We were a bit more careful after that.

John also writes wonderfully funny letters. I remember one he sent me shortly after he'd returned to London to become political editor of the BBC. He loathed the job and tore into the politicians and his new colleagues with savage humour. So when I had another letter from him recently I was puzzled. It was written on the headed paper of Roehampton University. It began:

> I am very excited to have been appointed Chancellor of Roehampton University and hope you will be able to join me at a ceremony to celebrate my new role.

44

There was something odd about this. Not that the university should have chosen John for the job or that he should have taken it. Anyone who saw him in his burka in Afghanistan will know that he'd enjoy the dressing-up bit, and obviously he would bring great gravitas and authority to the role. No, it was the language. He would have been flattered to be asked – even honoured – but 'very excited'? This is the man who liberated Kabul, who's been shot at and blown up more times than a firing-range target, and was once attacked by 'friendly' American fighters in Iraq; he bears the scars to this day. This is the man who can't see a war without wanting to be a part of it. He's so used to living dangerously he even had another baby when he was in his sixties. So was he 'very excited' to be appointed to a ceremonial post that required him to hand out degrees once a year and chair the occasional meeting? I don't think so. This was how the letter ended:

> I do hope you will be able to join us for what I'm sure
> will be a fun event.

A 'fun event'! Did that mean there would be a tombola during the Latin oration and an egg-and-spoon race while all the mortar-boards were being doffed? Perhaps the vice chancellor was going to do a pole dance instead of the usual speech and the new graduates a spot of mud-wrestling. I doubt it. The more mundane explanation was that John had not written the letter at all. He had given the university a list of names while he was rushing off to another war and the letters were sent out on his behalf – which explains the hype.

I had another invitation that week – this time to a debate about libel law between lawyers and journalists. It said:

> Join us for a heated discussion when we will ask how far we can really go!

How did they *know* it was going to be 'heated', and did they assume no one would turn up if they'd merely promised it would be enlightening or helpful? Hype again.

Of course there has always been hype. It has been with us since the birth of the modern advertising and marketing industry: a low-level noise to which we have become so accustomed we pay it barely any attention. What is different now is that it has moved beyond the world of the hucksters who are obviously trying to sell us something and has become pervasive. Hence the use of hype in the academic world. It has also become so much more . . . well . . . hyper. Maybe that's inevitable. The more of it there is, the more we become inured to it and the higher they have to raise the bar. The supermarkets are the masters of the art – always trying to persuade us how thrilling it will be if we share our shopping experience with them. Note 'experience'. We don't go shopping any longer. We have an 'experience'. This is typical of supermarket hype:

Exciting changes to your Nectar card!

That's the promise from Sainsbury's contained in one of those irritating flyers that fall out of newspapers and utility bills. What can they possibly be offering that's so exciting? A chance to do your next big shop for free, maybe, or a case of vintage champagne with every purchase over a fiver? Or even a guarantee that you won't have to wait for more than an hour at the check-out unless you do your shopping at three a.m. on Sunday? Not exactly. All is revealed in the next paragraph:

Ever wished you could use your Nectar points in more than just one Sainsbury's store?

As it happens, I've wished for many things in my life. I could probably offer you a list of a hundred things right now – everything from world peace and an end to poverty to a really good pint of bitter. But if I ever gave it a thought – which I haven't – I suppose I assumed that a giant supermarket chain with computers powerful enough to map the human genome had probably already made it possible for me to use my points in more than one of their stores. That's assuming I had any points in the first place – which I haven't because my local market and corner shops supply everything I need and (whisper it quietly) often more cheaply. This sort of thing gives hype a bad name.

I know a man who works in the furniture business

47

(strictly upmarket stuff) and once allowed a Sunday colour supplement to do a feature on his loft apartment. Incidentally, it seems that 'apartment' has finally taken over from 'flat'; I fancy they'll soon have 'closets' rather than wardrobes. Anyway, he'd done a big conversion job on the loft and he thought the story might drum up some business for him. How naïve. When he opened the magazine he discovered that his rather elegant home had become a 'House of Fun'. Worse, the strapline read that he had

turned a morgue into a space that knows how to party.

This puzzled him a bit – partly because he couldn't quite picture a partying flat, but also because he hadn't had a party there for four years. And that had been a pretty sedate affair. Hype again. Or maybe it was just a bit of creative imagination. Isn't that what writers must do if they are to have any impact?

Well, it depends on the writer. Here's a job advertisement that appeared in the spring of 2006. The bold heading read:

Create the Words to Communicate Britain's Health Policy

The job was as Patricia Hewitt's speechwriter. It may seem a touch pedantic to complain that a speechwriter does not 'create' words but uses existing ones to create a speech, but the phrase 'create the words' needs looking at. It implies that the words will not have the usual relationship to what they're supposed to describe. In other words, what is really needed is the ability to hype. It goes on:

> In this pivotal role, you will draft speeches for the Secretary of State . . .

'Pivotal' is a wonderful word and itself is full of hype. It suggests the world revolves around you, that nothing can happen unless you are at the centre of things. That the word 'pivotal' brings to mind spin is surely coincidental. And there was more:

> Demonstrable ability to craft lucid, coherent and persuasive speeches for senior politicians is crucial, tailored to the needs of differing audiences at high profile conferences, set pieces, lectures, seminars, debates and other significant occasions.

Let's pass over the bad English (is it the 'ability' or the 'speeches' that must be tailored?) and consider how many buzz-words employed in the services of hype are in that short paragraph. 'Crucial'. 'High profile'. 'Significant occasions'. But the phrase I particularly liked was:

> tailored to the needs

'Tailored' is a fine, relatively recent hype word conveying a sense of the meticulous, the personal, the pin in the mouth to make sure it all fits quite perfectly. No ordinary, straightforward, off-the-peg speeches for the Secretary of State. And what's this about the 'needs of differing audiences'? I wonder if anyone ever 'needs' a speech. Try to imagine them leaving the hall after an hour of Mrs Hewitt or any other politician and saying: 'By God, I needed that!' They may have appreciated it or even enjoyed it. They may have hated it. But did they 'need' it? I very much doubt it. The 'needs', of course, are those of the boss.

But for me the Big Daddy in the advertisement is the use of the word 'craft'. It transports us to the world of sawdust-strewn workshops and gnarled old artisans chiselling and sawing away, creating beautiful pieces of furniture using skills handed down over the generations. The work of a real craftsman speaks for itself – no hype needed.

Oddly enough, that's not quite how I picture politicians' speechwriters at work. Not that I'd go as far as George Orwell, who once wrote that political language 'is designed to make lies sound truthful and murder respectable and to give an appearance of solidity to pure wind'. It's hard not to imagine that the word 'crafty' was floating around in the mind of the person who put 'craft' in the advertising copy.

There is at least one word in the advertisement that means what it says and says what it means: 'persuasive'. Indeed, persuasion is the only 'skill' that's truly essential. If the politician is able to persuade the audience, the mission has been accomplished.

I suppose the job vacancy was filled pretty quickly. Certainly it paid well: £56,543 for an eighteen-hour week. Speech-writing doesn't come cheap, which is fair enough if it plays an important part in conveying politicians' arguments and giving us a better understanding of what they are trying to do on our behalf. But audiences, in my experience, have an unerring ability to sniff out hype and spot when a speech they are listening to has been written by someone other than the person who's delivering it. And they don't like it. They want to feel that the politician has been speaking from the heart, rather than faithfully regurgitating the words of a civil servant or highly paid adviser. Sounds obvious, but it's remarkable how many politicians go through the motions of delivering a speech even though they know they're probably more likely to be alienating their audience than persuading them.

The language of hype does not come with a big flashing sign saying, 'Hi, sucker!' Its vocabulary is limited to remarkably few familiar words: 'brilliant'; 'exciting'; 'fun'; 'simple'. But the users of hype need to be careful. Some of their words can be seriously dangerous. Take, for example, a favourite of theirs: 'perfect'. We stopped being perfect around the time when Eve picked the apple and started coming on to Adam. That has not stopped some NHS hospitals signing up to a scheme called 'Pursuing Perfection'.

One found itself in the headlines because it could not afford to pay enough porters and the bodies of patients who had died during the night were being left in their beds because there was no one to take them to the mortuary.

Among the most cherished words in the lexicon of hype is 'great'. If you took 'great' away from your average hypester, it would be like snatching a life-belt from a drowning man. Try flicking through one of those wretched advertising inserts next time and count how often it's used. But sometimes this tediously overused adjective finds itself attached to some very strange words. Try this, for example:

> We'd like to say to people: 'We're warm and breath-
> ing. We've got great product. Come and have a look.'

Those are the words of Stuart Rose, one of the best retailers in the business. He's the man who took over Marks & Spencer when it was on its knees and put it back on its feet. But 'great product'? Great knickers maybe, or great skirts, or even great fishcakes, but has anyone in the real world ever, ever said to anyone else, 'I really must nip into M&S. I'm told they've got great product'? And it's not as if Mr Rose is one of those executives who seems to be incapable of speaking a language we all understand. Here's how he described a disastrous revamp of the big M&S store in Birmingham:

'We screwed up big time. We pissed off a lot of customers.'

Not, perhaps, the language he might use in polite company, but it doesn't half tell it like it is. And I'd imagine that anyone who'd had an unhappy experience in the Birmingham store would greatly appreciate a bit of plain speaking. But plain speaking is to hype what garlic is to Dracula. I enjoyed (in a masochistic sort of way) the questionnaire on a Virgin train that came with the menu. It assured me, as these things invariably do, that Virgin were 'constantly seeking' to improve the service. The reason it wanted my 'feedback' was . . .

. . . so that we can ensure that we are meeting your needs, and exceeding your expectations.

Do people who write this stuff ever read their own words? If they are constantly seeking to exceed my expectations we're going to find ourselves in a gastronomic race in which they'll soon be having to serve me larks' tongues in aspic to stop me suing them for false trading. But even in the midst of such mindless hype, language can bring us down to reality with a thud. The menu itself was

. . . recommended for customers on shorter journeys, and for those who do not want to be interrupted as all components will be delivered at the same time.

53

Whatever happened to 'courses'? I've never thought of eating 'components'. We're back in the world of 'product'. But let's be charitable – if not sympathetic. After all, the menu was signed by the managing director, one Charles Belcher. You think he eats his own 'components' too quickly?

It's nice, though, isn't it, knowing that all these hotshot executives feel so close to their customers? A letter I received from BT was signed 'Kind regards'. True, it wasn't actually addressed to me (or anyone else for that matter) but it's the thought that counts. And it's good that they are so 'committed'. That's another favourite hype word. This letter began:

> At BT, we are committed to providing great value for all our customers, by constantly developing innovative new products and delivering high quality services.

'Great value', eh? Sounds good. A few quid off the next bill never comes amiss. But here's how my new friend at BT went on:

> To continue to do this, it's occasionally necessary to raise some of our prices a little.

Ah, I see. 'Great value', in this Lewis Carroll world, means higher prices. But what about these 'innovative new products'? I assumed that in the fast-moving world of telecoms that meant at least, say, better phones with batteries that lasted longer or little headsets you could wear when you were wandering around the house chatting on your cordless phone. This is what they mean:

> Customers on BT Together Option 2 or 3 can now benefit from savings. By signing up to a 12 month contract, you save £33 (£5.50 a month – that's half the price of BT Together Option 1 line rental £11**). So you pay only £11** for Option 2 (usually £16.50**), or £20** for Option 3 (usually £25.50**), for the first six months.

I'll spare you the detail of the asterisks just as I spared myself. It is entirely possible that, buried somewhere in that impenetrable paragraph, is a deal that really would 'meet my needs'. But I shall never find out because life is simply too short to spend precious hours trying to work it out. Sooner or later one loses the will to live. I feel the same about all those terribly tempting offers to buy my electricity and gas from somebody else. I managed to pass maths at O level half a century ago, but only just.

You need much more than an ancient maths O level to deal with train fares. I've just been listening to a man from the Association of Train Operating Companies trying to justify the ludicrous complexity of them. Twenty years ago there were five types of ticket on sale. Now the National Fares Manual lists more than seventy fares governed by 776 'validity' conditions. The result is that no one (with the possible exception of the people who run the railways) can make head or tail of them. Certainly not the passengers – or 'customers', as we must now be described. Yet the man from the ATOC insisted over and over again that the fares really do 'suit the needs' (that word again) of the passengers because so many people travel by train. Well, of *course* they do! They *need* to get to work.

It is vaguely reassuring to know that I am not alone in finding all this choice so off-putting, so alien to my real needs. Whole companies exist to help us, the wretched 'consumers', decide which supplier provides the best value for money. Wouldn't it be wonderful if the rail companies, the telecom operators and the energy suppliers threw all their 'innovative new products' in the bin and came up with something simple. Imagine if they were to say to us: 'Here's what it will cost you for every mile you travel / every unit of electricity you use / every minute you're on the phone.' Obviously we would pay more in peak times; we have always done so and we know why it's necessary. But if it were to be simplified, we'd be able to understand what we were being offered and we could make informed choices. Of course, that will never happen and the reason lies in one word. Hype.

Hype is everywhere. It has even infiltrated what I still think of as the musty offices of HM Customs & Revenue (the Inland Revenue in old money). They

decided recently they needed a new marketing manager to 'build the campaigns that build our image'.
You may wonder why. However you wrap it up, what
the taxman does is take money from us. Nothing
wrong with that. We may not enjoy paying tax but
we know it's necessary. It may occur to you that the
money they spend on marketing is our money and the
more they spend, the more they have to take from us,
but here's the bit of hype I liked: HM Revenue is

> . . . working with the largest customer base of any
> UK organisation.

Well, yes, they would be, wouldn't they? For the very
simple reason that we have no choice. If we choose not
to be their 'customer' there's absolutely nothing we
can do about it. So why make such a daft boast? You
know the answer.

There was a time when hype was the job of the
company's marketing department. Sadly, it is now
required of everyone: the bank manager; the hospital
chief executive; the head teacher; the airline pilot. Yes,
the airline pilot. Here we are, locked into a metal tube
hurtling through the air at 550 mph at 33,000 feet,
aware that it's so cold outside we'll be dead in ten
seconds if a window falls out, worrying whether that
shifty bloke in the row in front has a bomb in his shoe,
and we're invited to 'sit back, relax and enjoy ourselves' because

'Looking after you today we have a GREAT team!'

That presumably means that the team yesterday was rubbish. There does seem to have been a slight variation in airline language recently. Instead of 'enjoying the flight' we are often enjoined to enjoy 'the service'. Now, this is seriously perverse. It may be possible to enjoy the service if you had turned left when you boarded the plane and your only problem is which claret to select with your meal before turning your seat into a comfortable bed, but not if you are in cattle class becoming increasingly annoyed by all those stupid announcements telling you to enjoy yourself.

Especially annoying is the one that says they're about to try to flog you duty-free goods, which you will already have bought at the airport or will buy in the local market when you arrive at your foreign destination. Not that they put it like that. Instead they tell you that 'passing down the aisle' is what I have heard called an 'in-flight retail facilitator'.

Goebbels said that if you repeat a big lie often enough it becomes the truth. The sort of stuff I've been sounding off about is not made up of big lies. Hype doesn't work like that. It's about a legion of little ones. The insidious thing about hype is not so much that it pretends that something is what it's not.

It's rather that the sheer pervasiveness of the language of hype does indeed 're-create' what is around us so that we get used to seeing it in its terms. Hype may often seem just funny, even preposterous. But it colours a large part of the world we're living in and, for all its crudeness, subtly changes its nature.

CHAPTER THREE

Are You Shopping Comfortably?

In theory, one of the nice things about being on the radio and television is that you get lots of invitations to parties. I say 'in theory' because I can't quite see the fun in standing around for two hours drinking mediocre wine and spending exactly four and a half minutes talking to a succession of people whose names you can't remember. After four and a half minutes – at the precise point when you think you're about to remember the name and the conversation begins to get interesting – someone else comes along (whose name you also can't remember), chips in and you have to talk to them. There is sometimes a variation on this theme. This involves talking to someone who is so famous you really *do* know him, but who obviously finds you insufficiently famous to justify wasting his time and spends the four and a half minutes looking over your shoulder, hoping to find someone more important.

It is one of the mysteries of modern life that so many organisations waste so much time and money staging these grisly events, even though nobody ever admits to enjoying them but thinks they should 'put in an appearance'. Which takes me to the other nice thing about presenting a breakfast programme. It means you can turn down the invitations on the basis that you have to get up too early. So you get invited, which is nice because it makes you feel important and loved, but you don't have to go and can stay at home with a good book, which is even nicer – and you don't offend anyone. Perfect, really.

I had an invitation the other day to something that looked as if it might be reasonably interesting. It was an 'AWARENESS EVENT!'. These things always have capital letters and exclamation marks. How else would we know they were exciting? But I'd never been to an 'awareness event' before so I read on. It sounded pretty good. There was even a reward for going: two free plane tickets to a pleasant part of Spain with overnight accommodation thrown in. Yes, you've guessed, they were trying to flog me a time-share development. Obviously there's nothing new in hyping these things. Time-share hucksters get such a bad press – usually for very good reasons – that they need to keep coming up with something new to get us hooked. But why did they call it an 'awareness event'? If it had to be an 'event' at all, why couldn't it be an 'information event'?

Answer: because their marketing department would have told anyone who came up with such a boring, straightforward suggestion that they really had to start thinking outside the box, have a little imagination, jazz it up a bit. Information is dreary. It sounds so formal and serious. Also, give people information and they get picky: they start asking awkward questions. You don't want that. You want to flatter the punters a bit: any old fool can handle information – but 'awareness'? That's for a special kind of person. And awareness is not something you pick apart, it's something you just, like, accept and respect. Know what I'm saying?

I'm sorry to lurch into *faux*-American but I find it difficult to come across the word 'awareness' used in this way without imagining a bunch of Californians sitting around for hours talking in a monotone, never saying a word that might be even faintly politically incorrect, nodding in sympathetic understanding at everything and never once collapsing into giggles at the absurdity of it all.

Used in this way, the word changes direction by 180 degrees. Instead of referring to an awareness *of* something, it turns right round, ignores what's out there and concentrates on the person doing the aware-ing, so to speak. Awareness is all about an inner state.

It's rather like the word 'enjoy'. You're sitting in a restaurant, the waitress brings your meal and, with a sweet smile, says, 'Enjoy!' I want to say: 'Don't you know that "enjoy" is a transitive not an intransitive verb? You should say, "Enjoy it!" not "Enjoy!". Whatever do they teach in Polish schools, these days?'

As with 'awareness', the new, fashionable 'enjoy' makes our own experience, rather than the meal, the centre of attention. The message is clear. In a world of 'enjoy' and 'awareness' (rather than information), inner personal experience is what we must be thinking about – rather than what's out there.

But that's only right. Remember, all we're here for is to shop.

> 'Now, when I go out and buy a pair of trainers, they are not only cool, but some of the profits are going to raise awareness.'

That curious sentence came from the luscious lips of the actress Scarlett Johansson. She was talking about RED – capital letters again, I'm afraid, but that's how it's spelled. Bono, the singer who is famous enough to wear sunglasses indoors without everyone laughing at him, is the inspiration behind RED. You may remember him talking about it at the Live 8 concert in the summer of 2005. He got a group of companies together to sell some of their products under the RED label. Ms Johansson didn't get it quite right. The profits are not spent on raising awareness but will go into the Global Fund, which fights TB, Aids and malaria in Africa. And a very good thing too. But without wishing to be curmudgeonly about this, 'awareness' (in the old-fashioned sense of the word) doesn't appear to have an awful lot to do with it. Ms Johansson again:

'It's an available way of helping others, especially when you're doing something that's kind of mindless, like shopping. You don't have to write a cheque or travel to Africa to contribute, you can help out in your daily routine.'

It's true we can't all go to Africa to see what's happening for ourselves, but somehow the 'daily routine' of flashing our American Express RED card doesn't strike me as being very likely to increase our awareness of what's going on in the dark continent. And if it's *instead* of 'having to write a cheque' every now and then, it could be said to have the opposite effect. Here's how American Express put it in full-page newspaper advertisements:

Can desire ever have a virtuous side?
    Or, does popular theory prevail that it can only exist in spite of virtue? RED flies in the face of popular theory and believes Desire can be Virtuous. That's why we created the American Express RED card.

Let us resist the temptation to think ignoble thoughts here and put behind us any suggestion that American Express might see some commercial advantage in proclaiming its virtuous side. Anything that raises money for such a worthwhile cause must be a good thing. What's fascinating is the notion that desire – or 'spoiling yourself', as the advertisement puts it –

can be virtuous. Maybe Ms Johansson got it right. After all, an 'awareness' is being created – the awareness that we are truly virtuous people and can demonstrate it to ourselves without actually having to make the slightest sacrifice. Virtue does indeed have its own reward if we can prove we are charitable without making any effort and without it costing us a bean. This is how the article about RED in a Sunday supplement put it:

. . . the shopping revolution that's good for the soul.

It turns out that this shopping revolution (or 'conscience consumerism', as it's also called) is not so much about awareness of the world out there as about the soul in you. And, it hardly needs adding, what's meant by 'good for the soul', these days, is no more and no less than feeling good about yourself. Feelgood is salvation and the daily routine of tending to the soul is not saying a few Hail Marys or writing out a cheque for charity but, well, shopping. You could call it the New Awareness. Enjoy!

To return to the point about capital letters, it's a couple of centuries since nouns in the English language were routinely capitalised – not that anyone seems to have told American Express. But mostly we do the opposite now. It seems obligatory for 'rebranded' companies to have their name in lower case. Publicity material often gives lower-case letters to words in sentences that scream out for a capital. This is the title of an introductory brochure to LA Fitness gyms in London:

welcome! To your LA Journey

This is positively perverse. If ever a word demanded a capital it's that 'welcome!'. It cannot be an accident – the writer's finger slipping off the shift key – because someone would have noticed, wouldn't they? Perhaps one day a learned academic will construct an elegant theory around this sort of thing. My own view is that life's too short. I shall punish them by not joining an LA Fitness gym – which is not a massive sacrifice, given that I have never been much attracted to the smell of stale sweat, the sound of endless TV monitors blasting out hideous music and the sight of muscle-bound men showing off with those funny wide belts around their rippling stomachs. A trot around my local park suits me very nicely, thank you.

'Journey', you will have noticed, does have a capital letter. It's another of those gooey words like 'awareness'. It has an obvious physical meaning and, if you happen to be into this sort of thing, a metaphysical one too: life as a journey, the soul struggling along a path to . . . who knows where? There's another thesis to be written on that, but possibly not the sort of thing the gym people had in mind. For most people the gym 'journey' is a brief one. At approximately midday on 1

January they read the lifestyle articles in the news-papers, contemplate the amount of food and booze they have managed to consume over the past ten days and the effect it has had on their flabby bodies, and sign up at a gym. Some of them might even go more than once. But not many. It usually turns out to be a very short journey indeed.

But even more interesting than 'Journey' in the brochure title is the word 'your'. This little fellow is elbowing his way into everything, an insistent reminder of how things have changed. Where the world once consisted of lots of different things, free-standing and independent and among which 'you' were just one in six billion, now everything is presented as though it were just an extension of you, existing only as part of 'your personal experience'. Ms Johansson teaches us that. Marks & Spencer may have 'great product' but it also has a newish slogan:

Your M&S

It is disarmingly simple and it is untrue. M&S does not belong to the customers: it belongs to the share-holders. As the writer Lucy Kellaway points out, it 'implies that the product or service has been specially designed just for you personally'. It hasn't. The stuff is mass-produced for a mass market and the business – like almost every other large business around the world – is becoming less and less personal. Products are 'increasingly global and customer service is conducted via voicemail – or by a worker in India reading from a prompt sheet'. The splendid Ms Kellaway, incidentally, writes for the *Financial Times* – or rather, as it has taken to describing itself, 'Your *FT*'.

Words such as 'you' and 'yours' create a virtual reality that is very convenient for those who use them. They blur the edges of that awkward little space between two distinct players: the company and the customer. It is in this space that difficult questions get asked and conflict might break out. That danger is reduced if we are told: 'Look, it's not ours or someone else's. It's YOURS.' As the 'new awareness' tells us, 'you' are the central reference point of modern life, so why should you question what 'we' do on your behalf?

What all this concentration on 'you' is doing is reversing the Copernican revolution. You'll remember that Copernicus pointed out that the Earth wasn't the centre of the universe; it was just a planet orbiting the sun. And we now know there are billions of such suns, which makes us humans, perched on one little planet, pretty insignificant in the scheme of things. But that's not how we are encouraged to see matters any more. The new geography of the universe has You at the centre of it and around You is a comfort zone in which You should feel good about Yourself.

Advertising peddles this line all the time.

There's an advertisement for Italian furniture with a picture of a beautiful young couple relaxing in their elegant living room. The woman is stretched out on the sofa, the man squatting beside her, pouring tea into cups on a low table. The words over the picture read:

Comfort. Around You. Within You.

That's as good a definition as you will get of the comfort zone: we are encouraged to believe that the world should be exclusively for us. An inner sense of feeling comfortable about ourselves stretches out into the physical space we occupy. It may make you want to pour the hot tea down the front of the man's trousers and snap: 'Still feeling comfort within you?' But that would just show you are not keeping up with the times – which is similar to the feeling I have when politicians or their little helpers use such crass language.

The word 'comfortable' has had its own interesting career recently. At some point in the last couple of years – it's always hard to be specific in these cases – politicians and public servants started to be 'comfortable' with things. Usually it's a spin doctor or PR type who will tell you that the boss is 'comfortable' with this or that decision. It's a troubling phrase. It implies that the politician's peace of mind is what really matters – rather than whether the decision was right or wrong. It probably came from the United States and invites that curious Californian response again: the head nodding very slowly and a long-drawn-out 'riiiight'. It also invites a smart slap. Keeping democracy going is quite difficult in a 'comfort zone'.

But, not for the first time, we must turn to the world of showbiz and celebrities to take us a step further. The singer Cher decided to sell off some old junk – actually some pretty valuable stuff, including decent paintings and ballgowns that she'd had for years. You or I might have called it a 'clearout'. She called it

'rewriting my personal environment'

I imagine it remains quite comfortable.

Some of you, though, may require some guidance about how to make your life's comfort zone yet more comfortable. In that case what you need is 'Life Coaching'. I saw an advertisement for 'complimentary' life coaching, no less, which read:

An Executive Life coach can truly be, do or have anything you want. Unlock your potential!

Of course it was the execrable grammar that caught my attention but can it really be the case that just by hiring a coach I can 'be, do or have' anything I want?

If you are still not persuaded that, in our contemporary world, you really do sit at the centre of the universe in your very own comfort zone, able to command whatever you want, let me refer you to a higher authority, Noel Edmonds. His broadcasting career went through a lean patch when the gates of

Crinkly Bottom were finally slammed shut, but he was rescued by the startling success of *Deal or No Deal*. Let him who would cast the first stone at such a pointless use of television air time be prepared to admit that he has never been hooked by it!

Mr Edmonds is a formidable broadcaster but it seems he owes his success to more than his ability and a piece of inspired television scheduling. Cosmic ordering must be taken into the equation too – or, at least, he thinks so. It is all about asking the universe (the 'cosmos') for the things you want in life. This bizarre notion has been popularised by the writer Barbel Mohr, and her book, *The Cosmic Ordering Service*, has sold approximately a zillion copies. A modest lady, Ms Mohr, she even says that just by holding her book in your hand you have already 'changed your life'. Here's the pitch:

> Are you still waiting for your ship to come in? Looking for the relationship you can't seem to find? Working just to pay the bills until that perfect job comes along? Don't you wish that you could just place an order for the life you want? Well, Barbel Mohr says you can! And you don't have to chant, meditate, pray, fast, work, or do anything – just relax. And there won't be any bill to pay.

One of her many disciples in this country, Georgina Davies, told the *Daily Mail* that it works for her:

How you place an order is up to you, but rather than say 'I want more money', I imagined myself being rich. The next day my mother phoned and announced she wanted to pay for me to have a weekend away, I got a tax rebate of £700 and I also got two modelling jobs – all on the same day.

And no request is too trivial. Here's another believer, Heather Price:

From finding a parking space in a busy car park to landing the job of my dreams, cosmic ordering has brought many positive things into my life.

Including, it seems, her boyfriend:

Until then, I'd always gone for men I'd end up having unhealthy, possessive relationships with. I asked the cosmos to bring me a relationship in which we could both allow each other to be free and not make unrealistic demands on each other. I met my current boyfriend the week after making the order and we've been together for three years.

Georgina Davies ordered up her boyfriend too, but there must have been some crossed wires somewhere:

The only thing I asked for that didn't match was that he be called Jake – my favourite man's name. In fact he's called Pete, but I don't really think that's something to complain about. Cosmic ordering means I

73

never have to worry about anything, because it's given me an ability to trust that everything will work out exactly how I would like it to.

Hmm. I'm not sure Ms Davies was wise to accept a Pete when she wanted a Jake. He may well be a decent bloke, but it's the principle of the thing. Give 'em an inch and they'll take a mile. Next thing you know that cosmos crowd will want to be paid for the goods – even if they're defective.

I know it's easy to poke fun at all this (not that that's any reason we shouldn't) and I know there will always be people prepared to believe the moon is made of green cheese if a 'best-selling' book tells them so, but there's a serious point to be made. It's the notion that consumerism has finally taken over our way of understanding everything. The universe turns out to be a giant warehouse sitting somewhere out there, ready to supply all our needs without us having to make the slightest effort on our own behalf – not even a little prayer now and then. The cosmos as a just-in-time delivery service waiting to hear what we want perfectly fits the fiction of a comfort zone with ourselves and our appetites at its centre. It's all of a piece with the language of 'awareness' and 'journeys' and 'your' this and 'your' that and 'shopping revolutions' that are good for the soul.

But just in case I'm wrong, I've written out my own cosmic order and put it under my pillow. Well, you'd feel a fool if you didn't and it really worked, wouldn't you? So if you didn't hear me on the radio this morning it's probably because I'm a bit busy writing the acceptance speech for my Nobel Prize . . .

CHAPTER FOUR
Get a Lifestyle!

It's almost thirty years since I started presenting the *Nine O'Clock News* on BBC1. That was in the days when news studios did not resemble the inside of the Tardis just before take-off and newsreaders were not required to strut around the place looking like superannuated shop-walkers. My bosses assumed that the viewers were perfectly capable of following the news if it was read by someone sitting behind a desk instead of standing in front of vast screens, waving their arms a great deal and pointing at things. Nor did they much care what we wore. It's true that I was told to buy a new suit (even though the one I'd bought for my wedding fifteen years earlier was still perfectly good) but I never actually wore a suit on air – just the jacket. Since newsreaders were never seen below the waist, I tended to wear old jeans.

A few years ago a call came from Light Entertainment – known to everyone in the business as LE – asking me to present *Mastermind*. This is the glamorous bit of the BBC. If News is a fairly ropy (but reliable) old Ford, LE is a flashy Lamborghini. At LE they *do* care what you wear. And how. So I wasn't unduly surprised when, a few weeks before the first programme, I had a call from a young man in LE asking me if I'd spend the day with him shopping for new clothes. I needed, it seems, a 'makeover'. I would like to say that I resisted and that I pulled the same 'I've got a perfectly good suit' line from thirty years ago. But I didn't. When someone treats you like a star – which they most emphatically do not in News – it's difficult to resist. And, after a few muted protests, I loved it. I discovered what every woman knows from birth: clothes *do* make you feel different. If you march out on to the studio floor knowing that you're now in the entertainment business – even if *Mastermind* is at the serious end of it – it gives you a little boost to know that your clothes don't look as though they've come from a charity shop and your jacket could do with a visit to the dry cleaner's. I have even – possibly for the first time in my life – been complimented on my dress sense by one or two people below the age of thirty.

This is the relatively innocent aspect of the make-over culture. I use the word 'culture' because make-overs have taken over. Until relatively recently the word 'makeover' did not even appear in the dictionary – much less in the television schedules. Imagine the vast stretches of blank screen over the past few years if makeover shows had been removed. Everything gets one now. And the sinister truth behind them is that it's not just our houses or our wardrobes or our gardens that they are designed to change. It's us. It is *we* who need makeovers, who must be fashioned anew. Or, to use another word that has entered the dictionary only recently, it is our 'lifestyles' that need the makeover. And, as every student of modern culture knows, lifestyles are far more important than lives.

The shift is reflected in language. Sometimes you stumble across sentences that simply could not have been written twenty years ago. Here's one, from an upmarket newspaper:

> We like to connect with the values of the snowboarding lifestyle.

This bizarre sentence needs a bit of unpacking. Even those addicted to snowboarding may scratch their heads about why standing on a board and hurtling down a snow slope should constitute a lifestyle, as distinct from something you might just do every now and again. Even odder, why should such an activity, whether it constitutes a lifestyle or not, have 'values'? And what exactly are they? Honour? Loyalty? Frugality? Concern for others?

But perhaps the oddest bit of the sentence is the use of 'connect with' in relation to values. As I've always understood values, you might want to adopt them, or deplore them, or live by them, or preach them, but what has this timidly noncommittal phrase 'connect with' to do with values?

It might help to know who spoke the words: Anne Nenonen, the senior manager of global marketing at

Nokia, the mobile-phone company. She was explaining to the *Financial Times* how brands like hers seek out quirky action sports such as snowboarding and try to gain kudos with the punters by providing the sport with corporate sponsorship. Why the 'snowboarding lifestyle' should be important was explained by Casey Wasserman, the chairman and chief executive of Wasserman Media Group, who said of the snowboarders:

> 'This coveted and valuable audience with disposable income, a propensity to drink colas, energy drinks and bottled water, communicate using mobile devices, or wear fashionable shoes, shirts and shorts has become elusive.'

It makes them sound like a clandestine sect or, perhaps, a troop of rare baboons. You can picture David Attenborough spying on them from the undergrowth and whispering to the camera: 'This elusive animal with its extraordinary behaviour – so rarely seen outside its usual habitat of Notting Hill wine bars – gives us a fascinating glimpse into a world of which we know so little.' Once people are defined by their lifestyle they become what is known in the trade as a 'demographic'.

The snowboarding demographic, naturally enough, has its own values – or so the Wassermans of this world would have us believe. Except, of course, that in the real world values attach to life. When it's lifestyle we're talking about it's a different kettle of fish. As Joe Queenan, author of *Balsamic Dreams*, has put it:

> 'The measure of human success is no longer the life well lived but the lifestyle well lived.'

Lifestyle is a bit like football in the sense that it brings to mind that hoary old gag of Bill Shankly, the legendary manager of Liverpool, when he was asked about the game being a matter of life and death. 'No,' he said, 'it's more important than that.' Or maybe it's better represented by the young man in the jeweller's shop trying to buy his girlfriend the current must-have fashion accessory – a chain with a silver cross. He'd looked through dozens without finding what he wanted and the assistant asked what the problem was. 'Yeah, these are all right,' he said, 'but I really want one of them crosses with the little feller on.'

But there is no dodging the questions posed by Queenan's remark. What *is* the 'lifestyle well lived'? Ah, well, that depends on whether you're a 'civilian' – which is how Liz Hurley allegedly referred to those unfortunates who, unlike her, are not clothed in the mantle of celebrity. We should, perhaps, pass quickly over the fact that her celebrity is not exactly unrelated to her frequent appearances in public clothed in very little – most famously just a few scraps of cloth and some large safety-pins. Either way, the use of the insidiously patronising word 'civilians' in this context has caught on among the celebrity set. Anyway, the social classification is a little more complex.

Between celebrities and civilians sits another group. 'Sublebrities' is the word coined by the excellent Marina Hyde of *The Guardian*. It means civilians who have had a shot at becoming celebrities but not quite made it. Not that there is any shortage of 'real' celebrities. I had dinner with Marina a few days after she'd been asked by her paper to write a weekly column about the strange world celebrities inhabit. She was terrified that there would not be enough material to keep it going. She needn't have been. I suspect she'll be in a job long after Ms Hurley has fastened her last safety-pin.

So we now have a different social hierarchy from the one based on class and famously satirised by John Cleese, Ronnie Barker and Ronnie Corbett. Cleese was the upper-class character and he looked down on Barker, who looked up to him. Barker, who was middle class, looked down on Corbett, who looked up to both of them. A modern version would have Ms Hurley (a *real* celebrity) looking down on a wannabe celebrity – anyone who's been on *Big Brother* or *Pop Idol*, for instance. And in downtrodden little Ronnie Corbett's place, looking up to both of them, would be the equivalent of the check-out girl at the supermarket.

No doubt if you asked her whether she took celebrity life seriously, she'd say of course not, it's just a bit of a laugh. Except that you'll catch her poring over

Hello! magazine or doing herself up on a Friday night to look as much as possible like whoever happens to be adorning its pages. And perfectly serious newspapers are prepared to devote thousands of words to exploring the lives and opinions of people who have become celebrities for no better reason than that they married a footballer or pop star or enjoyed a fumble under the sheets at the *Big Brother* house. Celebrity life may be a fantasy but it's the dominant fantasy of our times.

In January 2006 the Learning and Skills Council reported that 16 per cent of the teenagers it had interviewed believed they would become famous, probably by appearing on shows like *Big Brother*. Many saw it as a better prospect than obtaining qualifications. They were sitting around 'waiting to be discovered'. The Council calculated that the chances of their actually becoming rich and famous as a result were roughly 30 million to one.

I don't suppose that made any difference because it is so hard to get away from it – as is clear from the phrase 'celebrity exposure'. Exposure was once something best avoided. You could die of it on a mountain or be destroyed by it in the red-top Sunday papers. These days it is usually grabbed with both hands. Enough exposure in the media (good or bad) can indeed guarantee an income for life – or at least until the papers tire of you, which will probably come sooner. Ask Rebecca Loos, who's done remarkably well out of sleeping (or not, as the case may be) with

David Beckham. Had it not been for all her exposure she might never have appeared on national television masturbating a pig. Let that be a lesson to us all.

There are moments in history when various elements come together to form the perfect combination. When the universe was young, hydrogen and oxygen fused to produce water. Life became possible. Messrs Rolls and Royce formed a partnership that gave us the finest cars and aircraft engines. Morecambe and Wise changed the face of television comedy. And then, in the summer of 2006, we witnessed the birth of a new force of nature. The WAGS were created.

Some people may affect outrage at the thought that the Wives and Girlfriends of the English footballers have earned themselves even a footnote in the history of this great nation. Well, let them. The WAGS had nothing more than their relationships (sometimes fleeting) with overpaid young footballers; extremely short skirts and long legs; the occasional surgical enhancement; a limitless capacity for booze and a truly heroic ability to shop. One more ingredient was needed in the mix.

As Laurel found his Hardy and Torville her Dean, so the WAGS found their partner: *the paparazzi*. A media starved of good British hooligan stories and with a desperate need to fill the many pages allocated by some Supreme Being to the non-event known as the World Cup provided the crucible in which this perfect partnership was fused. The English players themselves may have let down a nation, but not their partners. Marketing experts assured us that the girls would easily earn £5 million in the months after England's ignominious departure from Germany. Aleck Hornshaw of Get Me Media (I think we do) said: 'They have been catapulted into the limelight and will reap the benefits. They are aspirational figures and, from a marketing point of view, seriously hot property.' How right he was. One of the WAGS worked in a humble, low-paid job before Germany but after her exploits Mr Hornshaw assured us: 'She's a big star now.'

What turns stardom into hard cash is the opportunity to sponsor brands. As any half-awake follower of celebrities knows, an essential requirement of the celebrity lifestyle is always to use the right brands. The key here is to know precisely which celebrity is endorsing which brand at any given moment. Just a fleeting glimpse of a serious A-list celeb holding a particular handbag between limo and restaurant will do – even if she's only holding it for a friend. The PR people will do the rest.

Unlike 'makeover' and 'lifestyle', 'brand' is not a new word, but with its new friends it has acquired a whole new meaning. You could say it has had a makeover of its own. It comes from the Middle English word for 'burning'. In the sixteenth century it meant the mark made on something by burning it with a hot iron. The point about such a mark was that it was indelible. It provided a permanent means of identifying someone for what he was: a criminal, a slave. By the early nineteenth century and the beginnings of a consumer society, it had become a trade mark: again, the means of authenticating that something was what it was thought to be.

But 'brand' became bored with authenticity. Endlessly reassuring people that something is what it is thought to be and that no change has occurred – nor ever will – is hardly a life for an ambitious little word in such illustrious company. What if people could be persuaded to be less impressed by underlying realities and start instead to think what brand names might *suggest*? That would give some scope for the brand to conjure up all sorts of imaginary associations. Then we would start paying much more attention to these ephemeral but attractive associations than to dreary old reality.

Before long we would concentrate solely on appearances and forget all about realities. Eventually we might even come to believe that appearance *was* reality. Then brand would have ceased to be the dull slave of reality, authenticating that something was really what it seemed to be, and would have become the gadfly king of virtual reality, joking that anything could be anything, really.

Branding is now the art of getting people to think what something might be rather than what it necessarily is. It's about the manipulation of the virtual reality in which so many of us live. The manipulators include anyone with an interest in what we might think of them – not just big companies with products to sell but political parties with votes to win, design gurus with clients to attract – anyone, in other words, acting in some kind of market. They all have an interest in controlling their appearance to make us believe it is the reality.

Names are important if you want to control the image of your brand. The giant oil company, BP, has become 'bp', ridding itself of the imposing, powerful connotation of the capital letters in favour of the more modest, self-effacing manner of the lower-case. But it's gone further. In an audacious piece of rebranding, the company is trying to get us to think that the initials of its name do not stand, as we thought, for 'British Petroleum' but rather for 'beyond petroleum'.

It's not that this is a downright lie. BP is in the oil business and oil is running out. So it is spending serious money on exploring alternative sources of energy it hopes to sell us in the era 'beyond petroleum'. But the implication is that BP's vast profits have nothing to do with all that mucky oil that's polluting the Earth and everything to do with the pretty green and yellow flowers that adorn its winsome ads and are all part of branding it as a green company. Some makeover.

You might think that with such jiggery-pokery going on, branding needs to be a surreptitious activity in which the punters can't see the strings being pulled. Not a bit of it. In our post-modern world, where appearance is accepted as reality, the branding people seem to believe there's no harm in laying bare how their strange profession works. For many years a big chunk of the BBC was known as BBC Broadcast. It has changed its name – and is happy to tell us why:

> We wanted a name that reflected where we have come from. When we were Broadcasting and Presentation we were known as B&P. As BBC Broadcast we have been known as BBCB. So an evolutionary step was to play with the sound 'B'.
>
> The spelling as 'Bee' came from an internal brainstorm when we were looking at nature's expert navigators, because as a company facing the digital future we need to help the consumer become equally adept as navigators. We have always used Red as our colour property and this gave added strength to the name.
>
> We look forward to working with you as Red Bee Media.

Wonderful things, these brainstorms. But I'm leading us away from the important business of celebrity and how not to make a *faux pas* when selecting your own brands. That's important because your choice of brand is so vital in defining your identity. Neal Lawson, the chairman of the left-wing pressure group Compass, says we were once known by what we produced but now we judge ourselves and others by what we consume. It represents the triumph of the marketing men. The advertisers exploit it when they ask: 'What does your mobile say about you'?

It's such a pressing question you're going to need help.

No one is more capable of giving advice on keeping abreast of the celebrity lifestyle than Tyler Brûlé. He's the design guru who founded the hugely successful lifestyle and design magazine *Wallpaper*. He sold it to set up a design consultancy and now flits around the world providing advice wherever it's needed, picking up inspiration and persuading us that makeover is a permanent revolution – though possibly not in exactly the way Marx or Mao had in mind. In his breathless rush between flights, or probably on them, he manages to pen a weekly column for the Saturday *Financial Times* called 'Fast Lane'. He's keen to help us with our lifestyles, but it's not always easy.

I'm occasionally reluctant to reveal some of my favourite venues to eat, drink, shop and sleep on this page. It's not because I don't want to have breakfast with you on a side street in Copenhagen, compete with you for a prime pool position on Lago di Garda or watch you disrobe at an *onsen* outside Nagano. It's because some gems are best left unpolished. There's always a tricky balance between ensuring that a small café in Dornbirn, a kitchen shop in Chur or an *alimentari* in Chiavenna gets enough trade to tick over and pay the bills but not so much celebrity that it suddenly has the funds to renovate and install a cheap and nasty shop fit.

Indeed, indeed. One can perfectly understand his reluctance. One can't have the civilians polishing one's little gems. As for Mr Brûlé's own dream of the ultimate lifestyle, it's this: a little house 'hanging somewhere over Palm Beach' in Australia, where

> lots of friends will stop in to detox, refocus and rest.

You get the sort of demographic he mixes with from that one little line. It may possibly explain why, in listing the brands he advised us to have nothing to do with, he took a pot-shot at easyJet (or indeed 'easy-Anything'). It provoked this retort from easyJet's boss, Sir Stelios Haji-Ioannou:

> Not everyone can flit around the world like a faded aristocrat cherry-picking preferred upmarket brands and locations.

Which is more or less what you would have expected him to say. But what was interesting (and curiously heartrending) was another response to this little spat from an *FT* reader who said this about Mr Brûlé's lifestyle guidance:

> It is a revelation to me every week about brands and service standards that I have not experienced . . . yet.

No knowledge is superfluous, as Dante Alighieri said.

It was the 'yet' that was telling. The writer of the letter, Kenny Muncaster, lives in West Cumbria, one of the poorest areas of Britain and earns forty-five pounds a week delivering newspapers, starting at four fifteen in the morning. He went on:

> I may live in crushing poverty and have existed on a sub-standard diet for the past four years. But I know quality.

Such is the attraction of lifestyle and the power of fantasy.

Mr Muncaster's predicament does rather bring us back to reality and the challenge of how we are to pay for our chosen lifestyles. Note the word 'challenge'. We must expunge the word 'problem' from our vocabulary for a start. Far too negative. Happily, language comes to the rescue again to show us that it need not be much of a challenge at all.

I refer to the language of those enticing mailshots that pour through our letterboxes. You know them well. We have invariably been 'specially invited' to apply for a loan – but not just any old loan. We are 'a preferred MBNA customer' entitled to a 'Platinum Loan'. Some tell us we have been 'selected' for a loan – unless, importantly, we have been 'pre-selected'. The flattering implication of being pre-selected is slightly undermined by the final sentence inviting you to pass on this amazing offer to a friend if you're not interested. It's not as if the company would lend their money to any old Joe out there. Is it?

It 'couldn't be easier' to get your hands on the cash. A decision on your application can be made 'usually within minutes' and a cheque 'couriered to you within 24 hours'. As for paying interest, you'll enjoy 'a great low rate' – another phrase that's problematic only for the miserably pedantic. The important thing is that you shouldn't worry about any of it. Indeed, you can 'relax with 0% for up to nine months'.

Of course, you might be one of those people who's already stacked up quite a bit of debt. But don't let that disturb you. You can 'consolidate' your debts. Now that's a fine, solid word, is it not? You can convert them all into a single debt. That way you'll be able to 'rearrange your credit into one affordable loan' or end up with 'one low easy rate' to pay.

'Affordable'. 'Low'. 'Easy'. Such reassuring words. And there are others. If you go for a consolidated loan, your debt will be 'secured'. Now, how reassuring is that? So much wiser than, say, 'unsecured', wouldn't you think? Except that it means your debts are, for the first time, secured against your house. So if you don't keep up the payments you could lose the roof over your head. And the payments are 'easy' only in the sense that you have to make one big one rather than several little ones. They are 'affordable' and 'low' only because you're going to be paying them for very much longer.

A small footnote to the search for the elusive new lifestyle that may or may not be connected to the above: for the first time in history, personal debt in this country has passed one trillion pounds. That's an awful lot of noughts. The number of personal bankruptcies was forecast to rise beyond 100,000 in a single year.

If cheap'n'easy debt is not the way for you, there is an alternative route to the lifestyle makeover of your dreams. It was set out in another little leaflet that dropped on to my doormat and was entitled 'Never Stop Dreaming'.

> This week a sports car. Next week a round-the-world cruise. The week after that, how about a luxury villa abroad?

Sounds pretty good to me. The leaflet went on:

> A National Lottery Subscription gives you the chance to dream about ways of spending your winnings every week, because every week like clockwork, we'll enter your numbers into the draw for you.

Put aside any alarm you may feel that anyone would want to take out a subscription to a lottery and admire, for a moment, the clever piece of drafting in that sentence. Taken literally, it's silly: it says that a subscription will give you the 'chance to dream', as if you couldn't dream without a subscription. But, of course, we must not take it literally. The really slick little phrase is:

> the chance to dream about ways of spending your winnings every week.

So you'll be 'spending your winnings every week', will you? There's a problem here. To spend them every week would you not have to win every week? Indeed you would. But it would infringe every advertising law since Moses to guarantee something that is less likely to happen than Ms Hurley becoming a Carmelite nun. Which is why it doesn't actually say it . . . just allows you to think it. The great thing, though, is that a subscription means

> You'll never have to worry about forgetting to buy a Lottery ticket . . .

How wonderful to have the lifting of that particular 'worry'. And it's not the only worry they can help us with:

> . . . Or checking to see whether your numbers have come up. We'll take care of that too.

What nice people they are – and with such a homely, caring way of explaining how automatic computer systems work. All I need do, it seems, is sign on the dotted line – remembering, of course, to print my bank details clearly on the direct debit form – and . . .

. . . that's it. Once you've subscribed, all you have to
do is sit back, relax and start dreaming.

To sit back and relax seems to be the default
position of the fantasy lifestyle we are all being invited
to aspire to. For myself, I feel that if I had sat back and
relaxed as much as I have been encouraged to do over
recent years, I would have become permanently hori-
zontal long ago.

But I have to admit that I am not very good at sitting
back and relaxing. I keep getting bugged by this
thought. Such a posture, though comfortable, is perhaps not the best one for keeping your wits about you
while others 'take care' of your makeover, your lifestyle, your growing debt, gambling habits and anything else they can think of.

You don't suppose that is precisely why they suggest
it, do you?

CHAPTER FIVE
Now Isn't Soon Enough

As you would expect of somebody in my job, I have a great interest in sleep. An obsession with it would be more accurate. When you get up in the middle of the night several times a week, having enough sleep matters a great deal. I always want a little more. Some people feel the same way about food or drink and that, I suppose, is worse. At least sleep is relatively harmless and it's free. But will it stay that way? The *Sunday Times* reported a businessman saying this about snoozing:

> 'a 21st-century luxury which we, as a retailer of sleep, want to sell'.

The speaker was a chap called Wayne Munnelly and he rejoices in the title of director of sleep for Travelodge. So obviously he's got to flog the stuff one way or the other. But Professor Jim Horne doesn't, yet even he talks about sleep in a vaguely commercial manner. He runs the Sleep Research Laboratory at Loughborough University and he's been researching sleep for thirty years. He says there has been more interest in sleep and 'sleep products' in the past five years than in the previous thirty put together. Presumably selling sleep is only the beginning. How long before we learn about the appointment by another big company of a director of breathing? There has to be really, really serious money in retailing breathing, don't you think?

But then I came across an even more alarming headline. It read:

Say Goodbye to Sleep

The story was based on a piece in the *New Scientist* by Graham Lawton about a new drug that can apparently enable us to stay awake for days and get what amounts to a whole night's sleep in just a few hours. Yves, a thirty-one-year-old software developer from Seattle, has tried it:

'If I take a dose just before I go to bed, I can wake up after four or five hours and feel refreshed. I'm more organised and more motivated, and it means I can go out partying on a Friday night and still go skiing early on Saturday morning.'

The drug is called Modafinil and was described by Lawton thus:

a lifestyle drug for people who want off-the-peg wakefulness

That is a masterpiece of the language of consumer choice, each little element doing its bit. And there's our old friend 'lifestyle' again, used so casually in such a matter-of-fact way, with the easy assumption that we lead lifestyles rather than lives and recreational drugs are just a normal part of them.

'Off-the-peg wakefulness' beautifully captures the spirit of the times: the notion that anything we might want should be available instantly on demand. And near the top of any wish-list would be – why not? – a permanent 'wakefulness' that allows us to party all night and play all day.

In some ways, though, the most interesting word in Lawton's marvellous phrase is the most unobtrusive one: 'want'. It is obviously the word at the centre of consumerism and carries with it all those feelgood qualities of freedom and choice and liberation: you can decide what you want and, what's more, you can have it. The consumer is sovereign. We make choices. We choose what we want. But with this new medicine things are not quite so simple. As Lawton put it:

> We seem to be moving inescapably towards a society where sleep and wakefulness are available, if not on demand, then at least on request.

It's the 'inescapably' that's a bit troubling. An inexorable process seems to be under way in which

> . . . we are too far down the road of the 24-hour society to turn back.

So perhaps this is about more than simply 'wanting' – about being able to choose to party all Friday night and go skiing on Saturday morning – which is what the purveyors of 'lifestyle drugs' would have us believe.

The history of this particular drug is instructive. Lawton tells us it was originally developed to help people suffering from Alzheimer's to offset the effects of sleep deprivation. Then its use was extended into providing a 'lifestyle drug' to *facilitate* sleep deprivation among those who want to party and ski as much as they can. What might the next stage be? Once those who burn candles at both ends have set the norm, others may well be *expected* to take the drug to keep up with them. Before long the market for it stretches way beyond any sense of people 'wanting' it to those persuaded they 'need' it.

It is already being looked at closely by the American military. They can see its advantage to soldiers, who have to stay awake for very long stretches on special operations. But remember that we all now live in a twenty-four-hour society. Remember, too, that many people struggle desperately to make ends meet – sometimes because of all that partying and skiing, but sometimes because they don't earn enough to take the kids on a decent holiday once a year or to lead a reasonable life. The more desperate might see the advantage of working far longer hours – possibly even two jobs.

So the next stage could be a transition from 'lifestyle' drug to 'livelihood' drug. Employers might even provide it for free. After all, it's not hard to imagine the argument they'd use to get their workers to take it. It's a tough old world out there. Our twenty-four-hour society has come along at the same time as globalisation. With all those Chinese and Indians beavering away for a pittance, it's hard to stay competitive. Productivity is the answer.

It doesn't take much for the dream of free consumer choice to become the nightmare of necessity.

'Want' is not the only misleadingly simple word in the world of lifestyle consumer choice. Take another we bandy around without thinking about it: 'demand'. It's been part of the furniture since 1776 when Adam Smith tried to get our thinking about economics on to a more organised footing. Supply and demand have been the basis of the dismal science ever since.

The word 'supply' poses no problems: it expresses straightforwardly what producers can provide. But why should the word for what consumers might want be 'demand'? Why should we talk of 'consumer demand' rather than say, 'consumer desire', or 'consumer requirement' or even 'consumer request'? The point about a request is that it can be – and often is – denied. But 'demand' is different.

'Demand' suggests peremptoriness, rude insistence, grabbing rather than trading. It translates into 'gotta have it', the 'must-have handbag' and the clothes that are 'to die for' – though shouldn't that be 'to kill for'?

Above all, the word suggests childishness, the little horror staging a temper tantrum, stamping his feet and demanding he gets what he wants. We train children out of this sort of thing, persuading them that if they ask nicely they're more likely to achieve what they are after. But for some reason adults, as consumers, go on 'demanding'.

Poor Adam Smith didn't have this in mind at all. He was simply using a term that would relate the quantity of a particular product that people might fancy to the price at which they'd be prepared to buy it. There might very well be an infinite 'demand' from children for the latest PlayStation – but if its price is roughly what their grandparents paid for their first house it limits the number bought. Our everyday use of the word 'demand' has rather lost sight of the price bit. The sense is that whatever consumers 'demand' they must have – no argument.

That assumption, conveniently woven into the ordinary meaning of the word, crops up everywhere. The Department of Transport tells us that 'demand for air travel' will increase from 180 million passengers per year to 476 million by 2030. The assumption is that because there is this 'demand' it must be supplied. Another government department tells us we must worry about climate change and everyone knows that air travel is the fastest growing source of carbon-dioxide emissions. But demand is demand is demand – so the new airports will be built and the old runways extended whatever the environmentalists may say.

The real oddity, though, is that we consumers are not as demanding as the word might suggest. Taken to the water, we sometimes have to be made to drink. Otherwise there would be no need for all the advertising to 'create demand' for a product.

This is a phrase that becomes more extraordinary the more you think about it. On one hand you have all the associations of the urgent, the spontaneous, the uncompromising and the insistent resonance of the word 'demand'. On the other, there is the contradictory sense of work and effort, artifice and manipulation going into 'creating' it. When you think about it, it's a glorious oxymoron, on a par with Willie Whitelaw's famous comment about 'stirring up apathy'.

At least, it should be. But we take the idea of creating demand as an unremarkable part of our world. Perhaps it's because we have misunderstood something else. We tend to think of the phrase 'consumer demand' as meaning quite simply the demand of consumers. But maybe the preposition is wrong. Maybe it means the demand *on* consumers: the demand on them to, well, demand.

And, of course, once we've succumbed, the demands really are *on* us because now we must pay. So off we go to earn the money and if we can't earn enough we go into debt or maybe into the warm, dreaming embrace of the National Lottery or even one day – who knows? – into the grip of the off-the-peg-wakefulness drug.

And it really is 'inescapable': we're all in this together. Every economist I know says our relative economic prosperity of the past few years has been built largely on the back of consumer demand and the debt incurred to meet it. If we stop demanding, we're all sunk. Perhaps, in the end, it's just as well we have such a thuggish word to describe what we 'want' to keep the whole thing going.

Those of us in what Shakespeare rather hurtfully described as the seventh age may feel we are now largely exempt from all this. After all, we are not demanding off-the-peg wakefulness: just a bit of it now and again would do very nicely, thank you. As for the twenty-four-hour society, John McEnroe expressed it perfectly: 'You have GOT to be kidding!'

There has been an interesting shift here. Grandparents have always marvelled, with a mixture of pleasure and envy, at the things it's possible for their grandchildren to do but which they could only have dreamed of doing themselves. Now they wonder why anyone would *want* to do them.

Why, they ask, would someone choose to go to what they used to call a nightclub but which now *opens* at nine o'clock on a Sunday morning? Answer: because the demand has been created to go clubbing continuously from Friday night to Monday morning. What's the problem, Grandpa? If you've got the right drugs, lots of bottled water and plenty of readies . . .

An eighty-year-old told me that she hoped she wouldn't live too long because the world was fast becoming more unfamiliar, even more alien, than she could handle. As she put it in a perfectly cheery tone: 'I don't know how to "Visit our Website" and I don't bloody well want to anyway!'

But the elderly should not imagine they are going to be let off the important task of creating demand quite so easily. In the spring of 2006, when many of them may have been pootling around in their greenhouses pricking out the sweet peas, the big retail companies were forking out £700 a ticket to attend a one-day conference in London focused on helping them get their hands into elderly pockets. You can see why they'd want to. The over-fifties control 80 per cent of the UK's wealth, 60 per cent of its savings and 40 per cent of its disposable income. By 2010 they will constitute half of the population. The title of the conference was:

> Turning Grey Into Gold: Blending Cutting-Edge Population Knowledge With Innovative Marketing To Segment And Connect With The Older Market.

Pretty punchy, eh? What a joy it is to get back into the language of marketing executives. No, I shan't attempt to decode it (or even 'connect with' it) but one thing is worth noting: the word 'older'. The phrase 'the old' seems to be dying out. Judges are often given guidance on what is called 'inappropriate terminology'. They have been warned off 'old' because it carries connotations of being 'worn out and of little further use'. Well, quite. I recognise the symptoms.

Incidentally, if I had the power to issue guidelines I would decree that any reporter at the BBC (or anywhere else) who refers to old people by their first names should be strung up by their heels. It's not just a gross impertinence, it is deeply patronising. The assumption seems to be that once someone passes a certain age they become a child again and are no longer entitled to 'Mr' or 'Mrs'. When Gordon Brown met that remarkable old man Henry Allingham, the last living survivor of the Battle of Jutland who was celebrating his hundred and tenth birthday, the Chancellor was referred to in several reports as Mr Brown but Mr Allingham became 'Henry'. What a bloody cheek.

Anyway, the advertisement for the marketing conference referred to 'the older audience' and 'the mature consumer'. Best of all it said:

Leading speakers will deliver insightful case studies to propel your brand into the grey limelight.

What an extraordinary use of language that is. 'Grey limelight' is either completely bonkers or a work of marketing genius – though I suppose, in this strange world, it could be both. We would normally associate grey and old (or even 'older') with 'twilight' but here, with just a slight twist, we are invited instead to see the nation's wrinklies kicking up their heels and enjoying the limelight. It's all about feelgood, of course. Pick up any piece of Saga literature and you'll find seventy-year-olds whitewater-rafting or bungee-jumping all over the place. In a world where sixty-year-olds become mothers it's entirely plausible that marketing people should propel their feelgood brands into the grey limelight.

And if feelgood doesn't work in creating demand . . . well, there's always 'feelbad'. That's not in the dictionary because I've just coined it. The most potent feelbad tactic is to persuade us we're suffering from something not far short of an illness. This sort of advertisement, for instance:

> Growing Concerns: 1 in 4 women in the UK suffer from thinning hair

Advertisers love 'suffer'. I'd prefer to save such a powerful word for people with something a bit more serious than thinning hair. Obviously there's no reason why a company should not try to flog us something to help our hair grow back and if it really is one in four there's a massive market out there. But the advertisement implies that this commonplace and harmless condition is tantamount to an illness that needs treating.

It tells us that the effectiveness of the product is 'clinically proven' – just as a medicine has to be – and that it has the potential for 'helping thousands of women'. That's the sort of language that is more legitimately used when medical research comes up with a breakthrough for, say, breast cancer. To steal the words of the advertisement itself, 'feelbad' advertising is 'worrying, upsetting and damages confidence'.

In *Lost for Words* I drew attention to this trick of creating demand by inventing pseudo-illnesses. Some of it is pretty blatant. You take an ordinary condition, tack on the word 'syndrome' and you're away. Some of it is marginally more subtle. In my book I mentioned an advertisement that asked us in a very concerned way whether we showed 'signs of daily fatigue'. There's only one answer to that: who doesn't? But the real answer, we learned, was to take a little capsule and 'say goodbye to daily fatigue'. 'Saying goodbye' seems rather to be in fashion.

Since my book came out academics have got on the case. In early 2006 the journal *Public Library of Science Medicine* published no fewer than eleven learned articles from around the world on what one academic called the 'corporate-sponsored creation of disease' or, for the popular press, 'disease-mongering'.

Iona Heath, a GP in London, was quoted as saying: 'Disease-mongering exploits the deepest atavistic fears of suffering and death. It is in the interests of pharmaceutical companies to extend the range of the abnormal so that the market for treatments is pro-portionately enlarged.' That's as good a case of 'crea-ting demand' as I know.

The academics talked about the familiar cases, such as diagnosing naughty children with attention deficit hyperactivity disorder, but there were others. There's now something called 'social anxiety disorder', known to you and me as shyness. We're encouraged to wonder whether the mood-swings we all experience from time to time may not really be signs of bi-polar disorder, which can be a truly hellish disease. And then there's 'restless legs syndrome'. You may want to laugh at this – though you wouldn't if you suffered from it – but it's the language used to talk about it that is so revealing. This is how the giant pharmaceutical company, GlaxoSmithKline, puts it:

> It's estimated that 10–15% of adults suffer from restless legs syndrome, yet it is a very underdiag-nosed medical condition, which even when diag-nosed, often leaves people without effective treatment. About 3% of adults experience moderate to severely distressing RLS symptoms at least two or three times a week and are likely to benefit from treatment.

'Underdiagnosed' is a wonderful new word. I can perfectly well understand 'incorrectly diagnosed'. There was the remarkable case recently of a poor chap called Derek Kirchen who was diagnosed with lung cancer. Doctors were pretty confident that he had a bad tumour. For about eighteen months he'd had endless bouts of pneumonia, kept collapsing and had a seriously worrying lump in his lung. So he was admitted to hospital for an operation. When they inserted a tube, they discovered that the lump was not quite so sinister. It was a cashew nut. Mr Kirchen remembered that the last time he'd eaten one was two Christmases ago and it had 'gone down the wrong way'. When he came round from the operation, he said: 'All the nurses were laughing. They couldn't believe it.' He doesn't even like cashew nuts.

But 'underdiagnosed' is rather more puzzling than 'incorrectly diagnosed'. Presumably it means doctors aren't diagnosing the particular condition often enough – which might possibly suggest that not enough people are complaining about it. And that's a bit odd if they really *are* 'suffering' from it.

The other trick in the marketing books is to create demand by suggesting that a treatment offered for a specific condition suffered by a few might do us all a bit of good. That's the point made by Dr Joel Lexchin, of York University in Toronto, about Viagra and its makers, Pfizer. He alleges that the company has designed ways to 'ensure that the drug was seen as a legitimate therapy for almost any man' and that the message from its ads and website 'is that everyone, whatever their age, at one time or another, can use a little enhancement.'

Pfizer denies it, yet Viagra is increasingly talked about not just as a treatment for a medical condition but as a lifestyle drug. Versions of it are certainly widely available as such. I suppose you could call it a 'lifestyle drug for people who want off-the-peg wakefulness'. Of a sort.

It's certainly one way to say goodbye to sleep.

CHAPTER SIX

Formal Warning

The sociologist Zygmunt Bauman has said that to be a 'successful' consumer now defines what it is to be 'normal'. So it is not surprising to discover how many activities are now seen in consumerist or business terms. A British actor who appears on a Broadway stage is described as a 'talented export'. We no longer watch television news but, in the language of the broadcasting bosses, 'consume' it. The country itself is routinely called 'UK plc' – as though that's all it is. But the winner of gold in this category must be this – from a study commissioned by the United States Army:

> For the army to achieve its mission goals with Future Force Soldiers, it must overhaul its image as well as its product offering.

How much mightier would Churchill's oratory have been in those dark days of 1940 if only Britain had had its own Military Image Study:

> We shall fight on the beaches with our product offering. We shall fight in the hills and the marketing directors' expense-account restaurants. We shall

never surrender in the battle to defend our bottom line. And even if, which I do not for a moment believe, this great company were the target of an unscrupulous takeover bid, then our sales divisions beyond the seas, armed and guarded by our refurbished image and exciting new logo, would carry on the struggle . . . Let us therefore brace ourselves to our duties, and so bear ourselves that, if UK plc last for a thousand focus groups, men will still say, 'This was their finest hour.'

Well, it's not *that* far-fetched when you consider that a British education minister has referred to our universities as 'UK Knowledge plc', which needs to keep up its 'market share'. No less a figure than the Chancellor of Oxford University, Lord Patten, has spoken about his ancient institution as being part of 'the global university market', needing to 'trawl the world for the best students'.

I know that universities need to raise money wherever they can but using language like this has consequences. It's not surprising if students come to see themselves more as customers than as members of their universities. In one sense they are: they have to pay and they want value for money. Why not? But it seems that increasing numbers of them interpret that in the ordinary sense of customers' rights.

They're encouraged in that by marketing slogans such as:

Personalising your journey

That's ideal, you may think, for an upmarket travel agency offering two weeks' hiking in the Himalayas. But I'm told this is what students are to be offered at university. A friend runs a consultancy whose clients include some of our newer universities – the ones we called polytechnics not so long ago. He is being paid to advise them on how best to enrich the 'student experience' by 'personalising the journey'. If you are baffled by this language, don't fret. So is he.

The travel agency comparison turns out to be close to the mark. Baroness Deech is the first independent adjudicator for Britain's university sector and it has been an eye-opener for her:

> 'When I first started this job, somebody said education was like going on holiday – you get your glossy prospectus, pay your money and if there are cockroaches in the hotel you sue.'

In other words the attitude of some students was: 'I've paid my money and I've got to get an upper second and it's the university's job to make sure I do. I'm the customer, remember.' But it doesn't (and obviously shouldn't) work quite like that. Customers are frequently disappointed. When that happens in the world of commerce they complain. And that's exactly what they are doing now in academe. There were five times as many complaints from students in 2005 as there had been in 2004 and many of them, it seems, expressed in language you might use to complain about a rip-off merchant. Lady Deech was not impressed:

> 'In the course of looking at some complaints, we have seen emails from students to tutors which astonish me.'

Another effect of the tendency to interpret all our relationships with each other in commercial terms is that the language in which the 'supplier' speaks to us is changing. It is increasingly rare to come across straightforward statements that convey simple information in a purely formal way. Take this, for example:

> To ensure the ongoing quality of your swimming experience, the Club's swimming pool will be closed for annual maintenance from 3 April.

The club in question is the London Central YMCA and that notice appeared in the gym early in 2006. This is what the notice would once have said:

> The Club's swimming pool will be closed for annual maintenance from 3 April.

What's wrong with that? It tells the members what is going to happen and why. They will understand perfectly well that swimming pools need regular maintenance. But in this new relationship they must be dealt with as 'customers' so must be subjected to this nonsense. And the language is not only nonsensical, it's hideous.

'Ongoing quality' is entirely vacuous. Does anyone imagine that the people who run the pool would be happy for it to be nice and clean this week and filled with disgusting germs next week?

'Your' is once again meant to reinforce the idea that you personally are at the centre of their universe – in the same way that supermarkets stick up notices talking about 'your' store manager. He's not yours; he's theirs. Try getting him sacked because 'your' store is a mess.

As for 'swimming experience', it is an offence against the English language. In what sense is it an improvement on 'swim'? But then, we have 'reading experiences' these days instead of 'books' so I suppose we shouldn't be surprised. The education minister David Lammy gave an interview to the *Bookseller* magazine in which he said books are 'absolutely essential to the library experience'. Quite so. He should go far.

Does this silly language do any good? Of course not. That's partly because it inspires ridicule but it can also generate suspicion. Language so remote from the way we speak in the real world prompts the question: what's behind all that, then?

Gushing vacuity addressed to customers can have the same effect as excessive flattery: what's he *after*? When we're stuck on the end of a phone and the mechanical voice is saying, for the umpteenth time,

'Your call *is* important to us,' we know that it obviously isn't or they wouldn't have kept us waiting for half an hour and driven us to the edge of insanity with their ghastly Muzak. But sometimes it really *is* valuable to them. Literally. And that's even worse.

In 2005 we spent £1.6 billion dialling premium-rate phone numbers. That's more than any other country in the world – equivalent to thirty-five pounds for every adult – and I'd love to know how much of that is racked up while the mechanical voice tells us how valuable our call is.

On the other hand, at least you don't have to respond to the mechanical voice . . . not the way you do when you get a real person cold-calling on the phone. I had a call the other day from a chap at the *Sunday Times* Wine Club whose opening line was:

'I bet you weren't expecting this call!'

Good God, I thought, it must be Tony Blair offering to confess live on the *Today* programme tomorrow morning that he'd been wrong all the time about Iraq, or maybe the National Lottery telling me I'd won the jackpot – which would indeed have been a great surprise because I have never bought a ticket. Sadly, no. But the cold-callers usually start with:

'I hope I'm not disturbing you.'

How do they expect us to respond to that? 'Disturbing me? Of course not! In fact, I've been sitting by the phone for several days now waiting for someone to call and sell me life insurance I don't want and a new kitchen I don't need to fit into the house with double-glazing that I need even less. So *please* go ahead because I have absolutely nothing better to do than talk to you, and when this call has finished my life will be so empty I shall probably blow my brains out!'

Still, credit where credit's due. At least there is a certain courteous formality in the remark about my being disturbed – and formality matters. It can create a space between us that allows for a measure of independence and freedom. Take it away and that space is open to all manner of intruders, not all of them commercial. When, for example, did you last hear a public figure 'send their condolences' to someone who'd been bereaved? Not recently, I suspect. Nowadays, if there has been a disaster of some sort, it tends to be:

'Our thoughts go out to the loved ones . . .'

Or even:

'All our thoughts are with the families of those . . .'

It may be well meant, but it has the smack of insincerity about it – for the obvious reason that it's not true. 'All' our thoughts do not 'go out' to anyone. Of course all of us will feel a degree of sympathy, but for a politician to suggest that he is thinking of little else is patently false. And it can actually be insensitive to the people who have been bereaved. It is the equivalent of that ghastly and much parodied 'I feel your pain'. The truth is that no one can feel the pain or truly share the suffering of someone who has lost a child, parent or close friend. No one can feel someone else's pain. That's one reason why the pain is so hard to bear: it cannot be shared.

The difference between the old and the new way of expressing sympathy is a clear illustration of how changing language reveals something of the changing nature of our times. The old, formal expression of condolence was just that: the gesture was made and the bereaved were left to their grieving. The new, informal, supposedly more intimate expression pushes the person 'sharing the pain' into the centre of the picture. It sends a message about what *he* is experiencing. It tells us how *he* has been (or claims to have been) affected. No wonder a company's PR department always tells the boss, when disaster strikes, to use the less formal and more intimate language. It deflects criticism and blame by implying that the boss is suffering too – so let's go easy on him.

The new, enforced intimacy is everywhere. The Queen – widely admired for keeping her distance and exercising iron control over her emotions – is now expected to show she cares. It seems a bit odd. Does anyone really believe she somehow became a different person when she was put under pressure to let us know publicly that she was moved by the death of the Princess of Wales?

Formality is disappearing, too, in how we address each other. I knew a young woman in the sixties who got a job as secretary to the headmaster of a public school. After a week or so he said to her: 'Oh, Diana, you really don't need to call me "Sir". Just call me "Headmaster".' At the time we thought it comically stuffy. But that was before a British prime minister encouraged everyone to call him by his Christian name.

The first time I met Tony Blair after the election of 1997 I asked him off-air what I should call him. 'Tony, of course,' he said. I suppose I knew that's what he would say – we'd known each other for a long time and were obviously on first-name terms – but there's something different about being prime minister. It is, when all's said and done, the highest elected office in the land and deserves a special kind of respect. I once toyed with using Margaret Thatcher's first name when she was at Number Ten, but I chose life instead.

On one level this is trivial stuff, but it can matter. Old-fashioned civil servants have always wanted to keep at arm's length from their political bosses. They don't much like first names or approve of chats on sofas and prefer formal meetings around tables with officials present to take notes. There's a reason for that. Running a government is different from organising a village fête. Formality is linked to propriety and propriety is about doing things properly.

It's clear that a lot of the public value old-fashioned formality in the way we talk to each other. If I had a pound for every listener who gets het up when politicians use the interviewer's first name I'd be almost as rich as Terry Wogan or Jonathan Ross. People hate it, so why do the politicians do it? Well, the first thing to be said is that they are not all guilty. Margaret Thatcher never did it. Indeed, in one famous interview with the late Robin Day she called him 'Mr Day' throughout. Which would have been fine – except that he was 'Sir Robin' by that stage in his illustrious career.

Nor does it gain politicians any advantage when they pepper interviews with 'John' or 'Jim'. If they expect us to react like puppies having our tummies tickled . . . well, you'd have thought they might have learned by now that it doesn't work like that. Or maybe they expect us to respond in kind and use their first names too, thus giving the audience the impression that we're all friends together and it's really just a game. That isn't going to happen either. Any political interviewer on a serious programme who calls the politician by his first name should be drummed out of the Brownies. We should keep our distance. Formality is one way of doing so.

But there's an oddity about people's attitude to formality. You know what drives many Radio 4 listeners up the wall? Courtesy. Or, rather, too much of it. This is a common complaint:

The thing I find most annoying is the way you are all constantly thanking each other. For what? Doing your job?

It's difficult to argue with that. On my own programme you might very well hear Greg Wood thanking a guest on his business slot and handing over to me. I thank Greg and hand over to Gary or Steve for the sport and they thank me and then they thank whoever is the guest on their slot, at the end of which they hand back to me and I thank them and . . . well, you get the idea. But what's to be done about it? Yes, I know we're all being paid for what we do and, strictly speaking, there's no need to thank each other. But think about it for a moment.

The waitress is getting paid to bring you your meal in the restaurant, but I bet you thank her anyway. And don't you say, 'Thanks,' when you're handed something in a shop or the hairdresser trims your locks – even though you're paying for the service? And anyway, on programmes such as *Today* you have to end the interviews with *something* – even if it's been just a brief chat with one of your own correspondents.

Indeed, there are occasions when we cut off the thank-you and we shouldn't. The interviewer may have gone ten bruising rounds with a politician who has flatly refused to answer anything except name, rank and serial number. At the end of it the interviewer will say, through gritted teeth: 'Minister, *thank* you!' The minister's response will often be cut off by the studio manager, the person in charge of the technical end of things. I'd prefer to hear it. You can learn a lot from the way the minister responds. A cheery 'Thanks, John' tells you one thing; a snarl tells you something else. But in general there's no question that we overdo our thank-yous.

So it's not like the absurdity of those signposts that pepper our country roads with this message:

'Thank you for driving safely through . . .'

How do they know we were driving safely through their village? And if we were, it would be either because we had nine points on our licence and were terrified of speed cameras lurking behind laurel hedges or because we didn't want to smash into that huge tractor coming around the bend in the opposite direction. In either case, what was there to thank us for? And what if we're so busy reading the signpost that we drive slap bang into the village bobby? Not that there are any village bobbies any longer, so that's alright.

How formal the BBC should be is a controversial issue. Very few people want to return to the days when all announcers had to speak like the Queen, and the idea that the BBC should sound like one small middle-class corner of the south-east of England is preposterous. But there's a powerful argument for some of the formality that has been lost. On the old Third Programme it seldom got much more exciting than an announcer like Patricia Hughes intoning: 'It is ten past four and there now follows a recital of Czech part songs . . .'

You don't get more formal than that. What's interesting about this sort of delivery is that the listener had not the first idea what the announcer thought of the music that was about to be played. She might have considered it the most dreadful old cobblers and couldn't wait to rip off her headphones and nip into the studio next door for a bit of Sinatra. Or she might have sat there enraptured throughout. We had no way of knowing. She left it up to us to decide whether we wanted to hear Czech part songs and, having done so, to decide for ourselves whether it was a good performance or a wretched one. Now we are almost always told how marvellous it all was.

But it's probably the weather forecast that stirs the strongest passion in the breast of the Radio 4 listener. Many mourn the passing of the days when the weather was given straight – even if they had only the vaguest idea why areas of high pressure were a good thing.

A friend was telling me about his childhood holidays in North Wales in the early 1960s. You never knew whether you'd be stuck in the cottage all day, doing jigsaws and watching the rain, or paddling in the surf getting your neck burned red. So you needed to hear the forecast. Just before six every evening, he told me, his father would sternly call for silence. The wireless set would be turned on and a hush would descend on the room as the forecast was delivered. This was a serious business, make no mistake about it, and the seriousness was evident in the formal way the forecast was written. Today it is invariably cheery and chatty and don't forget to take your brolly or pack the sun cream.

You either like it or you loathe it. One listener told me that when he watches certain forecasters on television he immediately finds himself transported back to primary school where he is sitting in the presence of a smiling, reassuring and rather bossy young teacher. Whatever the detail, he says, this is what he actually hears:

> Well, it's going to rain, children, and we don't like rain, do we? But we've got to have it because it's good for us, haven't we? So let's all try to be a little bit grown-up and put a brave face on it. And, of course, we must remember to have our macs with us, mustn't we? And then, who knows?, the day after tomorrow the sun may shine on us all again. Now, I want to see a big smile from everyone . . . George, don't do that . . .

Some people find the formality of the hourly news bulletins, beautifully read by the likes of Harriet Cass and Charlotte Green, too sharp a contrast with the informality of the programmes in which they sit. But I suppose the biggest change has been in the way programmes are trailed and promoted on television. The purpose has always been the same – to encourage us to watch – but the old way was to deliver the information and leave it at that. It seemed almost a matter of indifference to the announcer as to what we did with it. Now the 'promo' is an art form. Cynics say that more effort goes into producing it than into the programme it promotes. And the announcer who does the voice-over bears about as much resemblance to Patricia Hughes as Mike Tyson to Mother Teresa.

On one level the reason for this is obvious: competition. Listeners and viewers have to be fought for. They cannot be taken for granted in the way they were when cable and satellite stations weren't even a gleam in Rupert Murdoch's eye and we could choose any radio station we wanted so long as it was the BBC. But the other reason is the death of formality. One might have expected – or even hoped – that the void would be filled with spontaneity. Instead, in this harsher commercial world, we have the hard sell: manipulative language delivered in slick, sleek packages that tell us we'd be mugs not to buy them.

Tate Modern is a wonderful art gallery – spoiled only by the banality of much of its content. But the building is magnificent and the view of St Paul's across the

Thames is stunning. Tate Britain is another kettle of fish. The Turners alone make it worth a daily visit. But the gallery does not have enough visitors and the people who run it have tried a fresh approach to attract more of us. They've produced new guides – booklets to tell visitors what to expect.

These are not the conventional, formal little guides that provide maps letting you know that the William Blakes are in Room X and the Stanley Spencers in Room Y. Rather, they're leaflets with a marketing spin. The particular sales pitch is to tell you that whatever your current preoccupations, whatever it is that's troubling you or affecting your mood, there's something in the gallery to help. The leaflets identify the pictures you need to look at and where to find them, and the curators have written brief helpful explanations of why particular pictures will do the business.

So, there's one leaflet entitled 'The Calming Collection', one 'The First Date Collection', one 'The Happily Depressed Collection' and one 'The I've Just Split Up Collection'. There are lots of others. The one that caught my eye is called 'The I Have a Big Meeting Collection'. Here's what it says:

> For maximum effect we recommend you experience
> this Collection twenty-four hours prior to a meeting.
> Whatever the reasons for your meeting, we are here
> to help you look good and to ooze confidence. Let's

start by putting you in the mood. Look at *Harvest Home* by John Linnell (room 7). You can almost breathe the fresh air from that golden afternoon. Fill your lungs with greatness. (Always make yourselves bigger before entering a room.)

So *that*'s what Tate Britain is there for – to help me ooze confidence! This is better than assertiveness training. And it's free. There's more:

It's time to take a look at the champion Greek archer *Teucer* by Sir Hamo Thornycroft near the Millbank entrance. He's one of the heroes of Homer's Trojan War. The tip here is never to lose focus on what you're aiming for. You may meditate on this last point over a coffee in the Café.

Ah, yes, the café: the most important place in any museum or gallery. Pictures are free but coffees are a couple of quid. And you can relax. Have a nice time. Watch the world go by . . . But I'm almost forgetting my big meeting.

Now we need to work on your look. Eyes are the most powerful weapons in meetings. Look at *Queen Elizabeth I* (room 2). Study her eyes and her pose. She's the model to follow.

Of course! That's why this is such a great picture. It'll help me to storm into a meeting tomorrow with the BBC Director-General, eyes blazing, looking like

Gloriana (only bigger – remember the first lesson). But we're not finished yet.

> With just a glance at *The Fisherman's Farewell* (room 21) you'll see a man saying goodbye to his family. But if you look deeper, you'll find determination and character. You should look like him by now.

Funny that. This painting strikes many people as being about anxiety and the reluctance to part, about the grinding necessity of earning a living and about the terrible fear of loss that's at the heart of love. But obviously we should look 'deeper' (or possibly even 'more deeply').

> Finally, spend some time in front of *The Battle of Camperdown* (room 9) – meetings are often like that. No one said it was going to be easy. But the painting still depicts the moment of victory. Bravery is the name of the game. Off you go.

Off I go indeed. This has really set me up. I'm a different person. By now I'm striding purposefully out of the gallery, resisting distraction from mere art to the left and right of me and probably already on my mobile barking new instructions to my secretary. Now I understand why we subsidise the arts.

But let's try to be generous to the sophisticated nabobs who run the Tate. Let's suppose they're just having a bit of fun – messing about with the notion of the post-modern, where texts both do and don't mean what they say. Maybe. Or maybe they're ticking boxes for bureaucrats. The people who dole out the cash have no doubt told the gallery that they must get visitor numbers up. They must increase 'accessibility'. They must make it all much more 'user-friendly'. They must make it fun. They must make it easy.

So, things have had to change at Tate Britain. Under the old formality, a gallery said in a neutral sort of way: 'Here we are. Here are some paintings. Come and look at them if you'd like to. Make of them what you will . . .' But that won't do any longer. The targets, God forbid, might not be met. So the calm, neutral space that was once created by the inexpressive formality of a gallery must now be filled with spin and salesmanship. We must be sold the line that art is 'relevant' to us. It's there to serve our needs. And there's not a single need, however trivial or mundane, to which it cannot cater. There's even the 'I'm Hung-over Collection', if that's your problem.

You wanted to know what the purpose of art is? It's obvious. It exists to help us all perform better and make life easier. You can almost hear a junior minister in the Department of Culture, Media and Sport making a speech about it:

> 'This has got to be good for everyone. It's good for individuals – people need help and it's our duty to provide it. It's good for the galleries – they don't

want to stay as fuddy-duddy institutions no one visits. They want to move with the times. And, above all, it's good for Britain. Don't forget – those big meetings really do matter. It's a tough world out there. If we're going to stay competitive in a global-ised economy, everyone's got to be able to perform at the top of their game. If the art world can help us do that, then it's a win-win situation!'

The only trouble with all this is that it destroys art in the process. It's what Marxists would call the 'com-modification of art'.

My own vague, tentative, no doubt ill-informed notion of what art might be derives from the ex-perience of seeing something, or reading it, or hear-ing it and feeling as if I'm being removed from the familiar clutter and preoccupations of my life. The effect of art is to take us out of ourselves, to transport us from the insistent parochialism of our daily existence. The experience may not always be comfortable or easy – even with a coffee thrown in. It may be disturbing, shaking the complacency with which we tend to see the world as a reflection of our own purposes and selfish little interests. If we deprive art of the neutral, unspun way it comes to us and instead recruit it as servant to those purposes, we destroy its power.

Those little leaflets remind me of the old cartoon of a flustered woman rushing into the Louvre and shouting at a startled attendant: 'Where's the Mona Lisa? I'm double-parked!'

What is revealing about the language of the Tate's leaflets is not that it's used to bamboozle us in the way a gallery of contemporary art might – and try to con us into believing that it is we who are at fault if we cannot see why a video 'installation', for instance, is truly a piece of art. It's the opposite. It seems designed to get us to overlook the fact that these paintings are great works of art and tells us instead that we can enlist them to serve our blinkered lives. But their glory lies precisely in their being able to take away those blinkers.

Formality may seem stuffy but it provides fresh air and freedom compared with this.

CHAPTER SEVEN

The Word on the Street

It really is true that there's no fool like an old fool. I have been a journalist for almost half a century – in broadcasting for most of that time – and I am living proof of it. I have delivered a lecture, engaged in debates and written several lengthy articles about the vacuous nature of much modern television – above all, the monstrous confidence trick that goes by the name of 'reality television'.

I do not deny that some of it is hugely entertaining. Indeed, one or two programmes have been superb. *Operatunity* was television at its best: deeply moving and utterly enthralling. It worked because there was no pretence: it *was* reality. *The Apprentice* and *Dragons' Den* work for the same reason. But most 'reality' television is a lie. It tries to create the illusion that we are watching, people behaving naturally in what are grotesquely contrived circumstances. Anyone who's been in television for five minutes knows that the camera changes everything. Here's how Tom Mangold, one of *Panorama*'s finest reporters, puts it:

'As one who's spent a lifetime being filmed, I promise you I only have to see a camera being unloaded
from a car and I pull my stomach in, adjust my
clothes and wipe my sweaty face. So does everyone
else.'

Indeed we do. Using a word like 'reality' to describe
something that is patently the opposite makes fools of
us all – and worse. The frightfully smart media types
who peddle rubbish like *Big Brother* (and who would
no more dream of appearing on it than they would
sacrifice their first-born) call people like me snobs.
The defence of the programme lies in the size of its
audience, they say. How can the masses be so wrong?
And, anyway, no one really buys into it: they know it's
just a game and they're in on the joke. Sure they are.

So what do I do when the call comes to take part in
a 'reality' show? Like a gullible teenager with stars in
his eyes and mush where his brain should be, I fall for
it. It's true that I had said no to lots of other shows. I
said no to *Big Brother* when I was invited some years
ago to enter the 'celebrity' house – partly on the
Groucho Marx grounds that I would never join any
'celebrity' group that would have me as a member. I
also said no to a spell in the Australian rainforest. So
far, so good. I was still a reality-TV virgin. Then I got
a call wondering if I'd like to take part in a new
programme for BBC2. The idea was that four 'famous'
people (how casually we throw around that word)

would spend a fortnight at the Chelsea Art College being taught how to draw and paint. At the end of the fortnight the work they produced would be exhibited and reviewed by distinguished art critics.

The working title of the programme should have alerted me immediately: *Celebrity Art School*. But I loved the idea. Like half of the population, I can barely draw a bath and I've always wondered whether that's because I was never taught properly. Maybe with a bit of expert tuition I could even sketch a dinosaur that does not resemble a nuclear explosion with a tail. It is deeply hurtful when a very small child looks at you with pity in his eyes and tells you how much better someone else's father is at drawing dinosaurs.

I began to get seriously suspicious, though, when I discovered which production company was making the programme: Endemol. That is the company (the very rich company) that came up with the idea for *Big Brother*. So I said no. Then the phone calls started. A stream of frightfully important people began ringing to persuade me that, no, of course this wasn't going to be some tacky reality-television exercise. But what about Endemol? Ah, this was Endemol *West* – an altogether more upmarket version of the parent company. So that seemed all right, then, and I eventually said yes. But it wasn't all right, and I realised from the first hour of the first day what an idiot I'd been.

The cameras followed us everywhere – not just in the art room but even when we were eating. At least, they did until I told them to clear off. And eventually – just as the producers had hoped and just as I should have grasped if I'd had even half a functioning brain – I lost my temper. I got angry with the producers, angry with the tutors (not that it was their fault) and angry with myself. It made 'good television', of course – which was the whole point. I've no doubt that if live cameras were filming the Second Coming and the Son of God decided to destroy, say, Manchester to teach us all a lesson, the producer would say: 'Shame about Manchester, but it was great television.'

So my tantrums made good television. They also made me look a fool. The *Observer*'s television critic said that if he ever found himself sitting next to me at a dinner party he would probably drive a fork through my hand. And I don't think he was joking.

And yet, in spite of everything, some good came of it. The other 'students' (Clarissa Dickson-Wright, Ulrika Jonsson, Keith Allen and the Radio 1 DJ Nihal) turned out to be great company and we all got on terribly well together – rather to the chagrin, I suspect, of the presenter who tried to entice us into being bitchy about each other. That makes better telly, you understand. But we did not oblige. I also learned a lot about language. It turns out, for example, that 'drawing' no longer means what it once did and neither, for that matter, does 'art'. The word survives but the meaning has been transformed.

Of course art has changed through the ages. Had it not, we'd have been denied the vision of the Impressionists or the radicalism of Picasso – not to mention the nonsense of Tracey Emin and the crude vulgarity of the Chapman brothers. Some of it has added to the gaiety of the nation. You'd have needed a heart of stone not to smile at the man who paid £6.5 million for the famous pickled shark, only to watch it rot gently away before his eyes. There's talk of replacing it with a fresher one – but would it still have the integrity of the original? The worry keeps me awake at night.

Whether or not we still have a firm grasp on the meaning of the word 'art' was a question raised too by the case of the sculptor David Hensel. He made a piece called *One Day Closer to Paradise* of a human head frozen in laughter and balancing precariously on a slate plinth. He submitted it to the Royal Academy for its 2006 Summer Exhibition. Somehow the head and the plinth got separated in transit. Nonetheless the Academy accepted his submission and displayed it. The strange thing was, though, that they thought the plinth was the work of art not the head, which was nowhere to be seen. As he put it ruefully: 'I've seen the funny side but I've also seen the philosophical side . . . It shows up not just the tastes of the selectors but also their unawareness.'

Yet, it's hard not to be impressed by the sheer marketing genius that lies behind contemporary art. Damien Hirst may or may not be the greatest artist of all time but he is, by a country mile, the richest. And Charles Saatchi hasn't done too badly out of it either.

I did not go to art school expecting great riches. I just wanted to learn a little. Indeed, I'd have been quite happy to spend the fortnight doing nothing else. I was even prepared to work hard at it, inspired by no less a figure than Leonardo da Vinci: 'Many are desirous of learning to draw and are very fond of it who are, notwithstanding, void of a proper disposition for it. This may be known by their want of perseverance.' Len, my boy, you said a mouthful there.

I was fully prepared to persevere – but my perseverance was never called for because technique was never called for. The first time I mentioned the word (in about the first hour, as I recall) I was met with an amused tolerance. Poor chap, you could see them thinking, he really is *very* naïve. By the tenth time the tutors were becoming a little irritated. Look, they said, this art thing isn't about learning technique. Sorry, I said, so what *is* it about? And that's the point at which the language became really interesting. It seems it is about the 'concept'. I thought I knew a little about conceptual art – not that I've ever been much impressed by it, but some of it does get you thinking. My problem was that I had failed to think deeply enough.

G. K. Chesterton said that when a man stops believing in God he doesn't then believe in nothing:

he believes in anything. He might have applied that to conceptual art. What I 'learned' during my fortnight at art school was that anything – and, yes, I do mean anything – can be art. And so can nothing. The concept is all. If the artist has a concept but is unable to execute it because he lacks the technique (or gets someone else to do it for him) might he still be a good artist? Yes indeed, they told me. In fact, the ultimate expression of 'conceptual art' is that the 'concept' remains just that: a concept. It is never executed. Yet it is art.

I was informed by the famous art critic who was wheeled in every evening to review our day's 'work' that anybody who couldn't see the artistic integrity in, say, an old bucket was stupid. That exchange came after the business with the mattress. Ulrika and I had been given a carving knife, a pumpkin and an old mattress to create a work of art. By that stage in the proceedings I was beyond boredom, so I vented some of my frustration by sticking the knife into the mattress. Our critic was mightily impressed. I had, it seems, 'brought out the mattressiness' of the mattress. Yes, really. I told her I thought that was ridiculous and she told me I was ridiculous for failing to appreciate my latent genius – which more or less sums up the intellectual level of our exchanges.

As it happens, there was an exhibition of work by Stubbs showing in London at the time. I ventured the opinion that he was rather good – not least because his horses actually looked like horses and came to life on the canvas. Her scorn could have melted tungsten. Didn't I know that things had 'moved on' since Stubbs?

A wonderful phrase that. 'Moved on' – when it comes from the mouths of highly knowledgeable but daft critics – invariably means the opposite of what is intended. Art may well have 'moved on' but only in the sense that Dan Brown with a word-processor has 'moved on' from Shakespeare with his quill pen.

I have always assumed that a work of art must be able to speak for itself. When Jane Austen wrote *Pride and Prejudice* she did not spend the first few pages telling us how funny it was going to be, and when Michelangelo created the *Pietà* he didn't warn us that we might be moved to tears by its beauty and simplicity. Nor did Mozart and Beethoven provide sleeve notes. They created the work and we judged it for ourselves. It doesn't work like that with conceptual art. We are told why the artist is so very, very clever and what he or she had in mind with this particular piece of genius. No doubt that's intended to pre-empt any notion that the emperor has no clothes.

It's always interesting to compare what happens in an exhibition of, say, the Impressionists and one of our great contemporary artists. When people approach a Monet they will stand and look at the picture – often for quite a long time. Then they might look at the notes, if any are provided. When they approach a Hirst or an Emin they will do things in reverse. The truly sophisticated will nod sagely – especially if they think they are being watched. The rest will look baffled and move on to the next piece of blurb. When my muti-lated mattress is finally exhibited at Tate Modern I shall insist on its mattressiness being explained in great detail.

So it became clear pretty quickly that I was not going to learn what I'd come for and that, like the naughty boy in the class, I'd get more out of messing about with the other kids than from what Teacher might have to say. Fortunately, as I say, the 'other kids' were great.

At first Nihal and I were slightly wary of each other. I suspect he thought I was a boring old hack obsessed with politics who knew nothing about modern music and cared even less. He was right about that last bit. What was more, I had not the vaguest idea how people like him earned their keep. I have never quite seen the point of DJs or understood why the best of them are more famous (and often richer) than the bands whose work they play. He set me straight on all that. He also taught me a lot about language.

Radio 4 presenters are expected to conform to certain norms, to speak a language with which the audience is comfortable. Nihal is under just as much pressure from his audience to challenge the norms. A Radio 1 DJ who does not speak the language of his (mostly) young listeners will soon be shown the door.

We made up our own language at school – mostly in the hope that the grown-ups wouldn't know what we were talking about. It seldom worked, but it does today. A teenager will use words that are often incomprehensible to his parents or mean the precise opposite of what they assume. And the language will be heavily influenced by other cultures and the all-pervasive rap.

I wondered if an ageing Radio 4 presenter could learn 'street' – not that I'd ever try to speak it, obviously. In one of his masterly *Letters from America* Alistair Cooke used a lovely expression to describe something unseemly. It was, he said, like nudging a pretty girl at a funeral. That applies to anyone over a certain age trying to sound like someone a generation younger. But Nihal humoured me and gave me a lesson.

He was good at it – and he has the most extraordinary talent for rap. You give him a subject – just about anything that comes into your mind – and in a couple of minutes he's off. I may not be one of nature's natural rappers, but I flatter myself that I have a reasonably good ear for language. I reckoned I could get away with a bit of 'Hey, man . . . how ya doin'?' and 'Know what I'm sayin'?' and using 'cool' at every opportunity rather than 'That's fine'. But, no, it doesn't work like that. Street language is inventive and rich.

I tried to imagine myself as a hip young dude meeting my equally cool young friend on the street.

(Yes, I know, you'll need a lot of imagination for this.) How would he greet me? Would we have to high-five each other? What would he say? Rather disconcertingly, Nihal told me, he might very well say nothing. There would be lots of touching fists, handshakes, hugs . . . very tactile (though only between men). It's part of being down.

'Being down'? I'd heard of 'being up'. One of the 2006 *Big Brother* saddos (a serious insult when used by one teenager about another) talked a lot about wanting to 'have it up, big time'. Or even: 'I like to go out there and blaze it up. I just like to have everyone up, everything, d'you get me?' Not really, to be honest, but Nihal had this explanation for 'being down':

> 'It's about being part of something. It's like being real. *You* understand where *I*'m coming from; *I* understand where *you*'re coming from. So it's like Freemasons: they have handshakes showing 'I'm down with you and you're down with me.' We're part of that thing. If you break something down you're getting to the essence of something. Being down is being at the essence of something.'

So what happens after the fist-touching and hugging? Not a lot, says Nihal: 'There's a million ways of not saying anything. Two people could walk up and say: "What's happenin'? Cool, man. What's goin' on with you? Good? All good? Things are runnin'? Peace. Safe."'

'Peace' means 'I'm outa here' (it's a long story) and 'safe' means 'We're safe with each other'; there's no animosity. The idea of things runnin' originates in Jamaica. A Jamaican who says, 'Big tings are gwang,' means: 'I've got lots of things running through my life at the moment . . . a lot of big projects going on.'

There is a well-known dark side to contemporary street rap. An alarming number of the words used to describe a woman imply that she is the property of her man, to treat as the mood takes him. And women are denigrated routinely. 'Bitch' is used for girlfriend and 'sket' is a loose woman. This is from NWA's Ice Cube:

Do I look like a mothafuckin' role model?
To a kid lookin' up ta me
Life ain't nothin' but bitches and money.

'Gangsta' rap has been around for nearly twenty years and it's pretty frightening. It's impossible to be sure, as David Cameron believes, that lyrics glorifying violence encourage people to carry guns and knives. It's obvious, though, that the genre has influenced fashion. The reason youngsters wear their trousers slung so low that the crotch is around the knees is because American convicts are not issued with belts.

Not that rap sanctions any language, however offensive. You would not, for instance, call someone a 'nigger'. Or at least, according to the subtleties revealed by my tutor Nihal, not unless you were careful how you spelled it. He explained that the word has been reclaimed by Afro-Americans. The film *Deep Cover* begins with a white cop asking a black cop about the 'difference between a black man and a nigger'. Eventually the black cop says the difference is that 'Only a nigger would answer the question.'

Here's how Nihal put it: 'If you spell it N-I-G-G-E-R, that's derogatory; if you spell it N-I-G-G-A . . . that's my boy; that's my friend! In America you have the phenomenon where nigga becomes just "friend".' I asked Nihal, who's Asian, if he would use it and he said he would not because he's slightly older. 'Those guys who use it (the ones in their twenties), they were never chased down the street by skinheads. They missed out on that. I didn't miss out on it.'

But he does use 'Paki' or 'TP' (typical Paki): 'If you're two hours late for a meeting, that's TP. I'd probably say that. It would be ironic, never with hatred or anger. It's like saying "idiot". A young Asian wouldn't be offended.'

This sort of language, though, treads on very thin ice. Chris Moyles, Radio 1's most famous DJ, got into a lot of bother when he described on air someone's ring-tone as 'gay'. He meant that it was rubbish. Does that mean gays are rubbish? Well, no. It's just that the word 'gay' has come to mean 'lame' or 'rubbish' among a certain group of young people. Even the BBC governors adjudicated that the word was in 'widespread current usage' in this harmless and in-offensive way among the young and that Moyles was only reflecting the fact. But that didn't stop some people complaining. They argued that for anyone from the BBC to use the term like this was 'cruel and scarring' for homosexuals. Funny how one little word can mean 'full of or disposed to joy and mirth', 'homosexual' and 'rubbish'. It just shows that context is everything.

Nihal told me that if you really do want to insult someone in 'street' you might call him 'chief'. No one seems quite sure why.

The point of this intriguing language, according to Nihal, is 'to separate me from you'. He says: 'It's like Latin in the Church. Knowledge is power. I've got knowledge on the street. That separates me from my parents. For example, I could be talking to my boys on the phone and saying, "I'm shifting keys at the moment. I've got some green coming in." That's talking about drugs. Keys equals kilos; green equals weed. If you said, "We were blazing hard the other night," you'd mean you were smoking lots of weed. If your parents heard you they wouldn't know what you were talking about.'

In fact, the moment older people *do* know is the moment the language dies. 'Bling' is a classic example, says Nihal: 'As soon as you hear commissioning editors at Channel 4 using it you know it's dead. Ali G killed off a lot of language. His creator was a nice, Cambridge-educated Jewish boy and he was taking the piss out of the way people speak. It was deadly.'

So who is speaking may matter more than the words themselves. And that's illustrated in Nihal's last re-mark. To hear him talk of 'taking the piss' is neither here nor there. But when others use such language it can cause a real jolt.

Stewart Daker, who described himself as a 'collec-tor for Christian Aid', wrote a thoughtful piece in *The Guardian*'s 'Face to Faith' slot during Christian Aid week. He mused on the reasons for hostility shown to collectors on the doorstep and included this sentence:

> I experienced too many doorstep transactions that revealed a public actively pissed off with religion.

Would he have written that a few years ago? I doubt it. Would a very senior politician have said what Margaret Beckett admitted to in an interview with *The Times* after she'd been promoted to foreign secretary? Again, I doubt it. She'd been asked for her reaction when Tony Blair told her she'd got the job. It was

> '. . . one word and four-lettered . . . beginning with the letter F . . .'

You might defend Mr Daker on the grounds that the rawness of his language expressed the strength of feeling he was reporting having found. But it may be that he thought using such street language would be more likely to get the readers' attention. As for Mrs Beckett, she's a plain-speaking woman at the best of times and, no doubt, was just being honest. But language has consequences.

The philosopher Mary Warnock believes there is a direct link between what she calls 'polite language' and polite behaviour. We are a rude society, she says, because we are not taught from childhood that there is a polite language 'different from the language we use with our mates'. A study by the think-tank Demos looked at the attitude of employers towards the current crop of graduates. One of the things they worried most about was their inability to deal politely with customers.

I learned a lot about language from Nihal though I doubt I'll be making much use of it on Radio 4. But I still can't draw a dinosaur.

CHAPTER EIGHT
Don't Diss It

At the end of the 2005 election campaign, Tony and Cherie Blair gave an interview to the *Sun*. The paper – as is the way with these things – boasted that this was a genuine exclusive: the first time the Blairs had given a joint interview. And, as is also the way with these things, it was mostly pretty dull. The fun came later when the Blairs posed in the garden at Number Ten for pictures – or, as the paper put it, 'cuddled under the cherry blossom'.

The photographer was one Arthur Edwards, a legend in his own darkroom, who is known as much for his cheeky-chappie relationship with his subjects as he is for his pictures. Arthur had asked Mr Blair – who'd just been voted (eat your heart out, Clement Attlee) Torso of the Week – to take off his tie for the pictures. Here is how the conversation between the three progressed:

TB: I'm not doing anything cheesy, Arthur, so don't ask.

CB: Oh, come on, Tony, strip off. Let's see that fit body we've been talking about.

TB: You can keep your hands to yourself, Cherie!

AE: So how fit are you, Tony?

CB: Very!

AE: What, five times a night?

TB: At least. I can do it more depending how I feel.

AE: Are you up to it?

CB: He always is!

TB: Right that's enough – interview over. And I'm not doing any kissing pictures! Come on, woman, time to cook my dinner!

As it happens, I was due to interview Mr Blair on the morning that that uplifting exchange appeared and it was the last thing I read before I nipped out of the studio for a pee. The nearest gents' is a small one: just two urinals. Standing at one – I didn't even know he was in the building – was the man himself. It is, I have to report, mildly off-putting trying to pee when you are standing next to the most powerful man in the land whom you are about (you hope) to reduce to jelly with the sheer brilliance of your interviewing. I wasn't having much success with the main purpose of my mission, so I tried some idle chitchat. Big mistake.

'I've just been reading about you,' I said.

'Oh, yeah . . . That stuff in the *Sun*, eh?'

The wise response was probably a smile. Instead I said: 'Yes . . . and if it was halfway true I'm surprised you can stand quite so close to the urinal.'

Big mistake, as I say. The first rule of conversation – engage brain before opening mouth – holds especially true when you are chatting with the Prime Minister in the gents' loo.

I was thinking of this when I came across the following remark of the great polymath, intellectual and all-round egghead, Jonathan Miller:

> 'There was a time in the early twentieth century when politicians and other figures of authority viewed the values of decency and sobriety as essential virtues of a civilised society. These values are certainly not celebrated by our politicians and our media now.'

What interested me was not so much Miller's sentiment as the almost throwaway phrase:

> politicians and other figures of authority

I rather doubt that *any* of the politicians I know would see themselves primarily as 'figures of authority' or, indeed, whether many of them would even want to be seen as such. The idea might appeal to their vanity, but the hard political calculation would probably be that it would cost them votes. Politicians have stepped off their pedestals and want to come across as ordinary 'guys' – and, no, that's not sexist: nowadays women are guys too.

It has a lot to do with underpants. John Major was wont to tuck his shirt into his. Or at any rate that is what Alastair Campbell 'revealed'. I have no idea whether he did – any more than Mr Campbell did. But Mr Campbell was a journalist at the time – happy to spread the sort of nonsense for which he would later castigate 'irresponsible' journalists in his new career as spin doctor. The effect of his 'revelation' was, as Campbell intended, to make Mr Major look a bit of a nerd and it allowed the *Guardian*'s brilliant cartoonist Steve Bell to portray him for ever after in (and sometimes *as*) a pair of Y-fronts. And, of course, they happened to be the wrong sort of underpants. Conservative leaders can wear only boxers or briefs, as we discovered when the two contenders in the most recent leadership election happily discussed which they wore on *Woman's Hour*.

But never mind about politicians, what about the rest of Miller's phrase: 'other figures of authority'? Presumably the figures he had in mind from the past were judges, policemen, vicars and schoolmasters – even, perhaps, bus conductors, caretakers and park keepers. Not to mention parents and neighbours. My own recollection of being a small boy in what we would now call a working-class community is that we knew better than to challenge adults because they were almost all 'figures of authority'. And there would be no point in appealing to parents over a perceived (or real) injustice. In any conflict between child and adult, the adult's authority was invariably upheld. As a result, we accepted the notion of adult authority.

I wonder what would happen if you filled a room with such a varied group of adults today and asked who saw themselves as a 'figure of authority'. No doubt judges would put up their hands immediately: without authority they're done for. But among the rest I reckon there would be a great deal of uncomfortable shuffling in seats and muttering that the word 'authority' was one they didn't feel very comfortable with. Not that they would *want* to lack authority, you understand, but it's not really how they would choose to be regarded.

The adult neighbours, I suspect, would walk out. They might excuse themselves by saying that the only safe common rule in communities now, is that everyone should mind their own business.

Parents would say that authority gets in the way of being friends with your children.

Vicars would plead that hardly anyone was listening to them anyway and there'd be even fewer if they posed as figures of authority.

The police would perhaps say that if you came down too hard on the authority thing you'd end up with unnecessary confrontation.

And schoolmasters would point out that they don't exist any more: they're now teachers – except for some of the younger ones who are encouraged to think of themselves as 'facilitators', enabling the child to learn rather than telling them what they should know.

In short, the word 'authority' is one for which we seem to have less and less use.

You can almost see the word disappearing before our eyes. The world of public administration was once stuffed with 'Authorities' of one sort or another. Now they are much more likely to be called Agencies, Regulators, Commissions, Directorates and the like. The body now running public transport in London was originally going to be called the London Transport Authority but became Transport for London instead. Privatisation turned the Thames Water Authority into Thames Water, and the British Airports Authority into BAA – though that may change now that the Spanish own it. Occasionally a new authority is set up – to organise the London Olympics, for instance – but it tends to be the exception and, in this particular case, doesn't quite have the ring of, well, authority about it. It's called the Olympic Delivery Authority. How exactly do you 'deliver' the Olympics? An image of milk floats comes to mind.

Nor do we speak much of someone being 'an authority' on something or other. We talk instead of 'experts'. But there's a difference. Experts are specialists. We think of them as knowing everything there could possibly be to know about their narrow little fields but suspect they don't know much about anything else. Someone who was 'an authority' on something certainly knew what they needed to know about it but the phrase conveyed the sense that they could see it in the round – that they had something beyond mere expertise, perhaps even a whiff of wisdom.

There are various reasons why the word 'authority' is fading away. One is that it's a difficult quality to define. You know it when you see it but you can't put your finger on exactly what it is. Our culture is impatient with the indefinable. It hasn't time to be faffing around, musing about fuzzy qualities like authority. It prefers the explicit, the quantitative, things that can be expressed in a number.

Another problem for the word is that it invariably kept company with its close relation 'defer'. That's what you do to authority: you defer to it. You might argue with it, express your own point of view with passion and logic, but if you do not ultimately defer to authority it is gone. 'Deference' has already gone – and a good thing too if it means deferring to people because they are posher or grander or richer or more famous than we are.

My father was a highly skilled man – a french-polisher of the old school who would no more use a spray to apply his polish than Renoir would have done his painting by numbers – but quite clearly working class. He told me once how he'd arrived at a grand house to polish the piano. The servant who opened the front door ordered him to use the tradesmen's entrance. My father turned on his heel and told the flunkey that if he had to use the tradesmen's entrance his master could polish the bloody piano himself. They let him use the front door.

Deferring to authority is different. It is often essential in a well-ordered society. But first we have to respect it.

'Respect' is a word you might expect to have gone the same way as authority. But quite the contrary: you can't get away from it.

I appeared on *Da Ali G Show* at the height of its fame. A few days after the broadcast I was walking through a fairly dodgy area of London late at night wearing a suit, carrying a briefcase and trying, as you do, to appear inconspicuous. A group of young men on the opposite side of the street, wearing hoods and looking vaguely menacing, saw me, muttered something to each other, and crossed over. Oh, God, I thought, should I run? Too late. One of them raised his arm and I cowered.

'Respect, man! Ali G!' He slapped me lightly on the shoulder and off they went. It's funny how you don't get that response from your typical *Today* listener.

'Respect' is a word that's been kept alive on the street. There, it has spawned a new word for which we didn't really have an equivalent: 'diss'. Until it came along we made do with circumlocutions, such as 'He treated me with disrespect', but 'diss' is catching on. Indeed, I heard a senior, Oxbridge-educated civil servant using it in an entirely unaffected manner just the other day.

Politicians have caught on and are now talking about respect too. We have a 'respect' agenda –

central, at one time, to Mr Blair's final term in office. We even have a 'Respect' Party, even if some people aren't entirely clear what its supporters are meant to be respecting: the party's principles or its leader's willingness to prance around on *Big Brother* and lick cream off a fellow 'housemate'?

So does this all mean that we now have more not only of the word but also of what it represents? The evidence is, at best, confusing. The purpose of the government's antisocial behaviour orders (ASBOs) was partly to shame young delinquents into behaving more respectfully. But, according to a poll for MTV, a third of young men regard them as a badge of pride and the holder of an ASBO is accorded respect on the street. Which was not what was intended.

Perhaps this is what's going on here. Respect is rooted in self-respect. That, in turn, depends to a large extent on the sense of being useful, of feeling that you are contributing something of value. And that may be harder to do now. When I was a callow youth based in Liverpool as a reporter for the BBC, I interviewed a man who had been working on the building of Liverpool Cathedral all his life. That was forty years ago but I remember our conversation as though it were yesterday. The man was a stonemason and I asked him why he didn't get bored, laying one stone on another day after day, year in, year out. He seemed genuinely puzzled. 'But that's not what I'm doing,' he said. 'I'm building a magnificent cathedral.' His pride – his respect for this great task and his part in it – shone through.

Now things are very different. The sociologist Richard Sennett has captured the problem we face:

> In place of craftsmanship, modern culture advances an idea of meritocracy which celebrates potential ability rather than past achievement.

Sennett's worry is that when a society singles out only a few for recognition – as our celebrity-based culture tends to do – we end up with a 'scarcity of respect'. Somehow, being told that you are a 'valued customer' isn't the same thing. And if that's all we are it may be impossible to regenerate the sense of respect most of us crave. Consumerism has instead created a society characterised by the British doctor who writes under the pseudonym Theodore Dalrymple as 'egotism informed by a sense of entitlement'.

So it may be that much of this talk of 'respect' is no more than waving the word about. Literally, in some cases. From Iraq it has been reported that American military personnel based there are carrying around 'talking-point' cards with phrases such as

> We are a values-based, people-focused team that strives to uphold the dignity and respect of all.

There is a whiff of desperation about the exercise – as there is in this country. We are left chanting the word like a witch-doctor invoking the spirits, hoping something will materialise.

When a word loses its moorings it becomes available to be exploited. Picture this advertisement in glossy magazines: a full-page black and white photograph of a handsome young father, dressed casually in a white T-shirt, with fashionable stubble and kindly eyes. He's holding out in front of him his baby son. Across the bottom of the photograph in big red letters (inevitably in caring, non-aggressive lower-case) is the word 'respect'. Across his chest is this:

> I earn respect in my role as a trainer for young people; they ask me for advice, we exchange knowledge and discover who we are. It's really rewarding . . .

At the bottom left, in small letters, it says:

> Meet Romain Tissot Charlod, father of a newborn son . . .

So what exactly is going on here? This is a photograph of a man who trains apprentices. Right. They 'ask me for advice'. Fine. 'We exchange knowledge' . . . Hang on. You're the trainer, they're the trainees, so what sort of knowledge have they got that they can exchange with you?

'We discover who we are' . . . Excuse me? Are these some sort of religious self-discovery sessions you're holding? Do you sit around cross-legged? Is there incense? Would Sir Alan Sugar fit in?

And what's the main message? It seems to be that respect is really what matters most and we must make it central to our lives.

Well, all right, but what is the advertisement actually for? In the bottom right-hand corner, discreetly in red, is the single word 'Toyota'.

So the *real* message turns out to be that what we need to know when buying a car is that it has been built by a handsome young dad who's good to his trainees.

D'you think someone may be dissing us?

Like the word 'respect', 'trust' is much in vogue. But, unlike 'authority', it's being attached to things rather than removed from them. We once had local health authorities. Now we have primary care trusts and hospital trusts. It's probably meant to reassure us. Where the word 'authority' might have suggested bossiness, the word 'trust' implies reliability and security. The idea of 'trustees' smacks of people who are disinterested (in the correct meaning of the word) and possessed of that great quality, probity.

When the government decided to give state schools more independence it first referred to them as trust schools. That was what we were encouraged to think they would be called. But they were also talked about as foundation schools. 'Foundation' is another of those reassuring words: a house built on strong foundations will not fall and all that. But it was all a bit confusing. So I contacted the Department for Education and they sent me this email:

> What we are calling 'Trust' schools are
> Foundation schools with foundations. At present,
> the vast majority of Foundation schools do not
> have a foundation, and most of the schools that
> do have foundations are voluntary schools. The
> existing terminology is confusing – to simplify
> things we intend to use the term 'Trust school'
> and 'Trust'.

Well, that's cleared that up, then. I think.

But rather like 'respect', the more we use the word 'trust', the less of it there seems to be. I'm always hearing from doctors who say their patients don't trust them as they once did. That's partly down to the Internet. When my young niece discovered she had breast cancer she didn't simply accept the diagnosis from her doctor, go away and do as she was told. She hammered away at every website she could find, tracked down every bit of information about every treatment and its effects, contacted dozens of other women with breast cancer through various support groups and ended up so well informed she could probably have qualified as a consultant in her own right.

Many doctors say this can only be a good thing. They would much prefer to treat people who have a genuine, intelligent understanding of what's wrong with them and who know how much or how little can be done to get them well again. But not everyone is as sensible as my niece and there are plenty of patients who are hopelessly misled or even conned by some quack 'expert' who destroys their trust in their own doctor.

Inevitably – in every case – it changes the relationship between doctor and patient. The good thing is that doctors can no longer play God. The bad thing is that we may not believe them when we should.

The philosopher Onora O'Neill said in her 2002 Reith Lectures, *A Question of Trust*, that we face not so much a crisis of trust as a crisis of suspicion. That is partly down to the new technologies. She thinks we should not be surprised that 'the technologies that spread information so easily are just as good at spreading misinformation'. With misinformation, of course, comes distrust.

It is because trust, at the most fundamental level, has disappeared that most of us are terrified of smiling at a child in the park or helping her if she seems to be in trouble. My local playground has big notices warning adults to stay out unless they have a child with them. Children are warned not to trust adults and adults don't trust other adults not to label them weirdos if they show the slightest interest in their kids. Teachers aren't trusted to slap a bit of sun cream on a child or even stick a plaster on a cut without a sworn affidavit from the parents, a lie-detector test and the Archbishop of Canterbury or the Pope vouching personally for them.

I'm sorry to inflict this image on you but as I type this I am sitting in a pair of shorts in front of an open window. London has just had its hottest June weekend on record. It's stifling. But (and I bet you know exactly where this is going) on my desk is a newspaper article about the primary school where the children have been told they must wear their long-sleeved jumpers all the time – unless their parents sign a 'consent form'. It's worth quoting the school's headmistress, Joan Lawlan, at some length:

> "We remind parents all the time and as the sun becomes more noticeable [sic] we remind them again. We add names to the list as parents give their consent. They must do that, it's very important. When we go out for PE the children must wear jumpers if they haven't got parental consent . . . When we were young certainly it wasn't an issue, but with the media attention now, it's very necessary. We know about the dangers and we are very vigilant."

I know these stories are now more common than fleas on a camel. Parents must sign 'consent forms' for just about everything except breathing. That's fair enough if the school wants to take the child up the Amazon in a dugout canoe hunting for crocodiles, but it's obviously absurd for parents to have to give written permission for their child's photo to appear on a noticeboard. So why is it required? It's to do with the fear of paedophiles. 'Hysteria' is a more accurate word. Of course everything possible must be done to thwart them. That is so obvious it hardly needs stating. But does anyone really think these daft new measures will make the blindest bit of difference? Even the Health and Safety Executive itself is worried about what it calls the 'cotton wool' culture.

There is something ineffably sad about this – and I'm not just referring to the poor little blighters sweating in the sun who might, in a more sensible age, have had a dollop of sun cream slapped on them by a concerned teacher. They'll survive. It's the head-mistress who has my sympathy. We may be tempted to scoff at her for not using a bit of common sense, but it's the line about 'media attention' that gets to me. The poor woman is so worried about what the media will do to her if one of her little charges gets red arms and the mother complains that she finds herself plas-tered all over the papers for doing what she thinks is the right thing to protect them. Media hysteria is a big factor in all this and let's not pretend it's only the red-top tabloids that do it. In place of trust such hysteria breeds paranoia.

Samuel Johnson said, 'It is happier to be sometimes cheated than not to trust.' Our trouble is we seem to find it harder to take the risk of being cheated. So, to make sure we won't be, we've started to depend on another word: accountability. Now there is a word with a solid – indeed a solemn – pedigree. The Good Book itself tells us that on the Day of Judgement everyone shall be required to give an account of themselves. Or, to use the language of modern accountability, they must be ready with data on their deliverables.

'Deliverables' is a word much loved in business management-speak. It means a target that can be specifically and explicitly identified as capable of being delivered, so that once it has been, everyone can pat themselves on the back and say how wonderfully successful they are. Trebles all round.

It is in the nature of deliverables that they deal only in quantities that can be measured and given a number. That's fine for most businesses because what they handle can usually easily be quantified. Accountability is quite close to accountancy. Businesses are used to reducing everything to numbers: profits, turnover, share prices. The bottom line is what counts. It's interesting, incidentally, how the phrase 'bottom line' is catching on in ordinary speech and is taken to mean 'the only thing that in the end need concern us'.

It's a bit more tricky with deliverables when the thing being handled cannot be counted easily. There's no problem in measuring the number of cars sold last month and the profit made on them, but what about measuring, say, the care of patients? Before accountability came along in this numbers-and-targets way the question didn't really arise. In our private lives we made do with a rather fuzzy, qualitative assessment of whether Granny was getting the sort of care she needed or the GP was up to scratch. We might not have been able to measure it, but we knew if the service was good and we knew if it was bad. More or less. We still do. It's called judgement. But increasingly that's not how the public sector feels able to do things.

It provides services which, by their very nature, have a strong element of the unquantifiable, the immeasurable. What, for example, defines a good education? Not an easy question but whatever it is, you cannot reduce good education to deliverables. Yet over the years politicians have painted themselves into a corner in which they are desperate to show they can do just that. They need 'deliverables' to be accountable to the voters. Hence something called the 'audit explosion': the setting of myriad quantitative targets throughout the public services and the ceaseless paper chase to check whether or not they are being met. The result is that the old qualitative way of assessing things has rather fallen by the way.

A friend was shocked by how far this had gone when he turned up to a parents' meeting. He asked the history teacher how his daughter was getting on and he was presented very professionally with a spreadsheet and a graph. *This* was where she was now and, on the assumption that her performance levels stayed constant, *this* was the trajectory she'd be following so *this* was the Key Stage Three grade that could be expected.

Yes, but did she show an interest in history? Did she seem to enjoy it? Did she contribute much in class? My friend didn't get very far with these questions. His attention was constantly redirected towards the graph and the performance indicators. Deliverability in action.

It happens in the private sector too. I talked to the headmaster of a small prep school in London a few days after it had had its annual inspection. The inspector wanted him to list, in descending order of importance, his ambitions for the school and its achievements. The first thing he wrote was 'A happy school'. The inspector was puzzled. What about exam results and reading standards and assessments of coursework? As it happens, they were all pretty good, but the headmaster had put them much lower down the list. Why? 'Because,' he told me, 'if the children aren't happy they're not learning.' The problem for the inspector was: how do you measure happiness?

Numbers are beguiling because they are simple to use. It's easier to glance at the star rating the critic has given the film than to plough through his five hundred words on why and make your own judgement. We seem to have a touching faith in numbers – or perhaps it's more like fear of them.

I forced myself (in the interests of research, you

understand) to watch one of those hideous programmes in which a bossy woman goes round to
some ordinary person's house and tells her how to
live her life. It seems to me to be a form of sado-
masochism – the soft-core version that's allowed on
before the watershed.

This one was about household cleanliness and the
bossy woman had a gizmo that measured hidden grime.
The housewife (the Scottish chapter of the Women's
Institute is debating banning the word even as I write)
had, of course, made it spotless for the cameras. When
the gizmo was pointed at the tell-tale area round the
fridge, it confirmed that all was fine. But when it was
directed at the wooden chopping board, the dial started
whirring, smoke poured out of its innards and the
numbers hysterically announced that there were at least
a gazillion lethal bugs lurking there, ready to strike
down the entire neighbourhood.

The poor woman looked utterly devastated.
Whether she survived the horror I have no way of
knowing. What I wanted her to do was seize the gizmo
from the bossy woman's hands, smash it over her
bossy head and scream: 'The figures mean nothing!
I've been using wooden chopping boards all my life
and so has my mother and her mother before her and if
there really are a billion bugs on mine I couldn't give
tuppence. I *like* bugs – now bugger off!'

As it happens, I once shared a kitchen with Gordon
Ramsay. I was competing with him to see who could

cook the best lamb curry. Yes, he won, but only just and only because I didn't buy my own chillies. (These chefs are *very* competitive. Almost as bad as journalists.) Anyway, we fell to talking about chopping boards. For the television show he has to use those horrible plasticky things ('elf'n'safety, of course). Guess what he'd prefer. Yet the statistics show the plastic ones are 'safer' and even Mr F-word himself is cowed by the figures.

The point about figures is meant to be that you can't argue with them. But, of course, you can. Cecil B. DeMille once said to a group of critics: 'Gentlemen, those are my principles. And if you don't like 'em . . . I've got others.' There are always other figures too.

Interviews with Gordon Brown have not been the most fun-packed moments of my life. P. G. Wodehouse once wrote that it is seldom difficult to distinguish between a ray of sunshine and a Scotsman with a grievance. He might have substituted 'a Scottish Chancellor with a statistic'. The point is that Mr Brown always has more statistics and they invariably serve his cause. Of course they do. That's why he selects them. Like any other politician in the history of politics – or any businessman for that matter – he chooses the statistics that make his point. There is another way of doing it: George Bush's way. He dealt with Trevor McDonald when he presented him with a set of figures to prove how America is polluting the environment by saying:

'Well, I just beg to differ with every figure you've got!'

When the need to demonstrate accountability is seen to be vital in building trust, 'deliverables' matter. But if the figures are, at best, capable of misleading and, at worse, meaningless, we have a problem. Here's how Onora O'Neill puts it:

Perhaps the culture of accountability that we are relentlessly building for ourselves actually damages trust rather than supporting it.

So how can we re-establish the reality of trust and respect and authority? Fortunately this is a book about language and not about how to put the world to rights. I leave that bit to you.

CHAPTER NINE
Talk Like an Amateur

Beneath the crest of the BBC are these words: 'Nation shall speak peace unto nation.' It is hard to think of a more stirring sentiment. If the BBC makes even a tiny contribution to this noble aim, then its existence has been justified. Yet there are times when I wonder if it should be replaced with this:

One either meets or one works.

Those are the words of one of the world's most successful management gurus, Peter Drucker. I grant you that, as a motto, it doesn't have the same ring to it, let alone the power to change the course of history in quite the same way. But what a thought – an organisation like the BBC committed to doing away with meetings.

Of course it will never happen. World peace is far more likely – a cinch by comparison. The people who would have to decide to end meetings in favour of work are the very people who spend their lives attending them. Take away the meetings and you take away the reason for their existence.

In all big organisations some people succeed by being very clever; some by being very lucky; some by working very hard; and some by being very good at meetings. They know when to keep their mouths shut and when to offer a judicious opinion. They can spot the way a meeting is going and support the boss's view even before he has offered it. It is a genuine talent.

When *Today* comes off the air and the team troops into the editor's office for the 'inquest', I stand in the doorway with one foot in and one foot out. I never sit down. Childish, I know, but it means I can claim that I never go to meetings. What *is* the point of them? If a couple of people get together they can reach a decision. If a dozen people get together they cannot.

People go to meetings either to guard their own backs or because they have nothing better to do. I once knew a very smart businessman who ran the European division of one of the world's biggest IT companies. Year after year its profits and turnover increased sharply. Then sales started to fall and kept falling. So he announced that during the final quarter of the year all meetings would be cancelled – except those with customers. The graph began to rise again. Many of those middle-management types who had spent their time talking to each other were talking to the customers instead.

So, Drucker is right. One either meets or one works. One reason to prefer working is to dodge the language that's spoken in meetings. There's not much point in nation speaking peace unto nation unless they can understand what each other is saying. When I hear some of my colleagues I frequently don't. Try this for size:

> The transition to an on demand digital environment requires a shift to an asset centric approach to media asset management, capturing meta data at the outset of the assets lifecycle. This in turn enables greater movement and sharing of audio & visual material across the BBC to deliver increased exploitation of assets.

Let me not suggest for a moment that the BBC is any worse than any other large bureaucratic organisation. They all have their equivalent of bosses who 'engender the buy-in of content creators', whatever that might mean. One qualification for being a manager is that you learn this silly language. Perhaps it doesn't matter very much if they spout it at each other behind corporate walls and leave the rest of us out of it.

In this sense the gobbledegook virus is a bit like bird flu. One does not like to think of chickens or geese getting it but that's not half as frightening as the prospect that it might jump the species barrier and infect humans too. Well, I have bad news. The gobbledegook virus has mutated and is infecting the wider population. Here is a random selection of phrases:

- Forward-looking companies invest in functional organisational capability.

- A vision of expanding contestability in the delivery of offender services.
- The consultants recommend parallel management matrix approaches.
- The process of external challenge needs to be robust . . . which is why we'll be looking at cross-cutting questions of resources.
- The transport secretary will have to reflect on whether the government could do more to leverage its relations with the security industry.
- Only geeks stuck in the 90s still go for compatible reciprocal concepts.
- I assure you that my prethinking will be rational.
- When we have looked at targets we've done the gap analysis so we know the bridges that we have to cross.

Some of those were generated by the Plain English Campaign gobbledegook computer. Most were spoken by politicians. If you can't tell which, then, as astronauts occasionally report to Mission Control, we have a problem. But it's worse than that. It is one thing for the virus to jump the species barrier between business and politics. Worryingly, it has crossed into the world of real people too. It has done it by first infecting the public services.

The general consensus among politicians is that what the public services need is not only an injection of market forces but much greater involvement of charities, or 'the voluntary sector', as they are now known. The government has something called the 'Civil Renewal Scheme' to bring them on board and most charities are more than willing to get stuck in.

The trouble is that volunteers (who tend to speak English) come up against bureaucrats (who tend not to). The chairman of a local Princess Royal Trust for Carers in Hampshire wrote to me some time ago in exasperation at his experience. His committee had been sent a six-page document called 'Government Support for the Voluntary and Community Sector' outlining how it was hoped that charities could help improve public services – or rather (infection having already set in) 'driving forward programmes to improve' them. The document included the sentence:

> The Infrastructure Strategy will join up with capacity building recommendations from linked pieces of work, to form an overarching strategy for implementing the capacity building and infrastructure proposals from the Cross Cutting Review.

As the chairman put it to me:

> 'None of our committee was other than perplexed by this foggy English.'

Even within charities the virus is spreading. That's because the term 'voluntary sector' is itself a bit misleading. It brings to mind draughty church halls with ladies of a certain age manning bring-and-buy stalls to raise funds to stop the spire falling down. It evokes the tin-rattlers who stand in the cold all Saturday morning outside M&S smiling gratefully as they stick a badge on you in exchange for a quid – not that they are allowed any longer to do the sticking themselves lest they be accused as assault.

But that's only half the story – perhaps less than half. The voluntary sector is, to a large degree, not voluntary at all. It's made up of full-time professionals paid to do a job. It could hardly be otherwise, given the tasks the charities have to perform.

As a result they're gradually changing the name to the 'Third Sector'. Its motto is supposed to distinguish it from the other two: 'Not-for-profit and mission-driven'. I think if I were in the private sector I might want to protest that I'd be out of business if I didn't make a profit. And if I were a public-sector worker I might want to say I felt pretty 'mission-driven' too. But as everyone is in a partnership, there are probably no hard feelings.

With the new professionalism of the Third Sector, though, comes the virus. Nick Aldridge, the director of strategy and communications at the Association of Chief Executives of Voluntary Organisations, has written a pamphlet trumpeting the potential for the Third Sector in public-service reform. It includes sentences such as:

> Third Sector providers are able to work across government silos, joining up funding streams and policies.

Anyone who can join up funding streams and silos in the same sentence will go far.

But back down among the volunteers it all seems rather baffling. A woman who works in a charity in south London told me it was a case of Indians and Chiefs. The Indians are the people doing what they have to do for the people they're helping; the Chiefs are the professionals in the office filling in the forms. They speak different languages. She told me:

> 'A lot of their language bears no relevance at all to what happens on the ground.'

Older volunteers, she says, are 'totally exasperated' not just with the alien language but with what it represents: the transformation of their charity from the kitchen table and the rattling tin to the computer terminal and the huge mailshots. They don't believe it helps them provide a better service.

She knows they have no alternative but to burble on about 'empowerment' and 'excellence' and 'best practice'. They have to speak this stuff, she says, if they have any chance of raising the money they need because much of that money comes from the government.

The rules require them, for instance, to demonstrate that they pursue what are called 'SMART aims'. And what are they? They are Specific, Measurable, Achievable, Realistic and Time-related. How bureaucrats love their acronyms. Now, that's fine except that 'achievable' and 'realistic' amount to the same thing. So couldn't the criteria be reduced to four? But then it would be SMAT aims or SMRT aims, neither of which has quite the same ring. So SMART aims it has to be, which means that form-fillers everywhere struggle to find something to write in the 'Realistic' box that hasn't already been included in 'Achievable'.

There are other ways of doing good works than joining a charity: become a school governor, perhaps. But don't imagine you will be spared language abuse if you do. A friend of mine (I'll call her Jane: she'd rather not be identified for reasons that will become clear) signed up to be a parent governor when her daughter joined a north London comprehensive school. If she had been expecting to stroll along to a few meetings and keep a benign eye on things she was in for a shock.

In one respect she was hugely impressed. The business of being a governor was taken extremely seriously. She found herself immersed in a highly organised Governor Development Training Programme. She was inundated with documents and scrupulously ploughed her way through them. It struck her that even when the language of bureaucracy was not jargon-laden and obscure, it often had nothing to say beyond the blindingly obvious. And then it said it again. And again.

For instance, she was given a 36-page glossy brochure about the borough's 'Healthy School Scheme'. She read a section, spaciously presented in bullet-point form, on how being part of the scheme helped schools. Then there was a section on how it helped pupils. Then one on what teachers who'd been part of the scheme had said about it. Then one on what the results of being part of the scheme would be. By now she felt she'd pretty much got the picture.

And then she turned to page nine. I am a bit reluctant to inflict this on you but it really won't do just to give you a flavour. You need to read the whole thing to appreciate what poor Jane and her fellow governors had to suffer. Here goes:

What Is a Healthy School?

- A Healthy School is a place which is an enjoyable and safe learning environment in which pupils can achieve their full potential and gain knowledge, understanding and skills to be able to lead healthy lives.
- A Healthy School is an inclusive school which values the diversity of its community and has policies and practices that reflect this.
- A Healthy School involves parents and the community in the promotion and maintenance of health.
- A Healthy School considers the health and well-being of staff as well as pupils.

- A Healthy School is active in promoting positive health and minimising potential health risks.
- A Healthy School will have a range of healthy school activities that reinforce the learning from the classroom.
- A Healthy School will be concerned about these topics: the environment and safety, healthy eating and physical activity, drug, alcohol and tobacco education, sex and relationship education, PSHE and citizenship, pupil support and consultation, staff health and welfare, teaching, leaving and achievement, partnerships and leadership and management.
- A Healthy School will also be concerned about its health-related policies, how health education is co-ordinated and planned, how pupils are involved and consulted, teaching and learning, how parents, governors, staff and the local community are involved, and how pupils' achievements are recognised.

In short

- **A Healthy School is an effective school.**

By now Jane was beginning to wonder if she had made the right choice. Instead of becoming a school governor perhaps she should have enlisted in the special forces and learned to abseil down buildings, crash through windows and force every bureaucrat in sight to eat nothing but crisps and drink nothing but

Coke while simultaneously smoking and engaging in unprotected sex. It's funny what too much of this sort of stuff can do to you. But she's tough, is Jane, and she kept reading.

Still to come were sections called 'Key Features of a Healthy School', 'What Is the Healthy School Scheme in Camden and Islington?', 'Principles of the Scheme', 'Aims of the Scheme', 'Achieving the Aims', 'Key Elements of the Scheme (details in Section Two)' . . . and this would take her only to page twelve.

There was also a schedule of meetings for new governors to attend. There were sixteen to choose from. Some seemed straightforward enough: 'Induction Part 1: Your Strategic Role'. Others she passed over rather quickly (she felt she was an expert by now on 'The Islington Healthy School Programme'). This one caught her attention:

Know your PANDA and your SMIF (Enjoy & Achieve)

You may think that enjoying a smif (let alone a panda) is not the sort of thing that should be happening in our schools. But, of course, the ADD (the Acronym Design Department) has been in action again.

'Enjoy and Achieve' is a reference to the government's 'Every Child Matters' initiative. Let's pause there a moment. Can you imagine any government launching an 'Only a Few Children Matter' initiative? Quite. A bureaucrat was then set the task of defining

'Every Child Matters: Outcomes'. These were: be healthy; stay safe; enjoy and achieve; make a positive contribution; and achieve economic well-being.

So, this meeting was all about category three. But what have enjoying and achieving got to do with pandas and smifs? Well, a panda (pay attention at the back, please) is the new Performance and Assessment Report and a smif is the School Management Information File.

There's also, in case you're interested, a SEF, the Self-Evaluation Form. So new governors might have been invited to a meeting to know their PANDA, their SMIF *and* their SEF. But one can have too much of a good thing – even enjoyment.

I'll spare you all the bullet points about pandas and smifs except one. It said that attending this meeting would

- Enable governors to consider and formulate some of the questions they might ask about the school's performance in their role as 'critical friend'.

Jane, an intelligent woman, wondered why she was deemed incapable of formulating the odd question without the aid of all this mumbo-jumbo. Might it be that only certain sorts of question would be welcome, even from a 'critical friend'?

She decided to forgo the pleasures of pandas and smifs but she did attend a meeting of new governors run by the outside professionals now responsible for her daughter's school. It was a bit like going to a revivalist meeting conducted in management-speak. It was full of boosterish language to do with how passionate everyone was about everything. But it was also peppered with words and phrases such as 'consultation', 'collaboration', 'partnership', 'addressing outcomes', 'sharpening up the action plan' and 'developing a proposal about your engagement'.

When, finally, she had had enough she blurted out that she hadn't the faintest idea what they were all talking about but it most certainly wasn't what *she* wanted to talk about. Her equally bemused fellow novitiates, who'd seemed a bit cowed by it all until then, joined in to back her up. The panda people seemed genuinely shocked, she told me. No one, it seemed, had ever complained that they were incomprehensible. It couldn't be true.

Jane's account made it sound rather like an episode of *Doctor Who* in which aliens, looking just like humans, are engaged in a dastardly conspiracy to seize real human beings, infect them with a virus and convert them into members of the conquering alien race. For aliens, read professionals; for humans, read amateur volunteers; for the virus, read language.

Deprive people of their own language and make them use another and they're a long way to being held captive. My friend came away from that first meeting with the impression (fair or unfair, she couldn't yet tell) that what those who ran the school were hoping for from their new governors wasn't so much an independent guiding voice but people who would simply nod through what they wanted.

The takeover of our affairs by pseudo-management language is no more than a reflection of our changing attitude to the amateur and the professional. It has turned a hundred and eighty degrees.

Not so very long ago the amateur was considered superior to the professional. That was partly for bad reasons, based on class (the players and the 'gentlemen'), and partly for good reasons. There was the sense that the amateur was more committed, was playing the game or running the race for the love of it. The origin of the word is *amo* and even people like me who gave up Latin after two years know what that means. Using the language of management-speak, it was the amateur, not the professional, who was 'passionate'.

Now 'amateur' is a term of abuse. An 'amateurish job' is one that has not been done properly; a 'professional job' can't be improved upon. We all want to be thought of as professional. That's fair enough in most ways. I wouldn't be terribly keen on having open-heart surgery from a keen amateur. But we badly need the enthusiastic amateur in so many ways. Even the panda people talk of schools needing 'critical friends'.

But friendship is not a profession and friends, by their nature, are not professionals. They are different from the doctors, psychiatrists, counsellors, probation officers and other professionals who advise us on how to live our lives. Our friends are amateurs and usually they give the best advice.

Volunteers are the friends of communities. If they are not left to speak their own language, if they are not allowed to remain amateurs but are coerced into being the hangers-on of professionals, they will disappear back into their private worlds.

There is the occasional ray of sunshine breaking through this gloomy sky. Read this and rejoice:

'My priority is to ensure that players feel more amateur than professional. Thirty to forty years ago, the effort was the other way. Now there is so much professionalism we have to revert to urging players to like the game, to love it, do it with joy.'

Bet you can't guess who said that. It was Big Phil, otherwise known as Felipe Scolari, regarded as one of the best football coaches in the world. He ran the Brazilian side when it last won the World Cup. And it was his Portuguese side that knocked England out of it in 2006. How extraordinary that a man at the very top of the most 'professional' game in the world, where players routinely earn £100,000 a week and are bought and sold for the price of a small country, should have come to such a conclusion. Mr Scolari was offered the job of managing the England side but he turned it down.

The brilliant sports writer Simon Barnes once argued that football matters too much. The person who can 'free himself from the straitjacket of professional concern and play the damn ball without thinking about it too hard' wins the real prize. And if he can do so with joy, so much the better.

Football, I'm afraid, bores me to death but even I can see the beauty in the game when it is played for the love of it as well as for the spoils of victory. A society run only by professionals is not one I much fancy belonging to. Apart from anything else, it would be one endless meeting.

CHAPTER TEN
Gissa Job

Does anyone tell the truth, the whole truth and nothing but the truth when they apply for jobs? I doubt it – but it may be that I'm simply trying to lessen my own sense of guilt. I'm ashamed to say that I tricked my first editor into giving me a job. I pretended that I had been a leading light at my school. To use the words of a former cabinet secretary, I was being at the very least economical with the truth.

The editor invited me to tell him what I'd been best at. Difficult, I said, given such a list of things to choose from, but it had probably been my prowess as a long-distance runner. The editor was mightily impressed: 'Just what's needed in a young reporter – plenty of stamina. You're hired.' Or words to that effect.

The truth is that I had made absolutely no impact on my school or it on me. I left at fifteen and when I went to see the headmaster for a reference it was perfectly clear that he hadn't the faintest idea who I was. He obviously knew what I had not done. I had not made it into the school rugby team, or the cricket team, or the hockey, tennis, swimming or falling-off-a-log teams. I hadn't even made it into the B teams. If I had been remotely athletic – or even particularly brainy – he would have known. He was one of those headmasters who were interested only in what we now call the 'gifted and talented' kids.

I suppose I shouldn't hold it against him, but I do. Some years later, after I'd achieved what passes for a modicum of fame in my strange trade, the school asked me back to speak at the annual prizegiving. I said I'd be delighted, then told them what I would say. The invitation was hastily withdrawn.

But all of that hung on my becoming a trainee reporter for the *Penarth Times*. My claim to be a long-distance runner was true as far as it went – but that was not very far. Every Wednesday afternoon in winter we were forced by our sadistic PE teacher to put on our daps (plimsolls, if you weren't born in South Wales, and trainers, if you were born any time after 1980) and run a few miles through the cold, wet streets of Cardiff. I think it was meant to be good for our characters.

Naturally the teacher didn't come with us: he was a sadist, not a masochist. I usually managed to grab my bike as we left the school, cycle round the course, stop for a gossip with someone, and get back reasonably swiftly without breaking too much of a sweat, but it was enough for that vital entry on my so-called CV and enough to impress my first editor. That was nearly half a century ago and, mercifully, I have had to apply for only three jobs since then. The rest

I managed to stumble into. For that, I am truly grateful.

It's not that there seems to be any shortage of jobs – not if you scan the media or public-sector appointments pages of *The Guardian*. The problem often is trying to work out what on earth they are. Employers seem to need some very odd creatures. Try these for size:

- A Common Assessment Framework Co-ordinator (Merton)
- A new Head of Innovation Clusters (Birmingham)
- Diversity Officers, decibel legacy (The Arts Council)

Haringey advertised, quite simply, for a 'Hints Visitor' and South Tyneside had a job going in 'Decriminalised Parking Enforcement Services'. I'd love to know what criminalised parking services are but it's probably best not to ask.

Beware, though, of guessing what a job ad might mean. A keen astronomer might think Staffordshire's post of 'Sub-Regional Observatory Co-ordinator' would be ideal for him – but not after he'd read the description. It's actually about 'providing cross-cutting information for Stoke-on-Trent and Staffordshire Strategic Partnership'. Obvious when you think about it, I suppose. Age Concern's need for a 'Signpost Agency Manager' presumably has nothing to do with all those road signs that clutter our streets. And I very much doubt that Swindon's 'Domestic Violence Co-ordinator' does exactly what their job title suggests. On the other hand, we do have a body called the National Domestic Violence Steering Group, so you never know.

Sometimes the language is so bizarre you may not progress even as far as getting the wrong end of the stick. As I write, the Camelot Foundation is advertising for tenders from bodies who might run this:

A Virtual Centre of Excellence on Self-Harm

I'm sure it will do a valuable job, but there must be a better way of phrasing it. Do the people who come up with these titles ever step back and imagine what such a group of words might appear to mean to those who are not already engrossed in the project? And does 'virtual' mean the salaries will be virtual too?

Organisations get into this sort of absurdity because they become so used to their own management jargon they forget that other people speak English. Kent Police, for example, advertised for a new 'Head of Project 2015'. The blurb said:

You will work in a highly politicised environment with significant exposure to external stakeholders.

I suspect they might be referring to the public. It did not say whether surgical masks would be provided.

Reading job advertisements is a bit like looking for somewhere to live and traipsing around one house after another. After a while you start to see the appeal of a camp site. With houses, it's other people's wall-paper, carpets and kitchen units that make your spirits sink. With job ads it's the language.

The people who place the ads seem to appreciate this and try to offset the effect by throwing in a few uplifting adjectives. But somehow it always seems a bit self-defeating. Thus, for example, this ad placed by head-hunters for the job of managing director of an unnamed company somewhere in the Thames Valley:

> This is a business critical role with an important division of a highly respected leading global organi-sation. With a strong reputation for creatively meet-ing market demand through an array of high value services, our client is at an exciting stage in its growth cycle.

When you get to 'creatively' you begin to realise this is just language wearily being wheeled in to do a job; by the time you reach 'exciting' you want to run away and do something that is genuinely exciting and creative, such as rearranging your sock drawer.

Once words like 'exciting' lose their oomph, sub-stitutes have to be found. The current favourite is 'passionate'. The London Development Agency ad-vertised for a public liaison officer. The ad explained how the successful candidate would be expected to do the job:

When we talk to stakeholders, our message is simple – we're passionate about improving London for the benefit of people living and working here.

Oh, come on! I'll grant the LDA may be keen, enthusiastic and committed, but 'passionate'? I don't want to be indelicate but passion is something that rather comes and goes. It's not something you can keep up all the time, so to speak. If I were a 'stakeholder' (perhaps I am, for all I know) and some young public liaison officer from the LDA kept coming over all passionate with me I think I'd run a mile.

The hype raises the stakes for what is expected of those poor souls looking for the jobs. Foxtons, for example – with the gloriously absurd slogan 'People Not Property' – advertised not simply for a Sales Coordinator but for an 'Energetic Sales Coordinator'. The blurb pitched it even higher:

Foxtons is recruiting for a Superstar to support a busy Sales Director at our stunning HQ.

This puzzled me because, in a separate ad entitled (for some reason that escapes me) 'Extreme' and with a photo of a young man in a wetsuit surfing the waves, it said:

Foxtons have revolutionised the property market in London by constant innovation in every area of our business to exceed our client's expectations.

You'd have thought if they had only one client they could take things a bit more easily in servicing him. Or maybe it's *because* there's only one client they so desperately need an energetic superstar. Seems a bit mean to pay only £25,000, though.

The effect of all this hype is not just to inflate the job but to set the tone in which applicants feel obliged to inflate themselves. Bizarrely, some job ads go as far as writing the script you must perform in the interview. An organisation called Creative Sheffield ('a mould-breaking, UK-first initiative aimed at creating one integrated lead organisation . . .') advertised for a chief executive. The text of the ad included this:

> Your undoubted passion for cities, coupled with a proven track record in managing complex regeneration agendas and economic master planning, will enable you to influence key movers and shakers . . .

Hang on. Isn't the point of an interview to discover whether candidates really do have an 'undoubted passion for cities'? Set the script like this and every candidate will feel compelled to show up proving they're on urban Viagra. Another paragraph began:

> Bringing a sense of urgency and a passion for change, you will rationalise and integrate the functions of . . .

If you were preparing for the interview after reading this ad, what strategy would you come up with? Turn up five minutes early, barge into the interview room and immediately set about rearranging the furniture before telling the marketing director to 'integrate' with the sales director or clear off?

This sort of language is not only silly but self-defeating. It forces candidates into a narrow role. The older, more formal way of advertising jobs didn't fall into this trap. The ads essentially did two things: they defined the job and tried to deter futile applications by including a sentence that read something like

> The successful candidate will have a degree and at least three years' experience in . . .

What they did not do was talk about 'you'. It meant that interviews could be more genuine opportunities for candidates to present themselves as they really were and – who knows? – some might even offer qualities whose value hadn't occurred to those trying to fill the post.

There is something odd, perhaps even slightly chilling, about the tendency to define 'you' so specifically that you have no option but to try to conform to the portrait they have already painted of you. Aren't they interested in who you *might* be? It's as if they're inviting you to hide yourself rather than present yourself. They see the interview as a performance – but one that is acted to their script rather than yours.

After the job comes the appraisal. You might think you've been doing reasonably well and so might your boss – but what about everyone else? A new phrase has entered the world of work: 'the three-sixty'. To give it the full title it's the '360-degree appraisal'. It means that everyone watches everyone else and then writes down what they think of them – anonymously, of course. You and your boss sit down and chew over what they've said about you. This can include anything under the sun – not just your professional competence, but your personal habits too. I can see some benefits in this. If *Today* presenters were ever 'three-sixtied' I would definitely report Jim for his habit of eating his polystyrene coffee cups. No doubt he thinks they're tastier than the coffee, but still . . .

Some people like it. One very senior civil servant told me she had volunteered (correction: 'proactively sought') a three-sixty when she changed departments because she had no other way of discovering how well she was doing. She argued that there were perfectly good reasons why all her colleagues – junior as well as senior – should have a say in how she did her job. Others hate it. One middle-aged curmudgeon told me he pores over his appraisal when it's handed to him, submits it to detailed textual analysis, works out precisely who must have said what about him, then devotes his life to plotting revenge. There is talk in some dark corners of the education world of allowing pupils to 'appraise' their teachers. There may be more lunatic ideas around, but I'm hard-pressed to think of one right now.

It's not so much the process that gets me as the language. Orwell would have loved it. Substitute 'surveillance' for 'appraisal' and at once Big Brother is watching you – only now your colleagues are the spies, keeping tabs on you from every angle. It was Orwell's case that once we buy into the language of something hitherto alien to us we are well on the way to accepting it. Here the alien notion in the phrase is that we should be under surveillance all the time and pounced upon if we transgress. Beyond work, we seem already to have accepted that with scarcely a murmur. There are more CCTV cameras in this country than just about anywhere else on earth and no one seems to mind.

Here's another phrase that has entered the world of work in recent years: 'work–life balance'. It's something we must all have, it seems. If we don't have one (and it must be the *right* one) we are doomed. Politicians keep talking about it and it's very hard to get through a day's newspapers without someone, somewhere, boasting that they've got theirs just right or they're desperately worried because they haven't. It is one of those verbal formulas whose terms we tend to take for granted. But if you think about it, it's quite odd.

If I had asked the mason working on Liverpool Cathedral back in the 1960s what he felt about his work–life balance, he probably wouldn't have known what I was talking about. He might have said that his work–*leisure* balance wasn't quite as he'd like it and that he'd prefer to spend a bit more time with his family. But as for his life, his work was so much a part of it that it made no sense to talk of it as something separate.

But he was a craftsman: the cathedral, or at least his small part of it, was his life's work. Most people don't have something solid they can point to in the same way. I don't suppose William Morris ever used the expression but back in the middle of the nineteenth century he saw that the retreat of craftsmanship in the face of industrialisation would mean that, for many people, work would be likely henceforth to cut against the grain of life rather than be naturally integrated with it. So did Karl Marx. The origins of our fashionable phrase could be said to go back that far.

A hundred and fifty years later some people are still lucky enough to feel their work goes with the grain of their lives. I'm one of them. My work–leisure balance is appalling but that's my choice and I make it because work and life for me are so intertwined. I keep getting called a workaholic but the truth is I'm one of those lucky people whose work is 'naturally integrated' with his life. I usually have three or four jobs on the go at the same time and can no more imagine retiring than I can retraining as a catwalk model. Work is as much a part of my life as leisure. I love building Bionicles (if you don't have a small boy to do it with it's best not to ask) or walking in the hills, but I also love asking questions of a politician on the radio or a *Mastermind* contender on television. The difference, by the way, is that one lot actually *wants* to answer the questions. I neither 'live to work' nor 'work to live'.

But if you look at some of the phrases used about our working lives it's not hard to see why for many people work and life are opposites rather than complements.

Have you, for example, 'reinvented yourself' recently? This is the buzz phrase for the new economy. We all know that the era of a job-for-life has disappeared. My parents could imagine nothing better for their children than a job in an office (ideally a bank) with a steady income and a pension at the end of it. In my own industry I know young graduates today who would willingly crawl over broken glass and set fire to their underpants if it gave them the chance of a three-month contract as a junior researcher. It is not uncommon for them to work for film-production companies for nothing. They might get their bus fares paid – if they're lucky. It is not that competitive in most other industries, but the idea of the carriage clock at the end of forty years' faithful service has gone the way of spats.

So we must now 'reinvent' ourselves. Some people will welcome the chance to vary their work; others will regret it. But as for the language, it is an extraordinary phrase to use about human beings.

Psychologists tell us that to make sense of life we must construct for ourselves a 'sustaining life narrative' that gives it meaning. I'm not quite sure how we do that if we need to keep reinventing ourselves. It might have been necessary for Lord Lucan when he went on the run or *Big Brother* 'celebs' when we've all forgotten why we ever knew them, but it's pretty tricky for normal folk. Think of it this way: how would you follow *Hamlet* if the hero popped up as Macbeth in the second act and King Lear in the third? Not easy. 'Reinvent' neatly captures the divorce between life and work that many people feel.

And here's another of the new buzz phrases to do with work that shows how alien it can be to life: 'de-layering'. Management consultants love it. It means breaking down the old hierarchical structures of companies in which everyone knew their place – and that's no bad thing. I had a friend who worked in middle management for Tesco when they had more grades of staff than cans of beans. The rule was that if someone was two grades above you, you called them 'Mr' (or, very rarely, Miss) no matter what your personal relationship. But at least there was some sense of belonging and of mutual loyalty. Now, when companies are de-layered they get rid of all those middle layers and there's just the powerful centre and you. It makes sense in some organisations – but it leaves people feeling exposed if they're not at the centre.

There's a lovely old cartoon that shows a boss with

his feet on his large desk and a sweating underling standing before him. 'Make it easy for me, Jim,' he says. 'You don't know how terrible it makes me feel to tell you you're fired.'

No, it wasn't meant to be Alan Sugar. In today's de-layered company you probably won't even get that face-to-face meeting with the heartless swine: possibly just an email telling you to collect your P45. As George Soros, the billionaire financier and philanthropist, put it: 'Transactions have replaced relationships in people's dealings with one another.' So perhaps it's not so strange that to many people work and life now seem opposed to each other.

In the midst of all this fresh-faced language of de-layering, reinventing and work – life balance a very old word has made a reappearance: 'happiness'. Even economists, who tend to prefer such dreary phrases as 'utility maximisation', have been heard using it. Politicians make speeches about it. Academics produce studies on it.

What's exercising them is the discovery that not only has becoming richer failed to make us happier but it seems to have contributed to our being less happy. And they've come up with an expression to describe the phenomenon: the 'hedonic treadmill'.

I had never heard the word 'hedonic' and assumed they had made it up. But there it is in the dictionary: 'hedonic (1656): of or pertaining to pleasure'.

The hedonic treadmill theorists claim that, in the never-ending process of working to earn to spend, we are now getting less satisfaction from the spending and more grief from the working. Wordsworth put it both more poetically and more clearly two hundred years ago:

Getting and spending, we lay waste our powers.

And he spotted that long before the consumer society got going. I doubt if he received much junk mail through the door of Dove Cottage offering to lend him a couple of grand to blow on a holiday.

The nineteenth-century American novelist Herman Melville warned us, too, about the seductive temptations of the hedonic treadmill when he wrote (with rather more style):

Seeking to conquer a larger liberty, man but extends the empire of necessity.

The fact is that sensible people have always known that money cannot buy happiness – even though it does make you a little more comfortable in your misery. The publisher Felix Dennis, who became so rich he wrote a book about it, says that although money does not make you happy it does improve your sex life.

But what gives all this recent talk of happiness and treadmills a bit more significance is that the predicament we've started to gripe about is no less than the utopia that the Western world has been striving to reach for the last five hundred years or so. We single-mindedly set about getting richer. We have succeeded. We in the world's richest countries have now achieved a level of material well-being (to say nothing of being able to live as long and healthily as we do) that would have seemed to our forebears like the realisation of utopia.

It was a utopia forecast by the economist John Maynard Keynes:

> There will come a time when we've solved the economic problems – at which point we shall be faced with the permanent problems of mankind: how to live wisely, agreeably and well.

How much richer do we have to get before we realise we've arrived? Yet having reached this utopia we seem to have discovered it's not what it was cracked up to be. We've now not only started talking about hedonic treadmills but we've begun to find a use for a word that means the very opposite of utopia: 'dystopia'.

That's a word that was previously so unused that the *Oxford English Dictionary* didn't even include it until 1972. Now it's become quite common to see modern life being talked of as a dystopia. And the need for the word seems not unconnected to treadmills because as another economist, John Kenneth Galbraith, remarked when talking about utopias, there are many versions of the good life 'but the treadmill isn't one of them.'

Still, that's probably not something to bring up at your next job interview.

CHAPTER ELEVEN
Back to School

An old friend from my years in South Africa had come for supper and I cracked open the last bottle of a case of wine I'd brought back with me thirty years ago. It had not improved with age but we drank it anyway – then started on a different case to take the taste away. So when my five-year-old crawled into my bed at about three in the morning my parenting skills (when did that ghastly phrase enter the vocabulary?) were sadly lacking.

'Dad,' he said urgently, 'we need to talk.'

I've noticed with clever little boys that they almost never say 'want': it's 'need'. I suppose they pick it up from us: 'You really need to brush your teeth/go to bed/eat some more of that broccoli.'

'What about?'

'Is Africa a bigger country than England?'

I sensed that this was not going to be easy but I tried to explain about continents and countries and said that, yes, Africa was very big indeed and much bigger than England. There was a short pause.

'Why did Jesus allow that?'

God help me. Perhaps if I'd done a philosophy

degree I might have tried explaining what a 'category mistake' is. Perhaps I could have gone down the theological route and dealt with Jesus as part of the Trinity or explained the Big Bang or the continental drift. But a combination of too much bad wine and too little sleep meant I was barely able to form a sentence. 'Ask your teacher' was the best I could manage. I'm not proud of it. Indeed, I'm ashamed. But there it is. Anyway, the teacher must have put the idea into his head in the first place.

Teaching is not easy and many teachers say it is made no easier by the demands of politicians and bureaucrats. It has never been so difficult to recruit head teachers. It was once the case that a school advertising for a new head struggled to choose from the mass of applicants. Now qualified teachers tell me they are almost afraid to walk past the school in case they are dragged in and tied to the head's empty chair.

They offer a number of reasons for this apparent lack of ambition. One is that schools have become exam factories and all that matters is that they manage more passes at better grades this year than last. The children are trained in the skill of passing tests, rather than getting the broadest possible education. The other complaint (not unrelated) is that teachers and heads are required to be managers and bureaucrats, endlessly filling in forms and meeting targets.

We parents may sympathise with them but there is often a touch of hypocrisy in our approach. Many of us speak with forked tongue. Yes, of course we want our little sprog to get a good, rounded education – but if he doesn't get the exam results we expected or do as well as his best friend we'll damn well want to know the reason why. And may the saints preserve the brave teacher who tells the pushy parent she's sorry that little Samantha hasn't done awfully well in her exams, but her talents lie in other directions.

The language of the teaching world gives some interesting pointers as to what is going on:

> The school has a policy of 'Eye Shine' days, whereby teaching staff are encouraged to, on occasion, suspend the curriculum and do 'a one-off' to excite and stimulate the children.

This comes from what is known in the business as a SEF – a 'Self-Evaluation Form'. It was filled in by a London primary school. It was in the box where schools are invited to note anything that might interest the Ofsted inspectors when they make their next visit.

On the face of it there's something rather charming about an 'Eye Shine' day. It suggests paintings of big yellow suns stuck on the school walls, their rays spreading out in all directions and a smiling face in the middle. But it suggests something else too.

It suggests that there is something special about an 'Eye Shine' day: that it is the exception rather than the rule. The implication is that only on special, earmarked days will the children's eyes shine with the joy of being taught at that school. Presumably the rest of the time, when the children are on the treadmill of the curriculum, plodding their way towards the next set of exams, their eyes are glazed over rather than shining brightly. Why else call the 'one-off' days 'Eye Shine' days?

No doubt many teachers will get cross about this and tell me it's not like that in their schools. I hope they're right. But there have been big changes in primary education since my elder children started school more than thirty years ago. We have had the national curriculum, more and more testing, school league tables and all the other apparatus for 'raising standards'.

Tests have become what would now be called the main 'driver' of everything. They matter to schools because they are the measure of how the school is doing in competition with others. They matter to pupils, of course, and they matter to parents because they will help determine which school their children get into next term. It creates pressures all round. That helps explain why a young teacher in a reception class said her four year-olds no longer had a sand table or water-play area: either might distract them from the serious business of hitting their targets.

One primary-school teacher told me how she has tried to create an oasis from all this by setting up a little poetry magazine to which pupils could contribute if they wished. There would be no marks, no points; it would be for the fun of it. It had been going for a while in a relaxed sort of way when an anxious middle-class mother came up to her at a parents' evening and said it was really important that her son had a poem published in the magazine. Well, fine, said the teacher, if he wrote something that she and the other children thought should go into it, it would. But that wasn't good enough for the pushy mum. It was *vital* he should have a poem in the magazine because it was 'needed for his CV'.

An eight-year-old with a CV? That's enough to dull the eyes of the brightest.

It seems a consensus is growing that all this may have gone a bit too far. The Qualifications and Curriculum Authority has admitted that 'the assessment load is huge' and announced that it wants to cut the number of tests in schools by a third. And a pamphlet, *The Shape of Things to Come*, published by the Department for Education and Skills Innovation Unit acknowledges the problem. Its author, the consultant and innovation guru Charles Leadbeater, writes:

> Many children feel education is something done to them, a period they must endure. This leads many to disengage from education or, worse, disrupt it.

The basic idea is that we need to replace the old 'send-and-receive' model of education, in which a teacher stands in front of a class and sends out teaching material the pupils are supposed to receive. Children don't so much need to learn 'stuff' as to 'learn how to learn'. Then they can do it for themselves. The solution is what is being called 'personalised learning'.

For this to happen (so the argument goes) the old organisational model of a school, in which pupils sit in classes following rigid timetables of fifty-minute lessons, needs breaking up a bit. Because children have varying ways of getting the hang of things, schools should be less rigid. Children should be free to explore ways of learning in small groups. Older children should help younger ones. There should be more one-to-one tuition and so on.

All of this amounts to 'personalised learning'. Leadbeater quotes Derek Wise, the head teacher of Cramlington comprehensive school in the north-east.

> Each lesson they come to should be organised into a cycle of activities – show the point of the lesson, connect it to things the children have already learned, introduce new information, allow the children to process that through an activity and demonstrate they have ingested it, debrief.

I confess, it sounds to me a bit like reinventing the wheel. That description is not a million miles from what competent teachers did with us when I was at school. In fact, getting children to learn how to learn is what good teachers have been trying to do since

Socrates. But perhaps the wheel really does need reinventing, and if schools have the resources to do more personalised learning, good luck to them.

What's new here, though, is the language in which this is couched and especially what it seems to say about our attitude to children. In the foreword to the pamphlet Valerie Hannon, the director of the Innovation Unit, writes:

> I hope *The Shape of Things to Come* provides a constructive challenge to policy makers and practitioners alike, helping to frame how we can begin to fulfil all of our aspirations for a personalised learning offer for every student.

If teachers still used old-fashioned blackboards that phrase 'personalised learning offer' would be the equivalent of a fingernail scratching down one. It's more than just a dreary piece of business-speak. It implies that a child is a client or a customer, the figure to whom the 'offer' is made. It becomes even more extraordinary when it's combined with what Leadbeater writes at the beginning of his pamphlet:

> . . . the ultimate goal of personalised learning [is] to encourage children to see themselves as co-investors with the state in their own education.

Come again? The ultimate goal is that children should *see themselves* as co-investors with the state? I reckon if a child came up to me and said she saw herself as a co-investor with the state in her own education I'd have serious worries about her welfare. I'd start wondering whether management consultants had begun to form sinister sects, grabbing kids in playgrounds and indoctrinating them in business-speak. Get 'em by seven and they're yours for life, as the Jesuits put it.

You may think this is just a silly piece of drafting and not worth fussing about. What he clearly meant was that the ultimate goal is to motivate children so that they are as keen to get themselves a good educa-tion as the state that's paying for it. Amen to that. But the language suggests a reluctance to talk about chil-dren as children. And that is because we couch so much of what we say in the jargon of business and markets.

All business relationships are between adults. So, to borrow the language of business, the 'stakeholders' come across as adults even when they are children. A child cannot be a 'co-investor' without in some sense ceasing to be a child. If we see people only as either consumers or producers or investors – and the lexicon of business allows no other categories – we lose the means to talk about children in ways that recognise they are children. *The Shape of Things to Come* seems peopled by children who are eight going on thirty-eight.

Leadbeater seems so imbued with this language that he even parrots a version of the oldest management cliché in the book – so whiskery that even managers groan when it's trotted out at business conferences by bosses wanting to say nice things about their staff:

> Our education system's biggest untapped resource is the children themselves.

I know what he's getting at but it's hard not to wince at the notion of children as an 'untapped resource'.

The shift away from language that allows us to talk about children as children is pervasive. Here, for example, is Eddie O'Hara, the Labour MP for Knowsley South, speaking in the House of Commons:

> 'At the end of this month, all Knowsley secondary schools will be closed and replaced with eight learning centres.'

This followed the abolition of the title 'director of education' and its replacement with 'director of children's services'. O'Hara said this was all part of the 'systemic, inclusive, corporate and holistic agenda' in Knowsley. The term 'learning centre' apparently reflects this.

I'm not at all sure that I know what that list of adjectives means but the words 'education' and 'school' are missing. They have been replaced: we now have 'children's services' and 'learning centres'. This is more than just another of those rebranding exercises. Changing something's name changes how we think of it.

The word 'school' has been used to describe many things but its basic association is with children. School is what everyone does between the ages of five and sixteen. It's a large part of what childhood means. 'Learning centre' does not have that association. Anyone can attend a learning centre. If children start going to learning centres something characteristic of childhood is taken away from them.

That may be deliberate. Some adults have always thought it would be a good thing if children were not treated so much as children but more as young adults. I think that's wrong. There is a difference between treating a child with condescension and attributing to him a maturity he cannot, by definition, possess.

But there is an even more important distinction that comes with the language. You go to a learning centre but you belong to a school. The difference matters because a school is (or should be) more than a learning centre, and what children learn there is more than their lessons. They learn what it is to belong to something beyond their own family – an institution with a life of its own that does not exist solely to serve their individual needs. A vital part of growing up is learning that the world is not just an extension of yourself but that you are part of something bigger.

To use a word we fret a lot about these days, a school really is a community. 'Learning centre' does not have that ring. It has much more in common with 'health centre' and 'leisure centre' – places that are there to serve you, not places that also make some demands on you.

Did I say 'demands'? Hmm. Dangerous word, that. Might, like, turn off the kids . . . know wha' I mean? Better not risk doin' their 'eads in, innit? I mean, wot we gonna do if they fink *Twelfth Night* is a pain in the jacksie to study? Obvious, innit? We do a revised version with lots of silly pictures and jokes and use language even the dopiest squid-for-brains can under-stand.

That appears to be more or less what Coordination Group Publications believes. 'Pain in the jacksie' is their phrase, not mine. It's on their website. And they happen to be publishers of educational texts widely used by schoolchildren from Key Stage One to A Level. 'Squid-for-brains' is what Macduff calls Macbeth in their helpful guide. Martin Samuel of *The Times* treated his readers to a flavour of how it works. You may remember that Shakespeare wrote these lines:

ROMEO: If I profane with my unworthiest hand
    This holy shrine, the gentle sin is this:
    My lips, two blushing pilgrims, ready stand
    To smooth that rough touch with a tender kiss.
JULIET: Good pilgrim, you do wrong your hand
    too much,

> Which mannerly devotion shows in this;
> For saints have hands that pilgrims' hands do touch
> And palm to palm is holy palmers' kiss.
>
> ROMEO: Have not saints lips, and holy palmers too?
>
> JULIET: Ay, pilgrim, lips that they must use in prayer.
>
> ROMEO: O, then, dear saint, let lips do what hands do;
> They pray, grant thou, lest faith turn to despair.
>
> JULIET: Saints do not move, though grant for prayers' sake.
>
> ROMEO: Then move not while my prayer's effect I take.

This, according to the guide, is what he meant to say:

> GIRL: What are you thinking about?
> BOY: Oh, just moons and spoons, in June.
> GIRL: Wow. Give us a snog, then.

Let's try a few lines spoken by Lady Macbeth:

> Was the hope drunk
> Wherein you dressed yourself? hath it slept since?
> And wakes it now, to look so green and pale
> At what it did so freely?

Guide version:

> Cowardy custard!

Or a few lines from Macbeth himself:

> Is this a dagger which I see before me,
> The handle toward my hand?

Guide version:

Oooh! Would you look at that.

Or:

> Thou canst not say, I did it; never shake
> Thy gory locks at me.

Which becomes:

Bloomin nora its (*sic*) Banquo's ghost.

Yes, I know it sounds as if I'm making it up, but you can check it for yourself.

It's not that we shouldn't try to make the greatest writer in English come alive for children. That is what good teachers do. But the point of studying Shakespeare is to engage with his thought, his language and his poetry because that will enhance students' lives. This sort of thing, as Professor Alan Smithers put it with what must have been enormous self-restraint, 'seems to be circumventing that engagement'.

Yet it works. It produces, in the language of commerce, satisfied customers. Last year more than 126,000 copies of the guides were sold to schools and in shops. No doubt it made Shakespeare – in the word that has come to epitomise all that is good in education and culture – 'accessible'. It delivers the service. Why bother to struggle with the complexity of Shakespeare's language when you can glance at the silly drawings and bowdlerised version and get the gist of it? The value of Shakespeare is in the beauty of his language. But 'value' means something else in the language of commerce.

The relentless onward march of technology is beginning to have a real effect on the language. Take spelling. The Oxford English Corpus – a massive database compiled by Oxford Dictionaries – monitors just about everything that's written these days from websites to blogs and newspapers to books. It has found a huge rise in spelling errors, most of which stem from the Internet. Some have changed the meaning of phrases that have been around for a very long time. A few examples:

strait-laced: 'straight-laced'
just desserts: 'just deserts'
sleight of hand: 'slight of hand'
fazed by: 'phased by'

Much more serious is the effect IT is having on the way our children learn. The neurobiologist Baroness Greenfield is worried about the distinction between those of us educated in the twentieth century and our children and grandchildren educated in the twenty-first. We had books; they have computers. What we get from books and the written word, she says, is guidance. The controlling mind of the author steers us through a lot of disparate material, giving us a conceptual framework of understanding. We may not agree with it, but we can read other books and gradually our own framework builds up.

One might argue that this is the basis of education – education as we know it. It is the building-up of a personalised conceptual framework, where we can relate incoming information to what we know already. We can place an isolated fact in a context that gives it significance. Traditional education has enabled us, if you like, to turn information into knowledge.

Children educated in this century are spending on average six and a half hours a day using electronic media – often 'multi-tasking' with two different devices on the go at once. Increasingly, the electronic media rely more on the icon than the word. But most of all, she points out, the quick-fire, fast-moving nature of much electronic media militates against building up a personalised conceptual framework.

Imagine that you are sitting in front of a multimedia presentation where you are unable, because you have not had the experience of many different intellectual journeys, to evaluate what is flashing up on the screen. The most immediate reaction instead would be to place a premium on the most obvious feature, the immediate sensory content – we could call it the 'yuk' or 'wow' factor. You would be having an experience rather than learning. Here, sounds and sights of a fast-paced, fast-moving, multimedia presentation would displace any time for reflection or any idiosyncratic or imaginative connections that we might make as we turn the pages, then stare at the wall to reflect.

I've talked to Lady Greenfield about this. She worries about a link between the time children sit in front of screens and the number of 'hyperactive' children being treated with drugs. If I were a half-awake fifteen-year-old, seeing adults first over-stimulate me, then sedate me with drugs, I'd feel I was being cheated.

It all comes back to shining eyes. At five, children's eyes are shining most of the time, even at those moments when they suspect Jesus may have cheated them about Africa. What we should want, once they have been taken off into the world of education, is for their eyes to go on shining perfectly naturally.

CHAPTER TWELVE
Bad Smells

The language of politics is changing. A generation ago the following sentence, which appeared in the *Financial Times* recently, would have been incomprehensible.

> Andrew Cooper, director of pollster Populus, said the Tories' opposition to ID cards and glorification was about 'brand positioning'.

Substitute 'selling biscuits' for the political stuff in that sentence and there would have been no problem understanding it. Selling biscuits or cars or trainers is all about brand and always has been. But it's new in politics. I'm not suggesting there was ever a golden age when politicians used only elegant argument to persuade the voters of their strongly held convictions. If you believe that, reading a little Trollope will set you right. What's new is the way in which politicians themselves acknowledge the reality.

It is no longer offensive or even controversial to acknowledge that politics is now essentially about marketing. About selling a product. About packaging a party and its leader so that both look appealing. It's about creating and positioning a brand in such a way that consumers/voters want to buy/vote for it.

So the advertising gurus have been in the driving seat – or, at least, doing the map-reading. One of the most famous and successful of them, Maurice Saatchi, was the first to have a really big success with a political client, Margaret Thatcher. Remember 'Labour isn't working'? But now he has announced that advertising in general is dead. That has implications for politics and for the role that language plays in it.

Among the reasons he gives for the death of advertising is that the digital age has bred something called CPA: 'continuous partial attention'. Lady Greenfield would know exactly what he's talking about. It seems that our minds – and especially the minds of our children, who represent the future – are distracted in ways they have never been before.

We are simultaneously distracted by mobiles and iPods, the television in the corner, the Gameboy we're playing and the magazine we're reading. So distracted that we can no longer concentrate long enough even on the slogans of political advertising – never mind detailed argument. Lord Saatchi comes to an intriguing conclusion:

> Each brand can own only one word. Each word can only be owned by one brand . . . The same applies to political parties or countries – Britain's Labour Party

won three elections with the word 'new'. America's one-word equity is 'freedom'.

As I write, the Conservative Party is in search of a new logo to replace the flaming torch ignited by Margaret Thatcher. We've had some harmless fun on *Today* inviting listeners to suggest a new one. What we should now do − all of us − is think of the one word with which our parties will be branded in future. Here are a few suggestions. You can decide for yourself which party deserves which:

- choice
- prosperity
- freedom
- peace
- contestability (no, I haven't the faintest idea either: ask Mr Blair)
- greed
- avarice
- sloth
- envy . . .

. . . whoops, sorry, getting carried away there.

But even the mighty Saatchi may be a little behind the times. It seems we may not need even that single word.

Now it may be all to do with smell. Fraser Nelson, the political editor of the *Spectator*, reports from inside the Conservative camp that the young Tory Turks have decided the real trick to winning power is simply to create an 'aroma'. Nelson quotes a senior policy maker as saying that 'vastly more important' than policies is the task of creating . . .

'. . . an aroma around the Conservatives so people naturally imagine our policies are the right ones'.

Stop sniggering! Smells are powerful. To this day I have only to smell old furniture polish and I am immediately transported back almost sixty years to my infants' school where we were allowed to rest our heads on our desk lids for a little snooze. Fresh bread takes me back to my grammar school, which was next to a bakery. The smell of freshly roasted bread and Chelsea buns (remember them?) was pure torture when it drifted through the classroom window. The smell of orange peel reminds me of the local flea-pit and Saturday mornings with Roy Rogers. So does the smell of stale pee . . . but we'd better stop it there. We all have our own set of smells and there will be plenty to analyse in the coming era of aroma politics.

Perhaps we shall have to develop a whole new vocabulary. Certain ministers will be fragrant; budgets piquant; policies complimented for their bouquet. But smells are also fleeting, will-o'-the-wisp, impossible to capture and pin down. Perfect, you might say, for what Robin Day called 'here-today-gone-tomorrow' politicians.

But until the time comes when I spend most of *Today* sniffing the air, there remains the task of dealing with the language politicians still use. Often, like a smell, it makes a big impact but is hard to pin down. For example, they frequently 'address the issue'. But what does that mean? It could be anything from considering setting up a working party to contemplate whether steps should be taken to forming a committee to recommend a policy review to come up with options for . . . well, to invading another country perhaps.

Or they borrow metaphors that sound solid in the original but evaporate into meaninglessness when they use them. So when things haven't gone quite as they should, they promise to 'raise their game'. If a crestfallen Andy Murray says it, you know he knows what he thinks he has to do. When a politician says it, it could mean anything. Or nothing.

One of the oddest of these phrases is 'redouble our effort'. Why not just 'double'? Does it mean they've already doubled their efforts once and that now we're in for a quadrupling? It can lead to delicious confusion. A Home Office minister used it at the time of the row over the releasing of foreign prisoners. A little later this headline appeared in *The Guardian*:

Reid Warns That Foreign Prisoner Crisis Twice As Bad As Expected

I don't think that's what the minister had had in mind.

Some favourite phrases sound tough but are intended to dodge answering very specific questions.

One is 'send a signal'. It is particularly popular in the field of criminal justice. Let's imagine that a politician proposes that young thugs be strung up by their toes while their victims throw stones at them. In response to the odd sceptical question from someone like me, he might well brush aside the objection, dismissing me as another 'cynic' who just wants to 'do down' honest attempts to deal with the problems, and argue that in any case details aren't what matter. No, what really matters is to get the right message across to the thugs. Not to adopt the measure would 'send the wrong signal'.

A relatively new phrase in the repertoire is 'direction of travel'. It's another device for dodging specific detail and talking instead about the 'broad picture'. I spotted it first when the government was trying to get its Education Bill through the House of Commons and was encountering some pretty determined opposition from its own back benches. It became quite difficult at times to know exactly what the rebels didn't like, especially after the government had made some concessions to them. We were told that it was the 'direction of travel' that upset them. In other words, the rebels could concede the government's good intentions but feared this particular direction of travel might be paved with them.

But we must not be too harsh on politicians. Sometimes when their language appears designed to dodge rather than address an issue it's only because they are representing us: it's we who are doing the dodging and they are taking their lead from us. Here's a much-used phrase:

We need to strike a sensible balance on this.

Most of the time that is precisely what they try to do – strike a sensible balance between the conflicting demands of tax and public spending, say, or an unfettered market and regulation. The problem arises when there is no 'sensible balance' to be struck, when the issue is so black and white that compromise is not an option.

Global warming is a good example. All the leaders of our main political parties agree that it is the most serious issue facing the world today – even bigger, says Mr Blair, than international terrorism. The experts agree that air travel is making things worse and is the fastest-growing source of carbon emissions. The number of flights from Britain will double over the next twenty years. But it is a very brave politician who will say we should fly less. They know we like our cheap flights so they say we must 'strike a sensible balance'. How exactly do you strike a balance between a cheap weekend in Prague and the future of the planet?

The 'sensible balance' lies not in dealing with the problem but in minimising a potential loss of votes. It's we, the voters, who abuse the phrase 'sensible balance'. The politicians merely utter it.

You may detect an unexpected sympathy for politicians in these remarks. And why not? It's much easier to interrogate them than to be one. We ask an awful lot of politicians – though, admittedly, they tend to encourage us.

When the government announced that it wanted to create 'dignity nurses' in every hospital to make sure that elderly patients were treated with proper courtesy (shouldn't every nurse do that?) a news bulletin said:

Ministers Want Patients To Complain

Do we really need ministers to get us to do something we're perfectly able and willing to do without them? I imagine the patient being approached by a concerned official as she lies in her hospital bed: 'Oh, you *must* complain, dear. We mustn't let that nice Mrs Hewitt down, must we?'

This assumption that politicians should be responsible for just about everything can lead them into some bizarre use of language. Here's a health minister talking on *Today* about child obesity:

'It's a hugely complex issue because it's not just about food, it's about exercise.'

Umm . . . True . . . It *is* about both food and exercise. But does that really make it hugely complex? The minister was responding to a report on obesity by no fewer than three watchdog bodies: the National Audit Office, the Audit Commission and the Healthcare Commission. It emerged that responsibility for reaching the government's targets was in turn shared between three government departments: the Department of Health, the Department for Education and Skills and the Department for Culture, Media and Sport. Beginning to get complex, isn't it? And now read what the boss of one of these bodies had to say:

> 'The challenge is that there has to be leadership from the government departments. That then has to flow down to the regional level so that at the regional level there is some clarity over funding and who's doing what. But that isn't sufficient. It then has to go right down to the local level. And at the local level what we're talking about is teachers working *with* children, *with* parents and also local authorities coming together as well to provide – because this isn't just a question of what children eat, it's also a question of ensuring that they get exercise . . . so it's quite a challenge for people locally to provide that advice . . . At the moment there isn't enough guidance for people really locally about what they can do that's effective. So what we need is more guidance and more examples about best practice to enthuse people locally.'

The blindingly obvious is made to seem 'hugely complex' simply because such a clutter of bureaucracy is created to deal with it. And that is because we demand politicians be responsible for so much.

Politicians have come up with a word to explain the nature of this complexity. The problems, we are told, are 'systemic'. This is a useful word for politicians. Charles Clarke used it about problems at the Home Office. It's useful precisely because it is not one we use in everyday language. It makes it sound as though it's something only experts would understand. But the real beauty of it is that it says it is the 'system' that is at fault – rather than any individual or specific group of people. If it were 'systematic' the fault would clearly lie with humans – and heads would have to roll.

One of the words that has most altered its meaning is 'debate'. I once lost a sweepstake over how many times a trade-union leader I was due to interview would use the word 'debate' (i.e. 'What we need is a debate about this') during a twenty-minute interview. I bet four. The winner guessed seven. The trade-union leader said it twelve times. I have some sympathy for him because I think he meant it. Mostly when politicians use the word they don't mean it at all. Or they mean something else.

It's a perfect illustration of the difference between textbook politics and modern marketing politics. In the textbooks, debates really do take place and decisions flow from them. In modern politics, decisions are often taken before the debate. It is rare for them to affect the decisions. Instead, when politicians say they want a debate it usually means they want to 'send a signal' rather than receive one. The signal is that they realise the rest of us may be het up about something so they want to be seen to be onside. But they don't want to lose control of an issue lest it affects (sorry 'impacts') their marketing strategy.

There is a helpful lexicon of phrases on which politicians may draw when they want to close down debate. Here's a sample:

- 'in the real world' (if you disagree with me you're bonkers)
- 'let's not play the blame game' (we only play this when it's the other lot who've cocked up)
- 'move on' (yes, we cocked it up last time but, hey, who's counting?)
- 'we mustn't hark back' (because we want to move on)

Bill Clinton, widely regarded as the most brilliant politician of his generation, liked to say: 'Never look back. *Never!*' What a luxury that would be in the world outside politics.

When politicians have to deal with crises of world-changing dimensions they sometimes resort to language that seems designed at worst to confuse and at best to distract. I wrote in *Lost for Words* about the curious word 'rendition', which was just creeping into our vocabulary. It transformed itself subsequently into 'extraordinary rendition', even though the activity it described was unchanged: moving prisoners from one country to another where the rules of interrogation were somewhat less restricting.

When Condoleezza Rice, the American Secretary of State, was asked about Iran she said:

'The invasion of Iran is not on the menu at this time.'

What a strange, homely phrase to use in such a context. When members of the Bush administration started having doubts about Guantánamo Bay because of the world's reaction, some began to regret ever having set it up. They referred to it as an 'impulse buy'.

Guantánamo Bay has provided some of the best examples of how wayward and adrift from reality political language can become. Sandra Hodgkinson, the deputy director of the Office of War Crimes Issues (itself a wonderful linguistic formulation) referred to 'the different care providers' at Guantánamo Bay. 'I was just down at Guantánamo Bay yesterday,' she chirruped, as though she were talking about having dropped in on her local nursery school. Rear Admiral Harry Harris, the camp commander, had his own, perhaps more characteristic way of talking about the same issue:

'We aggressively look for ways to build on the "safe and humane care and custody" mission . . .'

When people talk about the same thing in such radically different language, what is revealed is how differently they see the world – or, even more, how differently their jobs *make* them see it. This became strikingly obvious when three prisoners committed suicide in June 2006. Rear Admiral Harris described it as

'an act of asymmetrical warfare waged against us'.

I suppose he was seeing it as a military man. But another American official, Colleen Graffy, Deputy Assistant Secretary of State for Public Diplomacy, said:

'Taking their own lives was not necessary but it certainly is a good PR move.'

Ms Graffy had her knuckles rapped for that, but if you see the world only in PR terms you will end up assuming everyone else does too. It brought to mind the legendary remark of Metternich, the Austrian diplomat famed for his devious approach, who assumed everything everyone else did was equally devious. He had been engaged in intricate negotiations for months with the Russian ambassador, who suddenly died. Metternich said: 'I wonder what he meant by that . . .'

Yet some progress with more simple, straightforward language is being made. When the American government realised that the phrase 'War on Terror' was not having the desired effect around the world they came up with a new name. It is now called 'The Long War'.

There's no fancy packaging in that. This is plain language in plain brown wrappers. The only alarming thing is this. How do they already know it's going to be long?

Sometimes the simplest language is the most chilling.

Last Words

Confucius said the first thing he would do if he ever became ruler was to rectify the names of things. In his book *Unspeak*, Steven Poole imagines asking him why. This was the answer:

> When the names for things are incorrect, speech does not sound reasonable; when speech does not sound reasonable, things are not done properly; when things are not done properly, the structure of society is harmed; when the structure of society is harmed, punishments do not fit the crimes; and when punishments do not fit the crimes, the people don't know what to do.

That's a pretty good explanation of why it is important to pay attention to language. It's not hard to drift into a Confucian dystopia – you might call it 'a confusion' – where words no longer mean what they are supposed to mean and nothing is what it is said to be.

Nearer our own times, William Cobbett recognised the same danger when he wrote:

> Those who write badly think badly . . . Confusedness in words can proceed from nothing but confusedness

in the thoughts which give rise to them. These things may be of trifling importance when the actors move in private life, but when the happiness of millions of men is at stake, they are of an importance not easily to be described.

Forcing ourselves to write properly forces us to think properly.

In the view of many people, much of public life now suffers from the condition Cobbett feared. The American writer Joe Klein says in *Politics Lost* that 'the expectation of spin [has] deafened the American public to the possibility of substance'. If people do not believe that words represent real things they cannot act as citizens. The United States, according to Klein, has become 'a democracy without citizenship'.

But it's not just as citizens that we need to keep an eye on words. Our society, which treats us so much as an audience to be entertained and as consumers to be led to market, often uses language as an anaesthetic. If verbal blandishments can encourage us to sit back and relax, we can be taken care of in more ways than one. And unless we're trained to be alert to the use of language we're likely to end up duped.

It is young people who are most vulnerable to the wiles of the marketing man. Peer-group pressure is more powerful at sixteen than it is at sixty. We crusties tend to glory in our defiance of fashion – which is, I suppose, itself a kind of conformity. But the young are not taught to use and understand language as older people were – one of the main reasons I wrote *Lost for Words* – and that makes them even more vulnerable. It is that much more difficult to think for yourself if you don't have the language. And a society in which people don't think for themselves is dangerous. 'A society of sheep begets a government of wolves' was how the philosopher Bertrand de Jouvenel described the consequence.

The link between our independence and the need to be watchful over language is captured perfectly at the beginning of Philip Roth's fine novel *I Married a Communist*. The narrator is looking back to his schooldays and to his inspirational teacher, Murray Ringold.

'In human society,' Mr Ringold taught us, 'thinking's the greatest transgression of all.'

So, approving of transgression, he set about teaching them how to think for themselves. Roth describes the experience like this:

Mr Ringold knew very well that what boys like me needed to learn was not only how to express themselves with precision and acquire a more discerning response to words, but how to be rambunctious without being stupid, how not to be too well concealed or too well behaved, how to begin to release

239

the masculine intensities from the institutional rectitude that intimidated the bright kids the most.

'Expressing themselves with precision'; having 'a more discerning response to words'; learning how to be 'rambunctious without being stupid'. I'd be happy for Mr Ringold to teach my little boy.